"Hey, gorgeous, it's been almost two years, hasn't it?"

She nodded, her head swimming. He was still the most beautiful man she'd ever seen, still hard and handsome, still looking like a playful rascal and a bit of a rogue. His thick rust-colored hair seemed to have a constant breeze blowing through it, his mischievous blue eyes were framed by eyelashes so thick, it was almost criminal, and his mouth looked so deliciously sensual, it ought to be censored. That was Max, just as she remembered him. Lord how she'd missed him!

"So what are you doing here?" he asked, looking completely bemused.

"I came to...to sort of arrest you. In a way." She made a face. What a farce.

"Arrest me?" At last he focused on the security guards behind her. He frowned. "What did I do now?"

"Oh Max," she sighed. "Why can't you be good?"

"Kayla, my sweet," he said grinning at her, "you know that's not in my nature."

G000141530

Dear Reader,

This is the last book of a series of six about the lost princes of Ambria, a lovely, fog-shrouded, fictitious island nation off the coast of Western Europe. All the princes have been found and brought back home again. Their family, which was shattered and torn apart when their parents were killed by the Granvilli rebellion almost thirty years ago, is reconnected and healed about as well as it can be. Goodness and mercy are back in the land.

Too bad all our problems can't be solved so easily—but then, we're not royal, are we?

It's been something of a royal year, what with the Westminster Abbey wedding of Prince William and beautiful Kate Middleton and all the excitement and *celebration that surrounded it. This wonderful couple* brought back star power to the British monarchy, a sense of special magic that reminds us why fairy tales so often feature princes and princesses. Larger than life, the focus of dreams. No wonder we love it all.

Prince Max and the woman he loves, who is secretly raising his child, need a bit of that magic to find their happy ending. They have to struggle through misunderstandings, a kidnapping and a heavy shared sadness that almost destroys their love. I hope you enjoy being a witness to the way they manage to capture their dream.

Thank you for reading my story.

Regards!

Raye Morgan

TAMING THE LOST PRINCE

BY
RAYE MORGAN

All the characters in this book have no existence outside the imagination of the author, and have no relation whatsoever to anyone bearing the same name or names. They are not even distantly inspired by any individual known or unknown to the author, and all the incidents are pure invention.

All Rights Reserved including the right of reproduction in whole or in part in any form. This edition is published by arrangement with Harlequin Enterprises II B.V./S.à.r.l. The text of this publication or any part thereof may not be reproduced or transmitted in any form or by any means, electronic or mechanical, including photocopying, recording, storage in an information retrieval system, or otherwise, without the written permission of the publisher.

This book is sold subject to the condition that it shall not, by way of trade or otherwise, be lent, resold, hired out or otherwise circulated without the prior consent of the publisher in any form of binding or cover other than that in which it is published and without a similar condition including this condition being imposed on the subsequent purchaser.

® and ™ are trademarks owned and used by the trademark owner and/or its licensee. Trademarks marked with ® are registered with the United Kingdom Patent Office and/or the Office for Harmonisation in the Internal Market and in other countries.

First published in Great Britain 2012
by Mills & Boon, an imprint of Harlequin (UK) Limited,
Eton House, 18-24 Paradise Road, Richmond, Surrey TW9 1SR

© Helen Conrad 2012

ISBN: 978 0 263 89432 5
ebook ISBN: 978 1 408 97108 6

923-0512

Harlequin (UK) policy is to use papers that are natural, renewable and recyclable products and made from wood grown in sustainable forests. The logging and manufacturing processes conform to the legal environmental regulations of the country of origin.

Printed and bound in Spain
by Blackprint CPI, Barcelona

Raye Morgan has been a nursery-school teacher, a travel agent, a clerk and a business editor, but her best job ever has been writing romances—and fostering romance in her own family at the same time. Current score: two boys married, two more to go. Raye has published more than seventy romances, and claims to have many more waiting in the wings. She lives in Southern California, with her husband and whichever son happens to be staying at home at the moment.

This book is dedicated to Nick and Jenn, and most of all to CB, the new prince in our family.

CHAPTER ONE

PRINCE MAX leaned out over the edge of the wrought-iron rail on the balcony. A light rain was falling but he hardly noticed. He was at least the equivalent of five floors up. The castle garden below looked farther away than that. A strange, shivering impulse inside made him wonder what would happen if he jumped.

Too late now. A few weeks ago he could have jumped. He could have ended his worthless life with a flourish. No one would have cared.

But now he had a new life—new responsibilities. People were beginning to expect things of him. What the hell made them think he could possibly deliver?

Actually, this might be a better time to jump. Maybe he would find out he could fly. It looked so simple. All he had to do was spread his wings. He knew what it felt like to fly. He'd been flying ancient crates from past wars for years now. Flying planes was the one thing he knew he was good at. But taking that leap on his own would be different.

No, he wasn't going to jump. He wasn't going to

mock his fate by trying to fly without a plane. Self-destruction wasn't really his style. But he did have a peacock feather he'd picked up in the castle gardens. He held it out.

"Fly and be free," he muttered to it. And then he let it go. It began its long, meandering flight toward the ground and he leaned out even farther, watching it go. It flashed back colors, blue and green and gold. As it neared the ground, it started to spin crazily. He laughed. "Go, baby," he murmured to it. "Do your thing."

The feather hit the ground and his laughter faded away. Now it was caught, just like he was. A short flight to nowhere.

"Hey," a candy-coated feminine voice said to him. "Don't lean out so far. You'll fall."

He closed his eyes for a moment. Was he ready for this? Did he need it?

"You okay, mister?" she said.

He turned slowly, wondering if she realized who he was. Probably not. He was dressed for hiking, not for the ball. But he thought he'd seen her before, passed her in the halls. He recognized the look. And he knew the drill. Either he gave her a simple friendly nod and went on his way, or he smiled at her suggestively and things went on from there. His choice. He could tell she was ready. Eager even. A part of him groaned.

But he couldn't give in to that. What the hell? He was young. Life was there to be lived. And who knew how much longer he'd be free to follow where his urges led him?

"I'm fine," he said, and he smiled.

"You're wet," she countered flirtatiously.

He shook his head like a sheepdog. Water flew everywhere. She gave a little shriek and then she laughed.

"You'd better come on to my place and get dry," she offered.

"Your place?" he repeated questioningly.

"Sure. My room is on this floor. I'm only a few doors away. You need to dry off. You wouldn't want to catch a cold, would you?"

His gaze made an exploratory journey down the length of her, from her spiked, fire-engine-red hair, down to her full lips, lingering on her hourglass figure. His look was insolent. He knew it. And he also knew she was the type of woman who liked that sort of thing.

"Sure, why not?" he said. Anything was better than joining the other royals at this ridiculous ball the queen had cooked up. A few hours with this willing playmate might be just the thing to help him get rid of this feeling of doom that was hanging over him. "You're like an angel of mercy, aren't you? Always on the lookout for someone in trouble."

Her smile had a wicked sparkle to it. "Not really," she said. "I'm kind of picky about who I help."

He raised an eyebrow. "And I made the grade?"

Her eyes widened appreciatively. "Oh, yeah. You'll do."

He pretended to bow. "I'm honored."

She giggled and led the way.

* * *

Queen Pellea swept into the royal office and glared at
Kayla Mandrake. "So where is he?" she demanded.

Kayla jumped up from her desk, shaking her head.
That sinking feeling she'd been fighting since she'd
found out who the new prince actually was had come
back with a vengeance. "I haven't seen him at all," she
said. "I thought he was supposed to be here...."

Pellea grabbed the back of a chair, her knuckles
white. "Of course he was. He was given complete instructions. And he blew them off, as usual. Everyone
is waiting in the ballroom."

"Shall I make an announcement over the speaker
system?"

Pellea looked pained. "Oh, Kayla, you've been in
Paris all this time and you don't know how things have
been. This guy is driving me crazy."

Kayla held back a grin. That was Max. He drove everyone crazy.

"He'll settle down," she told the queen without really believing it herself. "Once he understands the way
we do things."

"The more he understands, the more he flouts the
rules. You're going to have to go out and track him
down."

Pellea made a sound of angry impatience and tossed
her head in frustration. She was wearing a spectacular
gown—deep blue silk threaded with gold, strapless,
form-fitting, with a skirt cut to move sinuously as she
danced...or walked. Kayla felt frumpy in her simple
skirt and sweater.

"And I hope you're prepared to kill him when you find him," Pellea said dramatically.

"Your Majesty," Kayla began, beginning *to give in* to a touch of anxiety. She was trying to think of a new excuse for him on the fly—but something that wouldn't get her fired. The queen did have her emotional moments.

"Don't." Pellea held up a hand like a crossing guard. "I don't want to hear any tales of woe. I don't want to hear explanations and confessions. All I want is Prince Maximillian here where I can punish him." She shivered with what looked like anticipation. "Or his head on a platter. That would do." Her dark eyes flashed. "Do you understand?"

Kayla nodded. Despite everything, she was working hard to suppress a grin. She didn't dare let it show. Pellea was so angry.

The trouble was, she knew very well that the Max she had known was sure to make Pellea even angrier as time went by. There was nothing she could do to avoid it.

"Yes, Your Majesty. I'll do my best."

"Just find him!"

Queen Pellea swept out like the storm she could sometimes resemble. Kayla took a deep breath and steadied herself. What now? How was she supposed to find a rebel prince who obviously didn't want to be found?

It was always this way with Max. Rules were made for other people, not for him. He was easily the most infuriating—and the most charming—man she'd ever known. Just the thought that she would see him again any moment gave her a thrill that was electric. But it also gave her a dull, pounding headache. How was she going to work this? Heaven only knew.

She started by making a few phone calls. There were guards everywhere and security officers working the monitors at special locations. If he was in the castle, someone must have seen him. And some had. She got a lead here and there, and finally, an actual sighting from a hall guard who'd seen him disappear into the apartment of a local girl who was well-known for partying.

"Of course," Kayla muttered acidly. "I should have known."

She started off toward the place like a rocket, but deep in her heart, she dreaded the whole confrontation ahead of her. What was she going to do once she got to the door? Barge in on a seduction? She shuddered as she punched in the floor designation on the elevator panel.

"Darn you, Max," she whispered. "Do you always have to make life so hard?"

She thought about the last time she'd seen him, almost two years ago, his thick, bronzed hair disheveled, his eyes bleary with pain. Emotional pain. They'd both been in agony that night, both mourning over the same tragedy. The next thing she'd known, he was gone.

The elevator doors slid open silently and she stepped off, heart beating, head aching. It was only a few steps to the doorway. She stood in front of it, wishing she were anywhere else. Her phone buzzed and she pulled it open. It was Pellea, of course.

"Yes?"

"Have you found him yet?"

She sighed. "I've got his location. I'm about to go in and see...."

"Watch him," Pellea warned. "If there's a balcony, he'll jump."

Kayla gasped. "You don't think he's suicidal, do you?"

"Oh, heavens no. He defies death for the fun of it. I swear he's got to be an adrenaline freak."

Kayla considered that seriously. "You know..." she began.

But Pellea wasn't waiting to hear other views.

"Last week, we had a gathering of the new princes at the ski chalet, a meeting for them to get to know each other better. We'd barely begun cocktails when Max and the chalet manager's two beautiful daughters took off on snowmobiles, racing off into the mountains as though it were nothing more than a free snow day. And they didn't come back."

"Oh."

"No excuses the next day, of course. He thinks his smile covers all bases."

"I see," she said for lack of anything cogent to add. She felt a little lost with the queen battering her with complaints like this. A part of her wanted to defend him, but how did you defend behavior like this?

"Last night it was dinner with the Italian ambassador. We're about to sign an important treaty with them. He didn't show. And what was the excuse? He'd stopped *in at a pub and got involved in judging a karaoke contest and lost track of time.*"

"Oh, Max," Kayla said in soft despair.

"So I say, watch the balcony. He'll tie a rope to the edge and pretend he's Tarzan. Don't let him get away."

"I won't." She only wished her determination was as stout as it sounded.

Pellea sighed. Maybe her tone hadn't been convincing. "Give me your exact location. I sent a couple of security officers up to help you. I'll key in directions for them."

That startled her. "Help me do what?" she asked after giving the queen her location.

"Make sure he doesn't escape. We'll tie him up and drag him in if we have to."

"We will?" She knew Max and she was pretty sure that wasn't going to be done easily. This whole thing was beginning to resemble a nightmare. She stared at the door to the target apartment. Max was supposedly in there. They'd told her he'd gone in with a woman. Did the phrase *love nest* come to mind? This wasn't the way she'd imagined their reunion might pan out.

"Now I want you to be forceful," Pellea encouraged. "You must take him by surprise."

Kayla gasped in horror as a picture of what that might mean spun through her head. "You mean…burst in on him without warning?"

"If you have to. Whatever you do, you've got to stop him from disappearing again. Call me when it's over."

"Yes, Your Majesty. Of course." She hung up just as two security guards stepped off the elevator and marched over to join her.

"Sgt. Marander, ma'am, at your service," the one who seemed to be in charge announced. "Here's the master key. We're here to back you up. We'll be right behind you."

She chewed on her lower lip. "Can I knock first?" she asked, rather forlorn.

His stare was steely cold. "I'm afraid not. Her Majesty specifically recommended a surprise attack. She's afraid he'll…"

"Escape by jumping off the balcony. Yes, she told me as much."

He glanced at her and frowned. He probably heard the reluctance in her voice and didn't approve. "Sorry, miss. Instructions from the queen are not to be taken lightly."

She took a deep breath. "All right," she said, straightening her shoulders and heading for the door. "Here I go."

She closed her eyes and turned the key in the door, letting it swing open. "Max?" she asked breathlessly, not daring to look. "Are you in there?"

There was an ominous moment of startled silence and then a deep voice cried, "Kayla! What are you doing here?"

She forced herself to squint through one slightly

opened eye. And there he was, standing before her, completely clothed. Very civilized. Not scary at all. She gasped in relief.

"Oh, Max," she said, half laughing. And as he threw his arms around her, she sighed and went limp in his embrace. "I can't believe it's really you."

He hugged her, kissed each cheek, dropped a quick one on her lips and, finally, leaned back to take a look.

"Hey, gorgeous, it's been almost two years, hasn't it?"

She nodded, her head swimming. He was still the most beautiful man she'd ever seen, still hard and handsome, still looking like a playful rascal and a bit of a rogue. His thick rust-colored hair seemed to have a constant breeze blowing through it, his mischievous blue eyes were framed by eyelashes so thick it was almost criminal, and his mouth looked so deliciously sensual, it ought to be censored. That was Max, just as she remembered him. Lord, how she'd missed him!

"So what are you doing here?" he asked, looking completely bemused.

"I came to...to sort of arrest you. In a way." She made a face. What a farce.

"Arrest me?" At last he focused on the security guards behind her. He frowned. "What did I do now?"

"Oh, Max," she sighed. "Why can't you be good?"

"Kayla, my sweet," he said grinning at her, "you know that's not in my nature."

But he was genuinely happy to see her. Taking her in was like a good shot of whiskey. One look and he was transported two years back in time, back to those sidewalk cafés with the red umbrellas along the Mediterranean coast, back to the balmy breezes and sunlight filtering through the palms, back to hearing suggestive songs played by small combos while they'd sat sipping chichis, the local drink that tasted a bit like a Mai Tai and packed a punch like an angry kangaroo. The things they'd done, the things that had happened, the choices made, the regrets—it all still churned inside him. He couldn't let it go.

But he also couldn't regret knowing Kayla. She'd always been a joy. It was fantastic seeing her again.

"This is Kayla," he said casually to the redhead who was standing behind him, looking terrified. It appeared she wasn't used to having castle security barge in through her locked door. "Her husband was my best buddy in the old days when we flew sorties out of Trialta together."

"Oh," the redhead said weakly. Her teeth seemed to be chattering. "Nice to meet you, I'm sure."

"Yes," Kayla responded and tried to smile at the girl.

Max saw the confusion in her eyes and realized she was still digesting the situation she'd burst in on. It was pretty obvious she thought she'd found him having a "moment" here. That was hardly the case, though the redhead seemed to have thought it might turn into one, too.

But he hadn't been able to conjure up any interest. He'd been polite. He'd chatted. He'd accepted one small drink and the redhead had worked hard at creating a seductive scene. But he'd found himself looking out at the stars in the inky sky and listening to the strains of the orchestra from below in the ballroom, and all desire for that sort of satisfaction had melted away.

But before he found a way to explain all that, the two guards stepped forward and began to slip metal restraints on his wrists.

He looked down, startled. "What the hell is this?"

"Sir," Sgt. Marander said in an unfortunately pompous tone, "consider yourself in the custody of castle security."

Max blinked. He couldn't accept this. Handcuffs? They had to be kidding. He quickly saw two or three ways out of the situation. He could easily handle the guards and...

But then he looked up and met Kayla's worried gaze. Her pretty face, her dark, clouded eyes and her long, silky blond hair all created in flesh a picture that had haunted him for two years. Adrenaline still sizzled inside him for a few seconds, then began to drain away.

He wasn't going to run from Kayla. Now that he'd found her again, he didn't want to lose her until they'd had a chance to talk. If he could mine her memories and join them with his, maybe he could slay some of the demons that kept him awake at night. Maybe.

"Please, Max," she was saying, reaching out and putting a hand on his arm. "It's really important to Queen Pellea that you make an appearance at the ball."

He smiled down into her anxious gaze. "There is nothing I'm looking forward to more," he lied smoothly.

"Now that you're here, I'll have someone to dance with."

She jerked back, pulling her hand away. "Oh, no. Not me. You're supposed to be meeting eligible ladies of rank. That's not me."

He stared at her. "Kayla, what's the deal? Do you work for the royal family, or what?"

She nodded. "Yes. I've known the queen since we were kids together and my sister's husband is in the guard. Pellea offered me a job and I jumped at it." She shrugged, palms up. "I love it here."

He frowned, not sure what to make of that. When they'd been in Trialta, he'd assumed she was as much of a vagabond as he was. Now to know she had royal ties…

But what was he thinking? He was the one who was supposed to be a prince.

Still, he didn't like being corralled this way. He could tolerate going to the ball if they let him come on his own terms. This way was just too much. Kayla or no Kayla, he was back to wanting to get the hell out of here. But his hesitation had meant he was locked up.

"Hey, I'll come with you willingly," he noted. "But could we get rid of these handcuffs?"

She hesitated, looking down at them. Then she gazed up into his eyes.

He smiled. She sighed.

"Sure," she said, wondering if she were risking everything but hardly caring. She looked at the security agents. "Let him go."

The sergeant glared at her. "But, Miss..."

"I'll take the responsibility," she said. "If he bolts, I'll tell the queen it was my fault."

The man shrugged and used the key, but he didn't look happy about it.

Max smiled and flexed his wrists and looked toward the balcony in the redhead's room. He could make it in two bounds and be jumping for freedom in seconds. Everything in him was ready to go. Why the hell should he stick around when he knew he was going to hate the results?

CHAPTER TWO

KAYLA could read Max's mind. She knew him too well. She saw the glance as a way out and she moved in smoothly, taking his hand in hers, lacing their fingers together. If he was going to run for it, he was going to have to drag her with him.

"You're all mine now," she told him archly. "I'm calling the shots."

"Is that right?" he said, looking skeptical, but amused. "I thought I was the one who was supposed to be royal all of a sudden." He raised one quizzical eyebrow. "You've heard, haven't you? Now they've got me pegged as one of the lost princes. Can you believe it?"

She shook her head, smiling at him. "I'm finding it hard. When I realized it was you…" She shrugged and closed her eyes as she relived those moments, and when she spoke again, her voice was shaky. "Max, I thought you were dead."

He looked at her for a moment, then managed a crooked smile. "Which time?" he asked softly.

Her phone buzzed. She knew it was the queen. Pressing her lips together, she shook her head.

"We'll have to talk later." She reached for her phone but she didn't let go of his hand. She'd learned a lesson or two over the years, and one of them was to look both ways before stepping off the curb.

"Yes, Your Majesty. We're on our way."

Ten minutes later they were in Pellea's public parlor while she flitted about and generally let Max know he was on thin ice with her. Kayla watched, but hardly listened. She knew the queen was crazy about him and was just trying to convince him to behave.

At the same time, she herself was a bit impatient with all this. She felt as though every nerve ending was vibrating right now. There were so many things to take care of, so much to consider. Max was back and she had to figure out how to fit him into her life again. She had a thousand questions for him. There was so much she wanted to know, so much they'd missed. So much they needed to discuss.

For instance, had he come close to marrying anyone in the last two years? Was there someone out there? She was hoping there was, but the signs weren't good. If he had someone serious in his life, she could move on without any lingering doubts. Couldn't she?

The funny thing was, she couldn't imagine him married. He didn't have a married way about him. His beautiful eyes had a look that said he was always searching for something and not very satisfied with what he'd found. You had a sense that there was something missing in his life, but he wasn't sure what it was and he knew he hadn't seen it yet. Just seeing that in him scared her.

But the queen seemed to have no forbearance left for all that. She knew what she wanted from Max and she wanted it now.

"The first thing we're going to do is get you into some decent clothes," she said, rummaging through her closet.

"What? You don't like my style?" He said it in a tone that might have seemed insolent if he hadn't paired his words with a look of pure innocence that caught Pellea by surprise, making her laugh.

"Now I see what the problem is," she told him, shaking her head. "You just don't know any better. You need to learn a thing or two about being a prince, don't you?"

"If you insist." His mouth twisted but he bent forward in a sweeping bow. "Anything for you, my beautiful queen."

Despite everything, Pellea colored slightly, then glanced Kayla's way. "You've got to admit, the boy's a charmer," she said out of the side of her mouth. "I think he's a diamond in the rough, too. We'll see what we can make of him." She smirked. "Heat and pressure. That's how you get perfect diamonds. Are you game?"

He didn't answer but she'd already turned away and was hunting through a closet again, muttering about sizes and ruffled shirts.

He looked at Kayla and shrugged, as though to say,

"They've got me this time," and she smiled at him, her heart full of affection for all he'd meant to her in the past. She wasn't sure what the future would bring. But things were never dull when Max was around.

Her smile faded as she remembered that there was something more lasting than memories between them, something more precious than life itself. And that was when she decided it was time for her to go.

"Your Majesty, if you don't need of me here…"

Pellea poked her head back out of the closet. "Go ahead, Kayla," she said. "I know you've got work to do. I won't keep you."

"Thank you," Kayla said, then she turned and gave Max a stern look. "You will be good, won't you?"

"At what?" he teased with a lopsided smile.

She glared at him. "The guard is outside so don't think you can get away with anything," she murmured to him out of Pellea's hearing.

He gave her a "Who? Me?" look. She shook her head and started for the door. "Have a lovely time at the ball," she said over her shoulder. "I'm sure you'll be the star."

And she was out the door before he had a chance to say or do anything else.

She hurried back to the office, hoping to get some work done that she'd neglected while she was off chasing princes. It had been a hectic week. Pellea had sent her to represent the DeAngelis royal family at a financial conference in Paris. She'd hated leaving for a whole week, but the fact that the queen had that much faith in her had been wonderful. She'd worked herself to the bone trying to live up to expectations and she was exhausted.

And while she was gone, the search for the last of the lost princes of Ambria had struck gold. First Mykal Marten, whom she'd met before she left for the continent, had been confirmed as the fourth prince. And then the news had come that the fifth and last prince had been discovered. When she saw the name—Max Arragen—in a newspaper account, she hadn't thought much of it, but then she saw a picture. It was blurry and taken from a distance, but the jaunty set of the shoulders had made her think of Max—her Max. She'd gasped and begun to wonder.

It wasn't until she'd returned home to Ambria a day ago that she'd seen a good picture and realized that Prince Max really was the man she'd known in Trialta as Max Arragen two years before. And that sent her into a virtual tailspin.

She'd only known him for about six months, but the time they'd spent together had been crazy and intense. He was her husband's best friend, and they'd both been working as contract pilots, flying reconnaissance missions against the tyrannical regime of the North African nation of Trialta on the Mediterranean. They'd lived like young people involved in war often do, working hard during the day, partying at night like there was no tomorrow. They were fighting for the rebels and thought they were invincible.

She couldn't believe he was back in her life again—at least in a peripheral way. He always managed to inject excitement and surprise into everything, like no one else she'd ever known. She remembered times in Trialta where it had seemed she and Eddie were in the lead vehicle in a continuous car chase—and Max was at the wheel.

And then came the day when Eddie didn't return from a mission. The wreckage of his plane was found, and all the parties stopped. Kayla had clung to Max at the time and they'd mourned together, hardly believing that the Eddie they both loved so much could be gone forever. No one else could have understood how deep their grief was.

But that was then. Things had changed, for both of them. Surely he'd had some life-changing experiences since she last knew him. And she'd had a beautiful, wonderful child.

What would it be like to be friends with Max now? She was a little bit afraid to find out. She wasn't the wide-eyed innocent she'd been two years before. She had some secrets of her own. And how would she keep them from him, now that he was going to be living right here in the castle?

She buried her worries in work, staying an hour longer than normal. And then, once she'd put away her papers and shut off her computer, she gave in to temptation and made her way down to the ballroom instead of going straight to her room.

She took a back entrance and climbed the stairs to a seldom-used interior balcony that overlooked the entire floor area. The orchestra was playing a waltz and the couples swept across the floor, around and around, the women like flowers in their beautiful dresses, the men resplendent in gold-edged uniforms of white or blue or crimson. Despite everything, it took her breath away and made her heart beat faster. A scene like this would make anyone want to be noble, especially if they'd been raised on fairy tales.

She watched for a few minutes longer, caught up in the magic. How wonderful to be royal and to live as though you were the star of it all. Just being here in the castle made her feel as though she were blessed. But it also made her feel a new and more intense responsibility to her country and her people. She wondered if Max would start to feel a little of that soon.

She could pick out most of the princes. So handsome, every one of them—so tall and strong. They looked like men who were confident in themselves and ready to take on the world. She could hardly believe Max was about to take his place alongside of them.

There was Prince Mykal, sitting on the sidelines, still recovering from a horrendous motorcycle accident from a few months before. Prince David, one of her favorites, was dancing with beautiful Ayme, who had recently become his bride. Prince Joe, still looking like a California surfer with his sun-streaked hair, was laughing with Kelly, his own new bride. And newly crowned King Monte had Pellea in his arms and was leading her around the floor with such obvious passion, you'd think the honeymoon was starting that night. That made her laugh softly to herself.

She searched the crowd. Where was Max? Her gaze lingered a moment on Princess Kim. She was glad to see her looking happy after all that she'd been through on the enemy side of the island with the Granvilli partisans. It was good to have her safe and sound, back in the castle where she belonged. But where was Max?

At first worried, she began to get angry. If he had slipped away again…!

And then she saw him.

Max was standing with a group of men she didn't recognize. As she watched, the men moved away and a beautiful dark-haired woman was brought up to be presented to him. Kayla felt a tug on her heartstrings, but she tried desperately to suppress it. She couldn't be jealous. There was no sense behind it. She had to keep it down. Max was not hers and never had been. Never would be, especially now that he was a prince. There was no justification for any jealousy. She couldn't let it happen.

She watched as they danced. He moved so well, as if he were floating on air. He was talking to his partner and she was blossoming in his arms. He could have been born for this—and of course, he really was!

The dance was over. She could breathe again. And now, she really had to go. But she watched for just one minute more, and suddenly his head was tilted up. He was looking right at her. And as she watched, he lifted a glass of champagne and smiled at her, giving her a toast. Her breath caught in her throat and she gasped. He gave her a nod, and then a lascivious wink. Her face felt hot as she pulled back, away from where anyone could see her. She was laughing, though. That wink was guaranteed to keep her warm that night. Trust Max!

But as she turned and left the balcony, her amusement evaporated. She couldn't do this. She couldn't be watching Max from afar and reacting every time he noticed her. Nothing good could come of this. Much better that she should stay as far away from him as she could get. If he really wasn't attached, it would be his duty to find a bride as soon as possible. Watching him fall in love would be tough to take. And if he ever found out…

No, keeping in touch with Max was much too dangerous. She had to find a way to avoid it.

She hadn't eaten since breakfast and she was starving. Glancing at her watch, she knew it was too late to pick up Teddy before he went to sleep. Her heart ached as she thought about that. She missed him. Her baby was only a little over a year old and she missed him when she had late days like this. Sighing, she knew she had to speak to Pellea about it. She really didn't want to be away from her child this long. At the same time, she was so lucky to have this job…

She stopped in at the all-night café and got a salad to eat once she got home.

Then she headed for her sister Caroline's room, just two doors down from hers.

"Hi," she called softly, opening the door with her own key. "How are they?"

"Sleeping like lambs," Caroline said, rising from the

couch where she'd been reading and coming to give her
sister a hug.

Just two years apart, they looked enough alike that
there was always someone who asked if they were
twins. Caroline wore her blond hair short, pixie-style,
and had a more sleepy, languid look about her, but otherwise, they were practically replicas and had always
been especially close.

They stood together looking down at where the two
little boys, one dark-haired like his father, the other as
blond as his mother, lay side by side, sound asleep.

Caroline's husband, Rik, was a rising star in the
Ambrian royal guard. Right now he was on a mission
on the Granvilli side of the island and would be gone
for a few days. Luckily, whether Rik was home or not,
Caroline loved having Teddy in to play with her own
boy.

"Why don't you leave him here for the night?" she
suggested. "He's used to sleeping here after the last
week when you were in Paris. And it was so hard to put
them down tonight, I hate to wake them up and have to
start all over again."

"Are you sure?" Kayla felt guilty, but she was so
tired, it sounded like a good thing to do.

"Absolutely. You're only two doors down. I can get
you over here fast if I need you. Just come on over first
thing in the morning and it will all be good."

She stayed for half an hour, sharing her salad with
her sister while they talked, watching her baby while
he slept.

And then she was back in the corridor, on her way home and looking down toward the public area, wondering how the ball was going. It was interesting to live this way, with everything happening so close at hand. The castle lifestyle was growing on her. She had been new to it a year before when she'd come to work here, but she was used to it now and it seemed a comfortable way of life. She compared it to living on a huge cruise ship.

She opened her own door and went in, yawning and kicking off her shoes as she did. A tap on a switch turned on a soft light in the kitchen, which did enough to light the path to her bedroom. She made her way slowly through the apartment, casting off clothes as she went, first her jacket, then her skirt, then her sweater.

She was thinking about crashing straight onto her bed and closing her eyes and not opening them again until morning. Heavenly peace. No dreams, please. Just wonderful sleep. Her eyes began to droop in anticipation.

But it was not to be. Two steps short of her destination, just as she was reaching back to unhook her bra, a dark hulk rose from her overstuffed chair in the corner.

"You know," the hulk said ruefully, "I'd love to let you go on with this, but I have a feeling you'd hate me in the morning. Just a hunch."

She screamed, grabbing her sweater back again and pressing it to her chest. At the same time, Max jumped forward and took her by the shoulders.

"No, don't scream," he said urgently. "I get into so much trouble when women scream."

She glared up at him, quickly pushing him away, startled and exasperated all at once. She could smell alcohol on his breath, but that was hardly surprising. Still, she was wary enough to be careful.

Handsome men, liquor and a moonlit night—the recipe for disaster.

"Then don't jump out at them from dark corners, maybe," she suggested sharply.

He shrugged as though anxious to make up for scaring her. "Okay, okay. It's a deal."

"*Oh, Max.*" *She glared at him as she tried to keep* covered in all the most delicate areas. "Why did you let me get this far before you said anything?"

His eyebrows rose. "Are you kidding me?"

"Oh!" She shook her head, but she was calming down. "Look that way," she insisted, pointing to the wall. "And don't turn around until I tell you to."

He turned obediently and she began to search her drawer for fresh clothes to wear. "What are you doing here?" she demanded at the same time.

"I wanted to see you. We need some time to talk. Old times and all that."

She pulled on a comfortable top.

"Maybe call first next time," she suggested grumpily as she dug for something to pull over her legs. "How did you get in here anyway?"

He chuckled. "Princes pretty much rule around this castle. You tell people you're a prince and they want to do things for you. The housekeeper couldn't wait to do me a favor."

"That's a problem." She sighed. "Okay, you can turn around."

He turned and looked at her and he was knocked out. Here he'd just come from a royal ball filled with beautiful women who'd all spent half the day in the beauty shop and were dressed to kill and no one he'd seen there turned him on the way Kayla did wearing a simple sweatshirt and black leggings, with her hair looking like a tornado had just come through.

"I think I love you," he said, taking in all her rumpled glory and smiling. "I know I've missed you like crazy. It's so good to see you again."

She gazed into his warm blue eyes and melted. She knew he was kidding, that this was his way of joking about emotions instead of dealing with them. But she also knew he was recognizing the ties between them and ready to embrace them, just like it used to be.

Still, she had to wonder if he remembered that last night as clearly as she did. He had done nothing to indicate it. As far as she was concerned, she hoped he had a touch of amnesia. That night had been a crazy rush of pain and grief and anguish and they hadn't handled it very well. Best to forget it. If they could.

She gave herself a moment to really look at him. Pellea had found him a striking uniform to wear to the ball, but he'd taken off the jacket and pulled open the shirt, displaying some gorgeous skin and manly chest hair. Now he looked less than formal. She shook her head at the sight, but despite everything, she enjoyed seeing him. She always did.

"How did you get away from Pellea?"

He shrugged. "It wasn't easy. The woman was watching me like a hawk."

She sighed and sank into a chair, gesturing for him to sit on the couch across from her. "She'll probably be calling me any minute to organize a search party."

He moved her discarded jacket and dropped down onto the arm of the couch, then leaned toward her. "You won't give me up, will you?" he said with a puppy-dog look.

"Are you kidding?" she told him crossly. "Of course I will. I'm not risking my job so that you can play hooky."

He laughed. "Good point." Then he frowned. "What is your job exactly?"

"I'm the queen's personal assistant. I do whatever she needs to get done but doesn't have time to do herself."

It was a good job and she was proud of it. As a single mother without anyone to count on but herself, she was lucky to have it. If she ever lost it, for any reason, she would be in real trouble. There weren't many good jobs for women in Ambria right now and the queen was a wonderful woman to work for. With a two-year-old of her own, Pellea understood the problems Kayla had to face and was ready to give her a lot of leeway.

"Ah," Max said, "impressive. Quite another level from the job you had in Trialta."

She smiled, thinking of it. "Selling T-shirts to tourists from a kiosk on the beach. Yes, I didn't get much chance to show my skills and talents at that one."

But it hadn't mattered then. Her days were spent waiting for Eddie to come back from a flight, and her nights were filled with wine, music and friends. For a few months, life had been carefree and exciting. But you had to pay for everything, one way or another, and she'd been paying the price ever since.

Max was staring at her as though he could see what she was thinking. "And yet, here you are, barely two years later, assistant to the queen."

She gave him a look. "I do have a university education, you know."

He appeared surprised. "No, I didn't know. When did you get that?"

She smiled. "Long before I first met you."

"No kidding." He frowned, thinking that over. "That's more than I've got. And they think they want me to be a prince."

Her smile wavered a bit. It was true. From what she knew of his background, he might have a bit of trouble. He'd never been shy about it. While sipping drinks in the sidewalk cafés of Trialta, he'd regaled them with tales of his childhood living on the streets, always making it sound hilarious rather than tragic. But she'd often thought the raw tattered ghost of deprivation lingered in the shadows of his eyes.

He'd had a rough childhood. Any breaks he ever got he'd worked hard to achieve. That was very different from what most royals experienced. The newspaper

accounts had filled in some of the parts of his background she hadn't known before, but she didn't know
how accurate they were.

"From what I've read in the newspapers and maga-
zines, they seem to think that you were spirited off on
the night of the rebellion," she said to him musingly.
"When the Granvilli family attacked and burned the
castle—when your parents, the king and queen were
killed, and all the DeAngelis royal children went into
hiding."

She shuddered just thinking of it. Those poor kids!

"Do you know how you escaped? Do you have any
idea who it was who saved you by carrying you off that
night?"

His shrug was careless, as if he didn't know and
didn't really care. "Whoever they were, they didn't take
very good care of me. By the time I was seven or eight,
I was fending for myself on the streets. Before that,
there were various strangers—at one point I think I
was staying with a pickpocket who tried to teach me
his tricks. But as far as I know, nobody was around for
long at anytime. There's no one I can claim."

It broke her heart to think of a child being abandoned
like that. She knew from his stories during their Trialta
days that he'd been taken in by a fisherman for a while,
but the man was cruel and he eventually ran away. It
wasn't until his late teens when he was given a corner
to sleep in and a job cleaning the chapel that he met a
wonderful older man—a pastor—and his kindly wife,

who made it their business to see that he was clothed and had a safe place to stay.

The pastor had a hobby of flying ancient aircraft—planes from twentieth century wars. Pretty soon he was teaching Max the ropes, introducing him to aviation, and after that life was much brighter. Max joined the Ambrian Air Force as soon as he was old enough. And that was pretty much all she knew.

"And no one ever guessed you were one of the lost princes," she murmured, looking at him wonderingly.

He laughed shortly. "Did you guess?"

She spread her hands out. "No."

"Neither did I. That shows you how long the odds were."

"Yes." She sighed. "How horrible for you to be treated like that as such a young child. I'm glad the Granvillis are paying the price for their treason now."

He stirred restlessly. "That's life. Sometimes you win, sometimes you lose."

"And sometimes they pull the chair out from under you, just when you think they've given you a throne to sit on."

He grinned at her appreciatively. "A cautionary tale, Kayla? Reminding me not to count on anything?"

She nodded. She couldn't help it. She'd always been a cautious one. Her only times of going crazy had involved marrying a flyer and then letting grief make her lose all control when he died. "Count no chicks before they hatch."

He cocked his head to the side. "Wisdom as well as beauty."

"Nice of you to notice." She rose, feeling a little too nervous to sit for long. "Would you like a drink? Iced tea? A cup of coffee?"

"A beer?" he suggested, following her to the little kitchenette.

"I think I have one." And she did, ice cold and ready to drink. She pulled it out of the refrigerator and popped the top for him.

He took a long sip, sighed with satisfaction and leaned against the counter, looking at her. "So what have you been doing all this time?" he asked her. "You didn't come straight here from Trialta did you?"

"No. I've been here for less than a year."

"And what were you doing before that?"

She hesitated. Her heart was thumping in her chest. It was time to come clean. She had to tell him. He would find out soon enough anyway. And if he thought she were trying to keep it from him, he might think...

She shivered.

"I...uh...I had a baby." She forced herself to look him in the eye and not waver. "A little boy. I call him Teddy."

"Teddy?" He blinked at her.

"Yes. He's at my sister's right now, down the hall. Maybe you can meet him tomorrow."

And she stared into his eyes, searching for doubt, searching for memories, searching for anything that would tell her he'd guessed the truth.

CHAPTER THREE

MAX's reaction came a beat too late. Kayla knew he'd had a quick second to think before he let his natural instincts take over. What was he thinking in that flash of time? What was he feeling? His crystal-blue eyes didn't show a thing. But that tiny hesitation did.

"Teddy," he said, sounding pretty normal. "You named him after Eddie, huh? Great."

He licked his upper lip quickly, then smiled and reached out to give her a one-armed hug. "Kayla, I'm so glad you have a piece of Eddie to hold on to. That is very cool."

He was looking right into her eyes now, seeming completely sincere. "I can hardly wait to meet him."

Glancing down, she realized, to her horror, that her fingers were trembling. Quickly, she shoved them under the hem of her sweatshirt.

"How about you?" she said, a little breathless. "I guess you're not married."

"Married!" His laugh was short and humorless. "You know me better than that."

"If Pellea has her way, you soon will be."

His deep, painful groan made her smile.

"Did you meet anyone interesting at the ball?"

"That wasn't all the ball was about, was it?" His groan was louder this time. "Oh, lord, do you think she's going to have more of them?"

"Of course. You have to marry someone. The others are all paired up already. Pellea wants to get you settled as well."

His sigh was heartfelt as he leaned wearily across the little counter. "Why don't you marry me? Then we can forget all about this nonsense and just be happy."

She looked away. The very suggestion sent something skittering through her like sparks from fireworks and she took a quick, gasping little breath, trying to suppress the feeling.

Marrying Max—what a concept. Luckily, that would never happen, not even for the sake of convenience. There was no way Max could ever take care of her and her baby. It wouldn't work. She'd been out in the world with him and she probably knew him better than she knew any other man, other than her husband. Max was born to be a bachelor.

Even Eddie had said so. "Max will never get married," he'd told her when she tried to have a go at a little matchmaking at one point. "He's like those animals that die in captivity. They can't be tamed. They can't even be gentled. Leave Max alone. He'll just break their hearts. And yours, too.'"

Eddie was right, as usual. Max was not a man to

hang your heart on. She shook her head and got up the nerve to meet his gaze again. "Sorry, Max. You're going to have to walk that lonesome valley on your own."

His mouth twisted with a bit of pretended chagrin, but he wasn't really thinking about what she'd said. His gaze was skimming over her face, searching in her eyes, looking for something in the set of her lips. She wasn't sure what he expected to see, but it was disturbing, and she turned away, heading back to the living room.

She could feel him watching her, as though his gaze were burning a brand into her back. She forced herself not to look, and finally he came after her and sank onto the couch.

"Come and sit down by me," he said.

His voice was low and there was a new element in it…something different, something mysterious. She felt wary and her pulse stuttered and then began to move a bit faster. There was a sense of being a bit off-kilter. Somehow, the room seemed warmer. A new tension quivered in the air. Every time her eyes met his, the tension seemed thicker, more insistent, like a drum-beat beginning to make itself heard across a rain-forest jungle.

She took a deep breath and held it for a moment, trying to calm herself. They were just friends, but she worried that he might be edging toward something more. She couldn't let that happen. Not again.

"Come on," he coaxed. He wasn't smiling but his gaze was warm. Almost smoldering.

She shook her head and dropped back into the chair. "No. I think I'll stay here."

"What's the matter?" he asked her.

She licked her dry lips. "I think we need to keep a demilitarized zone between us," she said, trying to sound casual and friendly at the same time.

His eyebrows shot up. "What are you talking about?"

She took a deep breath. How to begin?

"I'm serious, Max. I don't think we ought to be close. You're moving into a whole different sphere of life. I don't belong there. Let's not start anything that will have to be..." She shrugged, not sure she wanted to put it into words.

His bright gaze clouded and he appeared bewildered by what she'd said. "But you seem a part of this castle stuff and I'm just a beginner," he pointed out. "What are you talking about with this 'different sphere' business?"

She wondered for just a moment if he were really that naive about the class structure in their society. Ambria had always been a remote, self-absorbed little kingdom. Islands tended to breed peculiarities in animals and people if they were cut off from the mainstream for too long. Now that the monarchy had taken back control, after a twenty-five-year exile, and some of the old customs and rituals were being revived.

Royalty was royalty. It was special. That was all part of establishing authority and building back the old foundations. They were meant to be set apart from the common Ambrian. That was just the way it had to be.

"I'm an employee," she told him cheerfully. "You're a prince. Never the twain shall meet."

He made a face as though he thought that was complete tripe, but he would accept her judgment for the moment.

"We can still be friends, can't we? We can still talk."

"Sure."

He frowned. "I'm counting on you for that, you know."

That was just the problem. "Max…"

He took in a deep breath. "Here's the deal, Kayla. I don't know what I'm doing here." His gaze was hard now, insistent, and yet at the same time, completely vulnerable. "I don't know if I can stand too much of this prince stuff. It's not me."

"Oh." A flash close to pain went through her. He thought he couldn't do this. And yet, how could she be surprised? This was exactly what she would have expected if anyone had asked her. But that didn't mean she could let him go down this road without a struggle. He had to see how important it was.

"I'm willing to give it a go. For now. But I'm not feeling too confident. Most of my life has been lived on the other side of the divide. I don't know if I can adapt."

"Of course you can." She wished she could find the words she needed to get through to him. "Max, you were meant to be a prince from the beginning. Don't you see? The part where you lived on the streets was the mistake."

"I'm not so sure about that." He winced, then went

on softly, his eyes looking dark and luminous, his voice barely hiding the years of uncertainty he'd lived through.

"Sometimes I think I never got a family because I didn't deserve one. I was a misfit. A pretty bad misfit. And maybe I didn't ever get that kind of family love because…" He looked up and met her gaze. "Because I'm just unlovable."

She gasped. He wasn't joking. His expression was serious, questioning. Now she had to stop herself from going to him, from sliding down beside him and push-ing away his pain with her arms. And at the same time, everything in her wanted to do it.

"Max! How can you say that? Women adore you!"

He stared at her for a moment, then gave a half laugh, half grunt. "That's not love, Kayla. That's something else."

Her head went back in surprise. Who would have believed Max would be the one to see the difference so clearly? But still, he seemed to be utterly blind to his own strengths. He was always so carefree and debo-nair. She'd never known he had this insecurity at his core. She had to make him see how wrong it was.

"Oh, come on. What did we used to call you? Mr. Casanova. A new girl on your arm every night."

His sigh was full of regrets. "You see, that's just it." He took a long drink from his beer and stared into space. "Lots of new girls. No true love."

It was hard to believe that a man this appealing, this attractive, thought he couldn't find his soul mate. She looked at him, so handsome, so adorable. Her fingers ached to run through that thick auburn hair. It took all her will to stay where she was.

"Haven't you ever been in love?" she asked him.

"Not really." He squinted at her, thinking it over. "I don't think so. Not like you and Eddie." His smile was crooked. "I used to watch you two together and I think I hated you almost as much as I loved you."

"Oh, Max…"

"You know what I mean. It was pure jealousy. You two were so good together, so…so devoted." His voice broke on the word and she had to close her eyes and bite her lip to keep from going to him.

Devoted. Yes, that was exactly the way it had been. When she'd found Eddie, she couldn't believe her luck. They'd met in an elevator in their apartment building in Paris. As they traveled up the floors, people got off, but the two of them remained, until they were alone and looking at each other tentatively across the empty car. Their eyes met. Love at first sight. And when they finally got to her floor, he admitted his had been four stops before. How could she not invite him in for a cup of coffee? Two months later, they were married.

When he'd died, she had thought life was over. She moved in a dark, menacing fog, blindly searching for some way out of the pain, not really believing it was possible. For days, she was obsessed, thinking of ways to join him. And then she realized she had someone else to think about.

"Do you remember…?" Max's voice choked.

She stiffened. Here it came. She had to keep a cool front. Still, she had to tell the truth, at least as far as it was safe.

"I remember too much," she said softly.

"Me, too." He finished off his beer and looked at her. "I think about Eddie every day."

She nodded, closing her eyes. "Me, too."

She wasn't going to cry. She had to hold it back. For a moment, she let herself recall the way it had been being married to Eddie. Sunshine every day. Champagne for breakfast. Walks on the beach and dancing barefoot to a reggae tune. Driving with the top down. Love in the afternoon. Eddie was the best. The very best.

But she couldn't let herself think about him too much. That was a temptation that could sap her life away.

"Remember that day we went sailing in the bay," he said, "and your straw hat flew off and Eddie and I jumped into the water and raced for it?"

She nodded, trying to smile. "We had a picnic on that little island and we ate all those cherries."

"And then spent an hour rolling in the sand, moaning, with the worst stomachaches imaginable."

She managed a half grin. "I thought we were going to die."

He laughed. "I wanted to die."

His words seemed to echo in the room. Eddie was the one who had died, not long after that sunny day.

She closed her eyes again. They had to stop this. No *good could come of it. They were laying treacherous* emotional land mines all around. If they didn't stop, something was going to explode.

She wanted to stop. She tried. But somehow she couldn't keep the words from coming.

"I remember when you and Eddie would fly off into those big thunder clouds," she said softly, staring into the past, "like two falcons challenging the sky. It was so scary, but so magnificent. It made me shiver every time. I could hardly breathe. You were angels flying into the danger zone. And every time you came back victorious, another strike for the good guys, another strike for justice in the world." She turned to look at him, emotion almost choking her. "I was so proud of you both."

He didn't answer. Instead, he shook his head and looked away, and she knew his voice was probably too rough to use right now.

She should stop. She should push this all away into the past. But she couldn't. It was as though she had to get this out in the open in order to let it go. She tried not to say anything more, but the words came anyway.

"Everyone was proud of you. You were heroes. The best. The brightest stars."

She swallowed hard, then reached out across the coffee table and took his hand.

"And then, on that dark, rainy day in November, you took off together, as usual, but you...you came back alone."

She blinked, wondering why there were no tears in

her eyes. She usually had tears by now when she went over this in her own head. Why wasn't she crying?

"I stood there and watched your plane fly in, and I knew in my heart what it meant. But I didn't want to accept it. I kept thinking, no, he'll be coming. He's just had engine trouble or took a wrong turn or..." Her voice choked and she took a deep, shuddering breath. "I kept staring into the horizon, looking for that black spot to appear against the sky."

Her words seemed to echo against the walls as they both sat quietly, waiting for the pain to fade.

"Eddie was the best guy I ever knew," he said at last, his voice rough as a rocky beach. "It should have been me."

"No..." She held his hand as tightly as she could, with both her own.

"He was true and honest and brave. Not like me."

"No," she said fiercely. "Don't ever say that."

His face was twisted with pain. "Kayla, Kayla, it should have been me."

She was next to him on the couch now, and she wasn't sure how she got there. But she had to be with him, as close as she could get. She had to remind him of his own worth, his own value. She couldn't let him feel this way.

She took his beautiful face between her hands and stared right into his eyes. "Eddie was a wonderful man. But so are you. You're just as good and precious and worthy."

He looked at her and winced, as though the light was too bright in that direction.

"I would trade it all to have him back again," he muttered.

She shook her head. "I don't think you can make bargains like that. I don't think you can trade yourself. What happens, happens. We have to use it to make ourselves into better people."

"Yeah." He tried to twist away from her, then gave it up. "But it shouldn't have been Eddie. Not Eddie."

Her fingers dug into his hair and he looked down into her eyes. He was going to kiss her. She knew it and she knew she should stop him. She tried. But as his arms slowly wrapped around her and he pulled her body close, she could only sigh and raise her mouth to find his.

The moment was electric. They'd come together as though it were inevitable, as though they were pulled by a force they weren't strong enough to fight. Everything in Kayla cried out with need for Max. In this primal moment, he was hers and she was ready to surrender again. Just like before. She clung to him, clung and arched into his embrace, waiting for the touch of his tongue.

His face came closer. She could feel his warm breath on her lips. Closing her eyes, she sighed and offered her face to him.

And that was when the door to the apartment flew open and Pellea came storming into the room like a Valkyrie.

The two of them stared at her, mouths hanging open in shock, still tangled in each others arms. She glared back, her hands on her hips as the door slammed shut behind her.

"What the heck is going on here?" she demanded.

Max frowned, not letting Kayla go. "Doesn't anyone ever knock in this place?" he quizzed right back at her.

"You're a fine one to talk," Kayla said, sotto voce.

Pellea's nostrils flared. "I knocked. Nobody answered. I guess you were too busy with this…this…" Her hand waved around in the air but she couldn't find a word that would suit. Still, her annoyance was clear.

Kayla began to pry herself loose from Max's octopus embrace and rose quickly in order to show respect for Pellea's position, hoping Max would notice and follow her lead.

"Oh, Pellea, don't get upset," she said, half laughing at the crazy situation. "We're old friends. Max was Eddie's best friend. They flew together in the Mediterranean."

Pellea's mouth made a round circle for a moment. She looked from one to the other of them. "Wow," she said. "I had no idea."

Kayla looked back at Max. He was grumpy and she couldn't really blame him. But she was glad Pellea had interrupted them. If anyone needed an intervention, it was the two of them. She gave him a look and he slowly rose beside her.

"I didn't realize he was the man I'd known until

yesterday, when I first saw his picture in your office,"
Kayla explained.

Pellea frowned suspiciously. "You didn't say anything."

"I...I needed some time to get used to it. You see,
earlier I had thought he'd been killed in Somalia months
ago and..."

"Wait." Pellea held up her hand. "Your husband was
killed flying for the Trialta National Forces, wasn't he?"

"Yes. He and Max flew together there."

Pellea looked skeptical. "And you never had any idea
he might be royal?"

Kayla shook her head. "Never. I would have laughed
at anyone who suggested it."

"Hey," Max complained in a low voice.

"Oh, never mind." Pellea looked at Max, then at
Kayla, and shook her head and her look turned thoughtful. "That just makes it all more interesting, doesn't it?"

Kayla had to fight hard to resist rolling her eyes. "If
you say so," she muttered, wondering what the queen
had up her sleeve now.

She was carrying a portfolio, obviously something
she'd brought in to show off for some reason. But her
attention had been diverted. She glared at the recalci-
trant prince.

"I feel like I'm going to have to put a homing device
on you," she warned him.

He frowned, looking rebellious. He glanced at Kayla,
then looked straight at the queen. "Is this prince job a
twenty-four-hour commitment?" he asked suspiciously.

"Of course," Pellea said sharply.

"Of course not," Kayla said at the same time.

She certainly didn't want to contradict the queen, but she thought they'd better widen the discussion a bit before Max said something he would regret. The look on his face already set the stage for handing in his resignation as a royal. She didn't think the queen should portray it with quite such a heavy hand. Talk about scaring the quarry away! A little finesse was in order.

"The other princes don't have homing devices," she explained sensibly.

Pellea frowned at her. "The other princes don't need them."

Kayla shrugged reluctantly. "Good point."

And don't you forget it, Pellea seemed to say with her flashing eyes, though not a word passed her lips. She turned to Max and her face softened.

"Did you enjoy the ball?" she asked him hopefully.

He hesitated. Kayla bit her lip and prayed. For once in his life, was he going to be good? She knew there was a struggle going on inside him.

"Yes, Your Majesty, I did," he admitted at last. "You put on an amazing show. I was impressed."

Pellea looked pleased. "There, you see? If you would just relax and see what we're all about, you'll learn to love us in no time at all." She was smiling now, looking at both Kayla and Max with affection. "You'll see," she added, and then her smile faded and she took a deep, deep breath.

"But there's something else," she said, sliding the portfolio out from under her arm. "Take a look at this."

Sweeping aside the things on the coffee table, she pulled a poster out and spread it out on the flat surface.

"All right," she said dramatically, looking at Max. "Now explain this, mister!"

Max and Kayla stepped closer and looked down at the poster. Bright red with startling black writing, it displayed a large picture of Max and the announcement Max Arragen, Wanted, Dead or Alive!!!

CHAPTER FOUR

THE silence in the room was electric. All three seemed frozen in place. Finally, Kayla looked up at Max and asked simply, "What does it mean?"

He didn't meet her gaze. "I have no idea," he said softly, still staring at the poster. His mind was working like a buzz saw, cutting through all options and leaving shards of rejected possibilities behind. What could he possibly have done...?

Pellea crossed her arms over her chest and glared at him. "Okay, if nothing comes quickly to mind, let's go over the facts. As you can see, this was issued by the small nation of Mercuria. Have you ever been there?"

He raised his head and looked at the queen. This was a can of worms he would rather not have to deal with, but it seemed he would have no choice.

"Yes. I've been there."

"When? What were you doing there?"

Kayla was glaring at him now, as well. Interesting that they both seemed to assume he must be guilty of something. But then, he probably deserved that. If he didn't want people to suspect shenanigans, he should have lived a different sort of life. Was it too late to change? Probably. He frowned.

"I spent a few months there last year. I did some *work for the government. Actually, I helped* them set up their air force."

Pellea's eyebrows rose at that. "And then what happened?"

He thought about it for a moment. Funny how things that seemed so mundane at the time became so impossible to explain to anyone. This looked a little more serious than he'd expected. But try as he might, he couldn't remember having done anything illegal while he was there. He hadn't robbed anyone. He hadn't run off with the royal jewels. He hadn't stolen any plans. The only thing he could think of that might apply had been a broken relationship with a rather beautiful... Well, he wasn't going to tell these ladies about that. They wouldn't be happy to hear it. And anyway that had been over a year ago.

He faced them squarely and tried to look candid. "I have to think it over and see if I can figure out what they are actually talking about."

"You can't tell us now?" Kayla asked.

He looked at her and shook his head. "No. I'm sorry. You're going to have to wait until I get a bit clearer on just exactly what they're objecting to."

Kayla and Pellea were both staring at him with wide-eyed wonder. Both sets of eyes contained the same horrified expression. It was pretty clear that they both thought that anything that couldn't be explained right here, right now, in simple language, had to be pretty darn bad. He looked at them both and shrugged, hating to feel defensive this way. Why should he have to explain himself?

But he was trapped. Sooner or later, they would probably know everything about his life—even things he didn't know. Still, why make it easy for them?

"I haven't led a perfect life. I've done things I'm not proud of. Things I wouldn't want to tell you about."

Pellea nodded as though she'd thought as much, but Kayla appeared surprised and troubled. He regretted that. But he still wasn't going to tell her everything he'd ever done wrong in his life. He wasn't going to tell anyone.

"I'm sorry," he said simply. "But I'm going to find out what they are accusing me of before I start spilling my guts and go admitting to every crime known to have happened in the last ten years. You understand?"

He looked at them. They looked back, and it was clear they didn't understand. It was obvious neither one of them had ever done anything to be ashamed of in their lives. Or not much, anyway. They stared at him with huge eyes and didn't say a thing. He groaned.

Suddenly, he was a little angry. "You know what? I didn't ask for this gig. I don't know much yet about what it means to be a prince. And I'm starting to feel like it's going to crowd me a bit. I live my life pretty free and easy." He shook his head, looking from one to the other of them. "I don't know, maybe that sort of living is incompatible with royal structure. What do you think?"

They just stared and he began to feel uncomfortable. In his experience, women talked over everything. They never quit. What was with the silent treatment? Did they really think he'd done something so awful it couldn't be talked about at all?

He was about to ask about that when Pellea made a move toward him. As he watched, she walked up and grabbed him by the front of his shirt, pulling his face down inches from hers.

"Promise me you won't run away," she said fiercely.

That was a tough one. "Um…for how long?"

There was a pause while she seemed to digest his attitude and realize he was close to an edge she didn't want to reach. She closed her eyes for a second, then opened them again. "Promise me you will give this a month."

A month. Could he take a month of this constant royal oversight?

He shook his head. "How can I do that?" he said, his tone almost sarcastic. "I may have to go serve time in East Slobovia here." He gestured toward the poster, then pulled back and used his most disarming smile. "How about a week?"

She winced and made a concession to reality. "Two weeks."

He glanced at Kayla. She looked like she was holding her breath. He drew in a long breath himself and nodded as he looked back at the queen.

"Okay. I can give you that."

She let go and gave him a pat where she'd been grabbing his shirt. "Come to me tomorrow and be ready to tell me everything," she said as she headed for the door.

"I'll tell you what I feel you need to know," he countered as she opened it.

She whirled and glared at him. "Listen, Max. I hope you understand that you must take this seriously. So far, I've been able to keep this nonsense out of the king's notice. But if things get more dicey, I'm going to have to go to him with it."

Kayla bit her lip, wanting to stop Pellea. Didn't she see how he resented being talked to like this? Didn't she notice the sarcastic twist to the corner of his mouth, the veiled anger in his deep blue eyes?

She was actually surprised he hadn't said anything. He was used to talking back and walking out. It wasn't going to be easy for him to learn to hold his tongue and take honest criticism. Was he going to be able to handle it?

"Tomorrow," Pellea said. "And you will tell me all."

"Or at least as much of it as I know myself."

She threw back an exasperated look, but this time she didn't stop. In a few seconds, the door was closing and he and Kayla were alone again.

She turned to him, her eyes huge and dark in the lamplight.

"Max, what did you do?"

He took a deep breath and faced her. This was almost funny. Maybe someday they would look back and laugh. But not today.

"You know what? I don't have a clue." He saw the skepticism in her eyes and he looked away, swearing softly. "I've done a lot of things, Kayla. Nothing ever seemed bad enough to deserve jail time. Or death." He turned back and looked at her. "But you never know. People take things more seriously than you think at the time."

She shook her head slowly, almost in wonder. "Mercuria. It's a simple little country. You never even think of it. It's smaller than Ambria. What can they be so upset about?"

He shrugged, a little annoyed that no one seemed to have any faith in him. But he knew that wasn't fair. He'd given no one any reason to trust him. When you lived on the edge of a knife blade, like he had, you had to know that people were going to back away in horror now and then. It came with the territory.

"I'd have to see more than a picture on a Wanted poster to know that for sure."

He gave her a long, slow look, then shrugged again and headed for the door.

"I'd like to see a full description of my crime," he said, managing to sound lighthearted and carefree again. Free and easy. That was the way he wanted to live. "You've got to see what you're charged with before you can mount any sort of defense. Basic legal advice."

He turned and gave her a wink, then made it out the door and into the castle hallways.

Kayla watched the door swing shut and she drew air deep into her lungs. Secrets. He had secrets.

Well, funny thing. So did she.

The following morning when she got to work, Kayla found the queen involved in a dispute between a kitchen prep assistant and the royal chef. She was claiming the older man had promised to advance her and now he seemed to be spending all his time giving extra training to the pretty new pastry chef.

"Who knew my fabulously exciting days as queen would be filled with this sort of relationship management?" she complained to Kayla. "I might as well be working for the local department store." She sighed. "But I do feel sorry for her. He has been leading her on."

"Call the chef in for a nice chat, tell him that his grilled rosemary scallops are to-die-for and mention that reports of favoritism will be noted on his permanent record," Kayla advised. "And just to be safe, make sure he knows canoodling in the broom closet will be frowned upon."

Pellea shook her head. "You see it all so clearly, my dear. I know exactly why I hired you."

Kayla gave her a quizzical smile. "No regrets?"

Pellea pursed her lips and slid down into the chair opposite from where Kayla sat at her desk. "Okay. Let's get into it." She fixed her with a steady look. "Do I have anything to worry about?"

Kayla managed to look completely innocent. "In what way?"

Pellea gave her a look. "I think you know what I'm talking about. I have plans for Max, so it would be best if we put all our cards on the table, don't you agree?" She thought of something and her eyes narrowed. "By the way, where was your baby last night? I didn't see any evidence that he was with you."

Kayla's heart began to beat a bit harder. "He was nearby. He was staying down the hall with my sister."

"Oh." Pellea still looked skeptical.

Kayla leaned forward earnestly, determined not to let Pellea go down the road she obviously had been moving toward.

"No, it's not like that. Teddy often stays with Caroline when I work late. She watches him during the day, and her little one is the same age. He was already asleep…"

She stopped, realizing she was giving too much information. That was always the perfect way to sound absolutely guilty as charged. Taking a deep breath, she added simply, "I had no idea that Max was going to drop by."

Pellea blinked rapidly. "Just how close were you and Max in the old days?"

"We were good friends. Very good friends." She sighed and looked directly into the queen's eyes. "What you saw when you came in was a result of us both remembering Eddie and comforting each other over losing him that way."

Pellea held her gaze steady and slightly shook her head. "It looked like more than that to me."

Her heart rate made another lurch. "Pellea, I adored my husband," she said forcefully. "He was my life." She shook her head, hair flying about her shoulders. "Max loved him, too. Everybody did. He was a wonderful man." Reaching out, she took Pellea's hands in hers. "Please understand. Max and I were never…"

She stopped short, turning red. She couldn't really say that, could she? To her horror, she realized it was a lie. And she couldn't lie to Pellea of all people. She stared, wide-eyed, not sure how to get out of this trap she'd wandered into.

But Pellea didn't seem to notice. She nodded, searching her eyes with a sense of sympathy and compassion that didn't leave any more room for suspicion. "Okay. Oh, Kayla, I understand, and I'm sorry if it seemed I was implying anything more." She smiled with a sweetness that had once been her trademark, but wasn't often seen of late. "I won't do it again."

"Thanks." She smiled back, feeling a sense of relief that her friend and employer cared enough to make that pledge. And yet, in the pit of her stomach there lurked an aching tangle of guilt.

As of now, it seemed she was the only one who remembered what had happened that last night in Trialta. She had to keep it that way. But how could she do that when temptation was always lurking?

Somehow, she had to work at distancing herself from Max. She had to be unavailable when he was around.

It shouldn't be too hard. He was going to be very busy getting to know the rest of the royals and learning what his duties and responsibilities would be here in the castle. She would try to stay just as busy somewhere else. She might even ask for another assignment on the continent, one where she could take Teddy with her.

Yes, that was a good idea. She would leave the castle for a while. She would do something. She had to fix this. And she would.

"Did he tell you why Mercuria wants him to come back and stand trial?" Pellea asked.

"No. He didn't seem to know why."

"Hmmph." Pellea didn't sound convinced. "It's a real problem, you know. We owe that country a lot. They helped us during the war. Without their help, we might not have succeeded. And now that we've got a sort of truce going, they are the ones who act as go-between, our line of communication to the Granvillis. They're strong allies. I can't turn my back on a solid request like this. I can't ignore our friends. They won't be there for us next time if I do."

The worry in her voice sent Kayla's nerves quivering. They couldn't possibly be considering giving him up to the Mercurian royals—could they? Impossible.

"Send out the diplomats," she suggested, only half joking.

"Oh, definitely. Droves of them." She smiled, but it faded quickly. "I've got to admit, it worries me quite a bit. I'm going to have to make a call to them soon. I've got to tell them something. Max is going to have to level

with me. And regardless, we'll have to find some way
to either meet their demands or placate them."

"Meet their demands?" Kayla repeated, her dread
growing.

Pellea gave her a reassuring pat. "Placating is probably safer," she noted. Then she made a face. "If we
sent him back to them, lord only knows what he might
do."

Kayla was beginning to rebel. After all, he wasn't
all that bad. A bit nonconformist, of course, but all in
all, he was definitely a good guy, at least in her experience with him.

But Pellea was still thinking of examples. She shook
her head. "Last night at the ball, when he was presented
to the old duchess, my Great-Aunt Judis, I was afraid
he was going to say something like, 'Hey, Toots, could
you get me a refill on this drink while you're up?'"

Kayla's eyes widened. "He didn't!"

"No, he didn't." She raised a significant eyebrow.
"But there's something about him that keeps making
me scared he will."

Despite her regard for him as a man, Kayla knew
exactly what she meant. She frowned, trying to key in
to the heart of the matter.

"He just doesn't have the proper instincts."

"Exactly."

She looked up hopefully. "He'll learn."

Pellea sighed. "Of course he will. But can we wait
around for that to develop on its own? I think not." She

drew in a deep breath. "So I'm getting him a superior teacher."

"Really?" Kayla's heart fell but she fought against it. This was just what had to happen. He had to learn his place in the scheme of things and she had to keep her distance from the entire process. It was all for the best and she knew it. "Who is that?"

Pellea stared at her, lips pursed as though she were annoyed with her somehow.

"A wonderful woman. She's perfect for this assignment. Her only flaw is that she is rather slow on the uptake at times." She gave a sound of exasperation. "It's someone he already respects and has a great affection for."

"Really?" She was still frowning. She hadn't realized he knew that many women here. But what was she thinking? He always knew women, wherever he happened to be. "Do I know her?"

Pellea threw up her hands. "It's you, silly. And you have exactly one week to perform a magical transformation."

Max arrived at Pellea's office in a somewhat surly mood. He'd spent the morning thinking about what he was going to say to her and nothing very good had come to mind. He decided to go for the basics—to tell her why he'd been in Mercuria and how his work there went. Then maybe she could weave some sort of conspiracy out of it all.

"Good morning, Your Majesty," he said cheerfully

as she rose to greet him. He kissed both cheeks and smiled at her.

"You just missed Kayla," she told him. "I sent her on an errand." She gave him a sharp look. "But that will give us a chance to talk openly, won't it?"

He frowned, not sure he appreciated her implications that there might be things he could tell her that he wouldn't tell Kayla. Still, he followed her lead and sat across from her at her desk.

"I take it you have something to tell me?" she said, looking almost eager.

He shrugged and took a deep breath. "I've made some inquiries. I've got a few ideas."

"Good. Tell me what they are, because I don't have a clue."

He chewed on his lower lip, then admitted evasively, "I don't really have anything definitive."

She looked disappointed. "You don't know why the Mercurians are angry with you?"

He laughed shortly. "Angry, sure. Ready to lock me away in a dungeon...not so much."

Pellea's eyes were cooler now. "Why don't we start at the beginning?" she suggested. "Maybe there's something you're just not noticing. Why don't you tell me everything? All about your time in Mercuria."

He felt his jaw tighten, but he knew he really couldn't blame her. So he tried to do it her way.

"Okay. It all started when an old flight instructor of mine recommended me to the Mercurian Army as someone who might be able to help them get an air force organized and trained. I flew over, met the king and talked to the military people in charge. It seemed like a decent little country, trying to emerge onto the global stage, but without a lot of money and mainly ancient aircraft at their disposal. The jets were going to have to come later. Anyway, I thought I could help them. Why not? So I signed on."

"How long were you there?"

"Not quite a year."

She nodded, thinking about what he'd told her and frowning. "Were you successful?"

"I thought so. We got a good skeleton of a program started."

She nodded again. "Did you know they were helping us with our war effort?"

"Of course. That was one reason the project appealed to me. I'm Ambrian, too."

"Why did you leave?"

That was a harder question. There were too many threads making up that answer to get into right now.

"Actually, around that time some old flying friends of mine showed up and talked me into coming over to join the fight for the restoration of the monarchy here in Ambria. It sounded like fun. Aerial combat and all that. And I was growing tired of all the bureaucracy I had to deal with in Mercuria. I wanted to get back into real flying again. So I joined up." He looked at her expectantly, his story over.

She sighed, shaking her head. "Which tells me a lot," she muttered, "and nothing."

"Exactly."

She studied his face for a moment. "Were they angry that you left when you did? Did they feel you hadn't completed your commitment?"

He shook his head. "There might have been a little of that, but no one actually complained. They knew I was ready to go."

He leaned forward. She deserved a better answer, but he just didn't know what he could tell her that was going to give her the information she needed.

"Pellea, I did a lot of things that someone might look back on and decide were...out of bounds, perhaps. We were flyers. We raised hell. That's what we do."

Slowly, she shook her head. "I'm pretty sure this is more than raising hell," she said. "You don't say 'dead or alive' about a little carousing."

"Okay, maybe...maybe an old girlfriend decided to take some sort of revenge. Maybe an innkeeper decided to blame me for a fight that might have torn up his bar and is suing for damages. Maybe someone who felt slighted by me in some way wants a pound of flesh. I just don't know. And I'm not sure what you want me to do about it." He shrugged. "Do you want me to issue an apology?"

"What? No. Of course not. Not until we know just what this is about."

He bit his tongue, wishing he could lose the defensive attitude. He knew he hadn't been living an exemplary life. He regretted it. Talking with Pellea, he wasn't proud of it. But it was lousy being asked to ex-

plain it. Life was complicated enough without this stupid wanted poster arriving from Mercuria.

He sat back. "Leave it to me. I think I can handle
this. It might take a little time, but I'll get in touch with
people I knew when I was there. I'll let you know for
sure when I think I've really got it pinned down."

She nodded slowly. "Do that," she said. "But make
it soon."

Kayla knew Max was going in to see Pellea first thing
and she hoped they would be able to settle matters.
It might be better if she could be there to help things
along, but she had some business on the other side of
the castle and knew she would probably miss him. So
she left Max a message to meet her in the hall of portraits, and to her surprise, he was right on time.

The fact that there *was* a hall of portraits was a miracle. During the original rebellion, when the Granvillis
had burned most of the castle and killed the king and
queen—the parents of the current crop of princes, as
well as of King Monte, Pellea's husband—they had de-
stroyed everything they could get their hands on that
might remind anyone of the deposed monarchy. A lot
of paintings burned that night, but many of the most
important ones were spirited out by various servants
who hid them with relatives for the twenty-five years
of the Granvilli regime.

After the restoration of the DeAngelis monarchy,
when the castle archivist began to collect them and
bring them home, there was a wave of emotion in the

populace that touched them all. It was so very important to have these beautiful pictures to tell the story of what their history had been.

Kayla found Max gazing up at a huge stately portrait of his great grandfather. The fine-looking royal was wearing an ermine-lined cape and looking quite imperial and majestic.

"Quite a handsome bunch, your ancestors," she noted, sliding in beside him and looking up as well. She felt proud for him, proud for Ambria. She only hoped he understood what it meant to be a part of this.

"They certainly seem well-turned out," he agreed. "But then, you've always got artistic flattery on your side when you're royalty." He gave her a mock jab in the ribs with his elbow. "The artist makes them beautiful or he doesn't get paid, I would think."

"Maybe." She gave him a sideways look. "But from the evidence presented by your brothers, I'd chock it all up to good genes."

He shrugged and she frowned, not sure he was sufficiently impressed.

"After all, the blood of these very people flows in your veins," she pointed out.

He grunted. "Let's hope none of them were bleeders or vampires," he said lightly. "Don't those two things tend to run in this kind of family?"

For some reason him saying that made her absolutely furious. Did he really not understand how important his own family was? Or was he just trying to drive her crazy?

"There is no such thing as vampires," she said through clenched teeth.

"Maybe not," he said, his blue eyes sparkling with amusement. "But I'm going to start being more careful with the morning shave. You never know."

"No one in the DeAngelis family has ever shown any signs of hemophilia," she protested, trying hard not to let him see how annoyed she was. "Just forget it."

He gave her a look that infuriated her even further, then shrugged again and turned away as though it hardly affected him anyway. She took a deep breath and forced herself to calm down. She knew she was being overly sensitive, and that he was playing on her emotions like a skilled musician. She had to hold it back. She couldn't give him the satisfaction of showing her feelings like this.

Slowly, she followed as he examined one portrait after another. She'd been here often in the last few months and she didn't have to look at the labels to know who each one was. She was ready to answer any of his questions, but he didn't say another word and she wondered what he was thinking.

No matter what, he had to be fascinated by the imposing DeAngelis family. Who could help it? And to think that he'd suddenly found out he was one of them.

They'd walked the length of the hall and then they both went out onto the terrace that overlooked the royal fields. Leaning against the massive stone guardrail, he smiled at her and her annoyance with his attitude began to melt away. She really couldn't resist that smile.

"Did you talk to Pellea?" she asked.

"Oh, yeah. We had a little chat."

"And?"

He eyed her questioningly. "What? You think I'm going to tell you everything I told her?"

She pulled back quickly. "No. Of course not."

He laughed and reached out to push her hair behind her ear and then pull her closer again. "But you know I would. If there was anything to tell."

"You didn't come up with anything?" Her skin tingled where his fingers had touched and she frowned, trying to ignore it.

He hesitated. "Not anything sure. Or substantive." He shrugged and changed the subject. "I can't get over you being here like this," he said. "What are the odds that we would both end up in the Ambrian castle? That was certainly a stroke of luck."

"Yes, wasn't it?"

She looked at his beautiful eyes and the hard, tanned planes of his handsome face and she knew he belonged with the men and women in those huge, gorgeously painted portraits in the hall. Someday his image would hang there with them. That was his destiny. Surely he knew that. Didn't he?

"So how did Pellea find you, anyway?" he was asking her. "You said your sister had something to do with it?"

"I told you we'd known each other before. When my sister and her husband moved here, Caroline went to Pellea and told her about me and my situation and let her know I was looking for a job. It just so happened that she was looking for an assistant. So everything fell into place."

"Good timing. Life can happen that way sometimes."

She nodded ruefully. "Not often."

"No." A shadow flickered through his gaze. "Not often."

They stood silently for a moment, each thinking private thoughts. Kayla was remembering Eddie and she was pretty sure he was, too. But she didn't want to get started on that again. They had work to do.

"I guess you're wondering why I asked you to meet me here," she said at last.

He grinned at her using such a well-known cliché. "The question had crossed my mind a time or two," he admitted. "And then I decided you just wanted me to learn to connect with my roots."

"A simple goal, I would think."

He grimaced. "So okay, I looked each ancient ancestor in the eye and took his measure. And the women, too. And I was impressed." But he seemed a little impatient. "What else do you want from me?"

She drew a deep breath in slowly, wondering how to put this. She had no idea how he was going to take it. For all she knew, he might storm off and never speak to her again. Finally, she just blurted it out.

"Okay, Max. Here's the deal." She steeled herself. "Pellea wants me to teach you how to act like a prince."

CHAPTER FIVE

MAX stared at her and for a moment, Kayla thought he hadn't understood. But a faint smile quirked at the corners of his mouth and he repeated slowly, "Pellea wants you to teach me how to act like a prince?"

She nodded, waiting.

He gave her a look as though this was about as kooky as he'd thought things could get. "Really?" he said with a twist to his smile. "Who taught you?"

That was a good question and keyed right in to her deepest fears about this assignment. But she wasn't going to let him know that. She hadn't asked for this. In fact, she wished it hadn't occurred to Pellea at all. But it had, and here they were, stuck with a project to do.

"I'm very observant," she said cheekily. "Don't worry. I won't steer you wrong."

He grinned, watching her with a slightly lascivious expression. "I'm not worried at all. I have every intention of becoming teacher's pet in a major way."

She pretended to frown. "Don't count on that, mister. I'm a tough grader. You're going to have to earn your graduation papers."

"It's a deal." He pretended to look at his watch. "You've got two weeks to make me into royalty. Better get moving."

She wasn't crazy about the way he set it up like an adversarial position, but she'd known from the start that she would have to work fast. He didn't have to remind her. His attention span wouldn't last long. And he proved it by jumping to a new topic in seconds.

A man had walked by holding a baby, and they both looked up as the baby made a cooing sound. She met Max's wide eyes and they both smiled.

"Hey, when do I get to meet little...Teddy, did you say his name was?" he asked.

She felt a surge of unpleasant adrenaline.

"Yes, uh...Teddy."

He looked at her curiously. "Is he here at the castle with you?"

"He stays with my sister during the day. I'll...uh... make sure you get to meet him soon."

"Good." He frowned and she knew he was wondering why she was so hesitant. "I'll bet he looks just like Eddie."

Color filled her cheeks. She tried to force it back but it just kept coming. Had he noticed? Did he see how uncomfortable she was with this?

"He's a little young to look like anyone right now," she said breathlessly.

But he didn't seem to notice her reaction. He was

looking into the past, his brows pulled together, and thinking of how it had once been. "Thank God you had his baby," he said softly, reaching out to touch her cheek. "Thank God there's a piece of him left in the world."

Her mind was racing. She had to think of something. Hopefully, he would forget about Teddy once he was thoroughly invested in taking on the royal mantle. That had to be her goal: to convince him that becoming a prince was something he wanted to do, that it would engage his mind and spirit like nothing else he'd ever done. Once he opened himself to it fully, he would be so busy, so connected with what was going on here in the castle, that he would forget about her and her son. They would just fade into a pleasant memory for him, and then her life could go on as it had before he ever got here.

But he was still frowning at her, searching her eyes. She pulled away from his hand and turned to look at the distant sea. They were miles away, but she thought she could hear the waves pounding on the rocks.

"Listen, what about this Mercuria situation? I know you don't know exactly what their beef is, but you must have some idea of what set them off." She turned back to look at him. "Any clue at all as to what their problem was?"

He stared at her for a moment, then gave a bitter laugh. "You mean why they want to lock me away in their particularly nasty tower and torture me with bad food? No. I'm still not sure what that is all about."

She frowned. "Come on, Max. You must have a se-cret opinion. Or two."

"Oh, yeah. I've got some thoughts on the matter." He frowned and shifted his weight from one foot to the other, as though suddenly uncomfortable with those very thoughts. "But you wouldn't like them."

That gave her a momentary pang, but she was game. "Try me."

He made a face. "I'd rather not."

She looked into his eyes. He was serious.

"Max, this isn't a game. We have to find out the truth. This has to be dealt with."

He nodded slowly. "Of course."

She waited. He stood very still and watched her. She sighed with quick exasperation and tugged on his sleeve. "Max! Tell me! Delve down into your deepest intuitions and tell me what you think it just might be."

He grimaced, then looked back at her and shrugged. "Okay. If you really want me to do this, here you go. This is just a guess, but..." He took a deep breath, then looked out at the distant mountains. "I think they want me to marry their princess."

She stared at him in shock. He glanced at her and sighed.

"And here you thought this was the only royal gig I had lined up," he said grimly. "But no. I've got my choice. Lucky me."

Kayla swallowed hard. She hadn't expected some-thing like this. Staring at Max, she tried to get her mind around these new developments. Everything inside her was aching for a denial. He couldn't…could he? He hadn't…had he?

"Is there…uh…a reason they would be demanding this? I mean, their charges were pretty hard-line, even if they weren't explicit."

His blue gaze skimmed her features. "You mean, did I compromise the girl's reputation in some way?" he said with a trace of sarcasm and a touch of resentment. "No, Kayla. I did not."

"Oh." Relief flooded her, leaving her breathless. And then she realized she still didn't know any of the details. "Then…?"

"The Princess Nadine is fifteen years old," he told her, looking almost angry. "She decided to get a teenage crush on me. I didn't do a thing to encourage it. Believe me, I do have certain scruples. But girls that age…" He shrugged and looked toward the heavens for help.

It was ridiculous. Maddening. And ultimately, he had a feeling it would be quite embarrassing. There had to be a way to handle this without everyone knowing what the Mercurians really wanted.

Princess Nadine was a lovely girl, but she was much too young to be handed off to an old guy like him. He'd only seen her a few times and he'd managed to keep those visits short. He couldn't go back there. There was no telling what would be demanded of him. The family running the country was a few bricks short of a load at times. One might even say, crazy as loons.

"It's not a good situation."

"Oh."

"She decided she wanted me. And her daddy, the King of Mercuria, gives her whatever she wants."

"Oh, dear."

"Yes. 'Oh, dear'." He finally looked her in the eye. "So how am I supposed to explain this to Pellea? Especially when I don't even know if it's true?"

She thought for a moment. It was a problem. The queen was not going to be happy, and this put her in an awkward position in regard to an international relations situation that would just tangle things into knots. She could see why he hesitated to tell her about it.

But he would have to.

"You haven't said anything to her about this?"

"No."

She nodded. "Explain it to her just like you did to me."

He looked skeptical. "I don't think she'll buy it."

"If it's the truth, what else can you do?"

He gave her a baleful look and shook his head. "Run away?" he suggested, only half joking.

"Never," she said firmly.

He looked weary. "You know, this is just a guess. I don't have any evidence. I'm not sure this is the exact thing pulling their chain. For all I know..."

"You've got to tell her. Right now."

"Right now? But..."

She dug for her mobile and held up a hand to stop him. "I'll see if she's in," she said, punching in Pellea's office number. "She's not there," she said after a moment. "But her message says she'll be right back."

Leaning on the stone guard wall, he was watching her from under dark, lowered lashes. "You're bound and determined to make sure I do the right thing, aren't you? And by that, I mean the 'royal' right thing." His eyes narrowed further. "You remind me of a prison warden I once knew."

She looked up at him, doggedly set in her goals. "I'm going to make you into a prince," she said coolly. "And you're going to like it."

He didn't smile. His blue eyes looked as cold and hard as sapphire stones. "Or else I'll bow out," he said softly.

Holding his gaze, she shook her head slowly. "Over my dead body," she promised, enunciating each word carefully. "You're sticking this out, mister."

He stared a moment longer, and then his lip began to curl. "Damn," he said huskily. "Do you know how sexy you look when you're giving me orders?"

"Oh!" She turned and started away, furious with him again. Was he ever going to take anything seriously?

"Hey." He caught up with her and grabbed her upper arm, pulling her around to face him. "I'm sorry. I'm sure you thought that was condescending, didn't you? I didn't mean it that way. I was just being honest."

She glared at him. "Be honest with Pellea. She's the one who counts. And believe me, she's ready to give you every chance in the world. But you have to level with her. Come on." She linked her arm with his and gazed up at him, intense and a bit anxious. "Let's go on over to the office. She ought to be back any minute. And you can tell her yourself. She'll listen."

He gave her a skeptical look. "She'll try to see my side of things?"

"Oh, absolutely. She's really very understanding."

"I really don't understand any of this and what's more, I won't have it!"

Kayla recoiled. She'd never seen Pellea so angry. She glanced apologetically at Max, but he was scowling at the queen. Oh, brother, did she ever regret forcing this little conversation.

They had come back to the office and found Pellea just arriving, a sheaf of papers in her hand. Obviously, she'd had news. She'd greeted them both the way someone thoroughly annoyed might, and as things were going, that did seem to be exactly what she was.

Pellea took a deep breath, closed her eyes and tried to calm herself. "All right. I'm going to try not to shout. That sort of thing is never becoming in a queen." She gestured at them, slipping into her desk chair. "Sit down. We'll do this the right way." But her eyes flashed at Max. "Now tell me again, what exactly have you heard from Mercuria?"

Every muscle he owned seemed to be locked in stone. "As I said before, not much."

There was a hard line to his mouth that Kayla didn't like. She knew he resented being talked to the way Pellea had done, but she could also see that he was holding back. She only prayed that he was in control of his emotions. And that Pellea was, too. Sinking into a chair, she tugged on his sleeve to get him to sit down, too.

"I do have some calls in to some people and a friend is trying to look into this further, but..." He shrugged. "So far, not much."

"You're right," Pellea said evenly. "That's not much." She waved an official-looking document at him. "I'll tell you what I have. We've just received it. It's from their foreign minister." Her eyes blazed.

Max's head went back defensively and his eyes were hooded. "What does he have to say?"

She rattled the paper. "He says we have five days to the deadline and at that point, they expect us to hand you over."

A muscle pulsed at his jawline. "And if you don't hand me over?"

She glared at him. "They're going to invade."

Kayla gasped. "What? Oh, Pellea, that can't be."

The queen looked at Kayla, at a loss and showing it. "That's what they say, right here." She held up the embossed announcement, complete with signatures and an official stamp. "Read it and weep."

"They won't invade," Max scoffed. "They don't have the man power." But he perused the document carefully, reading every line.

Pellea seemed to be counting to ten. Finally, she said a bit breathlessly, "Maybe they won't actually invade. Maybe this is all bluster. But that doesn't fix everything. We still owe this country a lot. We need to pay them back, in kind if not in cash. What are we going to do to satisfy them? What are we going to do about their demand to have you extradited?"

His gaze was steady and firm. "We're going to tell them to pound sand, I hope."

"No." She shook her head emphatically.

His face registered a tiny flash of shock, then one eyebrow rose quizzically. "You want me to go and stand trial?" he asked incredulously.

"Of course not. But we don't get around it by yelling at them." She threw her hands up. "We consult. We sympathize. We question. We find ways to talk them out of their anger. We don't give them exactly what they want, but we make them think we did."

Max frowned, not sure he bought her song and dance. "But we still don't know exactly what they want from me."

"No. We don't, do we?" Pellea tapped the toe of her shoe against the tiled floor and stared at him steadily. "The only one here who could possibly know is you. So what do you think it is? If you were to venture a guess."

Max stared back. Kayla waited breathlessly, expecting him to find a way to tell the queen about the princess, just the way he'd told her. She waited. And waited.

But Max didn't say a word about that. Instead, his handsome face seemed to have cleansed itself of all emotion, all thought, and he said evenly, "I think you already have a theory. Don't you? Why don't you tell me what it is?"

"A theory? No." She pulled another large sheet of paper off her desk and brandished it. "But the foreign minister of Mercuria seems to have one. Here's what he says." She held it up and began to read, just skimming to the pertinent words and phrases.

"According to the foreign minister, while you were in their lovely country, enjoying their delightful hospitality…" She took a deep breath before going on, setting up a nicely dramatic pause. "You stole a horse, hijacked an airplane and made off with an important ancient historical national artifact." She lowered the paper and looked him in the eye. "And you say…?"

He was shaking his head, half laughing, but without amusement. "That's insane. I never took any artifact."

Kayla groaned and Pellea's eyes widened. "But the horse and the airplane…?"

He grimaced. This was all so stupid. "Listen, I can explain."

Pellea looked at Kayla. Kayla looked at Pellea. They both groaned.

"No, really," he said, feeling unfairly outnumbered. "There was no money in the treasury. They gave me the plane in lieu of payment for services rendered. I can prove it."

Pellea's eyes flashed. "Good. You'll have to. Do you have papers?"

He hesitated and then he shrugged. "I'll have to take a look. I must have something somewhere."

She nodded as though she'd known that all along. "And the horse?"

He drew in a long breath. "That's a longer story."

"Of course." She was glaring again. "And the artifact?"

His eyes blazed at that one. "Now there, I have no idea what they're talking about."

Pellea's eyes narrowed. "Oh, but I think you do."

"Do you?" His back was really up now. "Then why don't you tell me?"

She searched his eyes for a moment, then shrugged. "We're going to put together a letter of explanation," she said, completely dismissing the subject of the artifact for now, "and send an ambassador right away."

"For this?" he said dismissively.

She turned and looked at him. "Don't you understand how important this is? We have to soothe ruffled feathers as quickly as we can." Her eyes flashed and her hands smoothed down the bright red dress she was wearing, the outfit that was making her look like a Spanish dancer. "Unless you'd like to go back and explain it to them yourself?"

He winced. "I don't think that would be a good idea."

"Just so," she said, as though that proved some point she'd been making all along.

Watching all this, Kayla was at a loss. She knew Max was being cagey. Why hadn't he brought up the princess? Why did he treat Pellea like someone he had to keep things from? She wished he would lay it all out for her. If they didn't handle this properly, war could be the result.

Either that, or extradition. She shuddered.

"Pellea, does Monte...does the king know about this?" she asked her.

"No." Her face crumpled and for a second, Kayla was afraid she would cry. But she regained her composure quickly, taking Kayla's hand in hers and squeezing it as though grateful she had her support and understanding. "No, he's got his own international relations problems right now. I don't want to bother him with this. I have to begin taking care of these things on my own and not go running to him with everything."

Kayla nodded sympathetically. Working with Pellea, she had seen for herself what a precarious tightrope she walked trying to become effective without becoming either obsessive or too dependent. She and Monte had been like the perfect couple from the beginning, in more ways than one. Their royal marriage was a partnership and Pellea worked at it night and day.

Max rose, looking moody. "Your Majesty, let me just say this. The list you received from the foreign minister sounds like a bunch of excuses to me. I don't know what's really behind all this." He stopped and swallowed hard. It really wasn't easy for him to delve into his life and try to find explanations for this. But he would try.

"Why not wait until I find out something from my contacts in the country. Just hold on until then. Maybe we'll have something we can work with."

Pellea nodded, looking distracted. "Of course. You'll let me know, won't you?" She waved them off. "Until then, I'll be counting on Kayla to manage things. So go, both of you. Get some lunch. I'll talk to you later."

Kayla looked back as they closed the door. A jagged little piece of her heart tore at the look in Pellea's face. She bit her lip and turned away.

They walked away from the office. Kayla eyed at Max sideways and wondered how to broach the subject that was begging to be discussed. She kept expecting all this to be cleared up, and instead, she was just getting more confused.

"You want to explain all that to me?" she said at last, when he didn't volunteer anything.

He looked down at her and raised an eyebrow. "You mean, why I didn't tell her about Princess Nadine?"

She nodded. "You could start with that."

He shrugged and kept walking. "There was nothing about it in the complaint. So maybe I'm wrong. Maybe that's not what this is all about."

She stopped him and searched his eyes in wonder. "You don't believe that."

He glanced back at her, frowning. "Who cares what I believe, Kayla. What does it matter?"

"Of course what you believe matters. How are we going to get to the bottom of all this if we just throw out theories without exploring them?"

She saw the torture in his eyes and melted. "Listen." She grabbed his arm and pressed close so she could talk to him softly. "Whatever they think you did, whatever it turns out to be, we'll handle it. Nothing is going to drive you away. We won't let it." His gaze locked in hers. "I won't let it," she whispered, her love for him in her eyes.

He reached up and his hand cupped her chin, fingers trailing across her cheek. He didn't say a word, but something in his eyes said volumes. *I need you, Kayla,* they seemed to be saying. *Don't ever leave me. I don't want to live without you. Never again.*

She saw it as clearly as though he had said the words aloud. But she also saw what followed—a regret, a denial. She'd seen his true feelings, but at the same time, she saw why he couldn't act on them. It was all there. As Pellea had said, read them and weep.

He dropped his hand and looked away and she put distance between them and cleared her throat.

"Tell me about the horse," she said coolly.

Something flashed in his eyes and he turned away, then steeled himself and turned back and said, "Let's get some food first. Where's the closest place to get some food around here?"

She led him there and they entered the fast-food cavalcade, all chrome and neon flashing lights, with simple tables and chairs and a counter for ordering your food. Colors screamed from all sides and music was loud and aggressive. He scanned the place, then looked down at her and shook his head, his eyes amused.

"Are you going to tell me this is one of your favorite places?" he said skeptically.

She raised her chin and tried to keep from smiling,

though his gorgeous eyes were tempting her to laugh.
"Hey, I hang out here all the time." She glanced around
the room while he grinned at her obvious lie. "And anyway, you asked for something close."

He bit his lower lip and attempted to adjust the cri-
teria. "How about the closest decent food where you
can also hear yourself think?"

"Say no more," she said and led him to the escalator,
then around two corners and onto a quieter walkway.
"How about this?"

She would have thought the Two for Tea tearoom
might have been a little too precious for his taste, but
he smiled and nodded. "Looks great," he said.

She grinned. "I hadn't figured you for finger sandwiches," she said.

"That shows how little you really know me," he re-
plied, and escorted her in.

Every table had a lace cloth. The tea was served in
fragile cups and saucers and the trays of scones and
little sandwiches were passed from table to table by
girls in Victorian costumes. Music by Debussy, Liszt
and Chopin filled the air. Kayla sighed. Just what they
needed to calm the frantic mood of the day.

They sat, ordered and then smiled at each other
across the table.

"We came here to talk," she reminded him.

He made a face. "Yes." He sighed. "What was the
subject again?"

"The horse."

"Ah, yes. The horse." His eyes widened, full of innocence. "Okay, I did steal the horse."

She gasped. "What? I thought you were going to convince me it was all a misunderstanding."

"There was no misunderstanding. I stole him." Reaching out, he took her hand in his. "There was a good reason."

"Oh, Max," she said, swept up in a sense of despair.

"Let me tell you how it came to be."

She nodded, willing to hear him out. But tears were threatening and she knew he could tell. "Please," she said shakily.

He nodded, then took his hand away from hers and stared at the wall. "While I was living in Mercuria, I rented a room from a family, the Minderts, who had once been quite wealthy but through one thing and another, had lost all their money. All they had left from the old days, besides their house and land, was a stable of three beautiful, award-winning palomino horses, and it took all Dirk Mindert's efforts to make enough to keep them fed and well taken care of."

His eyes were troubled as he remembered how it had been for these people. "The whole family had one goal—keep those horses. But while I was living there, they had to get rid of two of them. They just couldn't keep up with expenses. They were about to lose their house and they couldn't...." He shook his head as though the words just wouldn't come for a moment.

"I would have tried to help them, but the Mercurian government wasn't paying me at the time. So I didn't *have much in the way of resources."* He looked down at his hands. They were clenched into fists. Slowly, he made them relax.

"But we managed to get together enough money to keep the most important one, a beautiful horse named Belle. He belonged to the Minderts' eight-year-old daughter, Mindy. She rode her every day. It was magical to watch the way she and that huge horse had a rapport between them. It would have been a crime to separate them."

Kayla murmured something and reached for his hand again. His fingers curled around hers, but he didn't seem to know it. He was wrapped up in his story.

"The public affairs minister and I had a falling out. Bottom line, he hated me. He tried to undercut me a couple of ways that just didn't work out. And then, all of a sudden, he took Mindy's horse away." His voice deepened roughly. "He had some trumped-up national security reason. They were supposedly confiscating all horses in the sector."

He turned to look into her eyes. "It was a bunch of bull. I went to him to try to get it rescinded. He called the guard, tried to have me arrested." He shrugged. "I got away." He gazed at the wall again and took a deep breath. "I found out where they were keeping Belle and I stole her back. I took her and I rode her right across the border."

He looked back at Kayla as though to see how she was taking that. She looked right back. So far, she wished he hadn't done it, but she didn't see how it was going to be a capital offense. These things could be explained...couldn't they? Maybe Pellea could authorize a payment?

But Max was still telling his story.

"I managed to have the Minderts meet me. They were about to lose their land anyway. It was time for them to go. I got them out of the country and on their way to Switzerland. They have family there." He took a deep breath and looked at her. "And Mindy has her horse back."

"Oh. I'm glad. But..." It did seem a large price to pay for a horse. She admired him for his instincts to help, but... "Max, you could go to prison for this." Not only that, but he could also be giving up his place in the royal family.

"Yes," he said simply. "I might." He stared hard into her eyes, his own silver with passion. "But, Kayla, I don't really care. There was something more important than that involved. And I would do it again. I would do it tomorrow."

CHAPTER SIX

MAX's hand tightened on Kayla's. "You see, there's more to this story. Mindy is a sweet and adorable girl. You would love her. But more than that, Mindy…" His voice choked a bit and he cleared his throat. "Mindy is blind, you see. Belle was her life companion, her only joy. You understand?" He searched her eyes, looking very serious.

She drew her breath in sharply, and then she nodded slowly. She did understand. She had to admit, Mindy's blindness made all the difference. The fact that he had thrown away everything he had in order to help the child…she was touched by what he'd done. "Yes. I think so. I do understand."

He nodded, as though satisfied with her answer and by what he could see in her eyes. "Good. It had to be done."

She stared at him. Yes, it had to be done. And he'd done it. He was a man who went ahead and did things. He didn't wait to see how the wind might blow. He

made things happen. Suddenly, her heart filled with affection for him. So he stole a horse—so what!

"And you...?" she asked.

He shook his head. "I never went back. It was time
for me to go anyway."

She took a deep breath and sighed as though she'd
just been through something important. "Wow. You
were a hero."

"No." He shook his head and appeared pained. "It
was my fault the horse was taken in the first place. I
should have been more obsequious to the minister. I
don't ever seem to be able to learn that lesson."

"And I don't suppose you were much of a hero to the
Mercurian regime, were you?"

He gave a short laugh. "Hardly."

"So by the time you left, they already had a pretty
deep grudge against you."

"So it seems."

Their tea was getting cold and the first round of
sandwiches had arrived. Luckily, they were delicious
and Kayla began to relax. It was wonderful what a little
bit of tea and some yummy finger food could do. She
was feeling so much better about everything.

He had reasons for taking the plane and reasons for
stealing the horse. Surely he also had an explanation
for the historical artifact. Whatever that was. But she
wouldn't bug him about that right now. All in good
time.

She definitely wouldn't let herself get caught up in
so much worry about it any longer. She had work to do.

She was supposed to mold him into a prince in a week. It was time to get going on that little job.

"We've got to get back to the essential things we've been tasked with," she told him between bites of a watercress delectable. She gave him a significant look. "Prince lessons."

He rolled his eyes but didn't balk. "I'm game," he said with resignation. "What do I do next? Cut my hair in a pageboy?"

"Nothing so old-fashioned as that," she assured him. "But I think we ought to make a list." She pulled a notebook out of her huge purse. She'd brought it along just for this sort of thing.

"A list?" His look was wary.

"A list of all the things the modern nobleman must be."

He gave her a crooked grin so endearing, she felt something move in her chest. He'd grinned at her with just that look before. She had a quick flashback to a day on the beach down on the Mediterranean, a day so bright and beautiful, it made her think her world had been enchanted. Max and Eddie were competing to see who could build the best sand castle. And she was just sitting to the side, watching them and laughing at their silly macho banter. The sea was turquoise blue, the sand was sparkling, the sun was liquid gold.

A perfect day. A perfect time. A bittersweet sense of nostalgia swept through her and she had to hold back tears. Nothing would ever be so special again.

She pulled herself back into the now and Max was still making fun of her list.

"I'll see your modern nobleman list," he teased her. "And then we'll raise the stakes and make a list of everything the non-noble should know before attempting to play the royal game. That one I might be able to shoot for."

She shook her head. "Don't worry. This doesn't mean you have to absorb everything all at once. It's more of a wish list." She wrote on the top of the page, The Attributes of the Perfect Prince.

"Perfect?" He groaned. "Might as well toss it right now."

"Will you stop it?" she said, raising her pen to her cheek as she thought things over. "I know. We'll start with physical appearance."

He seemed surprised. "You don't think I've got the looks for the job?"

She flashed him a satirical glance. "As far as the basics, you'll do. But there's more to it. There's a certain way that a prince carries himself."

He grinned. "Arrogance and disdain? I think I can handle that."

She pretended to glare at him. "No. Confidence and competence mixed with a certain sense of approachability. Leadership and the common touch, all wrapped up in one handsome package." She wrinkled her nose. "Do you understand what I mean?"

He looked back and then sighed. "I think I get it."

"Good." She nodded. "Work on that, please."

"Oh, sure. No problem."

"And then there is your manner of dress."

He looked down at his casual shirt and Levi's and eyed her questioningly.

Her look back was scathing and she shook her head. "I'll get together some pictures to show you what you can do on that."

"Spend money," he said cynically.

"Yes. But carefully. I'll teach you the tricks."

"No kidding?" His smile was nothing if not provocative. "I didn't know you had a few of those up your sleeve."

She grinned back and tapped him with her pen. "Be ready for anything."

"Oh, I will."

"But right now," she said, shifting gears and getting serious again, "I want to see how you walk."

He blinked at her. "What?"

"Your walk. Is it royal enough? Does it need more backbone? Insouciance? Perhaps a bit more savoir faire?"

"Listen, I'll do anything you want, but I'm not going French."

She laughed. "You only wish you could be French. The French know how to walk."

"I've never been put down for my walk before."

"Let's see it, then."

He blinked at her. She couldn't mean what she seemed to mean. Could she? "What?"

She gestured for him to stand. "Do it."

His eyes were clouded. "Do what?"

She leaned toward him, holding back a laugh at his hesitancy. "Walk across the room. Let's see what you've got."

"Here? Now?" He looked around the room, his face worried.

"Yes, here and now." She bit back a grin and decided it was time to take pity on him. "Oh, don't worry. Something simple. Just a quick turn and back again."

She almost laughed out loud at the look he gave her. It was obvious the whole concept was a huge embarrassment to him. Funny. Had he never been conscious of how he came across before?

"Just get up and walk over to the counter and pick up a tray of sweets and bring them back here. No one will know you're on display."

He took a deep breath, his look as close to a glare as she'd ever received from him. "All right," he said grudgingly. "But be kind."

Rising, he threw her an exasperated glance and started across the room. His walk was slow, strong and controlled and she knew right away there was nothing she could suggest to improve it. The set of his shoulders, the tilt of his head, the length of his stride—his manner of carrying himself might not be particularly royal, but it was about as good as it could get.

And then she noticed something odd. It was like a force field moving through the room. Every single woman, even those who couldn't have possibly seen him get up from where they were sitting, was turning her head in his direction. What was he—magnetized? She watched, eyes wide and hand over her mouth, as he picked up the tray and started back. They were all staring.

And it wasn't that he was so handsome. There were other handsome men in the room. There was more to it than that. There was a sense about him—a little bit of danger, a little bit of bravado and a lot of something else. She bit her lip, trying to analyze just what it was. Those gorgeous eyes seemed to say he knew things other people didn't—secret things about life and love. And whatever those secret things were, they seemed to draw the attention of every female imagination in the place.

"Wow," she breathed as he sat down again.

He lifted a dark eyebrow sardonically. "I was that good, was I?"

She rolled her eyes. "No," she told him briskly, not willing to let him know the power he had, just in case he wasn't sure of it yet. "I was just thinking what a lot of work we have ahead of us."

He winced and looked rebellious. "I can save everybody the trouble and forget the whole thing," he offered, only half joking. "If even the way I walk isn't good enough..."

"Isn't good enough," she echoed weakly, shaking her head. It was no use. He might as well know the truth. "Someone should call out the paramedics," she whispered to him wryly, leaning close so as not to be overheard. "Half the women in here are about to swoon right off their chairs after watching you walk across the room."

He eyed her skeptically, a cloudy, slightly bewildered expression in his eyes. Then he spoke with such honesty, she was taken aback. "Kayla, come on. Don't mess with my self-confidence like that. I'm feeling shaky enough about this whole royal thing. I don't need you, of all people, to be mocking me."

She recoiled in surprise. She hadn't meant to do that. She hadn't thought anything could ruffle his famously appealing feathers. Evidently, he wasn't quite as cocky as he seemed. To think that he had never noticed the effect he had on women was a revelation.

"I'm sorry," she said quickly. "I'm just as new at this as you are. I was trying to stick to a light tone and I guess I went a little too far." Reaching across the table, she took his hand in hers and leaned forward, looking into his eyes earnestly. "Max, you've got a great walk. Manly and noble and full of confidence. At least, that's the way it comes across and that is what counts. You were born to be a prince, no matter how you want to fight it. It's in your blood."

He squeezed her hand and didn't answer, but his eyes were smiling.

"But we aren't finished," she added quickly. "There are a lot of superficial things you need to learn. We still have a long way to go."

He nodded, agreeing with her. "'And miles to go before we sleep,'" he said softly.

She gasped and smiled. "A literary quote. Very good. Knowing good poetry is a real plus in a prince."

"Eddie taught me that one." His eyes clouded. "Too bad it wasn't Eddie who got the chance to be a prince. He would have done a bang-up job of it, wouldn't he?"

As she watched him, something caught in her heart. "Max, Eddie was great. I miss him constantly. It just kills me that he had to die. But..." And here was the hard part. It was true, but hard to say. "Max, he was no better a person than you are."

Max winced as though she'd slapped him. "Don't say that. Of course he was."

"No." She shook her head. "He wasn't perfect. He was a man, just like you are. He had his good days and his bad ones." She tried to smile. "He could be darn grumpy when the weather didn't suit him. You remember."

A slow grin erased Max's frown. "I remember."

Their gazes met and held. Max began to lean closer, his eyes filling with smoky memories.

"Kayla," he began huskily.

But he never got any further. A shriek filled the room, a sound like a fire engine coming through, and they both jumped back, startled.

"Oh, no," Kayla said as she leaped to her feet and whirled. And just in time. A child who could barely toddle was racing toward her as fast as his chubby little legs could take him.

"Teddy!"

He threw himself at her, practically flying through

the air, and she caught him and pulled him up into her arms, half laughing, half scolding. "Teddy, what are you doing here?"

"I am so sorry," Caroline said, rushing in behind him with her own little boy in her arms. "We saw you through the glass. And once he knew his mom was in here, there was no stopping him. He climbed right out of the stroller!"

Holding Teddy in her arms was like being close to heaven and Kayla always reveled in it. But there was another emotion lurking. Guilt. Leaving her baby with someone else was something she had to do, but the guilt never completely left her, no matter how busy and involved she was at work. She held him tightly and whispered soothing words against his adorable head, and he whimpered and pressed in close. And the guilt welled up inside her.

She looked up, realizing there were other issues that had to be dealt with. Her sister was smiling at Max, but she hadn't told her anything about him and she obviously had no idea who he was.

"Caroline, this is an old friend from back in my Trialta days. Max Arragen. He...he and Eddie were really close. They flew together...."

"Nice to meet you." Caroline frowned as she held out her hand for his. "Wait. Max Arragen? Aren't you...?"

He gave her one of his devastating self-deprecating smiles. "The new prince. Yes."

Caroline's eyes lit up. "Congratulations," she said,

glancing at Kayla. "I had no idea. Wow. You must be really excited with all this hoopla."

"Oh, yeah. Something like that anyway."

"I feel like I should do a little curtsy or something."

"No. Please." He seemed genuinely embarrassed and she laughed.

Kayla watched them and she had to smile. Her sister resembled her quite a bit, but her blond hair was cut short and perky. Caroline was the friendly, outgoing sort, while Kayla had always felt she was the shy one, the quietly competent one whose work no one really noticed. And yet, here she was, having lunch with a prince, working for the queen… Maybe it was time to reassess her self-image.

"Ma-ma," Teddy said, tugging on her collar and adding something indecipherable that probably meant, *Let's get out of here and have some 'mommy and me' time together.*

The words weren't there but Kayla heard the message loud and clear. She looked up at Max, waiting for him to finish chatting with her sister and notice the baby.

"We were on our way to the playground," Caroline was saying. "If you two have any lunch hour left, why don't you come along?"

Kayla looked at Max. He was staring at Teddy. Her heart began to race. What was he seeing? What did those sharp eyes catch? What were the vibes that were getting through to his instinctive reactions?

It was hard to tell. He was smiling, but something in that smile was beginning to stiffen up. Had he noticed?

Had he taken a quick assessment of whom Teddy might look like? It was an exercise that was completely familiar to her. She'd done it periodically ever since her baby was born. She was blond with dark eyes. Eddie had been the same. But Max had dark bronzed hair and shockingly blue eyes. And so did Teddy.

It didn't mean anything. Of course it didn't. There were all sorts of combinations possible with the logic of genetics. She knew that. He knew that. But still...

"This is Teddy," she told him, wishing her voice wasn't shaking. "Teddy, this is Max. Say 'hi.'" She made him wave, but his little baby face was rebellious.

Max hesitated. He didn't seem to have much experience socializing with babies and in the end, he smiled awkwardly and said, "Hi, Teddy."

Teddy turned and hid his face against her neck. Kayla searched Max's eyes, trying to guess what he might be thinking. She didn't see any clues. But she also didn't see the sort of appreciation for her beautiful child that she might have expected.

"I think he's tired," she said, knowing it sounded like an excuse.

"Oh, sure," Caroline chimed in helpfully. "He didn't have a nap this morning and he usually goes down for a half hour or so."

Teddy still had morning naps? Had she really been out of his daily routine for so long that she didn't know it any longer? She felt a sudden sense of remorse. She should be with her baby today. He needed her. She needed him. He was clinging to her and she was getting the message.

As she pulled him closer, he turned to look at Max. Teddy's expression didn't change, but his lower lip thrust out and his little hands dug deeper into the fabric of her blouse. *This is my mom*, his face said. *She belongs to me.*

"Cute kid," Max said shortly, but there was no warmth in his eyes as he turned away.

Kayla made her decision. "I think we're going to have to put off doing more work on our prince project," she told him. "I really feel I need to go to the playground with them. I've been neglecting Teddy so much lately. Do you...do you want to come along?"

She waited as he mulled it over, hoping he would say no.

"I've got a few things I've got to take care of," he said at last, his gaze touching hers, then veering off again. "I'll catch you later."

"Okay." Relief flooded her. This was just too nerve-wracking to keep up much longer.

She didn't look at Max again. Her attention was all for her baby. Caroline gave her a questioning look and she knew that her sister wanted to get filled in on a few details and get a fix on her feelings, but she wasn't up to discussing Max and all that he meant to her. Too much had happened too soon and she needed to reevaluate.

But right now it was Teddy's time. She turned her

face away and began a baby-talk discussion with her son. Her sister would have to wait.

Max wandered down into the main castle courtyard and out along the man-made miniwilderness where he could lose himself among the trees. A small babbling brook ran cheerfully past a large flat rock, and that was where he settled, out of sight of the walkways.

Normally, he wasn't much for introspection. He thought of himself as a man of action. He didn't tend to second-guess himself, to try to analyze why he did the things he went through or why the results had been good or bad. Navel gazing was just not his style.

But today he felt like a little self-analysis was in order. He'd just spent an hour in a meeting with two of his brothers—Prince Mykal, who had been identified as one of the royals only a few weeks before Max had, and Prince David, who had caught sight of him in the hallway and invited him to join them in a discussion of renovations to a still-destroyed area of the castle.

Much of the original and ancient castle had been burned on the night thirty years before when the Granvilli family had mounted a successful rebellion and taken over Ambria, killing the king and queen and establishing their vicious dictatorial regime. That night, each of the royal children had been spirited away by various servants or friends or members of the administration and hidden from the Granvillis. It had taken twenty-five years for the princes and princess to begin to find each other again. Their fight to win back their country had been successful and now there was only a remnant of the Granvilli faction that held a remote part of the island to deal with.

David was the second oldest prince and considered second only to King Monte in importance. Tall and dark, he had a serious air about him.

"Max, I'm glad to see you," he said when he met his brother in the hall. "I've been neglecting you, I know. There are so many issues coming up right now. I really want to get you more involved in management matters. We all have to share the burden of managing the castle, and eventually, the nation at large." He gave him a firm pat on the back. "I'm meeting Mykal in the blue meeting room right now. Why don't you join us?"

Max was glad to do just that. He was still new enough at the castle to be a little starstruck by his brothers and he wasn't sure he would ever get over being impressed by them. He'd been told a little of David's background. He'd been raised by a family in the Netherlands, and since he was six when he was taken, he remembered where he'd come from. But he also knew it had to be kept secret, and it wasn't until he was in his twenties that he and Monte found each other and began to plot their return to power. As the two oldest, they were regularly considered the head and heart of the family.

Mykal was almost as new to this as Max was, and it showed. Still recovering from a terrible motorcycle accident, he had trouble sitting for long, and by the time an hour had passed it was obvious the meeting had to be adjourned for the day.

But Max sat with them at the long, shiny table and made small talk about how he was settling in. Then the real work of the meeting had begun, and he was very quickly over his head. The talk was all architectural plans and cost estimates and zoning regulations, things he had never dealt with before. He listened carefully and filed information away to learn more about later. But he was definitely out of his element, and what's more, though he liked and admired them, he didn't feel any special connection. They were brothers, but it didn't feel the way he had expected that sort of relationship to feel. When they all rose, shook hands and parted ways, his head was swimming.

That feeling was still with him now. He was glad to have carved out an hour to be on his own. There was a lot to think about. He was feeling a bit shaky about what he ought to be doing and generally undecided about his own future. Bottom line—what the hell was he doing here living in a castle?

The whole prince thing just didn't feel right. He'd never asked for it. He'd been happily flying reconnaissance missions over the Granvilli territory when he'd been called in to the commander's office and asked to take a battery of tests. He still didn't know who had nominated him for testing or why.

If only he'd refused and walked away right at that point, none of this would be happening. He'd be off flying in someone else's war.

Still, what was stopping him from doing exactly what he pleased right now? He could go. He could find someone else to fly for. He would keep his promise to the queen, but once that was over, he wasn't so sure he was going to stick around. After all, what was really keeping him here?

Right now, he would have to say it was mostly Kayla. He hadn't expected to find her here, but now that they had reconnected, he knew he didn't want to lose her again.

Kayla was important to him. She always would be. He remembered those days in Trialta as the best days of his life. He and Eddie had hit it off like brothers, born to be together, and Kayla had been a huge part of that bond.

Funny. When he'd heard she had a child, he'd assumed her baby would be an extension of that. That he would love the kid as a small form of Eddie. But the reality hadn't fit in with the vision. There was something about that baby...

He was definitely a beautiful baby boy. But looking at him, something hadn't felt right. Something about the kid bothered him, made him want to look away quickly, and he didn't want to feel that way about Kayla's baby. Very strange. Maybe he ought to stay away from the kid until he was a little older.

A twig snapped and he turned his head, sure someone was coming into his little clearing. He didn't want company. He stared into the brush, ready to scowl a nonwelcome. But no one appeared. He stared harder, his gaze darting from one gap in the greenery to another, looking for movement. Nothing. Funny…he was sure he'd heard someone.

And it had happened before. He remembered getting the same feeling when he was wandering through the halls, earlier. A feeling that he wasn't alone.

Suddenly he had a prickly feeling on the back of his neck, and he stood, turning slowly, hands balled into fists. Yes, damn it, someone was watching him. Maybe he couldn't see it, but he sure as hell could feel it.

CHAPTER SEVEN

KAYLA looked up, startled, as Max came into the office. There was a thunderstorm brewing in that handsome face.

"Max," she said, but he walked right past her desk and confronted Pellea.

"I want to know why you've got somebody following me," he said curtly. "Don't you trust me? Has it really come to this?"

Pellea looked up and gaped at him, bewildered and showing it. "What are you talking about?"

"Look, I've made you a promise. I may be unreliable in superficial ways, but when I make a promise, I keep it. There was no call for you to send spies to watch over me. I don't like it."

She was shaking her head, looking at him as though he'd lost his mind. "I don't have anyone following you," she protested earnestly. "Really, Max. I swear."

His anger seemed to pulse in the small room. He took a deep breath, trying to calm himself. He knew he was over-the-top and taking it out on Pellea wasn't going to fix anything. This wasn't really her fault. He'd been angry when he thought it was, but her outrage told him differently, and he began to cool down. If he were honest with himself, he knew his own doubts and insecurities were more to blame for this outburst than anything the queen could have done. He needed to get a grip.

"I was just down in the courtyard, in among the trees, and someone was there watching me. I know it."

She shrugged. "There may have been someone watching you, but I didn't tell them to. Believe me, Max. I wouldn't do that." She made a face. "Not yet, anyway."

He looked at the ground and shook his head. For someone trying to learn to act like a prince, he was doing a lousy job of it. He looked up with a rueful smile and made a slight bow toward her.

"Your Majesty, please forgive me. This was rude and uncalled for. I had no right to attack you like this and I'm sorry."

Pellea's smile lit up the room. It seemed she knew earnest regret when she saw it. "Of course I forgive you. This is not supposed to be a fight. We're both on the same side." She rose from her desk chair and came out to throw her arms around him and then kiss him on both cheeks.

"Listen to me," he told her. "I will make you a pledge right now. I won't do anything behind your back. If anything happens, I'll tell you. If I decide I have to leave, I'll tell you. No secrets."

She nodded. "Good." One last pat on his cheek and

she turned. "And in the spirit of openness, sit down. I'll give you the rundown on our latest outreach to Mercuria."

He sank into a chair across from her, but glanced back at Kayla. She gave him a wink and a tiny approving smile. Ridiculously, he suddenly felt much better.

"All right, here's the news. We've sent our ambassador to Mercuria."

Max nodded. "And what message does he take with him?"

Pellea shuffled papers on her desk and brought up the pertinent ones. "In answer to their charges, we respond thusly—it is our understanding that the airplane was given to Prince Maximillian, formerly known as Max Arragen, in payment for his help in establishing the Mercurian Air Force and therefore not an item that can be reclaimed."

She looked up for his approval, and he nodded.

"As for the horse, we made it clear that we feel there was a misunderstanding and a wrong done to the horse's owner, who now has regained possession of the horse. If they like, we are prepared to pay damages for the loss of it to the Mercurian government." She nodded toward Kayla. "I've had that whole episode explained to me. Kayla repeated what you told her this morning."

He glanced back at Kayla again and nodded. "Sounds reasonable."

"As for the historical artifact, I let them know that we have no idea what this might be or how it might have come into your possession. We shall await clarification. Barring that, we are unwilling to count that as a serious charge against you."

"Wow. I'd say that pretty much covers all the bases."

Pellea nodded. "Now we wait to see how they take it. We should have their response tomorrow." She gave him a significant look. "And then, we'll see."

He heard the warning in her voice. She was seriously worried about this.

"You've said the Mercurians were a big help in the fight to regain Ambria for the DeAngelis royal family," he said musingly. "What made them come in on your side?"

Pellea shrugged. "As you know, Mercuria is a tiny stretch of land along the coast, not even as large or as important to this area as Ambria, whose main source of wealth comes from tourists, mainly in gambling. Some wags have called it nothing more than a casino with a nice beach. But they have been traditional allies of ours, and the fact that they have a monarchy, just as we do, cemented our ties more recently."

He nodded. "And they are the closest country to you, aren't they?"

"Yes. Just an hour by boat will bring you right to the foot of the Mercurian castle. You could almost consider them a neighbor."

"Do you know King Juomo personally?"

"No, I don't. I guess the families had personal ties back in the dark ages, but as far as I know, none of us have come face-to-face with any of them. As I under-stand it, they are rather reclusive."

He nodded. "Yes. Very reclusive. And very strange."

"So I've heard." She made a face. "That doesn't bode well. It's hard to judge how they will take this. What do you think?"

He shook his head. "I have no idea. King Juomo liked me, until he didn't like me anymore. And I'm not sure what made the change."

"Oh, well." Pellea waved a hand dismissively. "We shall see. And I need to get back to work." She smiled at him. "Cheer up. We'll get through this."

He smiled back. "Of course." Taking a deep breath, he rose, took his leave of the queen and pivoted to Kayla.

"Do you have time to go get a cup of coffee with me?" he asked, looking at her without any clear emotion.

She glanced at Pellea, who nodded her permission, and smiled. "Sure," she said, reaching to pull her tiny clutch purse out of her larger bag. "I won't be long," she promised the queen.

She almost had to run to keep up with Max's stride once they were out in the walkway. His walk was strong and aggressive, with a hint of residual anger still hovering over his mood.

"Will you tell me why you're so upset?" she asked.

He gave her a sideways glance and didn't respond as they came out onto the public corridor and up to the coffee bistro. It was packed with people and the lines were long.

"There's a vending machine a little farther out this way. We can get coffee and go out on the balcony."

They got their coffee in paper cups from the machine and made their way outside. The balcony was small, but there was a table flanked by two chairs, and they went to it after a quick look over the railing. The blue skies were gone and a cool wind blustered in and out of the crevices and still neither of them had said a word.

Max stared down into his coffee. She watched him. Finally he looked up and met her gaze.

"You know what?" he said. "I want to go."

Her heart jumped. His eyes looked hard and unhappy.

"Where?" she said.

He shrugged. "Away. Anywhere. Something new. Something different." His blue eyes held hers. "This isn't the life for me."

"Max..." She reached for his hand and held it tightly.

"I don't feel like I belong here. I don't think the way these people do. My instincts don't work here. I really feel I need to go."

"Max..."

His wide eyes stared right into her soul. "Will you go with me?"

She stared at him. How could he ask such a thing? Didn't he realize she had a life here? A son? She couldn't go anywhere she felt like. She had commitments.

He could read her refusal in her eyes. The child. Of

course. What was he thinking? She had the child. He pulled his hand away and looked out at the grey skies.

A cold wind blew in and Kayla shivered.

"Here, take this," he said, slipping out of the denim jacket and handing it to her. "Unless you still scorn it?" he tried to tease, his smile unconvincingly stiff.

"I never scorned it," she protested, shrugging into it and huddling gratefully in the warmth his body had left inside. "I love jeans jackets."

"Just not on princes."

She pulled the jacket in close and looked at him. "Not true. Max, I know you want to wear the clothes you feel comfortable in. And you should be able to. But you have to know what's expected of you in certain situations. That's all. We're not trying to change the fundamental you."

He grunted, and she leaned closer. "Tomorrow we'll go clothes shopping and I'll show you what I mean."

He stared at her and finally a smile began to tug at the corners of his mouth. "I guess that means you don't think much of my plan to leave," he said, eyes smiling sadly.

"I think it stinks. You promised Pellea two weeks. You'll manage to stick it out that long. I know you. You won't run."

He wasn't so sure she knew him as well as she thought she did. Running was what he'd done all his life—running from his problems, running from expectations, running from commitment. He knew it was time for him to grow up and stop running, but he wasn't sure how to do that.

"You won't run," she repeated confidently, and he merely smiled and let her think she had him pegged.

"At least you won't really need new clothes tonight," she mentioned. "Pellea has a dinner planned for all you princes, but it's beer and pizza and football on the television."

His smile evaporated in an instant. This was the first he'd heard about it. He scowled, but she wasn't cowed.

"You need to interact with your brothers more," she said. "Once you get to know them better, you'll feel more welcome here."

"Maybe." He didn't look convinced, but the sun came out from behind a cloud at that very moment, and it was as though liquid gold was streaming down all around them.

She laughed and went to the railing, enjoying the warmth of the sun, and he followed. The countryside around the castle looked magical. It was late afternoon and the shadows were long and colors intensified.

"Do you ever go walking down by the stream?" he asked her, pointing it out below.

"No, I've never been there."

He grabbed her hand. "Let's go," he said spontaneously. "You'll love it."

They took the elevator down and walked quickly through the corridors and onto the back patio, hoping to catch as much sunshine as they could before the cloud cover took over again. He took her hand and led her through the trees to his favorite rock. She scanned the area, enchanted with the rustling leaves and babbling brook. Then she got a thoughtful look.

"Is this where you were when you thought you were being watched?" she said accusingly.

"Yes, it is." He looked excessively innocent. "Why do you ask?"

"You just wanted me to come down here to see if I could help you catch the culprits, didn't you?" She pretended to take a swipe at him.

He laughed. "No," he said, fending off her mock attack and grabbing her wrists. "Though come to think of it, two sets of eyes are better than one."

He pulled her close until their faces were within inches of each other. She smiled into his eyes. He smiled back and something electric happened. He was going to kiss her. She could feel it. Her breath caught in her throat and she pulled back quickly, heart pounding.

"I don't see anybody," she said breathlessly. "I don't hear anybody. I think you're getting paranoid."

"No. Someone was there." He pulled her back against him. "But I don't care anymore."

He saw alarm in her eyes—denial, dismissal and a lot of worry, but like he'd said, he didn't care anymore. His mouth took hers as though he had a right to it, as though he'd gone through all the reasons why she wasn't his for the kissing and decided to throw them out the window. He wanted her. He'd always wanted her. And now that he had her in his arms, he needed to feel her heat, taste her warm sweetness, touch her beautiful body.

His hands slid under the jacket, under her sweater, up her slender back and she arched her softness against his hard chest. His kiss was hungry and hot and she answered it back the same way. The wind swirled around them. Leaves blew around their feet. The water from the brook sang a happy song, and time seemed to stand still.

It was meant to be a short kiss, just something quick and loaded with commitment and affection, but he never wanted it to stop. If it had been up to him, it never would have. But she knew it couldn't last.

"Max."

He was kissing the curve of her neck, tasting her skin, devouring her sweetness.

"Max!"

Pulling back, he looked at her groggily. She was laughing.

"Max, stop!"

He shook his head, then groaned and let her go. Running his fingers through his hair, he tried to get his balance back.

"Sorry," he muttered. "You just feel so good. I want to hold you forever."

She looked into his eyes, smiling, loving him, but not sure what to say. They couldn't do this. He couldn't kiss her this way. There was something intoxicating between the two of them. Once they started, they didn't seem to know how to stop. Reaching out, she cupped his rough cheek in her hand and smiled sadly.

And then, without a word, she stepped away carefully and sank down to sit on the rock. He followed and sat beside her.

"Eddie would have loved this place," he said softly, and then winced, wishing he'd kept his mouth shut.

She didn't look at him. She didn't say a word, but he knew she what she was thinking.

They were silent for a few minutes, watching the water, and then Max started talking about his brothers again, haltingly at first. And then he just kept going, talking as though they had never stopped.

"You know, there's a big difference between me and the other princes," he said at one point. "They all grew up in families. They might not have been the right families, but at least they had that. I think I'm the only one who sort of got thrown out with the trash."

His words might have been bitter, but she was glad to notice that his tone was more bemused.

"Actually," she told him, "Prince Cassius—the one we all call Joe—had a pretty rough time of it as well."

"Prince Joe? The surfer prince?" He had to grin. He'd met Joe.

She nodded, smiling. "That's him. Whoever was supposed to hide him that night didn't show up and the kitchen maid ended up taking him with her when she ran, hiding him under her shawl on the boat. She didn't know what to do with him, so she took him back home to England, whereupon she promptly died and left him to be raised by members of her family who had no clue who he was."

"How did he end up in California?"

"The family emigrated and then the parents got divorced and they all pretty much split up. I guess it wasn't much of a warm-and-toasty family after all. Sort of dysfunctional. The way I heard it, he took off pretty young and then he joined the military."

Max nodded. "Okay. Joe and I might just have a little bit in common. Maybe I'll have a chance to talk to him tonight." He made a comical face. "Pizza and beer," he repeated, shaking his head. "I guess she really does want to make me feel at home. That's practically my daily diet as it is."

"She's doing her best." She looked at him whimsically. "I don't think you realize how much better this is going to make things for you," she said simply.

He groaned and the anger flared in him again. That was the last thing he wanted to hear.

"Don't tell me how wonderful this is for me and how it's going to change my life. I don't want my life changed. I like things the way they've been. I don't want to be a prince."

She was frowning at him now. "You don't want to be a prince because you don't want to have to conform to rules and standards. You don't think anyone else should have a say in how you should act, do you?"

He blinked, not used to tough talk from her. "So? What's wrong with that?"

Her eyes flashed. "Grow up, Max. It's time for you
to stop playing at life and start living it."

Maybe I don't want to.

He didn't say it. The words popped out onto the tip
of his tongue, but he wisely held them back, and as he
thought them over, he realized how childish they were.
What the hell. She was right. It was time for him to
grow up. Grabbing her hand, he pressed his lips to the
center of her palm, then looked up at her, smiling.

"How did I do without you all this time?" he said
huskily. "Eddie once said to me that if anything ever
happened to you, he wouldn't want to go on alone. And
I can see why."

His words sent a shock through her. She closed her
eyes and thought about them for a moment. Then she
looked at him, trying not to be resentful. "And you're
wondering how I've managed to go on so normally
without him?"

"No," he said, looking shocked at the thought. "That
isn't what I meant to say at all."

"Then why did you say it?"

He shook his head, trying to remember what had
been in his mind at the time. "I just wanted to remind
you to remember how much Eddie loved you."

She pulled her arms in close. "I don't need reminding. I remember very well. I remember it all the time."
She still felt resentful as she looked at him. "I didn't
get to where I am without a lot of pain, you know."

He nodded, searching her face, staring into her
eyes. "I know that, Kayla. There was enough pain to

go around." He winced and looked away. "I felt it, too. After Eddie died, I went a little crazy for a while."

"Didn't we all?"

"No, I mean it." He looked back at her. "I took stupid chances, did stupid things. In some ways, it almost felt as though I couldn't live life normally anymore. If a guy as super as Eddie could get killed like that, what right did I have to be happy?" He frowned, remembering. "I began to make careless mistakes. At one point, I did something stupid and I had to ditch my plane. I bailed out in time, but it was a while before they found me." He shook his head. "That woke me up."

"That was when I saw the report on the news. I...I really thought you were gone, too."

He nodded. "It was hard to accept a world where the best people got snuffed out like candles. No real reason. Just here one moment, gone the next. To see a good guy like Eddie get killed so easily and a waster like I am get lucky every time—it didn't seem right. I was having a hard time with that."

"Max, Eddie's gone. I don't think you've completely faced it yet."

"Have you?"

"Yes. I've tried very hard. There's a part of me that will always love him and miss him horribly. But most of life has to go on without him. I either go on or I throw myself off the balcony."

His eyes darkened with horror. "You wouldn't do that."

"No. I couldn't do that. I have Teddy."

He looked startled, as though he'd forgotten.

"Teddy is my whole life now," she told him carefully, wishing she saw a smile or a look of affection or something friendly toward her son. How could this man not feel something? "Do you understand that?"

"Yeah, I think I do."

She thought about the fact that he'd never really lived in a family. Maybe he didn't understand what it meant to have a child, how it consumed your soul. It was true that as far as she could see, he didn't react well to Teddy and she didn't know why. But maybe this was a part of it.

Or maybe it was something else, something about Teddy's background that threw him off. And if that was what it was, she knew she didn't want to face that at all.

"I've got to get back."

He nodded. "I'll walk with you."

They started off and once again, they both fell silent, as if they had talked about things that needed some mulling over before they mentioned them to each other again. At the door to her office, Kayla smiled at him.

"Could I come by and see you tonight?" he asked. "After the pizza party?"

Her smile disappeared. "No," she said slowly, thinking it over on the run. "I think it would be better if we kept our relationship on a completely professional level. Forget that we're friends."

He looked as though he thought she was nuts. "Forget that we're friends?" He shook his head, his anger beginning to hint at a return engagement. "No. That's carrying things too far. I'll be circumspect during prince lessons, but once they're over, you're fair game."

"Fair game?" she repeated, puzzled.

"You got it. You can run but you can't hide."

"What are you talking about?"

"This." Taking her face in his hands, he bent down and kissed her softly. His lips were warm and his solid male earthy scent made her head spin. His kiss was sweet and sincere and somehow much more effective than the wild one out by the little river. It brought tears to her eyes and left her gasping, aching for more.

"And that's just a sample of things to come," he told her, giving her a triumphant grin and turning to go.

Speechless, she watched him go, her cheeks burning. It wasn't until he was out of sight that she remembered she still had his jacket.

She was fixing Teddy a nice peanut butter sandwich for dinner, because that was all he would eat besides eggs and bananas. He was dancing around the apartment, bobbing his head and pretending to play a little plastic guitar, when the phone rang.

"Hey, it's me."

Amazing how his voice could send sparkles through her bloodstream. She remembered the kisses and the sparkles intensified.

"Max. What is it?"

He paused, listening. "What's that noise in the background?"

"Oh, it's just Teddy. He's so funny. I wish you could

see him. He's sort of singing and dancing and banging things. But you may ignore at will. Go on."

"He makes a lot of noise for such a small kid."

"You don't know the half of it," she said, laughing. "He's only just begun."

"Hmm."

Once again Kayla got the impression that he didn't like her baby much, and she frowned.

"Well, I just called to tell you my place has been totally ransacked."

"What? How did someone get by the guard?"

There was an extensive network of security in the castle, but it was especially concentrated in the royal wing.

"That's a good question."

"Did they take anything?"

"I don't think so."

"What were they after?"

He paused, then said, "I think it's all related. The people watching me, the people going through my things. What do you think?"

"It would seem logical I guess. But you have no idea who they are, right?"

"Right. Still, I think it's related to this. Now if I could *figure out what they're looking for…*"

"How about an historical artifact from Mercuria?" she suggested, eyes widening as she thought of it.

"I was thinking the same thing." He paused. "Anyway, I just wanted to tell you to be careful. I've told the guards to watch your apartment more vigilantly than usual. So if you notice a lot of cops hanging around, you'll know why."

"Okay. Thanks." She frowned. "Do you think it's people from Mercuria?"

"I'm sure of it. No one else has a grudge against me at the moment. At least, no one that I know of."

"Are you still going to the pizza party?"

"Sure."

"Good. What are you wearing?"

"Kayla! I'm not a girl. Who cares what I wear?"

"No, I mean…I forgot to give you back your denim jacket. I left it in the closet at the office. Remind me later to give it back to you."

"I have another one."

"Oh. Hey, I guess you really do like them, don't you?"

He ignored that and when he spoke again, his voice was lower, almost husky, with a feeling she didn't want to name.

"Hey. I miss you."

Her heart gave a lurch. "No, you don't. You just saw me an hour ago."

"I know. But I still miss you."

"Max, don't. You can't…"

"I know. But I still miss you. Can't help it. See you tomorrow. Good night, Kayla."

"Good night, Max." She closed her eyes to stop the tears that were suddenly threatening. "Happy pizza."

* * *

They met for breakfast at nine. She flushed when she saw him waiting for her in the little crepe café. She couldn't help it. All that crazy kissing had made her jumpy for hours.

But he didn't seem to remember it. He had a lot to tell her about his pizza party with his brothers the night before. He'd obviously had a pretty good time, though he wasn't ready to call it that.

"It was okay," he said slowly as he savored the hot cup of coffee the waitress had served him. "I still don't feel really comfortable with them, but they are a great group. I like them all."

And then he went on to tell her in minute detail everything everyone had said. She smiled, listening to him, slowly picking at her blueberry crepe. Could it be that he was beginning to feel a little better about being here?

He had an omelet and a brioche, but he looked tired. And then he yawned.

She frowned. "Didn't you get enough sleep last night?"

He hesitated, looking a bit chagrined. "Actually, no. On my way back from the pizza party I met an old flying buddy I hadn't seen for a while. We went and had a few drinks and…"

She bit back the words that came to mind, but he read her thoughts in her eyes.

"I know, I know. I'm supposed to be learning to be royal, not carousing with old friends." He glowered at her. "The royal life is looking about as appealing as a term in prison."

"It's not that bad," she said, smiling at his funny face. "Royals go out with friends all the time. In fact, some even get in a lot of trouble all the time. Just read the tabloids. But…"

"Kayla, I know what you're worrying about. We're back to the need for me to grow up. I know. I'm working on it."

"I know." She made a face. "I don't mean to be your constant scold. That's not much fun for either of us. And you deserve to have fun." She gave him a silly grin that just oozed affection. How could she help it? She adored him and adored the way he told her what he was thinking all the time. There was very little about Max that was inscrutable.

And then she sobered. "Just don't forget how serious these times are. The war may be officially over, but there is more work to do. This truce with the Granvillis is going to lead to us taking over their area soon and who knows how that will go?"

He looked at her carefully. "You're sure of that, are you?"

"Of the Granvillis surrendering? Everyone says it's about to happen."

He raised his eyebrows. "Funny thing. This old flying buddy I met last night? He has some ties to the Granvillis and he thinks they are getting ready for a new surge."

Her heart sank. "Oh, no."

"He seems to think they're getting some international help they didn't have before."

She shook her head, knowing how terrible it would be if the war heated up again. "You'd better tell Monte," she said anxiously.

He looked away and shrugged. "I might," he said slowly. "I've got to think it over first."

"What?" The very thought that he might hesitate to tell his brother and king something that might be vital to national security floored her.

He glanced back, looking defensive. "It was a private conversation. Just talking with a friend. I can't back any of it up. I'm not sure if he was on the level or just trying to recruit me."

"Recruit you!"

He nodded. "They need flyers." He looked at her, hard. "That's what I do, Kayla. I'm a flyer. It's what I love. I told him I'd think about it."

"But..." She bit her tongue and turned away, horrified. Didn't he see that doing something like that would be tantamount to treason? She had to find a way to make him understand that he was now a part of the heart and soul of the Ambrian people, and of this royal family. Their destiny was his destiny. All the rest would flow from that.

Turning back, she looked at him, so handsome, so rebellious. She thought of Eddie. He'd been the kind of man who always did the right thing without effort. He was never tortured by doubts the way Max was. But he'd loved the vulnerability in Max as much as she did, and Eddie's own certainty was part of what drew Max to him, as she knew well. Two men, so different, yet both such quality guys. Max just didn't know the extent of his virtue yet. But he would work it out. She had faith in him.

"Max, you're representing the DeAngelis royal family now," she said quietly. "And the nation of Ambria. That has to be your highest priority."

He gave her a skeptical look and the corner of his mouth jerked down. She sighed, thinking about what she would say to him if only she could.

Max, you didn't really grow up here. You have love of country in your blood, but not in your experience. You need both in order to understand what the others take for granted. You will. But you need to be introduced first. How am I going to make sure that happens?

She ached to say those things, but she knew he wasn't ready to hear that right now. He was still feeling resentful.

"No matter what, I won't be a spy," he said, turning to look into her eyes. His jawline hardened. "I won't rat on my flying buddies."

She was so tempted to launch into a lecture on duty and patriotism and how those things had to come first, but she stopped herself. She was acting enough like a schoolmarm to turn Max from a best friend into an enemy. She had to learn a few things herself—things about when to hold 'em and when to fold 'em. So she bit her tongue and smiled brightly instead. After all, they were still trying to convince him that he should stay.

She knew one thing. Everyone who came in contact with him wanted him to hang around. But he was so bored with the whole thought of being a prince. She was afraid one of the other offers that kept pouring in would tempt him and he'd be gone.

CHAPTER EIGHT

HALF an hour later, Kayla and Max were taking the elevator down to the main floor, where the gymnasium was located. The gym had a marquee, like an old-fashioned movie theater, and today it was advertising a basketball game that night. But as they walked in, half of the pictures posted in the display boxes had to do with minor sports and most of those were fencing.

"Have you ever studied fencing?" Kayla asked him as they entered the cavernous room. All the princes had been trained and Max would have to learn as well.

"Never." He pretended to wield an imaginary foil. "We didn't do much of that in the crowd I ran with."

"Well, take a good look," she said with a sweep of her hand. "Because you're going to have to learn."

"This lame stuff?" He looked down over the edge of the railing and suddenly hoped his voice hadn't carried that far. Down below were numerous men in white clothing, holding very slender swords.

"Why don't you put on a suit and go in and give it a

try? It might just open your eyes." She snickered. "Or kill you."

He gave her a baleful look, but before he could make a rejoinder, someone hailed him from the floor.

"Hey, Max. Come on down here and give me some competition." The fencer pulled up his mask and slashed the air with his foil.

Max laughed, realizing it was his brother Joe. "I don't know one end of a sword from another. I'd probably end up stabbing myself," he called down.

"I was just like you a few months ago," Joe said. "Hey, I spent most of my growing up years on a surfboard in California. What did I know about these ancient ritualistic sports?" He grinned. "But I learned. And it's a lot of fun, actually. Gives you a good workout, too. We'll have to get you set up with lessons."

"Cool," Max said back. "If a surfer boy can learn, I guess a seat-of-the-pants flyer can."

"Absolutely."

"Though I don't know if I can fit it in," Max added, teasing Kayla, though he was still talking to Joe. "I'm real busy learning how to be a prince, you know."

"You have somebody teaching you?" Joe cried. "Hey, how do I get in on that gig?"

"I'll tell Pellea you're interested," Kayla told him with a laugh.

"Do that." He saluted them both. "See you later," he added as he pulled his mask back down and took the ready position.

"He doesn't need any lessons," Max said in admiration. "Look at him."

She did, then she turned back, eyes sparkling. "Max, you ought to look at yourself. You look just as good as he does. It's only a matter of time until you have the confidence to carry it off without a waver."

"Sure," he muttered out of the corner of his mouth. "Whatever you say, teacher lady. I'm here to learn."

Next stop was at the tailor. Mr. Nanvone's father had been the royal tailor thirty years before, and now his son had taken over. Max was less enthusiastic about this visit.

"Why don't we just wait awhile and see if we're really going to need formal wear and all that stuff?" he suggested as they reached the shop. Mannequins in tuxedos lined the show windows. "After all..."

Just then a smartly dressed man emerged from the shop doorway. It took a double take for Max to realize it was another of his brothers.

"Max," Mykal said jovially. "Come to get your fancy formal wear ordered?"

Max made a face. "Unfortunately, it does seem to be the goal here."

Mykal laughed. "We all have to do it. You want to play, you've got to wear the gear."

Max looked him over and blurted out, "What made you decide?"

Mykal looked wary. "Decide what?"

Max shrugged. "Whether you wanted to play or not."

They stared at each other for a long moment and then a grin broke through Mykal's reserve. "So you're still at that stage, are you? Wondering if it's all worth it." He patted him on the shoulder. "Been there, done that. And as you see, I'm still here."

He gave Kayla a wide smile, winked, then turned back to Max.

"Listen, come see me one of these days. We'll talk." And he was off.

Max watched him go, still favoring one side of his body over the other. Max sighed and then turned and followed Kayla into the tailor shop.

"I guess that motorcycle accident really did a number on him, didn't it?" Max murmured to her.

"Yes. He almost died. He had shrapnel in his back, very close to his spine, and they didn't want to operate because of that. But Mykal decided he would take any chance to be whole again, so he insisted on surgery."

Max nodded. "Brave guy." He squared his shoulders. "If he can do this, so can I. Where's the man with the measuring tape?"

Kayla laughed as Mr. Nanvone instantly appeared from behind the curtain barrier into the back room, a measuring tape in his hand.

His session didn't last very long, but by the time the measuring and other necessary particulars were finished, he seemed exhausted.

"The questions were the worst," he told her as they left the shop. "'Which do you prefer,'" he mimicked, copying the tailor's accent, "'ostrich- or pearl-gray, teal or military green, oxford or gold-ore brown.' Too many decisions!"

"Hold it," Kayla said, reaching for her phone. "There's a message from Pellea." She read it quickly. "She wants us to come in right away. They've had a response from Mercuria."

Her gaze met his and he reached out and took her by the hand.

"Let's go."

But as they walked toward the elevator, Max's mood grew more somber.

"I've got a bad feeling about this."

Kayla looked up at him, curious. "What do you expect to go wrong? Things like this usually go on forever. We send our ambassador, they send theirs, they talk, they negotiate, they go back to their respective corners and it all starts again. You hardly ever see anything actually resolved."

He considered her description as they got onto the elevator and punched in the right floor. "I'd feel better if I knew what that historical artifact they think I took was. I mean, one person's historical artifact could be another person's used piece of trash. I wish I had some idea of what we're looking for."

Pellea's face wasn't giving away any clues as they walked into the office.

"Thank you for getting here so quickly," she began. "I feel like things are escalating and I don't want them to spin out of control."

"Of course not," Kayla agreed. "What have you heard?"

The queen waited while they took chairs, then continued. "I think I explained to you how the charges were addressed by our ambassador. He handed our letter to King Juomo personally. Here is the king's response."

She held up a large, embossed and very official-looking document.

"'The plane and the horse are nothing to us. We are willing to let them go. The artifact is everything. We must have it back. There is only one way we will accept its return. Max Arragen must himself bring it back to Helgium Castle and offer it by hand to the Princess Nadine. No other method will suffice.'"

Pellea looked up and cocked her head in Max's direction. "Princess Nadine?" she said questioningly. "A new element has been added. Care to elaborate?"

Max sighed and looked guilty. "I should have told you about Princess Nadine."

Pellea's eyes flashed. "Yes, you should have."

Quickly he told her the same thing he had told Kayla, explaining how crazy this was, at least in his opinion. "She's just a teenaged girl with a teenaged crush. Nothing more."

"A teenaged girl with the power to start a war." Pellea glared at him. "And possibly have you executed."

Executed. That was an ugly and very serious word. Everyone in the room seemed to reverberate to the vibes coming off just the sound of it for a moment.

Pellea was the first to break out of the spell. "All

right, here's the rest. 'You have only three days left to comply with our demands. We are preparing for an invasion.'" She looked out at the others. "An invasion. The man is crazy, but then, those who invade other countries often are."

There was a long silence, and then Max looked up.

"Why don't I go? They can't hold this whole country responsible for me if I'm not here and haven't officially been made a part of the royal court. Just call me the black sheep, the one you can't control, the one you can do nothing about. They can't expect you to pay for my crimes."

"Impossible. You are a prince of Ambria. We can't let you go."

He looked down again, then up. "You know, I didn't do anything," he said softly to Pellea.

She half smiled. "Max, if I thought you had done anything at all with a fifteen-year-old girl, we wouldn't even be talking here anymore."

He looked relieved. "Of course not."

Kayla moved restlessly. "I think you should tell the queen about what happened to your rooms last night."

Pellea turned a questioning face Max's way. "Yes?"

"When I got in late last evening, I found my apartment ransacked. I think it was probably Mercurians after that darn artifact, whatever it may be."

"Interesting." She frowned. "Why weren't you better guarded?"

He shrugged. "I've talked to the captain of the guard. I think conditions will improve."

"Good." She frowned again as he told her the situation and what had been done to his things.

"You're sure nothing was taken?"

"As far as I can tell."

"And you think it was the Mercurians?"

He nodded. "I'm sure of it."

"Well, I guess we all had better be on our guard," Pellea warned. "Those darn Mercurians."

"Mercurians!"

That was the first thing Kayla thought when she opened the door to her own apartment later that afternoon. Everything looked normal at first, but she could tell. She had the distinct feeling that things were different. Strangers had been in her place. Nothing seemed to be missing. But there was a sense of invasion. Her personal space had been violated. She was sure of it.

She called Max right away.

"They tried hard to put everything back just the way it was," she said. "But I can tell. These creepy people have been all through my things. Ugh!"

"Did you call the security guards?"

"No." She felt a bit abashed. "I called you."

"I'll call them. And I'll be there in a few minutes."

"Oh, I don't want to bother you, Max. I know you have things to do."

"I'm coming over and I'm bringing my toothbrush and jammies."

"What? You can't stay here."

"Try and stop me."

She had to laugh after she hung up. He did have a
way about him. But amusement fled when the security
people arrived and claimed they couldn't find any evidence of a break in.

"How can you be sure your things were moved?
Suppose you moved them yourself and forgot you did
it?"

She had a feeling they were snickering at her behind
her back, but they got serious when Max arrived. He
wasn't pleased that they hadn't been watching her apartment more carefully, as he'd requested. They promised
to be more vigilant.

"You see, you don't have to stay," she told him once
they'd gone. "I'll be okay."

"Yes, you'll be fine. Because I will be here with
you."

"Really?" She gave him an exasperated look. "And
how long do you plan to stay here?"

"Until the Mercurians stop looking for the artifact."

She made a face at him. "That could take a long,
long time."

"Look, this is just for tonight. We'll deal with the
rest of our lives later. Okay?"

He had a few errands to run but he was back an
hour later. He'd been looking forward to his night with
Kayla with mixed feelings. It would be a delight to be
with her, even if the mood was platonic, but he knew
that Teddy probably came with the package. When he
arrived at the door and glanced around the room, sure

enough, there was the kid, sitting in a little plastic chair and playing with a stuffed dinosaur.

He wanted to like Teddy. The child was beautiful with huge blue eyes and a head of dark bronze curls. He looked adorable. But the kid hated him. He really seemed to have something against him. But that wasn't fair. He was only a baby. Babies didn't hate. Did they? They wanted what they wanted the minute they wanted it. Teddy wanted his mama and didn't want to share her with some strange man. Who could blame him?

Sure. He grinned to himself. That was all it was. He had to stop letting his imagination run away with him.

He'd thought about this ahead of time. He knew what he had to do. He went right up to the child. "Hi, Teddy," he said in a friendly manner. "What's that you've got there? A tyrannosaurus?"

The blue eyes glanced up at him and shot back down to stare at his toy.

There you go, he thought. *The kid hates me.*

He was at a loss. He'd never had any experience with children this age and he had no idea how to deal with them. He looked up at Kayla for help.

She stepped forward and he thought she seemed a little nervous. "Teddy, can you say 'hi' to Prince Max?"

Obviously not. Teddy's lower lip came out and he stared very hard at his dinosaur.

"All right, we'll work on that later," she said with forced cheer. "But you're going to have to learn to be polite to visitors."

"Leave him alone," Max murmured to the side. "Let

him get used to me." As if he knew the secrets to popularity with the Rugrat crowd.

She produced a batch of oven-fried chicken that was as good as anything the colonel made, along with crispy biscuits and a nice green salad. Even Teddy took a few bites. She'd also made some rubbery green gelatin squares that were so tough, they could play catch with them. Once he saw those, Teddy suddenly had an appetite. He came over to watch, hanging on his mother's leg and leaning his head on her knee, and when Max tossed a square into the air and caught it with his mouth, Teddy couldn't help it—he just had to laugh.

When it was time for bed, Teddy went down fairly easily.

"Help me tuck him in," Kayla urged.

"Why?"

She gave him a look and he reluctantly followed her into the bedroom. When Teddy saw Max, he hid his face in the covers.

"You see," Max whispered to her. "He doesn't want me to be here when you tuck him in."

"He's a child," she muttered back. "You're a grownup. You're the one in charge of the situation. Don't let him con you."

So he helped tuck Teddy in. But the kid still seemed to hate him. He wasn't sure why that should be—or why he cared. He'd known other kids who didn't seem to adore him and it had never bothered him before. Maybe it was the fact that he'd expected to have instant rapport with Eddie's boy. That hadn't happened.

He came out into the kitchen and helped her with the dishes, taking a towel and drying them as she put them up on the counter, sparkling clean. They talked about old times and laughed about old stories. And Kayla realized that Max was really her only link to Eddie, physical or emotional. The memories were all in his head, like they were in her heart. Was that what drew her to him so strongly? Was that what made her feel something very close to love whenever she looked into his eyes?

No. It was more than that. Much more. If only she could pin down exactly what it was.

She got him a beer and she made herself a cup of hot tea and they sat on the couch and talked softly.

She stretched and smiled at him. "You know what? In this very moment, in spite of everything, I'm very happy."

"Why?"

"Because you're here. And because you seem to be at peace in a way. Not quite as tense and restless as you usually are."

She was right. It was good being with her this way. She made him happy, too. He looked at her pretty face, her soft brown eyes, her beautiful lips and he felt an ache where his heart should be.

"You need to be kissed," he murmured, looking at her mouth a bit hungrily.

She shook her head and began to appear wary. "No, I don't."

"Yes, you do." Reaching out, he touched her chin,

then curled his hand around her jawline. "Or maybe I should say, I need to kiss you. That might be more honest."

Searching into his deep, mysterious eyes, she laughed softly. His hand felt so warm on her skin and his breath was even warmer on her face. She needed to pull away, let him know she couldn't let him keep the promise that was smoldering in his eyes. But somehow, that just wasn't happening.

"You don't need to kiss me," she said. "Kisses are for lovers. We're not going to do that."

A slight frown creased his brow. "You don't get it. I do need to kiss you. And you need to kiss me. Just me and you. And nothing about Eddie."

She closed her eyes for a moment, and then she looked into his again with a tiny, sad smile.

"I don't want you to do anything that you'll regret," she told him, half joking.

He frowned. "What is it that you regret?"

She shook her head, letting her sleek blond hair brush against his hand. "I don't regret anything. There was a time when I did. But I got over that quickly enough." Turning her face, she caught the palm of his hand against her lips and put a kiss there. "One look into my baby's eyes, and regrets faded away," she added softly.

He stared at her and a look of pain flashed in his eyes. "Kayla…"

"Hush." She put a finger to his lips. "Just kiss me."

And he did.

His mouth was hot and hard on hers and she moaned low in her throat, a deep, primal sound of pleasure. She'd been so lonely for so long, to feel his arms around her, to feel the joy of his true affection, seemed to bring her out of a long sleep and into the sunlight. Their tongues met, caressed, tangled, then seemed to meld together into one smoldering focus of heat and her whole body was ready to burst into flames.

"Oh!" she cried, pulling away and staring at him. "Oh, my gosh, Max. We can't even kiss without setting the world on fire. What the heck?"

He lay back against the pillows on the couch and started to laugh. She batted at him, then started to laugh as well, falling on him and holding him close as they both enjoyed the moment.

"Just let me hold you," he murmured, face buried in her hair. "I just want to feel you against me."

She nodded. "Me, too." And then she sighed. It took a while for her body to calm down. She knew in her heart that they would make love again and it would be soon. But not now. For now, this was enough. In fact, it was a certain brand of heaven.

A sound from Teddy's room made her get up to check on him. She looked down at her sleeping child and her heart was so full, for a moment, she couldn't breathe. She came out with a new determination. It was time.

"Max, we have to talk about it."

He looked up, startled at her tone. "Talk about what?"

"That night. That night after Eddie died."

His heart began to pound in his chest. "No. We don't have anything to talk about." His words were defensive and so was his tone. He was scared to talk about it. Anyone could see that.

She gestured for him to follow her. "Come here. I want you to look at this baby."

"No. Kayla…"

Reaching out, she grabbed his arm. "Come here. Look at him. You have to."

He came reluctantly, sure that this would do no good and make no difference. What was the point?

He looked down. Teddy really was a beautiful child. Something was fluttering in his chest.

"Look at him," she was saying softly, almost whispering. "His face is so sweet when he's asleep. Those big round cheeks." She turned to look at him. "If his eyes were open, you would see how blue they are."

"Kayla." He winced.

"He's an adorable, sweet little boy. And you're not letting him into your heart."

He closed his eyes, searching for an inner strength he wasn't sure he was going to find.

"Is he mine?" His voice was tortured, vibrating with pain.

"You know the answer."

He closed his eyes again and turned away, pushing his way back out to the living room. She followed, wondering if he'd felt what she wanted him to feel.

"How could we have done that, Kayla?" he was muttering angrily. "How could we have betrayed Eddie like that?"

"At the time we did it, it seemed like a sacrament. A tribute. An homage to his life. It was only later, in the sober light of day, that it seemed like a betrayal."

He nodded. "I remember it well."

Suddenly she turned on him. She threw a pillow at him and then cried fiercely, "Max, don't you dare regret it! Don't you dare!"

"Kayla…"

"That night, after we found out there was no hope of finding Eddie alive, we were in shock. The pain was so great—do you remember? We turned to each other to stem it. We told ourselves we were celebrating his life, but we were really trying to pay back the fates for what they'd done to us…to Eddie."

He nodded but he didn't say a word.

"All we could do was cry and hold on to each other. And somehow, we ended up doing something we never meant to do. But it happened." She pulled on his arm. "Don't deny it! It happened."

He turned his head away.

"A miracle came out of that, despite everything. My sweet baby. Our sweet baby. Don't you dare deny that."

Max took a deep breath and turned back to look her full in her tearstained face.

"No. I won't deny it. But I do regret it."

He took her in his arms and she cried and cried.

* * *

It was a few hours later. Max was asleep on the couch. He raised his head, wondering what he'd heard, and then he realized it was Kayla. She was singing softly to her baby. He listened, staying very still. There was something in that voice, something in the love she had for her child, that gave him chills. It touched him like nothing else and tears came to his eyes, stinging.

He'd never thought it would happen. He was the perennial bachelor. He was famous for it. No woman had ever been able to make her way through that tough shield of reality and reach his heart. Only Kayla had. And yet, he couldn't get around it. To love her was a betrayal of Eddie.

CHAPTER NINE

"LISTEN," Max said as he left in the morning. "I won't be able to stay with you tonight. Can you make arrangements to stay with Caroline?"

"Maybe." Kayla knew she sounded defensive, but that was how she felt. She knew he was upset, that things said and done from the night before had thrown him off again, and she resented it. "We'll see."

He hesitated, as though he wanted to argue with her, but then thought better of it. "Okay," he said. "I'll call you later."

And he was gone. She stared at the door as it closed, a lump in her throat. He was regretting again. She was losing him.

She fixed breakfast for Teddy and took him to her sister's, then hurried on to the office. Pellea was on a tear, racing from one project to another, barking out orders and ideas, and Kayla didn't have time to find out what had been decided as a response to the Mercurians. And then, suddenly, Max was back and he didn't have the scowl he'd had that morning.

"Look at this," he said, his blue eyes sparkling with new energy. "Research has come up with a picture of the artifact."

He had a thick book with beautiful photographic illustrations, and there was a huge picture of the item in question. They gathered around and stared at it and for a few minutes, no one said a word.

"Wow," Pellea said at last. "No wonder they want it back."

The historical artifact was a beautiful medallion on a thick gold chain. The background was encrusted with rubies and emeralds and the centerpiece was a huge, elongated, multifaceted diamond. It took a moment or two to realize that the gems formed a picture of a green field and a tree with rubies as apples. The diamond in the center seemed to represent a huge waterfall. On the next page, the image of the backside showed a date almost four centuries old and the name Mercuria.

"Wow," Kayla breathed, echoing the queen. "I've never seen anything so gorgeous."

"And probably worth more than ten small countries thrown together," Pellea said. "Max, did you ever have it in your possession?"

"Are you kidding? Do you think I could have forgotten something like this? Or mislaid it? I've never seen this before. And I damn well know I never held it in my hand."

They looked at each other.

"How about this?" Max asked after a moment of silence. "Do we have some sort of video communication system set up with King Juomo? If so, I could tell him face-to-face that I didn't take this and don't have it, without actually going there."

Pellea nodded. "We've got the capability. Heck, I could do it from my notebook. But as I understand it, it will take some time to set up the official, royal version that they can use, too," she said. "I'll try to have the technicians on it right away." Then she frowned. "In the meantime, you be careful. People have been known to do some ugly things to get their hands on a piece of jewelry like that."

"Don't worry. I've got my eyes open." He gave a simple bow to the queen and a faint smile to Kayla, and then he was out the door.

Kayla was glad to know he was now certain he had not taken the artifact, but she was not so happy with his new dismissive attitude. She was mulling over how to respond to it when Pellea walked up and leaned on her desk with both hands.

"What are we going to do about Max?" she said in a quiet voice, meant to stay clear of any eavesdroppers.

Kayla was startled. "Why? What's wrong?"

"Nothing new. Just the usual. I'm still worried about his lack of commitment to becoming a prince. His heart isn't in it. Not yet."

She only hesitated a moment before taking the plunge. "I'm afraid you're right. At least, in part. I think he's coming around, but it's going to take some time."

Pellea sighed. "The others seemed to be able to make the adjustment to royal status quickly and easily. I don't know if he's just too rigid in his ways or what. I'm really afraid that he might not be able to do it." She shook her head, looking worried. "There's something wild and free in him. Something that resists rules and borders. I'm not sure he'll be able to stay."

Kayla knew the queen was emotionally invested in Max's success, still, she was surprised to see she had tears in her eyes. Kayla reached for her hand and held it with genuine affection.

"Oh, Pellea, don't give up on him."

"Oh, I can't. We need him. The family won't be whole without him. Like a family portrait with one face cut out. Can you imagine? Impossible! It will kill Monte if he doesn't stay. Now that the war is basically won, now that Leonardo Granvilli is dead, he has such plans for this country."

"I'm sure he'll stay," she said, wishing she could sound more convincing. But that was hard when she wasn't sure what she was saying was true. "He just needs seasoning."

Pellea dried her eyes and gave Kayla a watery smile. "I still have hope. I do have one ace in the hole, you know. You see, I have one piece of bait, one promise, one prize that just might keep him here."

Kayla looked innocent. "What is that?"

Pellea laughed. "You!"

"Me? Oh, no, no, no, no."

"Yes, you my dear. It obvious the two of you are in love. Or hadn't you noticed?"

Luckily, a visitor arrived in time to save Kayla from

having to answer that. She went back to work, typing as
fast as she could, her cheeks hot and rosy. What Pellea
was suggesting was insane. She knew Max well enough
to know he wasn't husband material. He wasn't even father material. He was a wild man. And after last night,
she was afraid there was no hope of anything taming
him.

Kayla sent a message asking Max to come for dinner,
and to her surprise, he showed up, despite the fact that
he hadn't contacted her all day. It was funny how lonely
that had made her. In just a few days she'd become used
to hearing from him constantly and she missed it when
it wasn't there. She served meat loaf and mashed po-
tatoes and he had two helpings. Though he started out
seeming a bit distant, he soon warmed up as he told
her about talking to the king of Mercuria on the video
phone connection.

"We weren't exactly buddies when I was working
on organizing the air force last year," he said. "But
we did work together often and we got along well.
Unfortunately, he doesn't seem to remember all that."

"What did he say?"

"He insists I have the artifact. He says he has proof."

"Proof? What sort of proof?"

Max hesitated. Then he made a wry, apologetic face
and told her the truth. "He says that Princess Nadine
gave it to me personally when she knew I was leaving.
She supposedly gave it to me so that it would bring me
back to her." He looked at a loss. "Believe me, I barely

ever spoke to the girl. And she never gave me anything. I was hardly ever that close to her."

Kayla nodded, thinking hard. She had no doubt at all that Max was telling the truth. But how could the princess have thought she was giving it to him when she wasn't at all? And where was it now?

Teddy was playing about their feet as they finished their dinner. He had a large, open plastic bus and a small plastic horse and he was very intent on making the horse drive the bus. It seemed to make perfect sense to him that a horse would be driving. But at one point the horse fell out and the bus ran right over him.

Teddy gasped. Max reacted without thinking, reaching down to save the horse. "Poor little horsey," he said, pretending to make the animal neigh back at him. "The horsey wants to go back in the bus," he told Teddy, as though he'd understood the neigh. "Here." He put him back in the driver's seat.

Teddy stared up at him, eyes wide. Then, suddenly, he grinned right up at Max. It was a bright grin, a complete grin, full of joy, no holds barred. Max's heart almost stopped. He'd never known. No one had ever told him what a baby's smile could do. It knocked him out and then some. He felt something explode in his chest and realized it was his heart starting up again.

Teddy had already forgotten the moment and gone back to playing with the bus. Max turned and looked at Kayla. She smiled at him.

"Wonderful, isn't it?" she murmured.

She understood. He didn't have to say anything and

she understood. He glanced back at Teddy, at his own sweet baby. A baby who didn't hate him after all. He could hardly breathe, he was so happy.

They talked softly for a while longer, and the euphoria faded. He still didn't feel right about how Teddy had come to be. It had been wrong and he feared he would have to pay for that wrong, somehow.

"Are you okay?" Kayla asked.

He looked at her. She was so beautiful with the lamplight making a halo behind her beautiful hair. He wanted her—wanted her in his life and in his bed and in his dreams. Wanted her with an ache that throbbed inside and almost made him crazy. But he wasn't ready to tell her so. He had so many things to think about and he was having trouble keeping it all straight.

He might leave. Just go. He'd done it before. In fact, it was the way he normally operated. Stay in one place as long as it pleased him, then, when things got tough, just go. He might do it again. He didn't want it to happen. He was trying, really trying to change his ways, to find meaning in life and stick to it. But he knew himself well enough to know it might not work that way. He might just go.

He got up to leave. He had to go out on his own and figure out what was in his head and in his heart.

"Thanks for the great dinner," he told her. "Promise me you'll stay with Caroline tonight."

"I will. As soon as you're gone, we'll go over there." She searched his eyes. "Will I see you tomorrow?"

He avoided meeting her gaze. "I don't know. I've

got a lot to think about. I may go off on my own for a while." He shrugged. "And I have to decide what to do about Mercuria. I can't let them attack this country." He shook his head, looking bemused. "What a concept, huh? Like a comic opera. But they are just crazy enough, they might do it."

Kayla went up to say goodbye, then went on tiptoes and kissed him on the lips, surprising him. "I love you," she told him.

Everything in him cried out for him to take her in his arms and give her what she deserved, but he held back. He held her shoulders and felt her lovely rounded flesh, so warm, so inviting. But he held back. She didn't mean that she was in love with him. She loved him. She had always loved him, just as he'd loved Eddie. They had all loved each other. But that didn't mean they were in love. Was he in love with her? That was just one more question he had to deal with.

He had to figure this out.

"Goodbye. I'll call you."

She nodded and watched him go, then turned to her son.

"No crying," she told herself sternly. "We have things we have to do."

She packed Teddy's bag and then went into the closet to get some things of her own to take along to Caroline's. She'd finally brought the denim jacket back from the office and then she'd forgotten to give it to him again. Even worse, it had slipped off the hanger and lay on the floor. She picked it up and pressed it to her face, reveling in the scent that reminded her of Max. Then she put it back on the hanger, noting that it was an awfully heavy jacket. And she finished packing and grabbed her son and headed out to her sister's apartment.

The next day was unusually busy and different from their normal routine. In the morning, there was a meeting Pellea had set up that she wanted all the princes—and Princess Kim—to attend.

"I'd like all of the new princes to meet with the prime minister," she told Kayla that morning, "and begin to get an idea of what they need to study about our history and foreign policy matters. They need to begin developing what their duties will be. That, of course, will depend a lot on each one's individual skills and talents and how they can be used to best serve this country."

Pellea's face was quite serious, as though she'd given this a lot of thought. "Some of them still don't realize that they can't keep up the sort of lifestyle they are used to if they want to be serious about this royalty business."

"Yes, I agree with you," Kayla said softly, wondering if she mainly had Max in mind.

Pellea went on, completely filled with her own sense of purpose. "When you take on this way of living, you are taking on a responsibility for the lives, happiness and well-being of your people. And that means everybody in this castle, everybody on the royal side of the island, and even those rebels still siding with the

Granvillis. Because eventually we'll win them over, too, and the kingdom will be united again."

Kayla nodded. "Have you told them all where and when?" she asked, wondering if she ought to give Max a call to remind him.

"Yes. Ten o'clock in the blue meeting room. And then, of course, we have the picnic luncheon for the French foreign minister and his family, out on the south lawn. Practically everyone in the castle will be coming to that one. Free food does tend to gather a crowd."

The phone began to ring and the queen was soon engrossed in one conversation after another. Meanwhile, Kayla tried to get hold of Max. She called, she sent messages, she even emailed him, but there was no response. As time went by, she began to be concerned, wondering what could have happened to him. She knew he'd planned to go off on his own for a while to think things over, but surely he was checking his messages.

Unless...

Unless he'd left the island. Unless he'd decided just to go. Her heart raced and she got a sick feeling in the pit of her stomach.

"All right, I'm off to the prime minister's meeting with the princes. I'm sure you'll be able to handle things while I'm gone. I'll go straight to the picnic from there. And don't you forget to come to that. Afterward, we'll work on the response to Mercuria."

Kayla nodded, wondering how long it would be before she got a panicked call from the meeting telling her to find Max. When the hour went by without that call, she began to relax. Surely Pellea would have called her if he hadn't shown up. Maybe everything was okay. Maybe she was letting her imagination run away with her.

And maybe she would go to the picnic luncheon after all. Max might even be there. She put away her work and hurried over to the other side of the castle, glad she'd worn dark slacks and a crisp white shirt rather than her usual skirt and sweater. She was dressed for a picnic.

She came out on an upper level and looked down. From where she was standing, she could see the royal platform. And there were Pellea and King Monte and all the princes. All the princes except one. No Max.

Her heart fell. Where could he be? She bit her lip and tried to calm down. There was no point running around like a headless chicken. She had to be logical. The first place to look would be at his rooms.

Going back quickly through the halls, she made her way there in ten minutes. The usual guard was gone and when she knocked, no one answered.

Strike one. Where could she try next? Okay, he'd said he was going off on his own to think. He'd shown her his favorite place to do that, the flat rock by the stream. There was a balcony that looked right down over that area. That would provide the quickest access. She raced toward it.

There was an eerie feeling in this side of the castle today. The usually bustling halls were empty. Everyone was at the picnic. Kayla tried to calm herself down, but she was feeling a bit spooked.

Finally, out of breath, she reached the balcony, and with it, a sense of instant calm. She leaned out over the balcony railing, breathing in the fresh air and reveling in the feeling of freedom. White clouds scudded across a china blue sky. It was a beautiful day and a beautiful setting. Looking down, she didn't see Max, but she did see a glorious view of the countryside, and she knew Max was down there somewhere. Surely he would begin to feel better about everything after a few hours walking about the grounds. She knew she would. She leaned out a bit farther and searched the hills and valleys for a sign of him.

All in all, she was glad she had brought her baby here to the castle. She had a good job and a nice place to live. No complaints. The only element lacking was a daddy for her baby. Other than that, things were coming up roses.

Finally, a movement caught her eye, but it came from right below where she was standing. Two men were struggling with a large push cart. From her vantage point, she could see a large white van parked in a stretch of trees toward the main road. It looked like they were headed that way. But why not bring the van down to the castle and load their cargo in a convenient place? Only one reason she could think of. They were doing something illegal.

And that was certainly the feeling you got from watching them. Their movements were a little too

quick, and a lot too furtive. Funny. What could they
be transporting that they knew they shouldn't be?
Equipment they'd stolen? Machinery they'd found in
a storeroom? The entire contents of someone's living
room?

That reminded her of the way her place had been
manhandled and Max's ransacked. She looked at the
men more carefully. Was there anything about them
that could be said to seem Mercurian? Not really. They
looked like normal workmen. But still…

A siren sounded, making her jump. Sirens were not
unusual. There seemed to be a fire drill every week,
mostly because of the legacy of the castle burning during the Granvilli rebellion. But this was no drill, not
in the middle of a state picnic luncheon. She frowned
and looked down at the workmen. The siren seemed
to have panicked them. They were running now, pushing at each other and shouting. The pushcart hit a rock
and nearly overturned. The canvas cover came off and
their cargo was revealed. There was a man lying inside, scrunched into a curled-up position. The man was
either dead or unconscious, and he looked very much
like Max.

She gasped. The cover was quickly restored, but she
knew what she'd seen. Could this be the Mercurians?
They looked so guilty. Had they grabbed Max? She
wasn't at all sure that was who she'd seen, but still, just
the possibility threw her for a loop.

Her heart was pounding like a drum in her own ears.

Her hands were shaking so hard, she could barely use her mobile to call security. It rang and rang.

"Come on!" she muttered, nearly crazy.

And finally someone answered.

"Quick," she cried. "This is Kayla Mandrake. I've just seen two men kidnapping someone. I think it might be Prince Max."

"No, can't be," he said. "The princes are all at the picnic. I just saw them there."

"Did you see Max?"

He hesitated. "He's the new one, right? I don't think I've ever seen him, so..."

"Please, please, come quickly. They're going to get away!"

"Lady, listen, do you hear that siren? We're short-handed right now. We've got that darn picnic and now everyone else is out responding to the fire in the library area. There's no one here but me and I can't leave the phone. Listen, call back in about ten minutes. I'll see what I can do then."

"What?"

She couldn't believe it, but she didn't have time to argue. She tried Pellea's number, and then Caroline. Something was wrong; she couldn't get anyone. There was no one to help her. She looked down. They still hadn't reached the van. Maybe she could catch them herself.

Oh, sure. Catch them and do what? Yell at them a lot? Besides, she would never catch them before they got to the van. And then, who knew where they would go?

But wait. She did know where they would go. What had Max said? She remembered his words— "Mercuria is an hour away," or something like that. An hour away from where? The docks.

The docks! And that wasn't very far. In fact, she knew a shortcut. Caroline and her husband had twin motor scooters that they had used on weekend getaways before their boy was born. She still had a key to Caroline's scooter on her key ring. She could take that scooter and make it across the dunes to the docks before the van got past the traffic signals. There would be officials at the docks. Someone would be there to help her.

She raced down the hall to the stairway. She didn't have time for the elevators. The whole time she ran, she kept looking for someone who might help her, but the halls were empty. She would have to do this herself.

She made her way to the parking garage and found Caroline's scooter. Miraculously, the engine popped on with no trouble, and she was off, dashing for the dunes.

There was a small part of her brain that kept poking her, saying, *What if it is just a body? What if...what if...*

And she pushed it back, saying, *No! They may have said dead or alive, but everything they've done proves they want him alive. So don't even think that!*

She veered off the main road onto a dirt track that cut out about a mile of driving to the docks. The little scooter was racing along and she was feeling very scared, but strangely exhilarated at the same time. She saw the craggy outcropping of the rocky point ahead. That meant the docks were only a few minutes away.

As she came around a curve, the main road was spread out below and she saw the white van. It was turning around. She jammed on her brakes and pulled to a stop.

A man was running from it and another lay on the side of the road. A shot rang out, and then another. Her heart in her throat, she started down the incline, racing to get to the place where the trees stood near the road and she could get a view of the van as it passed without being seen herself.

If her guess were right, that should be Max driving. It looked to her as though he'd overpowered his kidnappers and taken off with their van, but she couldn't be sure. Ditching the scooter behind a small hill, she ran for the edge of the road and made it close enough to see, gasping for breath, just as the van came around the corner.

It was! She could see Max driving. It looked like he had a bloody head wound, but he was driving and as far as she could see, he was alone.

He'd done it! What a guy! Jumping for joy, she yelled and waved her arms, but she was still too far into the trees and he didn't see her.

She had a small, empty feeling when he drove on past and left her there, but she knew it wouldn't be long before she caught up with him again. She turned to run back to her scooter, and that was when she felt the dart go into her neck. She reached to pull it out, but her hands never made it there. In seconds, she was out like a light.

Max had been back at the castle for over an hour and had told everyone his story of being kidnapped by Mercurians. Even King Monte had come by to hear it personally. The whole thing seemed crazy, but everyone wanted to hear it.

Max had spent most of the morning out on his flat rock by the little river, thinking his life over and trying to make some important decisions. He knew Pellea wanted him at the prime minister's meeting, and he had come back to the castle for that, but just as he was coming in through the big double doors, someone had shot a tranquilizer dart into his neck and he had collapsed. He'd woken an hour or so later to find himself locked in a storeroom. This time they put him out with a rag soaked in chloroform, and he woke up in the back of the white van on his way to the docks. His hands were tied, but not very well, and he had no trouble working them free. Then he'd bided his time, not letting the two men know he was awake and that his hands were free. Finally he got his chance and he overpowered one of them. The driver pulled over to help his friend and Max threw the first man out and dealt with the second. Then it was a simple matter of grabbing the keys and taking the same transportation back again, minus the kidnappers this time.

"Though one of them did shoot at the van as I drove off," he told his attentive audience. "Luckily, he wasn't much of a shot."

Security at the docks had been alerted but they hadn't found the men.

"I'm calling out the army on this," Monte said with a scowl. "I want someone charged and put behind bars. We have to nip this sort of thing off right away. We can't have criminals running around kidnapping people."

By now, Max had asked where Kayla was a number of times and no one seemed to know. And then a call came in from the dockyard police saying they had found Caroline's abandoned scooter near the road to the docks, and Pellea and Max began to piece together different bits of evidence and get a vague idea of where she might be. Their conclusions were grim.

Once Pellea questioned the security guard who had been on duty that afternoon and found out someone had called in saying Max had been kidnapped, the picture became clearer.

"Kayla obviously saw the kidnappers taking you off and when she couldn't get security to help, she grabbed Caroline's scooter and went after you herself."

Max stared at Pellea, stunned.

"They have her," he said in a low, gravelly voice. "The bastards have her." He turned to look for his keys. "I've got to go."

CHAPTER TEN

"HOLD IT."

Monte held a hand up and stopped Max cold.

"You're not going anywhere."

Max's face darkened rebelliously. Right now he wasn't in the mood to take orders from royals, no matter who they were. But before he had a chance to say anything, Monte continued and explained his position.

"I'm not trying to pull rank on you, Max. But we have to stop and think things through before we act. We need to be sure we are doing the smart thing to get the results that we want and not just more bloodshed. You swimming the channel in a burst of adrenaline, showing up on shore with a knife between your teeth, is just going to get you killed. We can't succeed without a plan."

"What sort of plan?"

"I say we go in at midnight."

"Who's 'we'?"

"All of us royals. The warriors of the DeAngelis regime. We've got a very fast, very slinky boat that can enter areas without making a sound. I'm thinking four of us will take it."

"Four?" Mykal asked the question.

Monte nodded. "Sorry, old man, but I don't think we ought to risk you on this mission. You're not healed yet. We'll use you as a coordinator back home."

Mykal nodded reluctantly.

"Okay, so we've got Joe with his special forces training. And you, Max—you've been in combat. David is the best strategic thinker I know of. And I'm a pretty good leader." He shrugged. "What else do we need?"

"A plan," Max answered, still restless and not sure this was going to work. He liked to work alone. That was what he was used to. And every minute they delayed was a minute more Kayla had to endure whatever they were putting her through.

"A plan would be good," Monte admitted. "That's why we're going to take a few hours to think about it. We'll meet at eleven and go over our thoughts and put something together.

Max stared at him, trying not to let his resentment show. He knew what Monte was saying was smart, but he wanted to go now. He clenched his jaw and kept his opinion to himself. Monte knew what he was doing and he was exhibiting good leadership. He had to let this play out. Still, he ached to go right into their castle and save Kayla. If someone was hurting her, they were going to pay.

"I'm preparing a message for King Juomo and his ministers," Pellea said. "I'm telling the king that this nonsense has to end and that he'll personally pay for anything that happens to Kayla." She took a deep breath and looked around at them all. "You know it is possible that this is just a fringy, rogue element who has masterminded this," she said.

"You think so?" Max challenged her. "You don't think the king sending a poster saying I was wanted dead or alive was a little rogue, a little fringy?"

"Of course it was."

"Yes. The whole Mercurian royal family has been cuckoo for years."

"Which means you can't base your estimates of what they might do on normal reactions. Be ready for anything."

Max couldn't face going back to his room alone and thinking any more. He wanted to take action. It killed him to wait. He had to do something to take his mind off it. So he stopped by Caroline's apartment and asked to see Teddy.

Caroline was worried. He could see it in her face, and when he decided to take Teddy to Kayla's and fix him some dinner himself, she readily agreed, but caught him before he left.

"Are you going to save my sister?" she asked earnestly. "Can you guarantee me that she's going to be okay?"

He took her hand in his and gazed deep into her eyes. "I guarantee she'll be okay," he said gruffly. "Or I'll die trying to make that happen."

She stared back for a moment, then nodded, satisfied. "Okay," she said. "I'll hold you to that."

"Come on, Teddy," he said, looking at his little boy.
"You want to go with me?"

Teddy gave him a steady gaze but didn't look en-
thused.

"Go with Prince Max, honey," Carolyn said. "I'll bet
he could fix you a nice scrambled egg for your dinner."
She said as an aside, "He really likes scrambled eggs,"
and Max nodded, smiling as the little boy got up and
came to him.

"I'll bring him back in an hour or so."

He bent down and picked him up and they said goodbye, but Teddy was stiff in his arms until he saw that
they were going to his own apartment. Max realized he
probably thought he was going to see his mother, so he
began talking to him as they entered the room, keeping him occupied as long as possible, and it seemed to
work out all right.

They sat on the floor and Max began putting together
a set of fat train tracks meant for toddlers, while Teddy
pushed the train engine and tried to make train noises.
The tracks were going everywhere, and since the door
was open to the coat closet, soon they were going there,
too.

Max looked at the little boy he was playing with and
he couldn't help but smile. This child was his son. And
then Teddy looked at him and gave him that beautiful
smile again, and he felt it—the connection. Finally.
This really was his son. He could feel it now.

He got up to go fix Teddy some scrambled eggs. He couldn't eat anything himself, he was too tied up in knots, but he fed his boy. And then he paced the floor and thought of Kayla.

Suddenly he noticed a flash of light and he turned, puzzled. A sort of reflection was on the wall. He turned again, trying to figure out where it was coming from, and realized Teddy had pushed his toys into the closet and was pretending it was a cave. But something he was playing with had made that fantastic reflection, all dancing, shimmering lights.

He went into the closet and the first thing he noticed was his own denim jacket, lying on the floor. Realizing it must have fallen, he picked it up and put it on a hanger, then looked down at Teddy. The boy had a thick gold chain around his neck and he was playing with the pendant hanging from it. Max frowned and took a closer look, and then his blood began to pound in his veins and his heart did a flip in his chest.

"What the...?"

It was the artifact. He was staring down at a million-dollar diamond and his son was playing with it.

He turned away, struggling for breath. The historical artifact that threatened to ruin his life, the jewel-encrusted icon worth millions, was in the hands of a toddler. He turned back.

"Teddy, Teddy, where did you get that?"

Teddy didn't seem to know, but Max looked at his own denim jacket and realized what must have happened.

"It was in my jacket all this time," he muttered in hazy wonder. "And it took Teddy to find it."

And Teddy didn't want to give it up.

"Sorry, kid," he told him. "I've got to take this from you. I can't let it out of my possession again. Lives may depend on it."

Looking at it, he was sure this was what the king of Mercuria wanted. He didn't want Kayla. He didn't even want Max. This was basically the crown jewels of the nation and he wanted his treasure back.

How had it ended up in his jacket pocket? Maybe someone ought to ask Princess Nadine that question. He grabbed his denim jacket and put it on, then slipped the artifact back into the hidden, inside pocket, making sure it was secure.

"Thanks, Teddy," he said, picking the boy up and giving him a big kiss. "You're the hero tonight."

He got together the baby's things and he felt as though he were walking on air.

"Okay, Teddy," he muttered. "You're going to have to go back and stay with Caroline, because I'm going to get your mama back."

He knew he was supposed to wait for his brothers to go with him, but that was three hours away. He had to go now. Kayla was all alone and scared and he couldn't wait any longer.

Max had lived in Mercuria for almost a year and he knew all the little inlets along the coast and he could find them, even in the dark. He pulled his boat into a cove and tied it fast to a stand of pilings, then went ashore. It was a short walk to the castle. Mercuria was an old-fashioned country. The new, modern methods of security and border entry hadn't been introduced as yet. Very few people came to visit, because, after all, who cared about Mercuria? They had sat tight in their little isolated peninsula for decades and most people didn't even know they existed.

Max knew certain passwords, certain door codes, and before long, he was in the central living area of the castle, smiling at his old friend Sven, doorkeeper to the royal family.

"Hey, Sven," he said.

"Max!" Sven, a big, burly Swede, stepped out to clap him on the back. "Hey, good to see you, old buddy. It's been a while. So you're back?"

"Ah…yes, I'm back."

"And you're going into the royal center?"

"If you're going to let me, yes, I am."

"You don't have a pass, I suppose."

"Do I ever?"

Sven laughed. "No, can't say that I've ever known you to arrive with the proper pass." He shook his head with pure affection. "Come on in. Shall I announce you to anyone?"

"No, thanks. I'm going to go in and see who's available. Hopefully, I'll find the king isn't busy and has time to talk to me."

"Oh, sure. I think someone said he's in the greenhouse right now."

"Okay. I'll just hang around until he gets back."

"Sure."

He'd given a lot of thought to where they might be holding Kayla. There was a guest room on the first floor, off the library. If they were being extra special nice, they might have put her there. He slipped around the kitchen where he overheard two kitchen maids gossiping, and headed straight for the library, then the guest room. Empty.

That left the women's jail on the second floor. He took the stairs, hoping he wouldn't pass anyone on the way, and came to the fortified area that had been built especially to hold female prisoners. He'd known a housemaid who'd been accused of stealing and had been kept there for weeks. He'd felt sorry for her, visited her often and finally won her release when the real culprit was identified. He knew the way in and the way out and he could pick the main lock at will. A few clicks and he was in.

Two cells faced each other, divided by a corridor between them. In one cell, just as he'd expected, there was Kayla, sitting on a bare cot and looking unhappy but otherwise unscathed. But what he hadn't expected was to find Princess Nadine sitting in the other cell, face muddy with the effects of a lot of heavy crying. She looked up when Max entered, and her face brightened considerably.

"Max," she said, jumping up and going to the bars. "You came for me! Finally!"

But his attention was all on Kayla.

"Max!" She reached out her hand and he took it in his, pulling as close to her as he could.

"Are you all right?" Kayla asked anxiously. "How's your head?"

He'd forgotten all about his head wound. He touched it gingerly. "It's okay. How about you?" His gaze ran over every inch of her, searching for any signs of wounds. She looked a little mussed and had a bruise on one cheek, which made him swear softly. Her hair could use a combing. But she was the most beautiful thing he'd ever seen. "Did they hurt you?"

"No. Well, they did stick me with a tranquilizer dart."

He grinned at her. "Me, too."

She grinned back. "But other than that, they've been okay."

"Max!" Princess Nadine called, sounding like the spoiled child she was. "Come see about me."

He looked over his shoulder. "Why is she in here?" he asked.

Kayla shook her head. "I'm not sure. I think her father put her in here as a sort of trap for you when you returned to get her."

"Get her?"

"They seem to think you two have a love affair going on."

"In her imagination, maybe."

"Or maybe her father is just mad at her."

"I'm not mad at all, young lady," said a deep, sonorous voice.

Max turned quickly. King Juomo was coming down the center aisle. Dressed in eighteenth-century royal garb of brocade and velvet, he looked splendid and ridiculous all at the same time.

"My daughter is incarcerated for a very specific purpose." He smiled and made a slight inclination of his head toward Max. "I'm glad you made it. We've been waiting for you. Now we can get on with things."

"Your Majesty, with all due respect, I would like you to release Kayla right away. You have no right to hold her here. She has nothing to do with any of this."

He batted that pesky demand away. "I hear you're a prince now, my friend. What a lucky occurrence that is. Now my daughter will be doubly royal, won't she?" He put his head to one side, thinking hard. "Not to mention the unbreakable ties our two nations shall have with each other. Won't that be lovely?"

"Your Majesty," Max said bluntly, "I'm not going to marry your daughter."

"Oh, but I think you are. You see, I won't release your little friend here unless you do. It's quite simple, really." He smiled. "I've had the men in to fire up the old torture room in the dungeon. Quite a few nice old-fashioned machines in there. Can tear a body to ribbons, you know. I don't think your little friend will like it much. We will strive for historical accuracy, but still, her screams are going to be hard to take."

"Wait a minute." Max stared at the man as though he could hardly believe he was sane. "You're threatening to torture Kayla if I don't marry Princess Nadine? Are you crazy?"

"Not at all. I've been tested. I'm quite sane." He threw a dour look Kayla's way. "And not mad, either."

"I meant angry," she told him quickly. "Which is what I'm beginning to get. This is so absurd. I don't believe for a minute that you plan to torture me. You know very well international law forbids it."

He frowned. "Since when?"

"You don't keep up much with international affairs, do you? It's been that way for years. You can't get away with it. They'll string you up."

His laugh was jovial. "They'll have to catch me first."

"Really? And exactly where will you run to?"

He looked at Max. "I quite like your friend. She has a lot of spirit. Maybe I'll marry her myself." He giggled. "We'll have a double wedding."

"Daddy!" Nadine was sobbing.

"Hush, child. You wanted him and I told you I'd get him. Now he's here for you. Show a little gratitude."

"Tell you what," Max said sensibly, "I don't think anyone is marrying anyone at this point. But I do have a bargain for you. I might be able to produce your historical artifact."

"You'd certainly better produce the artifact. If you don't, you're all going to lose your heads."

"Oh, for heaven's sake," Kayla muttered just loud enough for Max to hear. "Now he thinks he's the Red Queen."

"If I can produce it," Max went on doggedly, "I'm sure you'll be gracious enough to let us both go free."

The king's eyes widened. "You and Nadine?"

"No. Me and Kayla."

He was frowning. "How does that help my little daughter? She loves you so."

"Daddy!" Nadine called.

"Hush. I'm negotiating here."

"But Daddy, I don't want him anymore. I hate him."

The king turned and glared at his daughter. "What?"

"I hate him. He didn't come back the way he was supposed to. I waited and waited."

"Well, he's back now. I went to a lot of trouble to get him for you."

"I know." She pouted. "I used to think he was really cute. But not anymore."

Max and Kayla exchanged significant glances.

"I don't understand," the plump man blustered. "I thought you couldn't live without him."

"Yeah, well..." She made a face. "He's not as cute as the new stable boy. Daddy? Please? I want the new stable boy."

Kayla grinned. By now she'd pretty much decided this whole thing was a thinly disguised farce. She couldn't believe anyone this silly could run a country.

"Maybe *I* ought to take a look at the new stable boy," she said brightly. "Who knows? Maybe I'll like him better, too."

Max turned to glare at her. He wasn't quite as ready as she was to assume this was an annoying but basically harmless situation. The king was off his rocker and pretty ridiculous, but that sort of person could go from farce to tragedy in a heartbeat.

But before he could say anything, there was a commotion in the hallway. There were shouts. A gun was fired, then another. And deadly silence.

They all stood very still, each holding his breath, listening for clues as to what this meant. Suddenly, the door to the cell room burst open and Monte appeared, with the guard Max knew as Sven in front of him with revolver pressed into his back.

"Your Majesty," Monte said to King Juomo, "so nice to meet you at last. We've come to take our people back, if you don't mind. The keys, please."

King Juomo seemed dumbfounded and very scared. Hands trembling, he produced the keys. David came in behind Monte and took the keys from him, opening the cell where Kayla had been sequestered and giving her a friendly smile.

"I always love it when they send in the cavalry," she noted approvingly.

"I don't know," Max said sardonically as he looked around at his brothers, "I thought I was doing okay on my own."

"It never hurts to get backup," Joe told him. "And anyway, thanks for trying to cut us out of the action."

"How did you know?" he asked, quietly admitting to himself that he'd never been happier to see a gang like this show up on his side.

"Caroline called Kimmee. Kimmee called Pellea."

"And we figured the rest out on our own," Monte said.

Max shook his head and grinned at his brothers. Reaching into the pocket of his jacket, he grabbed the artifact and drew it out. "Here you go," he told King Juomo, handing it to him.

The king looked at his daughter. "So you were telling me the truth?" he cried.

She nodded sulkily. "I put it in his pocket for safekeeping. I wanted it to be with him always, wherever he went. I knew it would bring him back to me, one way or another." She sniffed. "And now I don't want him."

"You see what folly it was to do that?" the king roared at her. "You see what trouble you caused?"

Her face crumpled but the princes were ready to leave her to her father's care and they began to head for the exit.

"It's been grand," Kayla said, saluting the king as she passed him. "Sort of like a visit to Freedonia without the Marx Brothers."

He looked rattled but it was evident he was starting to get color back in his face, and they hurried, not wanting to get bogged down in another discussion with him. Joe covered their departure, making sure the guards they'd disarmed on the way in weren't getting any ideas. And then they were on the boats and heading for home.

"There's something exhilarating about a good rescue operation," Monte said. "No casualties. Just some good clean fun."

"Fun." Max looked at Kayla, feeling drained.

She grinned at him. "All's well that ends well," she said.

Max groaned. "Another one of the quotes I'm supposed to learn, huh?"

She nodded and moved closer, putting her head against his shoulder and enjoying the cool, clean spray from the ocean. She loved Max. And she was in love with him, too. It was a good day that taught you a life lesson that big. She meant to savor it.

In the morning, Max went to Kayla's to have breakfast with her and her baby. He sat eating a delicious breakfast pastry that Kayla had picked up at the bakery and drinking black coffee and listening to Kayla talk to Teddy and feeling as though he'd won the lottery. This was great. This made him a happy man.

Suddenly he realized something. It broke over him like a shooting star, spreading sparkling gobs of fire all around. Being a flyer was important, but not everything. Being a prince was going to be his life's work. But the one thing he really cared about above all others, the one thing he wanted to do with his life, was to protect Kayla, to protect her and cherish her and make her happy. And loving Teddy was a part of that.

He sat back and marveled at how simple it all was once he'd let himself break free of all the old hurts and fears. He'd spent much too much time tied up in knots of doubt. No more doubts. No more regrets. He loved Kayla. Therefore, he would live his life to honor her. And that was all there was.

Could he do that? Could he be a father? Why the hell not?

He looked across the table at the woman he loved. "Will you marry me, Kayla?"

She pursed her lips and pretended to be thinking it over. "I don't know. I'll have to think about it. There's a lot to consider." She searched his face and shook her head sadly. "If only you were as cute as the stable boy."

He groaned. "I'm going to trade you to King Juomo. You'll be happy there. He really knows how to treat a lady."

She grinned happily. "Okay, I'll marry you. Let's do it quick."

"Before we change our minds?"

"Never." She held her glass of orange juice up as a toast to him. "I'll love you forever, Max. Forever and everywhere and always."

"Me, too."

Teddy made a noise. It sounded very much like words.

Max frowned. "Did he just say, 'me, too'?"

Kayla nodded. "It sure sounded like it."

"You know what that means?"

"Tell me."

"We're a family now."

Rising from her chair, she went to slip onto his lap and put her arms around him.

"Sealed with a kiss."

* * * * *

They had barely arrived at what appeared to be a postage stamp size courtyard of grass behind the twin white buildings when the bride and groom appeared.

"Congratulations!" the pretty woman in pink called, opening her little white container of bubbles and blowing, her lips pursed in a way that some men might have called sexy. Parker wasn't calling it anything. This woman was messing up his carefully planned day and his escape from all things wedding-related.

She gave Parker a stern look, which only made him more aware of those amazing and seriously sexy eyes of hers. That was wrong. He wasn't in the market for a woman of any kind, especially not a petite pirate who had boarded and was taking over his...

Wedding chapel, he thought, then quickly changed it to *building*. Darn it all, given the situation with his business and the board, the very last thing he needed in his life was a wedding chapel. Or interlopers. Pretty trespassers with full berry lips. And bubbles.

Praise for Myrna Mackenzie:

**** "A fun read with intriguing, emotionally
compelling characters."
—*RT Book Reviews* on *Riches to Rags Bride*

"Myrna Mackenzie writes such fine novels, everyone
should add her to their must buy list."
—*Cataromance*

INHERITED: EXPECTANT CINDERELLA

BY
MYRNA MACKENZIE

All the characters in this book have no existence outside the imagination of the author, and have no relation whatsoever to anyone bearing the same name or names. They are not even distantly inspired by any individual known or unknown to the author, and all the incidents are pure invention.

All Rights Reserved including the right of reproduction in whole or in part in any form. This edition is published by arrangement with Harlequin Enterprises II B.V./S.à.r.l. The text of this publication or any part thereof may not be reproduced or transmitted in any form or by any means, electronic or mechanical, including photocopying, recording, storage in an information retrieval system, or otherwise, without the written permission of the publisher.

This book is sold subject to the condition that it shall not, by way of trade or otherwise, be lent, resold, hired out or otherwise circulated without the prior consent of the publisher in any form of binding or cover other than that in which it is published and without a similar condition including this condition being imposed on the subsequent purchaser.

® and ™ are trademarks owned and used by the trademark owner and/or its licensee. Trademarks marked with ® are registered with the United Kingdom Patent Office and/or the Office for Harmonisation in the Internal Market and in other countries.

First published in Great Britain 2012
by Mills & Boon, an imprint of Harlequin (UK) Limited,
Eton House, 18-24 Paradise Road, Richmond, Surrey TW9 1SR

© Myrna Topol 2012

ISBN: 978 0 263 89432 5
ebook ISBN: 978 1 408 97109 3

923-0512

Harlequin (UK) policy is to use papers that are natural, renewable and recyclable products and made from wood grown in sustainable forests. The logging and manufacturing processes conform to the legal environmental regulations of the country of origin.

Printed and bound in Spain
by Blackprint CPI, Barcelona

Myrna Mackenzie grew up not having a clue what she wanted to be—she hadn't been born a princess, the one job she thought she might like because of the steady flow of pretty dresses and crowns—but she knew that she loved stories and happy endings, so falling into life as a romance writer was pretty much inevitable. An award-winning author, with over thirty-five novels written, Myrna was born in a small town in Dunklin County, Missouri, grew up just outside Chicago, and now divides her time between two lakes in Chicago and Wisconsin, both very different and both very beautiful. She adores the internet (which still seems magical after all these years), loves coffee, hiking, attempting gardening (without much success), cooking and knitting.

Readers (and other potential gardeners, cooks, knitters, writers, etc.) can visit Myrna online at www.myrna mackenzie.com, or write to her at PO Box 225, La Grange, IL 60525, USA.

CHAPTER ONE

"THIS wasn't exactly what I was thinking of when I decided I needed some time away from Boston," Parker Sutcliffe muttered to himself as he climbed from his black Rolls Phantom. He had stopped in front of a large old white frame building in a low-rent part of Las Vegas where there were no casinos or tourist attractions. The words "Forever and a Day Wedding Chapel" marched across the building in lurid pink neon. The building next door lacked signage but was otherwise a twin and appeared to be connected. He noted that there was no number on the door.

No matter, he thought. *This is the place.* These structures had belonged to a relative he'd never even heard of, but he'd been given the keys and told that he could take possession of the two empty buildings. The whole situation had been a surprise, and he disliked surprises, but the timing was right. This past year, after all that had happened...

He shied away from the thought, concentrating only on Sutcliffe's. The business had been his lifeline for as long as he could remember. It was failing now, and he wasn't going to let it slip away. So maybe what he needed was this. Coming here to claim his inheritance gave him a chance to get away, think, work and come up with an idea that would save Sutcliffe's. Plus, it was an excuse to escape the incessant suggestions by his board that he should marry to cre-

ate some badly needed positive buzz about the company
and himself now that his father had passed on.

Their insinuations that he wasn't a dynamic substitute as
the company representative, but that he could be its savior
if he'd only listen, had been a source of tension. This trip
offered a viable excuse for his absence while he grasped
the opportunity to brainstorm away from the fray. He desperately needed some quiet alone time.

But when he turned the handle of the abandoned chapel,
it wasn't locked. And when he entered, he discovered that
the building wasn't abandoned, either. Or quiet.

Immediately, a wall of off-key sound hit him. He was
standing at the back of the chapel, and a wedding was taking place. In the front, on a cramped raised stage, an Elvis
impersonator who looked as if he'd been in the business a
decade too long was belting out the ending to "It's Now or
Never." A bride and groom, who clearly weren't hearing
the music, were smiling.

For half a second, Parker wondered if he had walked
into a reality show. Or maybe someone was playing a joke
on him. But if his associates in Boston hoped to talk him
into a wedding by throwing him into the midst of one, they
had obviously chosen the wrong wedding.

That was all he had time to think. As the last of the lyr-
ics died away, a blur of pink came rushing at him from the
side aisle.

"I'm so sorry. You missed most of it." Parker looked
down at a tiny woman with long copper curls and a hid-
eous bright pink dress. She glanced at his dark suit. "You
must be a friend or relative of the bride or groom, but don't
worry. They're usually so excited that they won't notice a
late guest. Unless you're family. Are you family?"

"Not at all. I—"

"That's okay, then. Here they come. Take this." She

shoved something into his hand. "The reception is right down that hall and out the door."

Parker frowned. "Reception? You're mistaken. I'm not—"

"Quickly," she said. "They're coming, and with these smaller weddings, we need as much of a cheering section as we can get." Grabbing him by the hand, she tugged, trying to steer him toward the door.

He resisted. "Look, Ms.... I don't know who you are, but we need to talk."

"Mr.... I don't know who you are, either, but this is a wedding. They paid. This is the most important day of their lives, and talking can come later." She turned to go, then whirled back, a sudden look of fear in her big brown eyes. "You're not a bill collector, are you?"

Parker scowled. "No, but—"

"The police?"

"Do I really look like a police officer?"

She glanced at his suit. "Right. Not unless officers are wearing Armani these days. Okay, let's go, then. Talk later. Bring your bubbles."

"Bubbles?" he said half to himself, but the wedding party was closing in behind him, so he strode after the pretty, if bossy and insane, redhead.

They had barely arrived at what appeared to be a postage-stamp-sized courtyard of grass behind the twin white buildings when the bride and groom appeared.

"Congratulations!" the pretty woman in pink called, opening her little white container of bubbles and blowing, her lips pursed in a way that some men might have called sexy. Parker wasn't calling it anything. This woman was messing up his carefully planned day and his escape from all things wedding-related.

She gave Parker a stern look, which only made him

more aware of how amazingly expressive her eyes were. Immediately, he squelched that thought. He wasn't in the market for a woman, especially not a petite pirate who had boarded and was taking over his...

Wedding chapel, he thought, then quickly changed it to *building.* Damn it, given the situation with his business and the board, the very last thing he needed was a functioning wedding chapel or distractions from the very real problems he needed to solve. He certainly didn't want to have to deal with pretty trespassers with full berry lips. And bubbles.

Parker frowned, eager for this fiasco of a wedding to end so that he could find out what was going on. As he watched, the Elvis impersonator, the man who had officiated at the wedding and the woman who had played the piano made their way outside, the pink beauty gave them their containers and wands, and the bride and groom were treated to a rainbow of bubbles floating down on them and popping sloppily as they kissed.

The pink lady, aided by an elderly woman with a cane, turned on some soft music and uncovered a small wedding cake. Then the pretty redhead shifted gears, grabbed a camera and began shooting pictures as the bride and groom fed each other cake and shared a dance. Somewhere along the way, the papers were signed, the bride and groom left, and Parker found himself standing next to the pink princess.

"So..." she said, gazing up at him and finally losing the smile she had maintained for the past thirty minutes. Her brown eyes looked worried. "If you don't know anyone from that wedding party and you're not a bill collector or a police officer, who are you?" Then her eyes suddenly brightened and the smile reappeared. "I know. You must be a prospective groom. You want us to conduct *your* wedding. Forgive me for not thinking of that sooner. It was just…your suit… I'm not quite used to seeing that kind of quality, but don't worry. We know how to step things up a notch when we need to. I guarantee you won't regret coming to the Forever and a Day chapel."

"Too late," he said, frowning down at her. "I already regret it." He looked down to where some bubble solution had landed on his cuff.

"Oops, I'm so very sorry," she said, reaching out to rub it off. Her slender fingers brushed the back of his hand. As she moved closer, trying to undo the damage, he breathed in the faint scent of lavender, of…woman, and his entire body tightened. Ridiculous. She was a total stranger, and even if she weren't, he'd made too many mistakes with women. Serious, life-changing mistakes that had left him reeling and had nearly caught others in the crossfire. So… no. Definitely no.

The beauty must have felt the same way, because she quickly jerked her hand away. A pink smudge of cake frosting remained on the sleeve of his suit where her fingertips had slid against him, and he almost felt the small gasp whoosh out of her.

"I'm ninety-nine-percent positive that will come out," she promised with a blush. "You could give it to me. I could fix it."

Parker felt an unfamiliar urge to smile, but he restrained himself. There appeared to have been a lot of "fixing" going on, given the fact that the building was supposed to be unoccupied.

But the outcome of this wasn't going to be fun or funny. He lost the urge to smile. "I think not. We're done here," he said.

Those pretty brown eyes blinked. "Excuse me? Does that mean you won't be having your wedding here?"

"If I were ever going to have a wedding in this life-time—and I don't plan to—then no, it wouldn't be here."

"Because we're not up to your style?"

"Because I'll be selling the building and I doubt that the next owner will leave it intact."

Parker would have sworn that those big brown eyes couldn't have opened any wider or looked more distressed, but he would have been wrong.

"Sell the building?" Her words came out on a whisper. "But this is Tillie's building."

He thinned his lips. "I assume you're referring to my aunt Mathilda and she's…"

"She passed away," the woman said quietly. "You're her *heir*? She had *an heir*? A real live heir?"

The woman was clearly distressed to learn of his exis-tence…and possibly the fact that he was still among the living. "I'm Parker Sutcliffe," he said, "and I never met my aunt. And you are…?"

"I'm…well, I'm…" She had a look in her eyes that Parker recognized from experience. She was searching for a good story to tell him, so he gave her his best don't-even-bother-trying-to-lie icy aristocratic stare, the one he'd learned to use on the servants before he could even talk.

She blew out a breath that lifted those pretty copper bangs, took a deep breath and stood tall, or at least as tall as someone whose head barely reached his shoulder could. "I'm Daisy Lockett. I live here." She pushed her chin up. "*We* live here," she said with a touch of defiance. She ges-tured toward the woman with the cane, the minister and the organist who were gathered on the other side of the room looking worried.

"You *live* here," Parker repeated as if his brain had gone dead. And maybe it had. He'd been expecting an empty building and when it hadn't been empty he'd assumed that someone was simply borrowing the facilities, but…tenants? And not just tenants but a too-pretty woman with eyes like melted chocolate along with three frail elderly people?

Parker narrowed his eyes. He didn't care for this turn of events at all. Unpredictable, possibly messy situations were at the bottom of the list of things he liked. After all the drama of the past year and his disastrous personal relationships with women, he was ready for something a bit more boring.

But that was apparently not an option. Parker looked down into those worried dark caramel eyes. Daisy Lockett's hair looked soft and disheveled, the way a woman's hair would if a man had just taken her to bed and plunged his fingers into it. She had her index finger between her lips, either nervously chewing on her fingernail or not so nervously licking cake frosting off her pink fingertip.

He caught himself wondering which it was. Stupid. Did it matter? What mattered was that she was living under *his* roof. Admittedly a roof he hadn't even known about until last week, but one that he now possessed. Which meant that anything that went on inside this building could be tied to him, and right now—*especially* now—he didn't need any bizarre or provocative stories circulating about him.

"My aunt passed away a couple of months ago," he said. "So why are you still here? And why didn't the authorities or the real estate agent know that there were people in the building? Would you like to explain all that to me, Ms. Lockett?"

Parker crossed his arms over his chest and frowned down at Daisy Lockett. It was a look that had cowed employees much bigger than she was.

But to his surprise, the woman called his bluff. Tiny as she was, she stood taller. She crossed her arms, too, something which was, he surmised, supposed to make her look fierce, but given the generous curves of her breasts only made her look...interestingly hot.

Stop it, Sutcliffe, he warned himself. The woman's hotness quotient was the very last thing he needed to be thinking about. He and she were, after all, about to terminate their fleeting acquaintance. She would be leaving just as soon as he could hustle her out of here. And soon enough he would be returning to Boston and his business. A business that, despite its current difficulties, he could depend on and control.

It was obvious that Daisy Lockett was totally out of control. He needed to get rid of her, not examine her more closely.

"Well, Ms. Lockett, what's your explanation for this?" He held out his hand toward the remains of the sad wedding cake with its toppled plastic bride and groom, several half-used containers of bubbles, a puddle of foaming bubble solution forming on the cheap paper tablecloth and an MP3 player that needed new batteries. The low, distorted tones of a song playing on dying power sounded like a cow in distress.

"You don't like weddings, do you, Mr. Sutcliffe?" she asked suddenly, not answering his question. "I've met men like that before."

And clearly it hadn't been a pleasant experience.

He raised one eyebrow. "You're right. I'm not a huge fan of the institution of marriage, but that's completely beside the point. The point is that you're living in my building. Trespassing. What did you think would happen when someone found out you were here?"

She raised her chin. "I just... I hoped it wouldn't happen."

He blinked. A good businessman never made decisions based on hope alone. "Well, here I am. It's happened," he pointed out. "The question is, now that our paths have crossed despite your best hopes…what am I going to do about you?"

It would still be months before Daisy signed up for her first Lamaze class, but she knew that proper breathing was at the core of the program, so if she were in a class right now, she'd be failing. Fear was playing havoc with her breathing, and she was alternately forgetting to breathe and then having to suck in big gulps of air while trying to appear perfectly calm to this man who claimed to be Tillie's nephew. The man who also claimed to own this building.

"Tillie never spoke of you," she said, grasping for a lifeline. Surely Tillie, who had been like a mother to her, and also her best friend in the world, would have mentioned that she had a nephew….

Who looked more gorgeous than any man has a right to look. With great shoulders and great…other stuff, and a deep voice that—

Daisy blinked. What was wrong with her? Seriously. This man wasn't even nice.

She frowned. "It just seems as if Tillie might have mentioned a nephew if you were her heir," she said, glad that the man couldn't read minds. Or…he probably couldn't. Tillie had always tried to claim she was psychic and that Daisy was as transparent as they come. If this man was related to her…

"My aunt and I never met," the tall, dark-haired stranger said. "But according to her attorney, she died without a will and I'm her only living relative."

No. No. No. No. No. That couldn't be true, but…oh, just look at him. Look at the strong line of his jaw, the arch of his eyebrows. If she were playing a matching game, those features would be a perfect fit for Tillie's. Still…she needed time. She needed to think, to see if there was some way out of this crazy rabbit hole she'd fallen into when this man had stepped through the door.

"I'm sorry, but I'm going to need more proof than just your word." Men had told her so many lies over the years, they had hurt her so much. If she was going to get kicked out on the streets—*please don't let me get kicked out*—she wasn't going to go down meekly. Still, the look in those I'm-in-command green eyes told her that he was confident he would win. She tried not to think about what losing would mean for her and her friends and her—

She resisted the urge to curl a protective hand over her abdomen. Panic made breathing even more difficult. Her hands felt clammy.

The man looked decidedly irritated, and Daisy discovered that, even irritated, he looked just as devastating, a fact which really ticked her off. Life could be so unfair sometimes. "I don't generally carry around those kinds of documents," he told her with an imperious air.

A small sliver of hope grew within her. *Breathe. Breathe. Breathe,* she ordered herself. Maybe all of them could be safe for a little while longer.

And maybe a miracle could happen, a beam of light could lift me into an alternate universe where pink unicorns frolic and chocolate bars grow on trees, she chided herself. Or at least to a universe where there were no rich, handsome and, yes, rightful owners with the law on their sides wanting to throw her and hers out on the street. *Think, Daisy, think. You need real ammo here. You need to be smart.*

Okay. Here was the deal, all that she had. "Tillie was my very best friend," she said as forcefully as she dared. "She wanted me here. And I have proof, neighbors who will vouch for me." With the last bit of courage she possessed, Daisy lifted her chin.

The man ran a hand through his hair. Hair that had obviously seen the services of an expensive stylist. He turned those cold, deep-green eyes on her and frowned. "All right, you have me there. I never knew my aunt and I don't know anyone in Las Vegas. I'm not from here, but I assure you, Ms. Lockett, the law is on my side. I intend to come back and dispose of my aunt's effects. I'm going to do something with this building, and I'm afraid that you won't be allowed to stay unless you can provide legal papers that trump mine, the ones that really do exist. I'll be back tomorrow with proof of ownership, and if you're still here, I'll expect there to be a very good reason. A legal reason."

Daisy looked up into the man's gorgeous eyes and saw nothing that could give her hope. Tillie had been a total sweetheart, a surrogate mother and a friend, but she had also been a bit of a procrastinator. She'd disliked lawyers and anyone with authority. And like so many people, she'd thought she'd live forever and probably had never even considered making a will. In fact, given Tillie's spontaneous nature, it would be beyond surprising if she'd left anything legal that could save her friends now. And Daisy wasn't the only one at risk. Panic—sheer, terrifying panic—ripped through her. The others were too frail and old to deal with this stuff. She had to be the strong one now, the leader, the helper.

So, closing her eyes and biting her lip, she sent one swift wish for guidance into the ether. Reaching out, she touched the man's sleeve.

"Please don't send us out on the streets. We have nowhere to go."

She wasn't even touching his skin at all, but she felt as if a lightning bolt had ripped through her and left shimmering sparkles of electricity filling the air around her. As if she was somehow electrically linked to this man who was looking at her as if she had just declared that she was going to give birth right in front of him. The fact that that thought wouldn't be too terribly far from the truth if this was seven months into the future made Daisy blanch, but she held on. "Please," she added. "Not yet. I'll...I'll get proof about Tillie and all of us somehow."

"All of you," the man said. "There are more of you?"

"Just us four." She decided that it might be best not to mention the dog right now. Or...her pregnancy. "We just need a little time."

"Four. There are four people living in this building," he said, as if she hadn't told him that already.

Daisy nodded. "I'm sorry you didn't know before you got here. We didn't try to hide it." Although they *had* all known that the building didn't belong to them and that this couldn't last forever. They had been mailed a notice to leave and they just...hadn't left. But she wasn't sharing that with this man. He might have her cuffed and thrown into jail right now, and then where would the others be? She had to—somehow—gain them a little time.

She hazarded her best hopeful smile. "I guess...I guess you're our landlord now, Mr. Sutcliffe. We could start paying you rent." Even though she had no idea how they could scrounge together enough money for that.

For half a second, something that looked a bit like a smile lifted his lips just a touch. "You say that as if it's a novel idea. Were you paying my aunt rent?"

"We were working for Tillie. And we all contributed our share. We were kind of like a...sort of like a commune."

"A...commune? I see," he said, and it was obvious he didn't like what he saw.

"We could continue to be useful, running the chapel,"

she offered. "We make people happy. In a way, we make their dreams come true, and it pays a little."

If anything, Parker looked even more concerned. As if she'd just suggested that they take up raising rats. "I'm not a big believer in dreams, and I'm not interested in getting involved in the marriage business," he said. "But despite how things appear, I'm not totally heartless, either. I'll think things over tonight. Then tomorrow we'll start looking for somewhere for you to go so that you're not all homeless."

And just like that he turned to go. But she was still holding on to his sleeve. Daisy heard a tiny rip as he stepped away, and she let go, her hand flying to her mouth in horror. "I'm really sorry about that. I could…get it fixed for you."

"You're quite a resourceful woman, aren't you?"

That didn't sound like a true compliment, but then, Daisy had experienced more than her share of criticism in her lifetime. She'd had men turn their backs on her more than once. Men she should have been able to trust and depend on. She lifted her chin and stared straight into his eyes.

"You have absolutely no idea, Mr. Sutcliffe."

"I don't," he agreed. "I don't know a thing about you. But I know all I need to know."

And clearly he didn't like what he knew.

She opened her mouth.

"Tomorrow, Daisy." He cut her off, which was just as well since she didn't know what she would have said. Possibly something that would have made the situation worse, if that was possible.

As he walked away, Daisy couldn't help thinking that most women would probably get all excited at the prospect of a visit from a man who looked like Parker Sutcliffe.

Under other circumstances she might have joined their ranks and at least enjoyed looking at him. But these were not other circumstances. Her next meeting with Parker was going to turn her life upside-down even more than this one had.

She had better start preparing for their next meeting. Had she really handed the man—make that the *obviously rich* man—a homemade bottle of bubbles and a bubble wand? And gotten frosting on what had to be an incredibly expensive suit?

Daisy groaned. She had. And then, despite her precarious situation, she couldn't help smiling just a little remembering how horrified Parker had looked holding that bottle.

"The man probably never blew a bubble in his life," she muttered. "I could certainly teach him a thing or two about having fun."

Immediately she blanched. She'd be better off trying to think of ways to convince him that *he'd* be better off letting all of them stay here. Despite what she'd said, she could tell that he wouldn't be moved by her neighbors' opinions that Tillie would surely not have meant things to turn out this way.

What would Tillie do? she thought.

But all of the ideas that came to her were too preposterous…or illegal.

Maybe a miracle would happen, and a great idea about how to outwit Parker Sutcliffe would come to her in her dreams. Or maybe she'd just end up having a nightmare, one with a gorgeous but cruel villain…one who didn't like bubbles.

"Still, I need a plan. A fast plan," Daisy whispered. One that would help her save her family.

CHAPTER TWO

PARKER had called his secretary to tell her that he might be in Las Vegas an extra few days, and now Fran, who had worked for his family for years, was lecturing him.

"You know, you could simply hire someone to take care of that Mathilda situation."

He knew…even though his late aunt wasn't the only or even the main reason he was here.

Sutcliffe's is failing. I have to stop it. The thought slipped in. No surprise. The words had practically become his mantra. Still, he did need to take care of his aunt's belongings. Something was very wrong here, and it wasn't just the luscious and bold Daisy.

"No, it's up to me," he said, "because clearly someone else took care of Mathilda's situation years ago or I would have known that I had an aunt before she passed away."

"Parker, I'm sure that your parents had good reasons," she began.

"I'm sure they did." And he had a good idea what those reasons had been. "But they're both gone now, and I don't intend to leave here without getting what I came for. I don't like surprises, I didn't like *this* surprise and I intend to make sure there aren't any more. By the time I leave Las Vegas, I plan to know all there is to know about Aunt Mathilda including why the family didn't acknowledge her existence, and I'm going to sort the situation out myself. If I hire someone, important personal information may be missed. Or if there's anything incriminating—which I assume there is—it may become public knowledge and I don't want to risk having anything floating around out there that would be bad for Sutcliffe Industries." That was all that was needed to push the company off its fragile golden pedestal.

He also didn't want to think about the fact that Daisy might know things about his aunt that he didn't know. The wrong information in the wrong hands...

He frowned. There was something undeniably intriguing and enticing about Daisy, but that only made her doubly dangerous. He didn't want to be intrigued or enticed. His life had been devoted to his business, the one thing that had never let him down until now, and that was how he liked things. All he had to do was contain the trouble with Sutcliffe's. Then his world could return to its uneventful but satisfying path.

"You know," Fran began, breaking into Parker's thoughts. "Jarrod thinks this trip is a sham and that you've simply escaped to Vegas because he and the rest of the board have started picking out potential wives for you."

Well, there it was. Leave it to Fran to get right to the heart of things. Too bad she couldn't see his scowl through the phone lines, because she was definitely partly right. Jarrod, his cousin, had recommended an administrative assistant candidate to him last week who was clearly Boston royalty and knew nothing at all about the job.

"Jarrod may think that the board knows what's best for me and Sutcliffe's," Parker said. "But he and the rest of the board are way off base. Marriage isn't a good idea."

"Oh, I don't know. Remember how the stock of Ensign, Incorporated, shot up for months while Lloyd Ensign and his fiancée were engaged and inviting the public to sign in to their website and become part of the wedding-planning process? The company became a household name overnight."

"I remember. And I remember thinking that Lloyd Ensign was an even bigger ass than I'd always known him to be. Opening my emotional doors to the public for money? Not my style, Fran."

"I know, and you wouldn't have to take it that far, of course, but…people love the fairy tale, Parker. You know… billionaire bachelor finds the love of his life, his own personal princess, and has a romantic wedding with all the bells and whistles. And you and the board have agreed that you want to snag the public's attentions when you launch the new spa complex."

Which was true. Opening the Sutcliffe Spa Complex was the first major change in the company's long and successful history, definitely the first since Galen Sutcliffe had died and Parker had taken full control.

Parker's grip tightened on the phone. His father had been larger than life, a friend to every television screen. His image and voice had launched a hundred hotels and kept people coming back for more. Now there was a hole in the company where he had been, and Parker wasn't completely confident that the new spa complex could fill that hole. But this plan to boost the company's ratings by painting him as a Prince Charming in search of the perfect bride…?

"You, too, Fran? Trying to convince me the way everyone else is?"

"Why not me?"

"Because you know me."

She sighed. "Yes." And what Fran knew was that Parker wasn't interested in emotional entanglements. He'd had a lonely childhood until he'd found solace in work, and his

solitary ways hadn't translated well to his relationships
as an adult. Women found him too restrained, but they
liked his money; they wanted his name. And after the in-
cident when Evelyn had tried to manipulate him into marriage by pretending he was the father of her unborn child…
Parker's blood nearly froze at the thought. Besides the obvious betrayal and lies, the thought of raising a child…no.
No. Children needed so much more than he was capable
of offering.

"I know you don't want to get married, and I see your
point, but Jarrod won't give in as easily as I will," Fran
warned. "He's planted the idea of a big Sutcliffe wedding
in the minds of the other board members and it's starting
to take hold."

Parker didn't want to tell her that even he had examined the idea. Because while he'd been burned by women
and didn't want to try again, still he understood that his father's personality had been the secret to Sutcliffe's success.
If a meaningless wedding could breathe life back into the
business he'd built his life around… It was just one of the
things he needed time to think about, and he couldn't possibly think with Jarrod and the board singing the Wedding
March twenty-four hours a day.

"I have to go now, Fran. I'll tend to the spa situation
from here, and I'll keep you posted on what's going on,"
he promised.

"All right. I'll keep you posted, too. Just don't…"

"What?"

"I don't really think you should be handling this
Mathilda thing yourself. Now that you know there's
something odd going on and some strangers living in her
house…it's just…there might be dirt. The kind that might
harm you or Sutcliffe Industries."

He laughed. "I've been expecting dirt from the moment I learned that I had a secret relative. Doing damage control is part of why I'm here. If I'm lucky, I'll be able to bury anything unsavory and make it disappear before the reporters find out anything."

"Good luck with that. You know how they were with your parents' divorce."

He did. It had been ugly, brutal and had torn his young world apart, so he wasn't letting anyone from the press get close. Maintaining a low profile was part of why he was here alone.

Well, not exactly alone, he thought as he hung up. There was one impetuous redhead and her three pale sidekicks lurking in the shadows. What in the world was he going to do about his...tenants? About one tenant in particular?

For half a mad second, he wondered what the board would think of Daisy. They'd probably all start hyperventilating, scared to death that she might tarnish his shiny aristocratic most-eligible-bachelor image.

Or hand them a container of bubbles.

Parker almost smiled at that thought. But he didn't. He couldn't. Sutcliffe's had saved him when he'd desperately needed saving, and, with the company teetering, he had to do everything right. If Daisy had been living here illegally, what other secrets was she harboring? Was there something about the situation that could further harm Sutcliffe's if it came to light?

Probably not. He had, after all, been unaware of Daisy's presence before today. Still, this was a delicate situation and a possible PR nightmare. He didn't want to harm anyone, but the truth was that he was planning on relocating an entire crew of elderly people.

Parker blew out a breath. "Fine, it's delicate," he muttered. It was also ludicrous for a man who had eschewed marriage to inherit a wedding chapel. He would just have to deal with the situation.

"So get on with things," he muttered. "Do what you came to do." *Make a quick sweep of your aunt's possessions, hire someone to place Daisy and her brood elsewhere, make them disappear from your life and sell the building. Then figure out what's gone wrong with Sutcliffe's and fix it.*

Parker frowned. Clearly, he had plenty to keep his mind occupied, especially since the spa would open in a month. So, why were his thoughts stalling on Daisy's smile and the way she had stood up to him? The woman certainly made a man take notice. Even if he didn't want to.

Daisy was rushing. No surprise. She spent a lot of time rushing…from her part-time job as a tour guide to her even more part-time job as a freelance reporter for a local newspaper to organizing weddings. She also did her best to oversee her group and make sure that no one starved to death or forgot to pay a bill. And when they *did* forget, she wasn't too proud to try to schmooze the bill collector. Or evade him. Today shouldn't have been so different from that.

Except it was. Parker Sutcliffe was no ordinary bill collector. He had caught them in the act of mooching off him, and now he was going to put them out on the street. And it was clear as anything that she was the one who would have to try to get him to change his mind.

But, there had been no light-bulb moments in her dreams last night. Just a few erotic images of Parker with his suit off.

"Oh, that really helped a lot," she had grumbled when she woke up and remembered—vaguely—what she'd been dreaming. Undressing the villain didn't make him less a villain. It just made her look pathetic. Besides, she didn't have time for any of that.

"Lydia, help me make these pew bows look a little perkier. We weren't at the top of our game yesterday when Mr. Sutcliffe dropped by, so we've got to make this place shine before he shows up today."

"Do you think he'll like us better today, Daisy?" Nola asked, and Daisy wanted to cry. Or scream at Parker and beat her fists against his broad chest. Honestly, the man must go to the gym every day. What rich guy looked that fit without a personal trainer riding his butt all the time? He probably lived off arugula and bean sprouts while she and the gang ate a lot of mac 'n' cheese. The discount kind.

"Daisy?" Lydia sounded worried.

"He might like us better," Daisy said, trying to sound confident. "If we can wave some dollar signs in front of his eyes. I've met Mr. Sutcliffe's type before, men who are all about getting what they want. If we can convince him that the Forever and a Day has the potential to be profitable for him, he might want to leave things as they are. Maybe he'll agree to hire us and let us stay on here."

She looked at the cheery but inexpensive bows she and Lydia were affixing to the pews, but a part of her couldn't help seeing them through Parker's eyes. They weren't real silk. She remembered how his suit had looked…and felt. The man was not going to be impressed by this.

But he's not going to sneer, either, she vowed. She would punch him in the nose before she would let him make fun of Lydia or John or Nola. They had had tough lives and now they were old, but they had their pride. Tillie had been proud, too. And Daisy was not going to let some pompous rich guy look down his nose at them.

Just because they were squatting in his building. Breaking the law.

The truth hit her. It nearly did her in. They really had no right to be here. Parker Sutcliffe was completely within his rights to throw them all out.

She had three elderly people dependent on her...and her baby. *Her baby.* She still had trouble believing that she was going to be a mother. It was a scary thought, but she was determined not to mess up. Having no home for her baby would be messing up in a major way. So, what on earth was she going to do?

Something foolish, most likely, she thought. And that kind of thing had gotten her in trouble in the past. Big trouble. Put-you-in-handcuffs-and-write-bad-stuff-on-your-permanent-record trouble.

But that's not going to happen today. I'm not going to let things get out of control. Come on, Mr. Sutcliffe. I'm putting on my tour-guide face. I can fake it with the best of them. Let's do this thing.

The first thing that Parker noticed when he entered the Forever and a Day, documents in hand, was that someone had made an attempt to make the inside of the chapel shine. The pink bows affixed to the ends of the pews were more attractive than the ones that had been on display yesterday, there were two potted plants on the small staging area at the front and the cream-colored curtains that had been closed for privacy yesterday had been tied back to let the morning sunlight stream in. Unfortunately, while the sun made the place much brighter, it emphasized the fact that the pews were rather old, their upholstery somewhat shiny with age.

And apparently his inspection hadn't gone unnoticed. "We've been meaning to reupholster them when we get the funds, but we wanted you to see that this is a nice place to have a sweet, old-fashioned wedding. With just a small infusion of cash, it could be even better. We fill a niche that the bigger, flashier places don't. People who want something homey, loving, not overly commercial or expensive seek us out," Daisy said, walking toward him down the center aisle of the chapel. She had a determined smile on her face, but her eyes looked wary.

"Daisy," he drawled. "I told you—"

"I know. You're not interested in the marriage business. I went to the library and looked you up on the internet last night. I know what your company does, the properties you own and some of the women you've...um...dated. You're not exactly into small fish, are you?"

"I have nothing against small fish." He heard a giggle coming from his left. Daisy turned slightly and shook her head at whoever had been giggling. "I just have no interest in becoming the owner of a wedding chapel. It's not the kind of business I...invest in."

"You were going to say 'want to be associated with,' weren't you? Because I'm not criticizing. I know we're not exactly posh or anything like that. But I want you to know that we have real potential, and we're not too tacky, either. We're not one of those we'll-do-anything-you-want places. We don't do...I don't know...half-naked weddings. No one gets married in a bikini, even if it's a white one," she said, just as if this was a normal conversation. "At least, not anymore."

A slight pink flush turned Daisy's creamy skin rosy, and every male cell in Parker's body responded in a way that was completely inappropriate and unwelcome.

All right, this whole situation was totally preposterous and impossible. Parker managed to maintain his stern look, despite the fact that part of him wanted to smile. He held up one hand to stop Daisy, just in case she continued talking about women in bikinis. Already his thoughts were wandering into forbidden territory, wondering what Daisy would look like in a tiny white bikini. He needed to head her off. "I'm not worried about the tackiness factor," he said.

She gave him a you-have-to-be-kidding look. "Your family came over on the *Mayflower*, and you...you wear those suits that probably cost more than this building does."

Probably more than ten of these buildings did. "I'm not concerned about it because you won't be holding weddings here much longer. I thought I made that clear. I'm selling this place, going back to my life and my real business, and when I do..."

"You'll evict us," Daisy whispered. "But you said you weren't totally heartless."

"I also told you that I'd help you relocate."

"I know but...to where? Do you really think it's going to be easy to find affordable housing for all of us together? At least give us some time." She crossed her arms over the lilac fabric of her sundress, which only drew his attention to the curve of her breasts. Again.

He frowned. What was wrong with him? He'd never been one of those guys.

"I'll help you find someplace suitable," he insisted, glancing down and away, but not before he noted that the woman was wearing flip-flops. With lilac plastic flowers between her pretty and very bare pink toes. Did he even know another woman who would be caught out in public in those things?

She shook her head, sending those long red curls flying. "I was hoping you would reconsider once you got past the shock of finding us here, but since you haven't..."

Daisy looked toward the wall. "All right, you three, come on in." She turned toward Parker. "We're like family, and this concerns them every bit as much as it does me."

Parker turned as the three elderly people shuffled out. The harsh sunlight wasn't exactly kind to them, but he could see that they had done their best to dress to impress. Nola had taped a red ribbon around her cane. Lydia had a silk flower in her hair, even though it was beginning to slide out of its clip and droop a bit, and John was wearing a different threadbare suit from the threadbare one he'd worn yesterday.

"Mr. Sutcliffe, sir, I heard what you said about us having to leave, but…can you keep us together?" Nola asked. "Because we're a…a team. We stay together no matter what. Daisy says so."

"Yes," Lydia said, her head nodding non-stop. "Daisy leads tour groups and writes articles to help keep us in food, and we're really good at doing the weddings with her. She organizes things and takes pictures, I make cookies and play piano, Nola helps sew costumes and fixes flowers and sings and John…"

"John performs the services," Parker said. "Yes. I know."

"And sometimes Romeo serves as a ring bearer," John added. "He's very well behaved."

"Romeo?"

"My puppy," Nola said. "Romeo, come here, dear—"

"No!" Daisy called out, but it was apparently too late. A monster "Woof!" echoed through the walls, followed by the sound of something large pounding down the stairs. Within seconds, a huge German shepherd bounded into the room, ran up to Parker and gazed up at him, cocking his head.

"Romeo?" Parker asked.

"He was a groom's dog, but the bride didn't want him even though Romeo did his best to woo her," Daisy said. "He's one of the reasons we can't relocate just anywhere."

"He's rather large," John offered. "Too large."

"Don't say anything bad about my Romeo!" Nola said, and she looked as if she might cry. Daisy shot John a look, and he quickly apologized to Nola and patted Romeo's head.

"The thing is, we *are* a team," Daisy said, fiercely. "We go together. Everywhere."

And they had most likely been coached by Daisy to say all those things, to try to make him feel guilty. Daisy had her game on, all right.

"It's very nice that you're a team," Parker said, feeling a reluctant hint of admiration for Daisy's devotion to her aging friends. "But it's not really my concern."

"Mr. Sutcliffe," Daisy said, moving forward, and now all of that luscious flesh and intensity was much closer to him. His chest felt a bit tight.

Irrelevant, he told himself. He'd made some mistakes with women before, but getting any more involved with Daisy than he already was would be a much bigger mistake than he'd ever made…for so many reasons. Besides, she didn't exactly like him. And that wasn't going to change. He was still selling the building. In the end, she would have to leave her home.

Parker looked down into her unhappy brown eyes. He knew that his own were cold. He'd been told that before.

Daisy blew out a frustrated breath. Then she turned and whispered something in John's ear. Together the three elderly people and the dog wandered back into the other part of the house. "They can't go just anywhere," she said, fiercely. "Between them they don't have enough money to survive."

"You're the money-maker?"

"I work two part-time jobs, and between them and the chapel, we make enough to keep us from starving, but that wouldn't be true if we moved somewhere else. Besides, this place gives their lives meaning."

Parker looked around at the wedding chapel, a study in cotton-candy pink and white.

"A wedding chapel *doesn't* fit your image, does it?" she asked.

He wasn't going to lie. "It's definitely outside my realm of experience. My father built Sutcliffe Industries brick by brick, banking on a name, a reputation and a fortune that goes back generations. All my energies go toward making the business a success. And while we started out in the beverage industry and have our fingers in many pies, at the heart of the business is the subsidiary that provides luxury accommodations for people who happen to like their entertainment sanitized and their lives shielded from anything…"

"Common?" Daisy gestured to the slightly gaudy chapel.

"I'm not judging you, Daisy. I'm merely saying that I'm not planning on changing my line of work. Right now I'm on the cusp of an expansion into new territory, and that's the only business I'm interested in. Still, I'll do this much. I'll give you a little time. Two weeks. That should give you enough breathing room to find a new home and make some new plans."

She looked at him as if she had just found out that he was really a vampire intent on drinking her blood. He'd never had a woman look at him with that much distaste.

It shouldn't have mattered.

It did, but that still didn't change things. He'd learned at a young age how dangerous it was simply to follow one's emotions and impulses. He wasn't doing it. Not ever again.

"Two weeks rent-free," he reiterated. "And I'll get someone—a professional—to help you relocate."

Her shoulders slumped. "I thought you might have a change of heart. They're fragile."

"I see that they're fragile," he told her. "I don't intend to harm them."

Despite his desire to remain uninvolved, he couldn't help being moved by the sadness in her voice and her concern for her friends. He felt an unfamiliar urge to make a promise that he couldn't possibly keep, to tell her that her world wouldn't change. But he knew all too well how damaging lies could be. He resisted the urge to touch her.

"This is the only home they've known for years," Daisy said. "They fit here. They don't fit just anywhere. They're not interchangeable parts that you can plug into any old socket."

She was reproaching him. He couldn't blame her, not when she was clearly in pain. Still, he wasn't going to defend himself, either. That had never been his way.

"We'll find a suitable place. Or two," he said. "In a month it will be just like home to all of you. Better than this place."

She stared at him with those big accusing eyes and he felt as if a part of him he didn't even recognize had been seared. But he knew better than to let regret or...or feelings enter into this. That path offered nothing but disaster.

"I'll help you, Daisy," he reiterated. "Because you can't stay here. I'll be leaving soon, and when I go, this building will be empty and it will be sold."

Daisy stood there and stared at him as if she were taking a beating, not moving, not talking, just...letting his words rain down on her. But at last she gave a brief nod. "You didn't come to Las Vegas for us. You came because Tillie died and her property passed to you. You'll want to see what she left you," she whispered. "I'll take you there now. I'm afraid there's not much in the way of personal treasure."

For some reason he was reluctant to follow Daisy, even though this was one of the main reasons why he was here. After all, this building was her home even if she had no legal right to be here. Still, he couldn't allow himself to be sentimental. He needed to put Daisy on his checklist the way he put all his tasks on lists. In order of priority. Right now, finding her and the others a new home was high on the list of things he needed to check off. Discovering all he could about his aunt was up there, too. He wasn't really looking forward to either of those, but at least tending to Daisy and her situation and digging into his aunt's past was a respite from the board trying to entice him with every debutante in Boston. Right?

He gazed down at Daisy. Had he been staring at her for long? She was blushing prettily, that delicious rose color heating her cheeks, her chest and dipping beneath the bodice of her dress…

"Parker?"

He jerked to attention. Caught. "Sorry. My mind was wandering."

She raised an eyebrow.

"I was thinking about real estate," he lied. "The agent… I'll send one here tomorrow. You should compose a list of requirements…anything an agent should know about your needs."

"Such as how many bedrooms?"

"Yes. Such as that, and whether stairs are a concern. For Nola."

"I'm surprised you care."

Parker took a deep breath. "It's not caring," he insisted. "It's common sense. I told you that I'm all business, no sentiment."

"So you *don't* want to see any of Tillie's things before you tear the building down?"

Wrong. He very much wanted—and needed—to see Tillie's things. Not for sentimental reasons, but for business ones. But he wouldn't tell Daisy that. Tillie had been her friend, and she wouldn't want to know that his chief interest in his aunt was protecting his business from... whatever it was that had made his parents turn their backs on her. There was something hidden, something unacceptable. What was it? What had Mathilda done that had gotten her shunned? Knowing how his parents had been, it could have been anything. They both excelled at shunning people. There would be dirt, of course, but it might not even be very bad dirt. It didn't take much...

"Show me," he said. And then, looking into Daisy's eyes and realizing how cold and imperious that had sounded, he added, "Please show me."

"All right. It's just at the top of the stairs." She turned and began to lead him into the hallway that separated the two buildings. There was a set of stairs there and Daisy led the way.

Her hips swayed before him, and he did his best to put a leash on the quite natural heat that inspired. Instead he tried to concentrate on other things...such as her posture. Her back was very straight, very rigid and he knew that she didn't like doing this one bit. She didn't really want him to look at his aunt's belongings.

"Daisy," he said softly. "I promise I won't do anything drastic today."

Daisy suddenly stopped on the stairs in front of him, and he bumped into her, nearly knocking her forward. Automatically, he looped his arm around her waist to steady her.

That brought her body fully against his, and the soft give

of her flesh beneath his palm made his pulse quicken. Her pretty little butt was up against him, his chest against her back. Intimate. His body reacted. Instantly.

Wrong.

He hurried to steady and release her. "Are you all right?"

She nodded, but her back had become even more rigid, if that was possible. "I hadn't thought about the fact that you would probably pitch all of Tillie's stuff."

He wanted to tell her that he wouldn't, that she could have it, but…how did he know that? *Stuff* could be hard evidence and could be used against a person.

"We'll see what's there, but I won't do anything right away. Today I'm just looking. All right?"

She nodded, but her body radiated tension, possibly even anger. At the top of the stairs, Daisy pushed on a door that creaked as it opened. She flipped on a light switch and motioned Parker inside. Immediately, a sparkle caught his eye and he turned his gaze to the other side of the room where several clothing racks stood end to end. One of them contained nondescript middle-aged-woman outfits in cheap fabrics. The other two sparkled and glittered with sequins and fake jewels. Some of the outfits sported feathers. All of them were barely there.

He whirled and looked at Daisy. "These were…my aunt's? She was a…"

Daisy placed one hand on her hips. "Tillie was a showgirl, among other things." And then she must have noticed his confused look. What did *among other things* mean?

"Hmmm, I'll bet *that* won't play very well in Boston," she said. "Or with those luxury-seeking customers who like things sanitized."

He stepped forward, then froze. "Are you threatening me, Daisy?"

"Threatening?" Looking down at her wide, startled eyes,

he realized that he had been wrong. She hadn't been. And now, once again, he was close enough to touch her. That couldn't keep happening.

"No, of course not," he said, backing off. "But you said…among other things. What else was she?" His breath lifted a loose lock of hair at her temple.

Daisy reached out as if to touch him…or push him away, he didn't know which. "I'm not sure I can explain what Tillie was, and—" She took a big step back. Two steps. One more and she would be tumbling backward down the stairs.

He reached out to catch her again, but she shook her head as she turned and started down the stairs. "I have to go to work," she said. "I have a tour group, and we have another wedding tonight and one tomorrow."

And she fled down the stairs.

A short time later he sat staring at a fairly recent diary that—despite the fact that large parts of the book were still blank—left no doubt about at least some of his aunt's past indiscretions and colorful lifestyle. He was wondering what he should do with the damning book.

No doubt he should pitch it, burn it, shred it. He'd think about that.

But the beep of his cell phone reminded him that this trip—and Daisy—were just detours from his real life. Fran's text message that Jarrod was trying to finagle Parker's private phone number in order to discuss some of the female guests the board wanted to invite to the annual Sutcliffe Industries Ball was a reminder of just how intent Parker's relative-heavy board was on turning him into a living billboard for the company. They wanted him to adopt the role his father had taken as the aristocratic symbol of Sutcliffe's, a sort of Prince Charming waltzing to the Wedding March, all for the sake of marketing. If he was going to come up with a better alternative to pull Sutcliffe's out of its slump and make it a household name for the elite, he needed to come up with a brilliant plan fast. Only two things stood in the way of him devoting all of his time to finding that plan: his aunt and one caramel-eyed pixie with flowers between her pink toes.

"So do your research on Mathilda and find Daisy a viable home and get her off your plate," he ordered himself. "Quickly."

Good advice. With a little luck and a good real estate agent, Daisy and her "team" would be stirring up trouble for someone else soon. And he would have forgotten that he'd ever met her.

CHAPTER THREE

DAISY waited until Parker had left the building before she slipped back inside. She had lied about her tour. It had been canceled. That was money she couldn't afford to lose, but right now she was more concerned about what Parker Sutcliffe meant to her and her friends...and her child.

She didn't want to think about how crazy he made her feel whenever he got too close to her. Letting herself be even mildly attracted to the man could only end badly.

Sure, Parker was being nice by letting them live rent-free while he helped them find a place, but they were worlds apart, he was eager to get away and she had already had far too much experience with men who didn't stay.

Even more important, she was still getting used to the scary reality that she would soon be the source of... everything for a totally helpless baby. So, for now, for the sake of the others and her baby, she would accept Parker's help, but it had to be temporary. This situation was just more proof that she needed to become completely independent. No leaning on a man, no wanting a man. She had to make something better for her child, to find a secure full-time job and build a protective cocoon around herself and her baby. Getting dreamy about a rich guy who was on his way back to his rich world and his rich, sophisticated, not-pregnant women would be totally irresponsible. And irresponsible was number two on her list of things she didn't do anymore.

Number one was putting her trust in a man. She thought of that when Lydia asked her why she hadn't told Parker that she was pregnant.

"You should tell him," Lydia said. "You're not showing yet, but if you told him, maybe he would…"

Daisy shook her head vehemently. "He wouldn't understand. His type doesn't. And if he finds out about my past or thinks too hard about the fact that we're breaking the law by being here, he might report me as an unfit mother or something like that. Then I couldn't keep the baby." The thought terrified her.

"So…what are we going to do?" John asked.

Daisy took a deep breath, trying for the thousandth time not to panic at the thought of how dependent her friends were and how afraid she was of failing them. She wondered if Tillie had felt this way. For half a second she wondered if Parker felt that way right now, and she almost felt sorry for the man. He hadn't asked to have them all dumped on him. But she had no time to mull that over. John was waiting.

"Well," Daisy said, putting on her what-would-Tillie-do? thinking cap. "First I'm going to go be sick. No big deal. Just morning sickness. The usual. And then we're going to get ready for tomorrow's wedding."

The one thing Daisy could count on to take her mind off things was her role in planning the weddings. Even if she didn't want a wedding for herself, she loved planning weddings for others. The irony and sometimes the difficulty of creating weddings for people when she would never have a happily ever after didn't escape her. But she'd been helping Tillie since she was a teenager, and Tillie had loved weddings. Creating special ones made Daisy feel a connection to Tillie. And the next one was a fairy-tale wedding. Literally. Tillie's favorite and hers. Trying to forget her own troubles, she threw herself into planning a personalized ceremony.

It was only when Daisy got to the part where the groom/prince was supposed to say his special vows and take the bride in his arms that she suddenly remembered how she'd felt when Parker had caught her in his arms to keep her from falling. She'd leaned back against his chest, she'd felt his big palms on her body and—

Daisy's pen slid across the page. "Darn it! You wanted him to turn you around and kiss you. Having felt his hands, you wanted to know how his mouth felt, too, didn't you?"

Maybe. For sure she'd wanted to kiss *him*. It was a horrifying thought, except…it also made her smile. What would stuffy Parker Sutcliffe do if someone like her wrapped herself around him and kissed him?

Probably have her arrested. Or put her out on the street right now.

And that was just one of the many reasons why she had to stay away from Parker's body. The most important reason was…more basic.

Daisy glanced down at her abdomen. "I don't know how much you can absorb at this point," she told her unborn child. "But I want you to know that while you might not have had the best of beginnings—and I'm taking my share of responsibility for that—I'm glad that you're here and I will do everything possible to make sure that you have a stable life. I'm going to do my best never to do anything irresponsible like falling for men who might hurt us. So you should know right now that except for Nola and Lydia and John, it will always just be you and me, but that's okay. We'll be together and we'll be fine on our own. I'll see to it."

Still, Daisy sighed slightly at the thought of never being able to satisfy her curiosity about Parker's lips. And then, frowning, she pushed that thought aside. And went back to her planning. When she read through her notes later, she realized that in the midst of them she had written "No kissing."

That might be a problem at a wedding, she conceded as she crossed out the word *no* and replaced it with *lots of.*

Lips would be touching at this wedding. Just not hers and Parker's.

Parker wasn't happy when he approached Daisy's building the next afternoon. He opened the front door. Didn't they ever lock anything? Didn't they have any idea about basic safety? Adding a lock and a doorbell system? Anyone could walk right in and be inside the building that led to their living space and what would one petite woman and three senior citizens do if that happened?

He frowned, reminding himself that all of that would be moot soon. Besides, why was he even having those kinds of thoughts? Daisy was a stranger, one he really didn't want to know. Certainly, he didn't want to feel any sense of responsibility for her, did he?

"Uh-oh. The real estate agent must have told you something awful." Daisy's soft voice came from behind the piano, making him blink.

He walked over to the old, battered upright and found her sifting through sheet music. "Why would you say that?"

"Well, for one thing you're here when I hadn't expected to see you. And you're also frowning, but then..."

Right. He'd been frowning a lot lately. "Yes, well I do have some bad news. You were right. The agent said that the apartment hunt might be a challenge. She also suggested that you...consider ditching the dog if at all possible. It's definitely easier to place tenants without pets or children."

Daisy gave a tight nod. "So I hear." Her voice came out as a whisper. She turned away a bit. "What did you tell her?"

He hesitated. "I told her to keep looking." He didn't mention that the woman had told him that a landlord would most likely charge extra for the animal, which might make the price prohibitively expensive for Daisy. Or that the woman had insisted on giving him numbers of prospective shelters. Daisy might be an unwelcome impediment to his plans, but...she was here. He might not be capable of the deeper emotions other people felt, but he also tried to avoid trampling on those feelings whenever possible.

For some reason, he was pretty sure that Daisy would feel things multiplied by three. Which made dealing with her three times more difficult, especially since, sooner or later, she would probably have to face the fact that Romeo would need a new owner. Why he was putting off the inevitable when he didn't have time to waste was a mystery to him, one he didn't want to examine too closely. The answer was probably complicated, and he couldn't afford complications here. Still...

"We'll keep looking," he repeated.

"Thank you," she said, but her voice still sounded slightly faint. "Hopefully, we can find something quickly, and you and I can get past this and end our association."

"That was...very polite. I know that you don't like this situation any more than I do."

"No. I don't like being indebted to anyone and I'm not happy about the situation, but I appreciate the fact that you had the right to kick us out immediately and you didn't."

"Maybe I just didn't want my name splashed all over

the headlines as a greedy jerk who threw old people out on the street."

She blinked as if she'd never thought of that, and he almost wanted to smile.

"I never thought of that," she said, confirming his suspicions. "Is that why you let us stay?"

"I don't know." It was true. The thought had certainly crossed his mind, but he wasn't certain it was the only reason, and, like so many things with Daisy, the truth was complicated. Parker wished he'd stop having that thought. He grimaced.

She nodded. "Okay. I won't probe. Was that all you came for? To tell me about Romeo?"

"Not exactly." After his brief foray into Aunt Mathilda's possessions, he'd concluded that there was little of her history to be found here. Absolutely nothing about her link to his family. The diary seemed to point to a chaotic life, but it had been written recently, and most recently his aunt had been running a chapel and housing Daisy and her crew. Nothing was clear...which might slow down his investigation. It also made her more interesting: a secret puzzle piece from his past, but also a possible Pandora's box.

"I'd like to ask you some questions about my aunt."

She put down the sheet music she was holding. "Of course. Tillie was my favorite person in the whole world."

Which probably meant that Daisy wouldn't be telling him the kinds of things he wanted to know. It also probably meant that, given some of his reasons for wanting information on Tillie, tossed together with his relocation plans for Daisy, he might rank as Daisy's least favorite person.

The thought surprised him. Given his nature, he was used to people not warming up to him. He seldom cared... or even thought about it. Daisy, unfortunately, with her passionate loyalty to her friends and her eyes that seemed to be a window to every volatile emotion she possessed, had a way of making him look inward. He definitely didn't like that. It wasn't productive, and it wasn't helping him do the things he needed to do in order to move on to more important matters.

"Where can we talk?" he asked. They were still in the chapel, and anyone could walk in. "And don't you ever worry about intruders? Your door appears to be open all the time."

Daisy shrugged. "It's a wedding chapel. If we don't keep the door open, people take their business elsewhere. We do what's necessary to keep our custom...to keep people happy."

"I don't have anything against the word *customers*."

"I do. The people who come here are making a very personal decision. They don't think of it as buying something even if money is exchanged."

"And yet you almost used the word *customers*, a word that I would use."

She shrugged. "Maybe you're a bad influence on me. I'm a little more fixated on money today than I would normally be."

Because he had made her look at the going rate of apartments. Parker felt a twinge at that. He'd also felt a jolt, a slightly erotic jolt, when she'd said that he might be a bad influence on her. It was obvious that he was far too physically attracted to her.

"I won't tell anyone that you used the c-word."

She rolled her eyes at him. "It's a perfectly fine word and I used to use it, but it just doesn't apply here. Tillie was the one who showed me how important these weddings are. They're life-changing events. Emotional events. Sometimes I feel guilty taking people's money at all."

Parker almost groaned. How was Daisy ever going to

survive in a world where apartments cost money if she felt guilty taking money for services rendered? The businessman in him wanted to take her in hand and teach her about the world of finance. But he quickly nixed that idea. He was already wasting too much time here, and she clearly didn't want to spend any more time with him than she had to.

"Let's talk about Tillie," he said, getting back to the subject at hand.

She nodded. "We'll go into the garden."

He assumed she meant the patch of grass where they had held the reception yesterday.

"What do you know about my aunt?" he asked as he followed her into the small garden. The sun was at full tilt today, the tables were gone, and he could see now that the "garden" was really a bit of sleight of hand. There was an inexpensive green indoor-outdoor carpet with tiny patches of grass here and there at the edges, grass being a luxury in this desert environment. Pots of succulents and fake flowers were strategically placed, all of which created an illusion of a garden where there was, in fact, very little garden at all.

"I know she was a very generous woman," Daisy said.

Okay, this was going to be difficult. But what had he expected? Daisy had obviously loved his aunt.

"Tell me…how long were you with my aunt?"

"Since I was sixteen. Nine years."

He blinked. "Sixteen? How…was Mathilda a foster parent?"

Daisy laughed. "She would have liked that title. But no, she was just a woman who saw a kid headed toward major trouble."

He waited.

She stared him directly in the eyes, then took a deep

breath as she looked to the side. "I have a record, Parker. I did time in juvenile detention and I was wandering the streets and well on my way toward going back there again when Tillie took me in. I don't like sharing my past, but if you're digging up information on Tillie, my record will probably pop up. I don't hide it. I just don't advertise it. The point is, if you want to know about Tillie, it's important to know how generous she was. She took all of us in."

Parker felt as if the breath had been knocked out of him. "You're telling me that all of you are offenders?"

Those pretty brown eyes blinked wide. "No. Just me. The others had other issues. Homelessness, that kind of thing. Tillie saved us."

She was painting his aunt as an angel, but there had been Daisy's *She was a showgirl, among other things* comment yesterday. There had been that diary...and the fact that Mathilda's name had been erased from his family's history books. "I'm glad my aunt helped you, but..."

Daisy looked directly into his eyes. "But?"

"She couldn't have been a saint."

To his surprise, Daisy laughed, a totally enchanting sound. A thought which had no place here, he reminded himself. "Tillie would have been horrified to think that anyone thought of her as a saint."

"Did she have a criminal record?" He fired the question.

Daisy didn't look away, but those eyes... "I don't know."

Those eyes of hers didn't lie well. She knew something, and she wasn't telling. Even though she had just told him that if he went looking, her own juvenile record would pop up, she was hiding his aunt's record. He understood why—Daisy was loyal—but lies...how he hated lies. Lies had nearly cost him...so much.

"I read her diary," he said.

"I don't think any of that was real."

"Why not?"

"Tillie wasn't the type to brag about her exploits or past indiscretions."

"But a diary isn't exactly bragging, is it? It's a personal journal, purging one's soul."

Daisy took several steps closer, those brown eyes flashing fire. "I know that we owe you, Mr. Sutcliffe. You've generously overlooked the fact that we've stolen from you by trespassing here. If you wanted to have us thrown in jail, well, maybe you could, so don't get me wrong. I'm incredibly grateful that you've acted with restraint and for the fact that you're letting us stay here a little longer and helping us find a new home. No matter your reasons, it's... nice of you. But I thought you wanted to know about my Tillie, the woman I knew. Instead, it sounds as if you just want to dig up dirt on her."

They stood toe to toe now, Daisy looking straight up into his eyes. If she wanted to, she could strike him—and she looked like she wanted to. If he wanted to, he could kiss her, and even angry as she was, even throwing accusations at his head—or maybe because of how magnificently she was doing that—he wanted to feel her mouth beneath his. He'd never cared what people thought of him. He'd disengaged from those kinds of feelings at an early age, but—

"I don't just want to dig up dirt on Tillie. She's a missing part of my family history. I want to know everything."

Daisy's angry look deflated. She seemed to sink, just a bit. "Because you care about her."

It was tempting, so tempting to lie. Electricity was arcing between them. He knew that all he had to do was agree with her, and she might lean closer. He could taste those lips.

Slowly he shook his head. "I don't really know enough to care. But...I run a company, one whose reputation rises or falls on a tide of public approval. And I *don't* know why my mother's sister's existence was a total secret."

"You think that there's something about Tillie that could make your stock plummet?"

He opened his mouth to tell her that that was already happening, then closed it again. He was asking her to spill her secrets, but he never spilled his. And nothing had changed about that.

"I don't like having unknown variables," he said.

"All right," she said slowly.

"All right?"

"I suppose that if the reason for your interest in Tillie is your company's reputation, that you won't be sharing any of her secrets with the world?"

Her comment came out sounding more like a question. He raised one eyebrow. "Are you interrogating me, Daisy?"

"I'm in no position to interrogate the man who holds the deed to this property, but...yes, maybe I am. A little."

He nodded abruptly. "Okay, that's an honest response. So...no, I don't intend to share my aunt's past indiscretions, if any exist. I intend to bury them. Very deeply."

"For the sake of the company, not her."

He didn't bother answering. She didn't bother telling him, as other women had, that he was cold. Not that it would have made a bit of difference. He did what he needed to do.

Daisy let out a breath and stepped away. "I'll tell you what I know, but frankly, it's not that much. Because everyone here has a past, we didn't talk about our pasts. Frankly, even being associated with us might sully your company, Parker. You probably won't want to stay long."

"I don't intend to. Just until I've done what I came to do."

To his surprise, she smiled. "Getting rid of us being one of those things?"

He couldn't hide his amused expression. "I might not put it quite that way."

"Um. Bad for business to be that frank."

He wasn't denying it. People's main complaint with him was that he was restrained, not that he was tactless.

"Tell me what you know, Daisy," he said, his voice coming out a bit too deep, too much like a man asking a woman to take their relationship to a more intimate level.

He saw her visibly swallow. "I will, but not now."

"Excuse me?"

"I just heard a bell go off in the house. That means that we have only fifteen minutes before the next wedding begins. And I'm not dressed."

"Dressed?"

"Yes." She turned to go, then turned back. "You want to know more about Tillie? Then watch a couple of our weddings. There's a lot of Tillie in them."

She whirled away again, then stopped. Her body looked as if she was on the verge of crumpling.

"Daisy?" Parker reached her in two strides. She had her hands on her knees and she looked pale. "Are you all right?"

Of course she wasn't all right. All the color had leached from her face.

She held out one limp hand. "I'm…fine. Just dizzy. I turned too fast."

He started to reach for her, but she shook her head, a small, tight movement. "Got to go. Now." And she bolted.

He found John a few minutes later, and the man told him that Daisy was fine. But the man never looked directly at him, and Parker couldn't help thinking that something was very wrong here.

The thought almost made him laugh. Alarm bells had been going off in his head ever since he had first stepped into this chapel and been accosted by Daisy. This trip wasn't turning out at all as he had anticipated. So far it had been a disaster.

He hadn't discovered anything useful about his aunt and he had a building and tenants who were proving to be a distraction from his main goals. What was worse, he very desperately wanted to kiss Daisy, a woman with a juvenile record, a woman the board would most definitely not approve of. The only good thing, given the state of his company, the fact that another day had passed without him coming up with any earth-shattering ideas to save Sutcliffe's and the fact that his cousin Jarrod had started having Fran send him photos of prospective brides on his cell phone, was that things couldn't get much worse. Could they?

CHAPTER FOUR

DAISY blew out a breath as she got into her costume for the wedding. She wished that her morning sickness was more dependable. At least then she could plan for it. She'd almost betrayed herself with Parker, and their situation was bad enough without him finding out that she was going to have a baby. She was pretty sure that he wouldn't be pleased about adding a child to their apartment-hunting difficulties. He was being incredibly patient, but she wasn't going to fool herself. If she became too much trouble, he might turn everything over to his attorneys or the authorities and then where would she and her baby and friends be?

The man wanted her gone. And despite the fact—or maybe because of the fact—that she got lost in those green eyes every time she looked at him, she wanted *him* gone. Nothing good could come of an anti-marriage, elite corporate baron and a pregnant, former juvenile delinquent and trespasser spending time together, and the person most at risk was her…and her child. The only clear way out of this horrid situation was for her to somehow earn more money so that they could afford lodgings they were entitled to, ones with no connection to Parker.

She would have to shut down the chapel and find full-time work. Her heart ached at the thought. This chapel had become her home, a place where she had purpose. It was her and her friends' world.

And at least for today, she was still here, she reminded herself. And she had a wedding to tend to.

And Parker was most likely attending that wedding.

"Stop that," she muttered. The man might have gorgeous eyes, a jaw made for a woman's palm and a mouth that made her ache, but those were warning signs. They were keep-away-or-you're-going-to-get-hurt signs. And the fact that he was giving them more time instead of insisting that they get rid of their dog?

Nice but irrelevant. Christopher had comforted her after Tillie's death, but it had been a mistake to let her emotions cloud her common sense or to put her trust in a man. Once she'd gotten past her deepest hurt at Tillie's loss and realized how irrationally she'd acted in her grief, she'd been pregnant and alone. And scared. "But I can't afford to dwell on that," she reminded herself. "You're here," she whispered to her baby. "And I'm not going to fail you. You and me. Remember?"

Exactly. So while she was grateful for Parker's restraint, she wasn't leaning again.

Good, she thought. *Let's go make a wedding and forget that Parker even exists.*

She stepped forward and into the chapel. Immediately something felt different. More…charged.

"Are you wearing…what on earth are you wearing?" Parker's low voice came directly from her left, not two feet away, and Daisy nearly jumped out of her shoes. She'd known he would be here, but she hadn't expected him to be this close…or to speak to her. But then, the darn man had a disconcerting way of sneaking up on her, both in person and in her thoughts.

"What am I wearing?" she asked. Daisy looked down

at her costume, although she knew what she would see. It was better than looking at Parker and getting lost in those eyes again. "It's a Snow White wedding," she said. "One of our more popular themes."

"I see." Although she could tell by his slightly confused expression that he didn't see at all.

"Snow White not one of your favorite stories? I rather like it and identify with it myself. Snow White had loyal friends," Daisy said.

To her surprise, Parker smiled. "I wasn't criticizing Snow White. Believe it or not, I was a kid once, too. My nannies showed me all the requisite movies. I wasn't hatched at a bank."

Daisy couldn't resist an answering smile. "So you weren't the result of a stock merger?" She didn't comment on the fact that he'd mentioned movies and not books. Did rich kids have story time the way poor ones did? Even her own less-than-award-winning mother had made the attempt once or twice.

"Not the result of a stock merger? I wouldn't say that exactly." And this time he didn't smile. Well, what had she expected? Once a decade was probably all Parker could manage. More than that and his stockholders...or whatever...would start worrying that he was going crazy.

"My immediate confusion was because you're not dressed as Snow White," he mused. "So I take it that you're one of her...um...friends." The way he raised one eyebrow...there was something very intimate about that gesture, wasn't there? Something very knowing, very masculine. It made a woman want to check her lipstick. Except she wasn't wearing any, or any other makeup, either.

"I'm one of the seven dwarfs." And she was feeling rather frumpy in her loose-fitting brown costume and mad at herself for feeling that way just because Parker had raised his eyebrow when he'd looked at her.

He nodded. "Did you put this costume together yourself? It's very detailed." He reached out and touched the pick in the low-slung belt she was wearing. It was the most casual of touches, and there were layers of clothing between his flesh and hers. She couldn't even feel it, really, but he was standing so close...

Her heart rate picked up. "Yes," was all she could get out.

He drew his hand back, looking daggers at his append-age as if his fingers had acted of their own volition. Clearly he wasn't happy that their bodies had met again. "And this is a popular wedding?" he asked, just as if personal contact had never taken place.

Well, if he could ignore it, so could she. "Yes. Why do you ask?"

"No reason. I'm just...interested in how other business people present their products."

So there had been nothing personal about his touch at all. Daisy should have felt relieved that they were back on a more casual footing—and she did—but she also felt some-thing else. It couldn't be disappointment, could it? Because being disappointed that his touch had been the result of his interest in her...her *product* rather than in her as a woman was just insane. She should be happy that they had found some common ground, and she was, wasn't she? She fully intended to follow his lead and be one-hundred-percent business.

"I try to make each costume as authentic as possi-ble. Tillie used to make them before her fingers became arthritic. Now Nola and I do the sewing. We shop for props at garage sales and thrift stores. Details are important, especially for weddings like this. Children are very tough critics."

Parker froze. That was the best description Daisy could give. He looked directly into her eyes. "Children?"

Uh-oh. "Yes. We do a lot of second marriages, and either the bride or groom or both have children. They like having them be a part of the ceremony."

"So you include them." It was more a statement than a question.

"Don't worry. I'm pretty good at shepherding children. They won't get close to you. I'm fully aware that not everyone likes kids."

Now, he looked slightly angry. "I don't dislike them. Just because I don't intend to have any children of my own doesn't mean I have anything against them."

"No children? Won't you want an heir? I mean, you're rich, your father built the company and you'll want to pass all that inherited history and wealth along to family, right?"

Daisy recoiled from the look he gave her. "I apologize. That was rude beyond belief," she said. "Tillie always told me that I was too direct. It's absolutely none of my business what you do with your company or whether you have children."

The anger died in his eyes. "No, it was my fault. I was the one who blurted out my intention to remain childless, which was…crude of me. Let's just say that I have my reasons, and none of them have anything to do with disliking children. But I'm not good with them, not comfortable. Children are sparse in my family. We seem to produce only the requisite amount so that the business never goes to the wrong people. All pregnancies are carefully thought out and planned. Purely business decisions. Very…efficient. It's the Sutcliffe way. In my case, I have a cousin and he has one child. No heirs are needed."

"Okay." Daisy nodded shakily at Parker's version of family planning. She wanted to shield her abdomen to protect her baby from such harsh comments. Producing babies only when absolutely necessary for business purposes? How cold. And yet…was it any worse than producing a child by accident?

No. Not when an accidental pregnancy resulted in a fatherless child. Parker might not want children, but she was pretty sure that he wouldn't father and then abandon a child, if only because it wouldn't play well to potential customers. She was also positive that he would be appalled at her accidentally pregnant state. It was definitely not the Sutcliffe way.

At that moment, Lydia began to play the light, airy tune that signaled the beginning of the wedding. "Better retreat," Daisy whispered to Parker. "Here come the children."

She held out her hands and looked to either side, her signal to the bride's children to join her in their matching dwarf costumes. As the three little boys, one barely a toddler holding on to his brother's hand, skipped in to meet her and to begin the procession down the aisle, she couldn't help noticing that Parker had indeed retreated but only halfway down the pew.

Smiling into his eyes, she was met with a haughty stare. Oh, the man didn't like the fact that he wasn't comfortable with kids.

But that doesn't change reality, Daisy. He isn't comfortable and he won't be having children. You, with your baby on the way, would probably be his idea of a nightmare.

Parker tried not to pay too much attention to Daisy. He was sitting through this wedding only so that he could continue interviewing her about Tillie after the ceremony was over, wasn't he?

Still, she looked incredibly cute in that baggy outfit and she was difficult to ignore. The hood was supposed to hide her red curls, but they kept slipping out. There was just something about her that practically glowed. He couldn't seem to stop watching her.

Which wasn't a good thing. He was here to observe the proceedings. That was all. Still, when the toddler fell going down the aisle, sprawling with his chubby arms and legs splayed, it was clear that there were going to be tears, a halt in the proceedings and a bit of drama. Without so much as missing a step, Daisy reached down, scooped the little boy into her arms, whispered something against his cheek and they all kept proceeding, all of which made Snow White, moving to meet her groom, smile more broadly.

At the front of the chapel, as the ceremony began, Daisy seemed to be everywhere, making sure that the children were settled, cueing Nola and John and Lydia, who were also dressed as part of the Seven Dwarfs entourage, making sure that everything went according to plan as Snow White and her prince went through a brief enactment of the story and the waking kiss and then recited their vows. And yet for all of her work, Daisy made herself seem almost invisible. Only someone watching her closely—as Parker was—would note all that she was accomplishing.

Not that his reasons for watching her were anything other than business, he reminded himself. He was merely observing an apparently accomplished micromanager do her job efficiently. It was always a good idea to keep tabs on exemplary business practices. And that was the only reason he even noticed when Daisy suddenly looked a bit strained and pale just as John pronounced the couple man and wife and the music began to play. She bent slightly, placing her hands on her knees, then righted herself.

Parker knew that Daisy would be rushing off to organize and oversee the reception, but her expression...

He slid to the edge of the pew and strode down the side aisle, Daisy in his sights. Before he could reach her, though, a heavily made-up thirtyish blond woman sitting in the first pew cut him off. "Well, I thought I knew everyone here, but I don't know you. I would definitely remember you if we'd ever met. Do you work for the chapel?"

"No, I'm sorry, but I don't." He started to continue on his way.

"Well, in that case, let me introduce myself. I'm Miriam. The bride's sister. It was a glorious wedding, wasn't it?"

Parker wouldn't know. He didn't consider himself a judge of such things, but he also didn't intend to sabotage his temporary tenants who seemed to need this money. "Unique," he agreed.

She smiled one of those toothpaste-commercial smiles. "I know," she said, clutching his sleeve. "Wasn't it just precious? And the way she gave all of the children parts to play? Don't you just love children, Mr....?"

"Sutcliffe," he said automatically. "It was very nice meeting you, but if you'll excuse me, I need to go...help with the reception."

The woman looked confused. No doubt because he had just told her that he didn't work here. But then he was confused, too. Why should he care if Daisy looked ill?

I'm not a monster, he reminded himself. And yet when he saw the children standing directly in his path en route to Daisy, and the cherub smiling up at him, a child with a child's naive expectations that knew nothing of adult failings or shortcomings, he forced himself to smile back. A strained smile.

The little boy seemed to take that as an invitation. On chubby, tottering legs, he walked up to Parker and tugged on his pants leg as if trying to get him to lean down. When Parker didn't comply, the child leaned back and looked at him. His big, blue eyes looked puppy-sad, as if he couldn't understand why this big person would ignore him. "Pease," he said, tugging again.

Visions of his own father walking away from him slammed through Parker's mind. His father had always been walking away. Or worse. And the child looked as if he might crumple. "Pease," he said, cramming his fingers in his mouth.

What could a guy do? Parker awkwardly went down on one knee. "What's wrong?" he asked.

The little boy pulled his wet hand from his mouth and patted Parker's tie. "House," he said, and Parker realized that the Sutcliffe logo, a hotel, on his shiny tie tack had caught the child's eye.

"House," Parker agreed, not knowing what else to say. He tentatively patted the child on the head. Hell, he was so bad at this.

"There you are, you little munchkin," the Snow White bride said, picking up her child. She gave Parker a smile, then moved away.

He wanted to breathe a sigh of relief. He might not be a monster, but he was incapable of the types of emotions other people had every right to expect. He could still see the distress in the child's eyes when he'd been ignored. He could remember what that type of indifference felt like.

"Parker? You look pale." Daisy's voice came from his right. He turned to her. She no longer looked ill.

"I'm fine." He gave the standard response.

She leaned back and raised a delicate eyebrow. "I'd say you've been slimed." She pointed to where the cherub's wet hand had made contact with his tie. "And your pants have cake on them again."

He looked down to see a large white smear.

"We certainly appear to be hazardous to your wardrobe," she said.

And my peace of mind, he thought, remembering the child, and now looking into Daisy's worried eyes.

"I have more suits."

"I'll just bet you do."

"You're not going to goad me," he said, and this time he managed a small smile.

"I saw you headed my way earlier. Were you looking for me?"

"Yes." But now that she looked all right, he didn't want to admit that he'd been worried about her.

She nodded. "I'll be done in about an hour. Then we can continue our talk about Tillie. That's what you wanted, wasn't it?"

"Of course," he said, and he tried to convince himself that the words were true. Lies of omission were still lies, and he'd always hated lies, especially since his disastrous relationship with Evelyn.

If ever a man didn't want to have children, Parker was the man, Daisy thought. He'd looked at that little boy as if he was a hand grenade with the pin removed. And she'd seen the bride's sister trying to glom on to him. The woman had looked as if she wanted to ask Parker to father her baby right there and then.

He'd politely extricated himself and moved on. That kind of thing must happen all the time. Well, it was good to know, wasn't it? The more she reminded herself of all the things that stood between herself and Parker, the less likely she would be to make an idiot of herself the way that woman had.

She even felt a little sorry for the woman. But not much.

The sister was seriously pretty. And she was still following Parker with her eyes every time he crossed the yard. Which he did often, since the bride and groom were so enthusiastic that they kept sending John to the office to retrieve more souvenir brochures and Parker somehow ended up directing people to the exit and the washroom.

"It appears that your wedding was a success," Parker said at her elbow, making frissons of awareness run down her spine. What was it about the man's voice that made her think seriously stupid thoughts? Like what Parker would look like if he ever took off that suit? Maybe she and the blond sister had more in common than she wanted to admit.

Daisy wanted to frown. Instead she pasted on a smile. There was no way she was ever going to let Parker know that she was just as susceptible as every other woman in the world.

"Yes, well, Snow White is always a big draw."

"I see that. A number of people seemed to want business cards. How many different types of weddings do you do?"

"Can't say. Sometimes I customize them. And each one is always a bit different even if it's not a custom job. Something unexpected always happens. You can't always plan for the best stuff. Or the worst."

"Like needing to soothe a child's tears during the procession?"

Why had he brought that up? "Oh, that was nothing. Small stuff."

"It didn't seem small to me, yet you handled it like a pro. So, what's the big stuff?"

She shrugged. "Fistfights. People who show up drunk. Brides or grooms that don't show. Or that leave in mid-ceremony."

"Does that happen often?"

"More than you would think. Especially the abandoned brides." She couldn't hold back her frown.

"What do you do then?"

"I try to console the bride and her family. As much as anyone can."

Parker was studying her too intently. She could only imagine that he not only had women drooling over him, he had walked away from his share...which made him an extremely bad choice of companion for a woman who had been abandoned as much as she had. "It sounds as if running a chapel is a challenge," he noted. "A woman working two jobs might start to feel the strain."

She looked up into his eyes. He'd apparently seen when she'd almost been sick again. She'd had to slip out and drink in big gulps of air, but she was better now. And she was not going to explain any part of that to him.

"I'm an adult, Parker. I know when I've overstepped my limits and how to handle the situation. Why do you care?"

He shook his head slowly. "I don't have the vaguest idea. But then I have lots of employees. I've been responsible for other people for years."

"I'm not your employee." She certainly didn't want anyone hanging around her out of some misguided sense of obligation.

"No, you're not my employee. You're my—"

"Thorn in the side," she offered, knowing that he disliked having tenants.

"I wouldn't have put it exactly like that," he said, but he didn't deny the truth of her flippant words, either.

"I could give the bride's sister your phone number. She wants to have babies with you. That would be a real thorn in the side. I just want to be able to continue conducting weddings in your chapel."

He smiled. He actually smiled. "Trying to paint yourself as the lesser of two evils, Daisy?"

"I'll do whatever it takes. What is it you want me to do?"

He stared at her...for too long. For half a second she was sure that he was looking at her lips. Suddenly she was aware that she had a woman's body beneath this baggy costume and she wanted to squirm. She felt the power of his gaze and understood why a man like this was able to run an empire. He'd probably been born with the ability to make people squirm and want to tell their secrets, to make women want to please him. If there was such a thing as royalty in the States, he would be it.

Parker sighed. "What do I want? What are you and I about? Tell me a Tillie story. I need to know things, and you seem to be the gate."

Daisy looked up at him. "Then I'd better go put on my gatekeeper costume." She held up her droopy sleeve. "I'll be back in ten, Parker. Just as soon as I clear all these fairy-tale people out of here, you and I will discuss reality."

And she would darn well keep her mind on reality, too. Reality was that Parker might be interested in her lips, but he didn't want to be. Reality might be that she was just as interested in his lips and arms and...everything, but she darn well couldn't afford to be. He was off limits and out of reach. He was man-dynamite for a woman like her, and her entire world would blow up in her face if she ever forgot that.

So, while she was gone, she gave herself two pep talks, assured her baby one more time that Parker would never, ever even come close to being her daddy and that that was a very good thing. She readied herself to be professional but distant.

And hoped that she could follow through on that.

CHAPTER FIVE

PARKER waited in the garden. He had turned his cell phone back on while Daisy went off to change. There were several voice mails and text messages from Fran. Apparently Jarrod and the board had decided to take things to the next level and were planning on bombarding him with debutantes at the annual Sutcliffe ball. This year's ball was being held just before the opening of the new spa complex three weeks from now, an attempt to build to a crescendo. Obviously the board thought that if he could just single out one perfect socially prominent woman at the ball, the speculation about the budding relationship and, hopefully, hints about a possible Sutcliffe bride combined with the new spa complex would vault Sutcliffe's back onto its pedestal.

He hated the idea. But he'd been here in Vegas for several days and he hadn't come up with a better one. Moreover, he hadn't really even learned anything about Tillie and his family's secrets. Her past was obviously a bit wicked, but not so much so that he could see any reason to blot her name from the family tree. There had to be something more significant and possibly damaging to his family or business in her history.

Daisy was the key, he thought as he flipped through the texts and photos of women Fran had sent along. Irritated, he flipped the phone closed and swore beneath his breath.

And looked up to see that Daisy was staring at him. And at his phone. She had to be wondering what the images were about, but to her credit, she didn't ask.

"Well," she said, "let's talk about Tillie."

"Yes, let's do that." Because he sure as hell didn't want to have to explain the photos. There was something a bit creepy about having one's secretary shop photos of women to him as if he were choosing a potential wife from a catalog. Besides, one look at Daisy's flip-flops with butterflies hovering over her pretty pink toes and he found that he couldn't quite remember any of the details Fran had included about those women other than that they were all beautiful and sophisticated and socially desirable. Of course.

"Butterflies?" he asked.

She raised one delicately arched eyebrow. "You have something against butterflies?"

"Not at all." And she had been right to question his question. Her toes or her butterflies should be nothing to him. That wasn't, after all, why he was here when he needed to be working on a way to draw customers back to Sutcliffe's. "Tell me more about Tillie," he said as Daisy sank down onto a white wrought-iron bench. "I know she was your friend and a former dancer and she created costumes for the weddings. What else do you remember most about her?"

"You don't want to go through the rest of her belongings? There might be something in there that would help you get to know her."

"I will. After we've talked, although I have to say that pawing through her belongings makes me a bit uncomfortable."

Daisy laughed. "Well, there's something I can tell you about Tillie. She wouldn't have hesitated to go through *your* things. She always said that you could tell a lot about a person by the things they bought."

He gazed down at her butterfly-studded feet.

She slid them beneath her, beneath the bench.

"Sorry," he said. "They're very...eye-catching."

Daisy gave him a you-have-to-be-kidding look.

"What?"

"You can't have my flip-flops. They're too gaudy and they don't go with that suit."

He realized that she was teasing him. Because he had made her uncomfortable? Well, it wouldn't be the first time in his life he'd done that to someone. His inability to join in and casually express what some considered normal emotions made it easier to exercise his authority, but it also made people nervous. It created distance. Not that there was anything he could or would do about that. Distance could be a good thing.

"I'll bet you've never worn flip-flops in your life," she said.

"You've got me there."

"Tillie did...occasionally. Mostly, though, she wore ballet slippers. She wanted to be a dancer long after she could no longer dance. It was her dream." Daisy's voice was sad.

"You wanted her to have her dream."

"Why not? Isn't that how it is with people you love? You want them to have the things that make them happy?"

"I suppose it must be." Not that he knew from experience. It occurred to him that the only person in his family that he'd never met seemed to be the one person who inspired deep emotions. He wondered what it would have been like to have known his aunt.

Daisy studied him more closely. That could only lead to more personal questions he didn't want to answer...and it could lead to trouble.

"Did you ever see Tillie dance?" he asked.

She shook her head. "No, but she had friends who told me about it. I guess she was something. If she hadn't fallen and broken her leg, she might have danced for much longer. As it was…well, she was philosophical about it. Tillie didn't believe in looking back. Remembering what a person couldn't change didn't serve any purpose, she always said."

"And yet she kept all her costumes."

"I know." Daisy's voice was even sadder now. "But when a person doesn't want to talk about their past, you don't ask questions. Not if you care about them."

He tilted his head. "I'm going to ask questions, Daisy. She was my aunt."

"And you've already told me that not having known her, you can't really care about her on a personal basis."

"Don't hold it against me. Even if I had known her, I'm just not a very emotional man, Daisy."

"I suppose some women don't care about that kind of thing."

Parker blinked. He frowned, confused. And saw that she was blushing.

"The women on my phone? I've never met any of them."

Now it was her turn to look startled. "But they're on your phone."

He shrugged. "My board wants me to get married. For marketing purposes. They're sending me potential mates."

"Isn't that a bit…cold-blooded?"

It was. Even he wasn't that cold-blooded, and yet…a part of him—the desperate part—was considering it. "It's business, and business is the—"

"Sutcliffe way?" she suggested.

His slight laugh wasn't amused, even though she was pretty much on the money. "I was going to say that my business is the focal point of my existence, but yes, I guess that's the Sutcliffe way."

"Are you going to do it?"

"I don't know. This wouldn't be simply a quiet, private wedding. The whole point would be to build public interest, to create a spectacle, a show. It would involve acting. I'm not good at acting."

"I am." She looked up into his eyes, and he was mesmerized. He wanted to lean closer.

"Are you proposing giving me acting lessons, Daisy?"

"Maybe."

"What would you want in trade?" Not that he was really considering having Daisy coach him. He just wanted to hear her answer, to know just where they stood.

"Let us stay here."

He shook his head. "I can't."

Her brows drew together in a frown and she still looked pretty to him. "Why? Don't you own lots of property?"

"I do. But not here. And—"

She waited.

"I don't know why Tillie was a secret, but I know there's a good reason. Finding out I owned these buildings, that I had an aunt...it's a bit like discovering that you've inherited a haunted house. You need to find out where the ghosts are and how much of a danger they present so that you're armed. Then you need to seal the house up so the ghosts never escape again."

"You think that there's something really bad about Tillie."

"I don't know."

"There wasn't. There couldn't be."

"You don't know that."

"I do. I knew her."

"Really. What do you know?"

"I know that she was good and kind and she took Nola and Lydia and John and me in. I know that she had friends."

"And what do you know about her past?"

Daisy opened her mouth. Then she shut it again.

"You don't know any more than I do," he whispered.

"I know that Tillie was more than her past," Daisy said angrily. "I know that a person's past shouldn't follow them forever if they change their ways. People make mistakes."

"I know that. But I still need to know the truth. And I'm still planning on selling the buildings. I'm sorry."

"If I can help you discover...whatever it is that you're looking for...if we should find that there was nothing in Tillie's past that could harm your company...is there any chance you would reconsider shutting everything here down and closing all your connections to Las Vegas?"

He wanted to say no. Even though he wasn't sure why, Parker was pretty certain that when he turned his back on Daisy he needed to make sure that it was final. But the clock was ticking away, and he had discovered nothing. Maybe that was because there was nothing to discover. Maybe Daisy was right. Either way, finishing up here would leave him free to concentrate entirely on Sutcliffe's. And that was crucial. The financial reports Fran had sent him this morning showed that the company was still on a downward path.

"Do you think you can help me?"

"I can try. I *do* have some experience as a reporter. I know how to conduct research, and I'm more than familiar with Tillie's turf and at least some of her acquaintances."

"All right, then. If you can help me find what I'm looking for, and it turns out that you're right and I've jumped to conclusions about my aunt, then you can all stay here."

She gave a tight nod. "That's...fair. We wouldn't be able

to afford to rent the chapel, too. Plus, the business was Tillie's. By rights, it's yours now."

By rights he could shut down the chapel today, but that wouldn't have been smart for anyone, not at this juncture, anyway. And part of him was a bit fascinated by what it was about Daisy's weddings that drew people to this out-of-the-way place. As someone whose business was suffering, he was curious about those that were thriving.

"John told me that he's been performing a record number of weddings at the chapel," Parker said, skirting the issue of his ownership of the Forever and a Day. "So…how do you manage your other jobs?"

Daisy shrugged. "The tour job is part-time—I only do a few a week on a regular basis and I sub for other people on an as-needed basis. The reporting is…more sporadic. It was a spinoff I started after I took the tour job and I fit it in during my spare time. It doesn't bring in much money."

So if the chapel folded, that would be a problem. Unless Daisy found alternative employment.

"If you assist me in doing research, we'll consider that rent rendered, and for now we'll keep the Forever and a Day operational, but I won't be here that long."

"I understand." Her sad expression told him that she did, but she didn't argue. For some reason, he wished she would.

"Do you want to see Tillie's things now? To go through some more of the boxes?"

"I—yes." He wasn't sure. What he'd seen the last time didn't seem to offer anything promising, and he'd felt like some sort of stalker.

As they entered Tillie's room, he glanced around at the cupboards, the boxes, the closet. "I wonder how she would have felt if she'd known that a total stranger would be mucking through all of her things."

Daisy's mouth tightened. She hugged her arms around herself, then as if she realized how negative her reactions were, she stood straighter, letting her arms fall to her sides. "Would you like me to stay?"

He gave her a quizzical look. "As a...chaperone?"

She smiled. "A chaperone for Tillie's stuff. I think she'd like the weirdness of it. Tillie loved the unusual."

"And you are a very unusual woman."

"I'm not sure that's why she loved me. At first, I think she loved me because I needed her, and later just because... she did. You know how it is."

"Not really."

Her eyes opened wide, startled, but then she nodded. "The Sutcliffe way. The baby-planning. The nannies." She didn't say more. She didn't have to.

"Don't get that sad tone in your voice. I had every luxury a child could have. Servants at my beck and call, anything I needed."

Almost. A near-forgotten memory of himself running up to his father and being told he was too demanding, that his father had important business to tend to, dropped in. People didn't love in his family. Not in the way Daisy was talking about.

But he wasn't going to dwell on that. He sat down on the end of the bed with Daisy a foot away from him. The diary that he had looked at earlier lay on a nightstand. He glanced at it.

"Fiction," Daisy said.

He said nothing. Instead he opened a box. Inside there were feather boas, hats, scarves and jewelry. Nothing expensive, no heirlooms, but all different kinds of costume jewelry.

Another box revealed more hats. And more in another.

"Tillie loved to play dress-up," Daisy offered. "But I know that's not what you're looking for."

"I don't know what I'm looking for."

"You're looking for something scandalous."

He glanced up from the box into her eyes, intending to deny what she'd said. But he couldn't.

"And if you find it," she said, "you'll lock it away so that the world will never know the truth. It must be nice to have enough power to be able to conceal anything unsavory that threatens you."

"I wouldn't know. I've never done it."

That got her attention. She blinked, her eyes wide. Her legs were crossed, one luscious knee far too close to him, close enough to touch. The foot she had been wiggling so that her flip-flop had nearly fallen off stilled.

"You've never used your power to make sure that things you don't want the world to know never see the light of day? I thought you had. You're obviously intent on doing that with Tillie and you seem so forceful, so single-minded and…"

"Cold," he said. "I've been told that before." But sitting inches away from Daisy with that guileless expression on her face, with her legs nearly bare, with her looking at him open-mouthed, he didn't feel cold.

"I didn't mean you were actually cold."

"You did. I am." But she'd reached out her hand as she spoke, touched his arm as if to make her point, and if there had been a drop of ice in his veins, it melted instantly. It turned to flame. With one fluid movement, he slid closer, placed his hand at her waist and pulled her to him. He tilted his head and brought his mouth down on hers.

He tasted her, fully, as he'd been wanting to since that first day. With only those two points of contact, his hand at her waist, his mouth on hers, his whole body reacted.

His brain ceased to function. He pulled away and returned again, swooping in for another kiss. And another.

She kissed him back. She started to loop one arm around his neck.

Then, as if the movement of her arm had caught her attention, she froze. She scooted back. "No. Not this time," she said.

And oh, he wanted to know what she meant. But at the same time, he realized she'd done them both a favor. He would have kept advancing. He'd had no thought of stopping. That would have complicated the situation in ways he didn't want to imagine, since he was definitely leaving here soon. He had enough trouble at his fingertips already. Daisy…Daisy would be heavenly trouble, but she was indebted to him now, and—he'd had those kinds of uneven relationships before. They had been hellish, uncomfortable and had prompted people to feed him those lies he'd hated. He didn't want another.

Obviously she didn't want what was sizzling between them, either. He was absolutely not going to ask what *not this time* had meant. No. He wasn't.

"This time?" he asked, totally ignoring common sense.

She looked uncomfortable. Then she sat up straight and gave him a proud and indignant look. "I imagine that I'm not the first woman you've kissed. Did you think that you were the first man *I've* kissed?"

No. Of course not. So why was he struggling so hard not to think of Daisy being kissed by someone…not like him. Someone not cold?

It couldn't matter.

"I'm not that naive. A woman like you would have many men wanting to kiss you."

She blinked as if he'd said something wrong. He supposed that he had. "A woman like me?"

"It wasn't an insult. I wasn't referring to your morals, but to your appeal."

She blushed, ever so slightly. It was charming. Beautiful. Tempting. "I'd better get back to the boxes," he said.

"It doesn't look as if you're going to find anything helpful."

She was right. They didn't find anything helpful. But they did find something.

"Isn't that you?" Daisy suddenly asked. She pointed to a newspaper clipping that had fallen from a folder as he'd lifted it.

Parker sucked in a deep breath, startled into silence for a moment. Finally, he nodded. "Yes. That's me. It was the first Sutcliffe ball I ever attended. The year I officially became a part of the company."

"A rite of passage? The year you left boyhood behind and became a man?"

"You might say that, but…in my father's words, there are no Sutcliffe boys. We're in training to be men from the day we learn to speak and obey."

To his surprise Daisy crossed her arms. "I have to tell you, Parker, the Sutcliffes don't sound like a boatload of fun."

"We're not," he agreed, but to his surprise he smiled as he said it.

"Why is that funny?"

"I suppose…because you dared to say it to my face."

"No one has ever insulted you before?"

"Not in quite that bold way."

"I'm sorry, but it seems criminal to deny a boy his childhood."

"You had a happy one, I take it?"

She hesitated. Then she plunged on in that direct Daisy way of hers. "I know what one should be like. I have an image of the perfect childhood." She folded her arms more tightly over her middle. "So Tillie had at least one photo of you," she rushed on. "That proves something."

"It doesn't prove anything. She was still an invisible relative, someone who was never mentioned in my presence." But a part of his mind was short-circuiting. That photo... his aunt...once again it occurred to him that he hadn't been the only person his parents had turned away from.

"Well, maybe you didn't know anything about her, but she sure knew that you existed. That photo proves that. And—"

"And what?" Parker asked, turning to her. Her eyes had gone wide; her face was pale.

She raised her chin and gave a curt nod as if trying to jolt the words from her mouth. "If she knew you existed, then maybe she really did mean for you to have the Forever and a Day. Maybe it wasn't just an oversight. Maybe if she had lived longer, you would have met her and unraveled the mystery and your family would have been reunited."

Parker thought about that, about how his parents had been, about the diary and the barely there dancer costumes. There was no chance that his family would have ever had the kind of big, happy, teary reunions one saw in the movies and sometimes in the news.

He gazed down at Daisy who had those Daisy lights shining in her eyes. "You don't just make up those stories for the weddings, do you? You believe in fairy tales."

She shook her head vehemently. "No. I don't. At all. But I want to."

And that was just one more reason why he shouldn't be kissing Daisy anymore. But that didn't mean he didn't want to.

CHAPTER SIX

DAISY had spent all of last night lying awake trying to think of ways to help Parker find his connection to Tillie— because she wanted to keep this apartment, but also…she needed to end her association with Parker. Like it or not, she was susceptible to him. Maybe it was because he hadn't kicked them out when he had the right, or because he hadn't closed the Forever and a Day even though he clearly wanted to or…something else that made her melt in seriously stupid ways when he was near.

Whatever it was, she couldn't allow it. Being attracted to any man right now would be a mistake. Being attracted to Parker? Phenomenally crazy. The man had made it clear he wouldn't consider marriage under normal circumstances but was considering marriage in a bid to save his company. And to the only kind of woman who would do: a debutante.

Daisy wanted to shriek. And run away. Fast. She patted her still-flat belly as if to reassure her child that "mom" was in control. But she knew she wasn't. She couldn't seem to control her reactions to Parker. When he'd kissed her, she'd turned into one big bundle of nerve endings. Wanting him. She wanted him right now.

"That's so irritating," she muttered. "And not smart."

So what *could* she do? *Help Parker find what he's look-*

ing for. The answer was obvious. If she did that, he'd be gone in an instant.

And she'd be safe from her ricocheting emotions.

So first things first. Make a good plan. She liked that idea. But after a sleepless night, ideas were short. Finally, she hit on one thing. One very small thing.

Daisy picked up the phone and dialed the number Parker had given her. *Just punching in the numbers felt too intimate,* but when his voice came on, the intimacy factor kicked up about fifty notches.

"You're up early, Daisy."

"I know. Just woke up. I'm still in bed."

Darn it! She wanted to slap her hand against her forehead. That had been a stupid thing to say. It brought up visions of sheets, near nakedness, Parker beside her.

And he hadn't answered her.

"I hope I didn't wake you," she rushed on, "but I thought you might like a Tillie tour."

"Excuse me?"

"A tour of places Tillie liked. Maybe visit some of her friends afterward. They might know more than I do."

"Of course. Friends." He said the word as if it was a foreign term he'd just learned. "That's an excellent idea. How about ten o'clock?"

"Perfect." That would give her time to call those friends and to round up other people for the tour. It would be better if she wasn't alone with Parker. That kiss was still flashing into her memory at frequent intervals. No one had ever kissed her in such a commanding and heated fashion. She couldn't afford to get used to it. Even though she had liked it. A lot.

So…stay away from Parker's hands…and lips. Plan the tour. Call Tillie's friends. It was a start. Just as soon as she got dressed and settled her stomach, she'd take care of the calls.

But in the end, it didn't work that way. A sleepless night threw everything off, including Daisy's chemistry. When Parker showed up an hour early, she was in utter misery.

The minute she heard his voice at the door, fear joined forces with misery. She bolted, hurriedly telling Nola that she was going for a walk and would be back soon. The last thing she wanted was for Parker to see her like this. Their meetings were already lurching up and down like a roller coaster. Throw a baby into the mix with a man who blanched at the very word *children* and he might decide to lock all the doors, end everything right now, hire a private investigator and forget about their deal.

Quickly Daisy headed toward a park down the street. All she had to do was get past these few dizzy moments and she would be able to paste on a smile and return to Parker looking normal.

Surely that wasn't too much to ask, was it?

Parker smiled at Nola and the older woman smiled back. Tentatively. Very tentatively. Had he done something to offend her?

"That was a very lovely wedding yesterday," he offered. "I especially liked the costumes. That's part of what you do, isn't it?"

Her smile became less tentative, but not completely. She was twisting her fingers together.

Parker wanted to sigh. How could a man be a businessman and have this effect on people?

"Daisy's not here," Nola blurted out. "She went for a walk."

He blinked. "I know I'm early, but...a walk? As in exercise?" He supposed that giving tours, arranging weddings

and writing articles didn't allow a person much time for
fitness, and his being here probably hadn't made things
any better.

"Not exercise. Just a walk. She does that a lot lately."

Now *that* didn't sound good. It sounded as if she was
stressed. "Do you know which way she went?"

"Oh, yes. There's a little park at the end of the street.
That's where she goes."

Parker turned toward the door.

"I probably shouldn't have told you that," Nola admitted. "But I worry about her. Especially now."

He didn't wait to hear if *especially now* was a lead-in to
how stressed he'd made Daisy. Instead, Parker just headed
toward the park. It wasn't hard to find, and it wasn't exactly
a park. More like the remains of one. A large broken fountain was the centerpiece and there were a few hardy succulents here and there. Parker stopped where the shadow
of the huge fountain dropped the temperature slightly...
and where Daisy had also stopped.

"Nola said you were here. She also said that you'd been
stressed lately and going for lots of walks."

"Nola is a sweetie, a sweetie with a big mouth, and she
worries too much." But her face belied her words. Clearly
Nola had reason to worry.

"We can work something else out. You don't have to
help me find information about Tillie. I'm used to hiring
people. I'll do that."

"No! We had a deal."

"I'm not going back on my end of the deal."

"I don't see how you can't. If you hire someone to interrogate Tillie's friends, I won't be helping, and that was
the deal."

"Daisy, I came in the front door and you went out the
back. I think—no, I *know* I owe you an apology. Clearly

my presence has upset your world in numerous ways. To begin with, I should never have kissed you."

"I kissed you, too, and no, we should never have—"

She closed her eyes. She swayed on her feet.

"Daisy?" His voice rose. "What's wrong? Here, sit down." He gestured toward a bench a few feet away, reaching for her at the same time. Forget not touching her. He was damn well going to touch her.

"No." Daisy could barely get the word out. Sitting would only make things worse. Only one thing could make this situation better, but the public restroom here was only open when an event was taking place in the ball fields beyond. With no time to lose, she rushed toward an area at the back of the park where there was mulch...and where she would be out of sight. And then illness overtook her.

When she finally felt better, she rose shakily and wiped her mouth with the handkerchief she'd learned to keep in her pocket. Eyes downcast, embarrassment flooding her, she returned to where Parker was standing.

"I—I'm so sorry," she said.

"*You're sorry?* Daisy, *I'm* sorry. I just...stood here."

"Yes, I know. Thank you. I hate for people to see me like that. I appreciate you keeping your distance. It's always so embarrassing."

"This has happened to you before? Have you seen a doctor?"

"I—yes, I— It's okay."

"It's not okay."

She stopped, still catching her breath, then looked up at him. "Has anyone ever told you how dictatorial you are?"

"Quite a few people, actually."

"Well, it's probably natural and just due to the fact that you're a rich—"

"Jackass?"

She blinked and managed to forget her illness momentarily as a smile came unbidden. "I was going to say businessman."

"You were going to be polite."

"You're not a…what you said."

"Oh, now you really *are* being polite. You can't even say the word."

"It's not a nice word. Tillie would have washed my mouth out with soap…or at least she would have threatened to. She never really did it. Anyway, you're not so bad."

He gave her an amused look. "Thank you. I think."

"Well, I can't have you thinking that my being ill has anything to do with you."

"I brought a lot of extra stress in your life. Now, in addition to all the jobs, you're having to think about how to help me dig up my aunt's past, and I know you're worried about the future."

"Isn't everyone at least a little bit worried about the future? You're worried about Sutcliffe's."

"That's different. I was born to that."

"I have to tell you, Parker, you're spoiling my ideas of what it's like to be rich. When does the good stuff start?"

He surprised her by chuckling, although she almost wished that he hadn't. He was even more gorgeous when he was laughing. Still…

"You need to do that more often," she said.

He shrugged. "I'll consider it."

And then it was quiet, and she realized that all her teasing was a cover-up. Maybe a good one. He hadn't asked her about the cause of her sudden illness. Maybe if she could keep him talking, he'd forget about it. Or maybe he already had. That would be good.

"Anyway, I want you to know that I don't want you to

hire someone else to research Tillie. I'm a good researcher and she was my friend. Her friends are good people, and I'd rather not sic an investigator on them. You know that saying about 'what happens in Vegas stays in Vegas'? Well, there's a good chance that some of Tillie's friends have things they left behind, too. An investigator would only make them uncomfortable. Besides…"

"What?"

"When you leave here, you want the door closed on Tillie. And when you leave here, I want to feel as if we've earned back the time we trespassed. We weren't trying to hurt anyone, because we didn't think Tillie had any family, but we weren't entitled to free rent. I can't pay you back any other way, so let me do this. I need to wipe the slate clean."

He was staring at her. Intently.

"What?" she asked.

"How are you feeling now? You're talking a lot. Are you trying to distract me from asking more questions about why you're sick?"

She didn't want to answer that last question. "I'm fine. We should go back. It's probably almost ten o'clock and time for the tour."

"No."

"Yes. Don't you have to get back to Boston soon? You need to find out what you can find out about Tillie and do damage control if necessary before that ball and before the spa complex opens. I told you, I'm helping. Even if you don't want me to. I have some pride. Besides, I have a vested interest. Tillie was like a mother. Her reputation matters to me. If I can prove to you that she couldn't possibly be a threat to your company or your name, I want to do that. Okay?"

He didn't answer, but he held out his arm. When she reached out, he swung her into his arms.

Daisy shrieked. "Parker, what are you doing?"

"Carrying you. You shouldn't be walking in this heat if you're ill. And then I'm taking you to the doctor. The Tillie tour can wait."

His arms banded around her, and Daisy was all too aware of how strong Parker was. For a businessman, he had some major muscles. Which she shouldn't even be noticing. She certainly shouldn't be letting him carry her. It made this moment feel far too personal and made *her* feel too…feminine. Desires she'd vowed to set aside started simmering. That couldn't be good. At all.

"I've been to the doctor," she said suddenly, trying not to lean against Parker, trying not to feel.

"He must not be a very good one if you're still sick."

"I'm not sick. This is normal."

And then he finally got it. He looked at her abdomen as if he could see right through her. "You're…pregnant?"

She nodded tightly. She didn't like telling him. People tended to pass judgment. To his credit, he didn't ask her who the father was. Maybe he didn't care. Most likely he didn't care.

But he certainly cared about the rest. "You're pregnant. You're going to have a baby in a matter of months."

"A little less than seven," she clarified.

He looked at her abdomen as if an alien baby might appear there at any moment. What on earth had happened to Parker where children were concerned? It was more than the Sutcliffe way, she was sure.

Not that it was any of her business. What mattered was that Parker was dead set against having kids and she was absolutely, positively giving birth this year.

Don't forget that, she told herself. It was one more reminder that a man—especially a man like Parker—would only distract her from what was important in her life now: her baby, her friends and creating a secure future for all of them.

By now they were back at the apartment, and Parker set her down. Gently. Uh-oh.

"Just because I'm pregnant doesn't mean I'll break. I still intend to conduct that tour."

"You were just sick."

She lifted one shoulder. "It's a daily occurrence. I'm told it will pass."

Daisy glanced up and saw that Parker was looking like a smoke cloud. He pinioned her with a look. "Why didn't you say anything before?"

"I don't announce it to everyone I meet. I didn't see any reason to tell you."

But, of course, that was partly a lie. She sighed and looked down. "At first I was afraid that you were looking for arguments to make us look bad. You know, in case you decided to sue us or something. I was afraid you might paint me as an unfit mother and that I might risk losing my baby."

He swore beneath his breath but she heard it clearly, and automatically covered her abdomen.

Unfortunately, her automatic action was caught by Parker. The man didn't miss a thing. Well, except for her pregnancy, but that was understandable. There had been no hard evidence.

"You thought I would harm a pregnant woman?"

"Not physically."

He swore again. She resisted the urge to protect her baby's ears…or whatever…this time. But the effort to hold back cost her. Her hands clenched just a bit.

"I apologize," he said. And then, "You said 'at first.' I take it that you eventually decided I wasn't that evil."

"You're not. You didn't throw us out. But by then, I knew about your feelings toward babies."

"About me *having* children. I harbor them no ill will. As I explained earlier."

She nodded. There was obviously more to this story, but then there was more to her story, too.

"I wish you'd said something," he said, just as if he could read her thoughts.

"Why does it matter?"

He looked to the side. "It shouldn't. I guess it doesn't. I dated a pregnant woman once. The baby wasn't mine, but she threatened to tell the newspapers that it was in a bid to get me to marry her."

Daisy froze. "I would never do that."

"I didn't mean it that way."

"I think you might have. At least a little." She put her hands on her hips. "Parker, I want you to know that *I'm* not getting married."

"Really?" Her response seemed to have stunned him. "Then…isn't it difficult being surrounded by all those ecstatic brides and grooms?"

"It's not the same. I love the creative side of planning weddings, and it's nice carrying on Tillie's work. I've learned to compartmentalize my clients' situations separately from my own, to be happy when they're happy. Because I have solid reasons for my decision to stay single. I'm…just not good with men. I don't know. Maybe I'm allergic to them," she said, trying to lighten the mood.

He surprised her by smiling again. "I don't think so."

Uh-oh. "You don't think so about what?"

"About you being allergic to men. You're not allergic to *me*. I kissed you last night and nothing happened."

Oh, he was so wrong about that.

"You're right. I'm not allergic to you, but I don't want a man and I have no plans to marry. If you thought I might in any way be planning to foist my child on you, you were dead wrong. My baby will be loved and wanted."

Parker froze. He turned pale beneath his tan, but he looked her straight in the eyes. "Touché. I had that coming."

Maybe. Maybe not. Seeing the pain deep in Parker's eyes, Daisy was sure there was more to the baby issue than the dishonest and scheming girlfriend. And she was pretty sure that the words she'd just uttered had struck deep. She certainly didn't feel better about herself. She was, after all, no angel.

Still, this whole situation only emphasized how important it was for her and Parker to get past their brief interlude together, to do what needed doing, cut the connection and move on. Their paths might be crossing now, but they were a bad match. Nothing in common, different goals in life.

So get to the goals, Daisy, she told herself. "Let me change clothes. I'll meet you down here in ten."

"You're sure you want to do this?"

She managed a smile. "Are you trying to renege on our deal?"

"Are you daring me, Daisy?"

"I—yes."

He tilted his head, held out his hand.

She swallowed hard and slipped her palm in his. Both of them stood there for longer than was customary. Daisy could feel his pulse against her skin, his warmth. The look in those green eyes was dark and dangerous.

"Handshake deals are pretty much a thing of the past, but let's shake on this, Daisy. I have my failings, but I promise I won't renege on our deal. From now until we find the information we need or I have to leave and seek other resources, we're partners. We'll have to trust each other."

"You should know that I have trust issues," she whispered.

"Clearly, so do I."

"All right, I'll do my best to trust you, and to fulfill our bargain."

"And I'll be right there with you."

She looked down at her hand, still folded into his. He released her. But when she returned ten minutes later, as promised, her hand still tingled. As if Parker had left a permanent imprint on it.

That couldn't be good. When he was gone, she wanted no memories of him, no regrets, no sense that something had gone unfulfilled.

She wished she had some way of wiping him from her heart and her mind. As it was, tying up all the loose ends was her best bet to ending any lingering thoughts of Parker.

They walked out the door together.

CHAPTER SEVEN

THE tour Daisy took Parker on was enlightening even though it didn't turn up anything helpful regarding why his parents had never mentioned his aunt. Daisy was, Parker acknowledged, a natural with people.

"Doris Dugan, this is Parker. I've brought him to your lovely tea room because you have such great stories. Especially the stories about my aunt. And wonderful tea, too. And cookies. Doris's cookies are absolutely the best," she told Parker.

"Oh, this one, she's a charmer," Doris said, patting Daisy on the cheek. "You want stories, hon? I'll tell you stories."

And she launched into a tale of how she and Tillie had once taken in a whole group of people whose tour bus had broken down. They'd entertained them and fed them. They'd told the children stories. "Tillie was a natural-born entertainer and she was always good with kids," Doris said. "Maybe because she'd never had any of her own. There was such an intensity, almost a frenzy, as if she needed more hours in the day to do all the good deeds she wanted to do."

"She sounds like a wonderful person," Parker said.

"Well, don't get me wrong. Tillie was no angel. She liked a glass of wine or beer, she *really* liked men. But yes, she had a kind heart."

It was that way wherever they went. Everyone greeted

Daisy like a daughter. "Here's Klaus," Daisy said. "Tillie used to dance in his nightclub back when he had a nightclub."

Klaus gave Daisy a hug. He expressed regret that he didn't see her more often and told her how he missed Tillie. "Tillie was something else," Klaus said to Parker. "That woman—oh, she could make a man sweat. A little like Daisy and you, eh?"

There was no way that Parker was going to tell Klaus that it wasn't like that for Daisy and him. Because frankly, it was. She *did* make him sweat and ache. She made his hands shake and his lips burn, and denying that would seem like an insult to Daisy. But admitting it could be worse. The truth was that he didn't want to want Daisy. She didn't want to want him. Their goals were just about as opposite as goals could get. But...

"I think Daisy...sparkles," Parker said.

She blinked. "Excuse me?"

Klaus was nodding. "Yes...that's a good way of putting it. Daisy, how about this guy? He's got a good way with words for a guy who isn't a reporter like you. I would have liked to use that word *sparkles* to advertise one of my dancers way back when. It's a good word, isn't it?"

She smiled. "It's a very good word, although I'm not so sure that I sparkle."

Parker and Klaus exchanged a look. "You do," they both said.

"I think it's the attitude...and the flip-flops," Parker said. *And the everything. The smile, the eyes, the body, the...Daisy.*

"Not a flip-flop man myself," Klaus said, "but she's cute. Don't hurt her, okay? Not like the other one."

Suddenly the atmosphere turned more serious. "That's not in my plans," Parker agreed.

"And...we're out of here. We have to go," Daisy chimed in. "But Parker's very interested in the dancers and, of course, I'm always interested in Tillie. If you ever remember... I don't know...anything you think I might want to know, will you call me?"

Klaus stared at her. "I had a lot of dancers, Daisy."

"I know. But wasn't Tillie pretty special? You told me that many times."

He laughed, a huge belly laugh. "Caught me. You're a sneaky one, Daisy."

"I know. Sometimes a girl has to be sneaky." She didn't look at Parker when she said that. He wondered if she was thinking about her living in the apartment after she'd been asked to leave or about not telling him that she was pregnant. Probably either one of them. He was pretty sure that given the chance to do things differently with the apartment, she would do the same thing. But in this case, they were talking about Tillie, too.

"Tillie said a lot of things like that," Klaus remembered. "She started many sentences with *Sometimes a girl has to*... Tillie was a survivor. She did what she had to do. Remember that."

Parker tried to envision his aunt. A survivor. Had she, like him, survived the Sutcliffe way?

"I remember Tillie's *Sometimes a girl has to*...every day. I live by that mantra," Daisy promised.

"Good. I worry about you," Klaus said.

"Don't worry. I'm fine."

"Raymond treating you right?"

"Raymond eats out of my hand."

Then they said their goodbyes and Daisy and Parker walked out in the sunlight toward Parker's car. They had driven only a few blocks down the road when he turned to her.

"Raymond eats out of your hand? I'm assuming he's not a dog."

Daisy rolled her eyes and laughed. "Definitely not. He's very much a living human being."

One who apparently adored Daisy. Which was totally none of Parker's business. His hands clenched on the steering wheel. "Is he the father of your baby?"

Daisy gasped. And then she coughed.

Immediately Parker pulled over to the side of the road, afraid that he had done something to make her ill. He reached out and, not knowing what to do, rubbed small circles on her back. He tried not to think about the fact that her skin was warm and soft beneath his palm. "Are you all right?" he asked.

"No. Yes," she said shakily. "Parker, I'm fine, but—"

He drew his hand away reluctantly.

"Raymond runs the tour agency where I work. The father of my baby isn't here. I don't know where he is. I just—he was a friend. I *thought* he was a friend. After Tillie died, I was pretty messed up. Chris was there. He was kind. I was stupid and did a stupid thing."

"You slept with him." Of course she had. *That's how babies are made, Sutcliffe. As if you didn't know that.*

"I'm not going to make excuses for myself. I was on shaky emotional ground at the time, but, even so, I was an adult."

Parker scowled. "He knew you weren't thinking straight. He took advantage."

"No," she said, her voice sad. "No. I'd really love to be able to say that, to let myself off the hook, but as I said, I'm not making excuses for myself. I'm responsible for what happened, at least in part. And yes, I do blame him, too, but only because I trusted him and he left as soon as he had what he wanted. When I learned that I was pregnant,

I called him. It wasn't a pleasant conversation and the next day he changed his phone number. I hate that I put my trust where I had no business putting it."

Parker knew all about that. About people who used other people. He wouldn't have let the guy off the hook so easily. Instantly, he disliked the man, but he couldn't lie to himself. It wasn't just because the man had impregnated Daisy and deserted her. It was because the guy had spent the night in Daisy's bed, an experience he would never have.

"The man was vermin," Parker insisted.

Daisy touched his arm. "I don't waste time feeling sorry for myself, Parker. To what point? I have to concentrate on the future. Part of that future is making sure I have a job and a home for my child and another part of it—for now— is fulfilling my obligation to you."

And when that was done, he would leave, one way or the other.

He turned to her. "You're an honorable human being, Daisy."

"Even though I stole your building for a while?"

"Even so."

"Thank you. That's the nicest thing anyone has ever said to me, I think."

He chuckled as he drove off. "Better than saying that you sparkle?"

"The word *sparkle* makes it sound as if I have glitter all over my body."

Parker nearly ran off the road at the thought. Fortunately, he was a man who never let his emotions get the best of him. And for once in his life, that characteristic served him well. He kept his hands steadily on the wheel and his eyes off Daisy.

For the most part.

* * *

Well, that had been invigorating, Daisy thought. And rather frightening. Why on earth had she made that comment about having glitter all over her body?

But the answer was almost worse. She had been shaken by Parker's concern for her—and by his touch. These reactions were getting out of hand. She needed this to be over. Until Parker left town, her life was going to be a mess, and she'd had more than enough of that kind of thing—going all the way back to her father deserting them, to her mother's death and her life on the streets, to Tillie's death and...

She looked down and touched her still-flat stomach. "You were an accident, but a wonderful accident," she whispered. "I'm never going to walk away from you."

Then she took a deep breath. Okay, enough introspection. Time to get to work. Klaus's reminiscing had given her an idea for an article. She wanted to write about his nightclub and the dancers there. The women of The Row. Including Tillie. It would be her final farewell to her mother/friend.

But she knew that she had to share her decision with Parker. Which was how she found herself standing on the sidewalk outside the luxury hotel where he was staying. She'd called, but he was in the midst of something and he'd sent a limo to pick her up. Sitting in the cavernous, luxurious limo, she'd understood fully just how big a gap there was between her and Parker. And if that hadn't been enough—

"Mr. Stenson has the entire top floor. Here's the key to the penthouse elevator," the woman at the desk told her.

Daisy opened her mouth to tell the woman that she had no interest in any Mr. Stenson, then shut it again. Obviously Parker hadn't announced his presence here. Otherwise, people would be bombarding him with questions about his business, about the new spa complex, possibly even about the bride to be...if that was public knowledge.

Daisy remembered the women in the photos, the potential brides who had been model-thin, self-assured, sophisticated. She looked down at her own short skirt and her flip-flops and wiggled her bare toes as the elevator rose. When it opened, she was caught off guard.

"Cherries?" Parker said as he glanced at her feet.

She looked up into his eyes. He was smiling. Her heart did some weird flippy thing. Idiotic heart.

"Every flip-flop gets a turn."

"Ah, a woman with a sense of fairness. I like that." His voice had dropped lower, softer, so it took an effort to appear flippant and unaffected, but Daisy did her best.

"I'll just bet you're used to women melting whenever you say 'I like that,' aren't you?"

He blinked, looking a bit startled. "Actually, no." He stepped aside to let her past. "Does that mean you were melting?"

She grinned up at him. With effort. "I was joking."

"I see."

He didn't. She was *totally* melting. "I want to talk to you about a project I'm planning. Tillie might be involved." She outlined what she planned to do as she followed him into the depths of the huge open suite with the floor-to-ceiling windows. All of Las Vegas was laid out beneath her.

"Wow, Mr. Stenson certainly can afford a nice place."

"Wealth has its moments. And Mr. Stenson appreciates those moments."

He offered her a seat, but Daisy was too wide-eyed to sit down. "I'll probably never see the inside of any place like this again in my lifetime. I'll wander, if you don't mind."

"Wander away." But, of course, now she was conscious

that he was watching her. She turned to him. "What do you think of the idea?"

"I think it's interesting, that people who like history will enjoy it and Klaus will be thrilled."

"How about you? I'll have to mention Tillie's name."

"Her last name is relatively common and it isn't the same as mine. She's been here all these years, and apparently no one made the connection. You don't need my permission."

"I know, but it felt…right to ask."

"What if I had said that I'd rather you didn't write it?"

"I wouldn't have written it."

"Just like that? Because some man forbade you to do it?"

"Well, I don't think anyone mentioned the word forbade, but no, it wasn't that, anyway. It's just…whether you knew her or not, you appear to be all the family Tillie had when she died. And she kept that photo of you."

"Photos."

"Excuse me?"

"I packed up that box and brought it here, folder and all. She had lots of newspaper and magazine clippings of me. I hadn't meant to keep that from you."

She shrugged. "You don't have a responsibility to tell me anything."

He smiled. Just a small, fleeting smile. "I suppose I'm taking a page from your book. Tillie was special to you and you were special to her. You have a right to know what was in those boxes."

A tight lump formed in Daisy's throat. She whirled away. "Would you look at that? The fountain at the Bellagio looks so beautiful from up here."

"I hadn't noticed."

"You should. It's really special, but I guess you're used to things like that, places like this." She kept walking with him right behind her and then she came to the end of the wall and turned. And stopped.

Laid out in front of her was a huge table with what looked to be a model on it, complete with a little sign that read Sutcliffe's Spa Complex.

"Wow, you really need some new marketing people. That is one boring name."

He laughed. "It's just a placeholder."

"Are you kidding me? I thought the complex was on the verge of opening."

"It is. I haven't come up with a name I like yet. No one has."

"So you'll open with this name? Surely there won't be time to get a sign that size made if you wait too long."

She looked up at him. His eyes were smiling. Stupid expression, but it was true, more or less. It was the first time she'd seen him like that. "Not a problem?"

"Not a problem," he agreed.

"I guess if you're drowning in money then the sign makers will work around the clock for you. Still, you need something better. Like Decadence, the Rejuvenation Zone or Silken Waters."

"I have people working on it. They'll come up with something."

Daisy stared down at the board. "Does Mr. Stenson always travel with a model of your current project? Don't the maids wonder what's going on?"

"The maids receive excellent compensation for not noticing a thing. Okay?"

"Okay."

"You can stop worrying that you've outed me by coming here, too. No one knows of our association."

She *had* been worrying a bit about that. She'd made a point of never using his last name on the tour yesterday.

"All right, I understand. You've taken care of everything. Money talks. Mr. Stenson is the only man in this room."

"Thank you."

"So why do you carry your model with you?"

"Latent juvenile tendencies?"

"No. I've seen those. People on the tours act like kids all the time. You don't."

This time he didn't smile. "Well, I never actually did."

Right. The direct route to manhood. She hadn't forgotten.

"I have it with me, because I'm the architect and I'm looking for ways to tweak it."

"It's beautiful." Even though it was a model, it was a gorgeous model, all aqua blue and glass. Very polished.

"Something's not right," he said.

She shook her head vehemently. "No, it's gorgeous. Really gorgeous."

"It has to be more than gorgeous. It has to be spectacular, memorable, a winner, the kind of thing to get people talking."

"Or the company will suffer?" she whispered.

"Yes."

"And people will blame you because it's your building." That was a lot of responsibility. She imagined that there were tons of people working at the Sutcliffe hotels, scores of jobs relying on the success of the name and the chain.

"*I'll* blame me."

"But you're not the only person in charge. You told me, you have a board."

"And I've ignored their wishes since my father died. They want me to be him. I was never him. He was—"

"The man who wanted you to skip boyhood."

He gave her a long and patient look. "I told you, my childhood would have been the envy of most kids."

She wasn't so sure of that. "When did you first start working for the company?"

"In an informal fashion, when I was twelve. Not directly, of course. But I started studying Sutcliffe's then. The history, the divisions, even the finances. I took tours, read anything I could get my hands on. I made suggestions. Good suggestions. I loved the company. It gave my life definition."

"And you still love it."

"Yes. I know that probably seems rather crusty and boring, but I'm good at the behind-the-scenes part. I'm just not good at being 'The Sutcliffe.' Unfortunately, the role of 'The Sutcliffe' is apparently mine, like it or not and it's an important role. It's up to me to fit into that title. Unfortunately, the company has been fading since my father's death. It's bleeding. Dying. On the verge of toppling."

"And even the smallest thing—such as a tiny scandal— might tip it the wrong way," she whispered. "That's why you were so appalled to find all of us living under your roof, and why you need to find out why Tillie became a ghost relative even though the truth could harm Sutcliffe's."

"Yes."

"And now you have a pregnant tenant. If it will help, I'll make an announcement or write an article swearing that you and I never met until a few days ago."

He shook his head. "Bad idea when no one is questioning your pregnancy or even knows about it. Or about us."

"Right." Especially since there was no "us" or would ever be, not in a romantic sense. "Bringing up things people haven't even noticed would just attract attention, I suppose. Besides, you're really Mr. Stenson as far as everyone in Las Vegas is concerned, aren't you? As Mr. Stenson, you can do whatever you want to do. Who's going to know or care?"

"Mr. Stenson will."

Daisy shook her head. "The fact that Mr. Stenson is talking about himself in the third person worries me. And... he seems a bit uptight, tense. Maybe he needs to relax for just five minutes."

"Says the woman who works around the clock. What do *you* do for relaxation, Daisy? Tomorrow's Saturday, play day for most people. What will you be doing?"

But, of course, he must already know the answer. She tried not to look sheepish, but failed utterly. "Okay, you win. I'll be overseeing a wedding tomorrow. Two of them. But they're unusual ones."

He smiled at her. "You workaholic, you. May I watch you again?"

If she were any other woman, Daisy thought, she wouldn't start thinking steamy thoughts at that innocent question, but she was a woman high on hormones. All the man had to do was open his mouth and her mind went straight to visions of herself and Parker together. On a bed.

She hoped against hope that she wasn't blushing. She realized that he was still waiting. He'd asked a simple question and deserved a simple answer. *Say yes,* she ordered her mouth.

But because she wanted to say yes so badly, she knew she should say no. Whatever Parker's reasons for wanting to attend the weddings, her reasons for wanting him to be there were suspect. Wrong. She was responding to his voice, to that masculine something in his tone that made her remember his lips on hers. She felt like one of those women on his phone. Hopeful. Maybe a bit desperate. But she would never be one of those women. She wouldn't be chosen as his bride and she wouldn't choose putting her fate in a man's hands again, either. But she was still susceptible to Parker's lazy gaze.

"You don't like weddings," she reminded him.

"I don't *dislike* them. I just don't especially want to be one of the starring players."

"But you might end up being one."

He didn't answer. "I won't come if it bothers you. Obviously it does. These…unusual weddings…what's so unusual and embarrassing that you don't want me there? Since you told me that you don't have them anymore, I'm assuming that there won't be any half-naked people," he said.

Had she really said that? She had. How utterly degrading.

"You needn't have reminded me that I said that," she said.

"You're right. I apologize for teasing you."

"And no, there won't be any half-naked people unless you take *your* clothes off," she quipped.

And suddenly the huge room seemed smaller. The air conditioning didn't appear to be working. Daisy's clothes felt too tight. Parker's arms and mouth seemed too far away. *Don't. Danger!* flashed through her mind. "Sorry about that," she said. "I sometimes push things too far and I always did have a big mouth."

"It's perfect." He was staring at her lips.

She clenched her hands on the folds of her skirt. "What's perfect?"

"Your mouth. It's perfect."

"I should go."

"I know." He nodded.

She started to back away, then stopped. "Why *did* you ask to come to the weddings?"

Parker shrugged and the air of danger drifted away. "Don't worry, Daisy. My reasons were strictly business. Weddings are very much a people field. You have customers. They seem to like what you do. I'm always interested in successful businesses. But…it's not a big deal. Don't worry about it."

"Strictly business?" Daisy breathed easier. She smiled. He couldn't have said anything that would have done a better job of turning this wayward conversation around and putting her at ease.

"Come," she told him as she walked to the elevator and stepped inside. "I'll save you a choice seat."

"Will there be dwarves and a prince?"

"Even better. Leprechauns." She grinned at him.

To her surprise, his eyes turned dark and seductive. "You make me crazy," he told her just as the door closed. And she didn't get to ask whether that was crazy in a good or a bad way.

Or…was there such a thing as a good or bad way? Any way you looked at it, her interactions with Parker were getting more and more dangerous.

"I need to end this," she whispered to herself that night. It was time to be more proactive about finding dependable work outside the chapel and finding an affordable place for all of them to live. And she needed to do it herself. Depending on a man for anything—leaning—just wasn't a good idea.

She didn't want to distress Nola and Lydia and John, so she'd have to hunt during her free time. She dreaded telling them that they really were going to have to leave the Forever and a Day behind soon. Her heart ached at the thought of hurting them and of leaving this place that had been her home.

But the sooner the better. Spending too much more time with Parker was going to have an emotional cost. Already she was starting to like him too much.

That's seriously scary, Daisy thought. *Not smart at all.*

I have a bad history with men, and Parker was born to break hearts.

She knew better than to get too close. But she was pretty sure that there would be closeness. Because she wanted to kiss him at least one more time before they parted ways.

CHAPTER EIGHT

PARKER entered the chapel forty minutes before the wedding was to begin and found no sign of Daisy. Nola was wringing her hands. Lydia was tight-lipped. John was pacing. "She's always here at least an hour before things start," he said. "That's the deal with Daisy. We all have jobs, but she's the rounder-upper, the cheerleader, the glue. There was never anything formally announced but when Tillie got too ill to do all those things, Daisy stepped in. I'm not sure we can do this without her."

"I can't imagine Daisy leaving you in the lurch," Parker offered.

Lydia looked indignant. "Of course she wouldn't. If she can be here, she will. But we don't know where she is. I called Raymond, and she didn't have a tour today."

For a minute, Parker felt a thread of panic slip through him. He understood exactly why Daisy's elderly posse was so upset, but then a bell went off in his head. "Research. She told me she was going to write an article that would include some information about Tillie. She's probably interviewing Klaus. Or someone."

"Really?" Nola looked like a little girl, so eager and scared. And even if he wasn't completely sure, he knew he was going to say whatever he had to.

"She told me that yesterday."

Nola gazed at him adoringly. She patted his arm, then rose on her toes and kissed his cheek.

He froze. No one ever treated him that way…or hardly ever and never in such a guileless fashion. Casual affection had always been frowned on in his world. He'd never learned how to deal with the stuff, and he knew he must look like a very cold robot.

"I—" He didn't know what to say. "Thank you," he managed, wondering if one thanked a person for such things, wishing he knew the right words.

And then he saw Daisy coming down the hallway. She had a funny look on her face, as if she knew he was uncomfortable. And possibly why.

"Parker was just telling us that you were probably researching an article," John offered.

Was that guilt on Daisy's face? "Yes, I did tell him about that." Which wasn't exactly an answer, was it? What had Daisy been doing? And why didn't she want anyone to know? For one crazy moment, Parker remembered her comment about Raymond eating out of her hand, and a foolish surge of jealousy rushed through him. Unacceptable. He thrust it aside, his only excuse being that Evelyn had been cheating on him with the father of her child while plotting to marry Parker and raise her son as a Sutcliffe.

But Daisy didn't want to get married. To anyone.

Right. He was being an idiot. Probably because this situation and the one with Sutcliffe's had him a bit on edge. Well, no more. He didn't belong at the Forever and a Day. He was only here to observe what brought customers here when there were so many more convenient and trendy chapels.

"Well," he said. "I suppose we should let Daisy get ready and…er…put on her leprechaun costume."

John looked confused. Daisy laughed. "Sorry," she said.

"I must have made a mistake when I told you that. This one is actually a Regency wedding. As a matter of fact, if you were in costume you'd fit right in. You do have the look of a Regency romance hero about you."

Parker didn't quite know what to say to that, but the others murmured their agreement. Then they headed off to their respective chores, their panic over now that Daisy had been found.

He raised one eyebrow. "So there were no leprechauns? And it was a mistake?"

She actually looked guilty. "Well…maybe *mistake* was too strong a word. But really, I was just teasing you. Doesn't anyone ever tease you?"

"Not really. I don't exactly have those kinds of relationships."

"You mean the normal kind?" Then she slid her hand over her mouth. "Just forget I said that, okay? But…no teasing? Not even the fun kind, because you know that's was what I was doing, right? I wasn't mocking you."

"I think you were. A little. But that's okay," he said with a slight smile. "I know I'm rather pompous at times and I probably deserve to be mocked. So…no leprechauns at all?"

"We did once have a wedding with leprechauns. Really. It was a St. Patrick's Day wedding. Fun. Light-hearted."

"I can only imagine."

"Next time I'll videotape it and send you a copy."

Because next time he'd be in Boston and he would either have sold the building or set up a manager. Better never even to think of Daisy once he'd gone. He would have his company…and maybe his suitable bride. She would have her baby.

He slugged in a deep breath of air. "So…a Regency wedding."

"The bride is a big Jane Austen fan, and we always try to fulfill the fantasy when we can."

He saw as much once the wedding had begun. The music had been chosen carefully. The decorations, while inexpensive, reflected the period. As did the flowers, the costumes and even the vows. When John spoke about the couple, it was almost as if he knew them. But surely they weren't locals.

He caught up with Daisy after the service. "How do you do that?" he asked.

"Do what?"

"Make it seem as if the wedding couple are old friends of yours."

She shook her head. "There's no magic here. I interview them at length when that possibility presents itself. If I can, I try to meet with them a day or two before the wedding. Even when we don't have much lead time, I try to talk to the couple beforehand about their interests, how they met, what their dreams are. Anything that can personalize the service. I try to make it seem as if the service is being conducted by friends who care about them. And I do care. Everyone who comes here should have a memorable wedding."

"What if—what if you don't like the couple?"

"I pretend."

"You lie."

"It's not a lie. Just because my first impression of a person isn't favorable doesn't mean I'm right. Making a snap judgment about someone seldom yields the truth. It's so easy to be wrong. A person may seem wonderful, just what you want in your life. And you can be dead wrong."

Parker was pretty sure that they weren't talking about the Forever and a Day anymore.

"Point taken," he said. And then, when she didn't speak... "You're very good at the pretending business."

"Thank you. I think. Most of the time it isn't pretend, though."

He couldn't help wondering if she—like the women who'd wanted his name and his money—was just pretending to like him. He owned the buildings and the business she depended on to survive. Wouldn't she want to stay on his good side? To try to influence him?

Parker hated having those kinds of thoughts, but he couldn't ignore the possibility. He also couldn't ignore the fact that Daisy was very good at her job. The Forever and a Day wasn't fancy, but during the course of a wedding, you'd swear you were in whatever world she created.

Even if the scene had to be set in a hurry. As soon as everything was cleared away from the Regency ceremony, Daisy made a rush for the door. When she came back, she had changed clothes.

"Cowboys and cowgirls?" he asked.

"Yes," she said. "And...Nola's leg is bothering her more than usual. I wonder...since you're here...would you be willing to take her part or is that something The Sutcliffe can't do?" He'd merely observed during the last wedding.

Parker couldn't hide his disbelief. He gave her his best stern Sutcliffe look. "I don't think that would be a good idea."

"Just like that? No maybe? No 'I'll think about it, Daisy'?"

"As I said...not a good idea."

"You could think of it as...Halloween coming early. Trying on your costume well ahead of October."

"Halloween costumes weren't big in the Sutcliffe household."

She blinked. "Not even simple stuff? A sheet turned into a ghost or a toga?"

"We usually left town on Halloween. My father didn't want grubby children clamoring for candy and storming the gates of the estate."

Daisy froze. "I'm sorry, but that is seriously messed up."

He couldn't help smiling. "Probably. Still...I lack Halloween experience. I'm sure I'd spoil your wedding."

Daisy gazed up at him. "No. You wouldn't, but...you're right. This is probably too undignified for a Sutcliffe, and if word got out, your board members would probably be appalled. I shouldn't have asked. I'll just run down the street and get a neighbor to help, or we'll get by with just the three of us. We've done that before." She turned to go.

Parker caught her hand and stopped her.

She looked at him, confusion in her eyes. "I have to go. If I have to find someone, I'll need time."

"You'll have to run faster."

She lifted a shoulder in dismissal, because he was obviously right.

He swore beneath his breath. "No. No. Absolutely no. A pregnant woman should *not* be running down the street or doing the work of two people."

She gave him a look. "Do not go all Sutcliffe on me, Parker. I have work to do."

"I know. You do. And you're right. I'm acting like an ass. And Nola does need rest. All of that trumps my objections, my dignity, my lack of Halloween experience, the board members and my bad attitude. So...I'll help. Just tell me, what do I have to do? Play dress-up, I assume? Interact?"

The relief in Daisy's eyes lit up her face. Parker had the good grace to feel guilty for making her wait.

"You're sure?"

"No. I'm not. But I'm doing it, anyway."

"Okay, then. Yes, you've got the general gist of things right. And…thank you. I promise this one won't be too bad, Parker. It's only a simple cowboy wedding. I wouldn't ask you to wear the back part of the horse costume or a bunny suit or anything really undignified."

"A bunny suit? You do that?"

"Hardly ever."

He repressed a shudder, and he knew that his questions were really just an attempt to kill time, to avoid the inevitable. Because here was the deal. He'd seen how Daisy and the others jumped right into their parts. The very thought of trying to make small talk and act a part made him feel a bit ill. The fact that there might be more children made his palms sweat.

Daisy touched his hand, sending heat spiraling through him. "I'll help you. It won't be that bad. You won't regret it."

He couldn't help laughing at that. "Frankly, I think we're *both* going to regret this. A lot. But, I'll give it my best shot if you're not afraid that I'll horrify your guests."

"If you mess up, we can always say that you're a city slicker," she teased. "I take it you don't have any jeans here?"

"I'm not sure I even own a pair of jeans."

She gave him a startled glance. "Sometimes I forget that you and I were born on different planets, and then you say something like that, and I totally remember."

Parker shrugged. "We don't need jeans on my planet."

She gave him a mock disgusted look. "Well, you can get by without them for today. Just tell Lydia that you need a vest, a hat and a bandana. And take your jacket off. You'll pass, cowboy." She poked him in the chest.

He captured her hand. "You're starting to enjoy this, aren't you?" he asked. "Taking me out of my element?"

"Maybe a little. And you sure you're okay with this?"

"I'll try to look at it as a research experiment. I'm interested in how you accomplish what you do, and I'll get a better idea of how things work if I'm not making all the attendees nervous by sticking out like a sore thumb. And... I'll do my best to fit in and be useful."

"Thank you. Why don't you begin by greeting the guests? Nothing fancy. Just make them feel welcome."

"Like a butler."

She grinned. "Like a cowboy butler. Go get 'em, cowboy."

"I'm not sure I'm going to get 'em, but I intend to do my best to help you create another success, Daisy," he said, smiling down at her now that they were on to teasing. He liked sparring with her. She was a worthy and clever adversary. And—he took in her costume—she was charming and pretty in a pair of tight jeans, a white collared shirt open at the neck, a hot-pink vest and pink boots. A white cowgirl hat hung at her back.

"No flip-flops?"

"Special occasion. Try saying 'We aim to please, ma'am,' instead of 'I intend to do my best.'"

"No. Absolutely not."

"Why not? You're a cowboy."

"You're just trying to get me say something undignified, aren't you?"

"Maybe. But I'll bet if you try it out on a few of the females here, they won't laugh." Her voice was low, suggestive, hot. At least he felt hot; he wanted to drag her into his arms, but she winked at him, then turned and left, smiling as she moved off to tend to her duties, orchestrate the entire affair and make sure that no one left unfulfilled.

At first Parker greeted people with his customary, "Very

nice to meet you," "Welcome to the wedding," and "How nice that you could make it."

People smiled politely and looked at his expensive pants. Obviously, there was a bit of disappointment even if no one was saying so. The bride and groom had, after all, paid for a full-fledged cowboy wedding and now he, a stuffed shirt, was messing with the fantasy.

Frustrated but not surprised at his inability to break through—he had always been uncomfortable in social circumstances—Parker frowned.

"I'm really sorry to bother you," a middle-aged woman said, fussing with her bandana, "but could you tell me where I can get a program?"

A vision of Daisy laughing at him merged with his frustration. He closed his eyes, then opened them again. He suppressed a sigh and took a deep breath. "I surely can, darlin'," he said, sweeping up a program from a nearby table and presenting it to her. "And if there's anything else you need, you just come find me. This cowboy aims to please. All right?" Even though his delivery was a bit stilted, he smiled at her as if he meant to sweep her into his arms at any moment.

"I surely will," she said on a breath. "Thank you. I really appreciate your help. My niece told me that the Forever and a Day was known for personal service. I—I guess she was right."

He took his hat and held it over his heart the way he'd seen in a Western or two. "Thank you, sweetheart." Then, thinking that he might have gone too far—did men really say 'darlin'' and 'sweetheart' all the time, and wasn't that a little politically incorrect?—he tilted his head. "Or have I offended you with my familiarity?"

The woman reached out and touched him on the cheek.

"Sweetheart, you can call me *sweetheart* any time you like."

Parker decided that, successful as that had been, he needed to tone it back a touch. But from then on he relaxed a bit, and even though he ditched the dialect, people seemed to respond. There weren't any children here, and he was ashamed to be relieved...but he was most definitely relieved. He escorted guests, helped Nola with the food and danced with women who had no partners. At least when they were waltzing. Square dancing was a bit beyond him, even though Daisy had hired a caller.

"Thank you. I hope you know that you've added a touch of excitement to the proceedings that we don't usually have." Parker turned to see Daisy at his elbow, even though he hadn't needed to turn to know that it was her. He'd felt her presence. He knew her voice.

"It was...my pleasure. I enjoyed it. I can see why people come to you for their weddings. The bride told me that the poem she read was the first she'd written since she was young. She'd given up writing poetry when a teacher discouraged her and you not only somehow got her to share that with you, you convinced her to write a poem to the groom. She was thrilled. The groom was thrilled. I think people love the fact that you pay attention to the little things."

"Apparently, you pay attention to the little things, too. I had several ladies tell me that you made them feel like princesses...or princess cowgirls. What did you tell them?"

He frowned and shook his head. "That all they had to do was ask and I would try to make sure they were taken care of." It was the kind of thing the Sutcliffe concierges were famous for. That was where he'd gotten the line.

Daisy gave him a long look, then fanned herself with a

program. "Well, I can see how having you available to fulfill their every whim would make a lot of women happy."

He smiled at her. "We aim to please, darlin'."

She gave him a look. "I said a lot of women. Not me. *I*
am immune. As you know."

He knew that was what she'd told him, but he also knew
that she'd melted in his arms before. Clearly, she didn't
want to want him, though. He needed to respect that, to
somehow…stop wanting to kiss her.

To stop wanting to *know* her. How was he supposed to
do that? He didn't have a clue, but he knew that it was important. Falling for Daisy would be disastrous.

And right now…the two of them were more or less alone.
The guests were gone, but the music was still playing. Nola
and Lydia and John were heading upstairs.

Alone, he thought again. Parker wanted nothing more
than to take Daisy into his arms and kiss her.

"Dance with me, Daisy," he said, instead.

"That might not be wise."

"It *isn't* wise. Do it, anyway. It's just a simple dance."

Even though he was pretty sure that there would be nothing simple about whirling Daisy in his arms.

"All right." She moved into his arms. "We'll pretend
we're just a cowboy and cowgirl."

"No. No pretense. We are who we are. Exactly who we
are. Two people from different planets, with different goals.
Some of my goals interfere with yours. You're going somewhere I would never choose to go."

She nodded slowly and he breathed in the lemony scent
of her shampoo, of her. They turned into the dance; he
pulled her closer…and felt the kick of being near her.

"You're so good at pretending," he whispered. "It's none
of my business, but…how will you paint your child's father

to him or her? Will you say that he was an opportunistic jerk?"

"That may be what I'll want to say, but..." She smoothed her hand over her abdomen. "I don't know the right answer or if there is a right answer, but I want to make sure that this child has a better start than I did."

"Daisy..."

"No. I didn't say that to inspire pity, but the truth of the matter is that my father wasn't around, either, and when I grew up and tried to find him, I learned that he'd left by choice. He didn't want to know me. I'm determined to make sure my child is as happy as possible. I'm going to cocoon this baby and let her know that we're a complete unit, no father needed. So I'll probably simply say that he was a good man, but that circumstances prevented him from ever being with us."

"In other words, you'll lie."

"For the greater good."

Parker frowned.

"You don't have to approve," Daisy said. "I'm doing this for my baby."

"You don't need my approval, and I understand why you're doing it. Just..."

He blew out a frustrated breath. "Just dance," he said, because, after all, maybe this was as close as they would ever get, all the touching they would ever do, and maybe that was a good thing. There were too many barriers between them.

Still, he wondered if Evelyn had thought she was lying for the greater good when she'd professed to love him. He didn't know, but he knew one thing. That had turned out badly. He wasn't going there again.

He and Daisy might share some smiles and teasing, even a dance, but in the end, his life was in Boston with

Sutcliffe's; hers was here planning weddings that made her glow. If he tried to take this any further and she went along, he would always wonder if she was simply pretending because he held the strings to her life, and appeasing him was "for the greater good" of her and her friends.

He wasn't even going to think about the baby.

CHAPTER NINE

Daisy hung up the phone and immediately called Parker. "Klaus found a box of Tillie's old stuff. After we spoke with him and I told him about the article I wanted to write, he started cleaning out a storage closet that was mostly used to store props. Some of the dancers had boxed a few things up. It's probably nothing."

"I'm not getting my hopes up," Parker agreed, "but I'd like to look at it. Will Klaus mind if we bring it back to my place?"

"He said that you could keep it."

Which was how Daisy found herself entering the lion's den again. "Will you mind if I stay to look?" she asked as she followed Parker into his apartment. She tried to tone down her reaction, but this find was different from what was in Tillie's room. This was stuff Tillie had forgotten she had. It might have been from when she first came to Las Vegas.

"This is as much your search as mine." Although it wasn't really. She knew that Parker was sure his aunt had skeletons in her closet. His was the greater need. After all, she'd had Tillie for years and there was nothing in those boxes that would bring Tillie back, so the most important quest was Parker's.

But when they'd finished going through the box…

"Mostly costumes. Nothing that would supply a clue about her past."

"Except for the letter," Daisy offered.

"What letter?"

"The one hidden in the zipper lining of one of her costumes." Daisy held it out. "Klaus told me about it. She must have treasured it if she hid it away."

But the single letter didn't offer any clues. "There's no mention of her past," Parker pointed out.

"There's the line about how the woman—Liza Brett—has been such a good friend."

"Yes...but you implied that Tillie had a lot of friends."

"I know, but this letter implies a closer friendship than Tillie shared with most of the people I know. Plus, I never met this woman. Klaus says that she worked at the club for a few months thirty years ago. I don't know when Tillie first came here, but if this woman and Tillie were good friends, they might have shared secrets."

"Does Klaus know where she is?"

"Not at all."

He stared at the letter. "If she's alive, I can find her. But if she knows Tillie's secrets—and they're not good ones—are you sure you want to know?"

"Are you sure *you* do?"

"Better to know than not to know."

"Absolutely. I want to exonerate Tillie. She's the closest thing to a grandmother my baby would have had."

"And if the news is bad...will you lie for the greater good?"

"It won't be bad."

"But if it is?"

"Then I'll tell my child about the woman *I* knew."

"I'm...sorry," Parker said. He raked a hand back through all that lovely dark hair.

"What for?"

"It must seem as if I'm being very callous, the way I'm coldly digging into the past of a woman who kept photos and clippings of me and whose possessions I've inherited. My methods…"

"Are part of the Sutcliffe way?"

He smiled. "I should have known that expression would come back to bite me. Sounds a bit pompous…but then, we are rather pompous. We're taught to be self-sufficient at an early age."

Daisy was beginning to realize that "being self-sufficient" meant not showing any signs of weakness, no hugging, no outward affection…or maybe no affection at all. Had she thought Parker was dangerous? She'd underestimated.

"A man like you could be downright terrifying to a woman like me. So many of my decisions are based on how big the emotional payoff will be."

"I can't think of anything much more terrifying than that."

She smiled. "Parker, you don't know terrifying." But she was pretty sure that he did. Children weren't born without emotions. Having parents who encouraged him to bury all of his feelings must have made for an anguishing childhood, no matter how much wealth he had. No wonder he didn't want children with their hugs and sticky emotions. Or maybe he simply knew he couldn't provide what a child needed. Either way, she should be grateful that he'd warned her. And she should definitely keep her distance.

"Regardless of how we're approaching this, we're both interested in Tillie's past."

"So, I'll track down Liza Brett."

"A private investigator?" she asked.

"Only if necessary. I told you, I'm all about facts and

figures. I can handle the tracking part. I may need you once I've found her, for the personal bit, the interview."

"Yes, you can be a bit...overwhelming at first."

"Rigid."

"In control," she countered.

"You don't have to be nice to me. I'm not holding anything over your head. We've set the apartment-hunting aside."

"I know you have, but I haven't. It occurred to me that waiting to see what happens and then simply reacting was no longer a smart way for me to operate."

"No longer?"

"It's how I've done things in the past. Maybe you're beginning to rub off on me."

"That's not necessarily a good thing. Have I mentioned how impressed I am with the way you run the Forever and a Day? Lots of waiting to see what happens and reacting quickly there."

She shrugged. "Agreed. But I need to be more proactive about life now. I've been looking for an apartment. And work."

"Daisy?" He frowned. "I can help you with those things. I told you—"

She held up her hand. "I *want* to find my own apartment, not to be indebted to you for the place I sleep every night."

He groaned; his eyes grew dark as he stared at her.

"For a man who isn't very emotional, you do know how to make a woman feel as if she—"

"Drives a man insane? Makes him wish things were different? Does referring to the place you sleep every night make me want to slip those flip-flops and everything else off you and find a bed right now? Yes. Even the least emotional man would feel hungry when he looks at you. That doesn't mean I *want* to feel that way."

Daisy's heart raced. Her hands itched to reach out and place her palms against his chest, pop the buttons on his shirt and smooth the lapels open to bare his chest to her touch.

She took a deep breath. "I don't want to feel that way, either," she said, her voice a bit shaky. "So maybe I should rephrase my comment. I need to find my own apartment. I'm going to be a single mom. I have to be self-sufficient."

"And you're looking for a job, too? What about the Forever and a Day?"

"That's…yours. The more I know you, the more I know I can't stay there."

He looked as if she had slapped him. Daisy wanted to reach out and soothe him, but almost as soon as the wounded look appeared, he replaced it with that cool exterior she recognized all too well. He was once again The Sutcliffe.

"What I meant was that you and I need to end our association when this is over. I realize that now."

"Then you have no reason to continue with your quest to find Tillie's past. I offered you the apartment as incentive."

"You know that's not my incentive."

"You're doing it to clear her name in my eyes."

"In part. I'm also recreating her past for my child. I'm creating a family, a world. And I'm not stopping now. You and I are in this together until we're done. Even if both of us know we're in dangerous territory."

He studied her for several seconds. "Agreed. Would you like me to…limit my contact with you to our search for Tillie?"

Yes. That would be so much safer.

"No. We still owe you, and this business with Tillie doesn't count as payback considering that I have a vested interest in the results. Even if I didn't, it wouldn't cover what we owe you for rent. Plus, the chapel is really yours and the money made from it really should flow through you."

Uh-oh, now he was looking angry. "I don't want the money. It was never about the money. The amount we're talking about is inconsequential."

"Not to us."

"Exactly. Keep it."

"Not unless I give something back. You were decent not to throw us out on the street. What we did—what *I* did—was theft and I gave that up years ago."

She twisted her fingers together and blew out a breath. "Daisy," he said, taking her fingers into his big hands.

"No, I mean it. I never told you what I went to juvie for, but it was theft. I stole food and not just once. I can't condone stealing from you."

"Daisy."

"What?" Finally, she gave in and looked up at him.

"Shut up, Daisy. I wasn't angry that first day because you stole from me."

"I know. You were angry because we were in your way."

He grimaced. "That was rather blunt."

"I'm a blunt person."

"But it was true."

"*I know, and that's why I have to make it up to you. I* don't want to hear that it's not necessary." He was still holding her hands, she had taken a step closer to retain her balance. They were so close to each other that she could feel his body heat. Parts of her she didn't want to think about ached. That wasn't good. She needed to concentrate.

"It's not necessary," he insisted.

"It *is*. To me."

"Let me finish. What I was going to say was that it wasn't necessary to repay me, but I understand why you want to do it."

"Why I *need* to do it. How can I look my baby in the face if he thinks his mother was a thief?"

Parker's hands tightened on hers for just a second before he loosened his grip. She really should stop mentioning the baby around him. It wasn't fair, Daisy thought.

"Have you ever noticed that sometimes you call your baby him and sometimes her?"

"Just covering the bases."

"Even in utero, you don't want to offend?"

"You never know what a baby can hear. I want to project positive vibes, to make sure there's no question that he… or she is *wanted*."

He tilted his head. "So…you want to repay me because you need your child's self-respect?"

She gave him a don't-you-dare-laugh-at-me look. "I need to do it for me, too. You said that you were interested in how we ran the chapel from a business perspective. What else can I do for you?"

He growled, then released her. Daisy, flustered at how suggestive her innocent words had sounded and frustrated because even though "not touching" Parker was for the best, she craved the connection.

"Um, sorry about that. Thank you for not saying something crude and obvious," she said.

"Daisy, I'm not the best of men, but despite the fact that I find you intensely desirable and am having trouble keeping my hands to myself, I hope I'd never be crude with you."

He looked unhappy.

"Or obvious," she teased, trying to lighten the atmosphere that had grown far too charged.

He laughed. "What can you do? How about looking at my model again and telling me how you would do things differently?"

Daisy let out a sigh of relief. She wanted to touch Parker so badly that she practically ran to the model of the Sutcliffe Spa Complex.

"Any word from your secretary?"

"Yes. The list is growing. The board is grumbling at my continued absence. They want me to do a commercial. I'm lousy at that kind of thing."

"Maybe you could put on your cowboy hat and throw a few 'darlin's' out into commercial land."

"Might be worth it just to see the board have a group apoplexy."

Daisy smiled. Satisfied that she and Parker had lowered the heat to a low, bubbling simmer, she looked at the model. "I told you before, it looks beautiful."

"And I think I might have intimated that beautiful wouldn't be enough."

"All right, let me look more closely, but I have to tell you, beautiful is going to be enough for some people. It always is."

"Are you speaking from experience?"

"I've met plenty of grooms—and some brides—who seem to have made their choice based on exteriors only."

"Ever hear how long those marriages last?"

"No. And I don't want to know. I'm guessing not long."

"My point exactly. So don't worry about offending me. Just give me your unblemished opinion."

"As a businesswoman?"

"Yes, and as a pretend potential customer and also as simply—"

She glanced up and found him studying her. "You," he said simply. "Just be you."

"I'm not your target customer."

"Just be you," he said again.

"That's not really fair. If it were me… I'm into comfort, fun, pleasure. I don't think that was what you were shooting for here."

Oops, she thought. *Pleasure*? *Really, Lockett*? Why had she said something suggestive again? Had she really worried about Parker being obvious when she was the one being more than obvious?

"Maybe what I was shooting for wasn't the right thing."

"And maybe it was. It's your business. You're the expert."

"Daisy…" he drawled.

She let out a deep sigh. "I don't know what your customers expect, but if I wanted to go to a luxury hotel, I'd still want comfort and, you know, it's probably just me, but I'd still want fun. I like fun."

"And pleasure," he added.

"Just forget I said that."

"Not likely."

She gave him a don't-push-me look. "Let's just stick to the facts here, Mr. Facts and Figures. So…what are the rooms like?"

He gave her the basics and showed her a picture.

She nodded…but then she frowned.

"What?"

"I don't know. It looks nice on paper, but then aren't photos of hotels made to look nice? The photographer chooses an angle and a filter that show the room to advantage, but it's not exactly what your customers will feel when they walk in. Still, looking at this, I'd say that everything looks wonderful. Totally wonderful. Except there's no gathering place in the room. If I was going to a luxury hotel, I'd want to invite some friends to visit. If only as proof that I was actually there. I like people. Crowds."

She liked crowds most of the time. Except when she was with Parker. But she didn't like the fact that she enjoyed being alone with him.

"Anyway, that's probably not what you were shooting for. Is it?"

"Not at the time. No."

"See? I told you that I wasn't your target audience."

"Still, you like people. And people like you. You have a better sense of how people act and react than I do. I was thinking…do you have a free day anytime soon?"

"We're closed on Sundays and Wednesdays and I don't have any tours this Wednesday. When your colleagues are elderly, they can't work seven days a week. Besides, they have friends. Book groups. Luncheons. Maybe senior date nights. They don't always tell me. I don't ask. But they have…stuff."

"Stuff." He smiled. "Well, then, while the gang does their stuff on Wednesday, would you consider visiting the spa with me? We're only flying to Chicago and I can have you back by early afternoon the next day."

Daisy's mind went blank for a second. Her hands went cold. "Go to Chicago? With you? To your hotel? And we'd be flying?"

He smiled. "If we drove, it would take days."

"Of course. I knew that. It's just—why do you want me to do this again?"

"I want your first impressions? Real impressions. Not just looking at a model. It would be immensely helpful."

And she had told him that she wanted to be helpful, to repay him. But traveling alone with Parker? And flying?

"It's all right," he said. "Not my best idea. A bit spontaneous for me."

And that was what got her. Parker had grown up weighing all the odds, doing the right thing, being the perfect non-demanding son and employee. Now he was trapped into being The Sutcliffe. He had responsibilities being heaped on him, expectations, possibly a marriage just for show. Sutcliffe's was his passion, but he didn't handle spontaneity well. The fact that he was doing it now…

Daisy jumped.

"Just tell me when and where. I'll be there. But I should warn you, if I'm going there to give my opinion, I'm going to give it. First thing out of my mouth. No holds barred."

"I wouldn't have it any other way."

"Because this is business, right? Important stuff."

"Very important. Absolutely business. But Daisy?"

"Yes?"

"I want you to be yourself. Don't leave your flip-flops at home."

Her temperature rose slightly. When had a discussion of her shoes made her feel so sensual?

No question. Only since Parker started noticing them. Daisy dragged in a deep breath. "Right. Be myself. But I have one question. Does any of this even make sense? I mean…when is the grand opening?"

"In two weeks, two days after the Sutcliffe ball."

"The one where all the brides-to-be will be paraded before you for your pleasure."

He grimaced. "That one."

"What could you possibly change in two weeks?"

"Maybe nothing, but…where Sutcliffe's is concerned, I can do a lot. At least in terms of the building."

"Only the building? I think you underestimate yourself."

"In what way?"

"In your role as The Sutcliffe, your skills extend beyond

the building. People want to please you. They want you to like them, to be near them, to smile at them."

He froze.

So did she? What was she saying?

And then he slipped one hand beneath her hair and cupped her neck with his long, elegant fingers. He leaned forward and kissed her. Just once. Very gently.

She felt it down to her toes.

"More and more I see why the Forever and a Day has a steady crowd despite the fact that the building and the location aren't ideal."

"I meant all those things in the most professional way," she insisted, her voice weaker, softer than she wanted it to be. And she *had* meant what she'd said in a professional sense. But she'd also felt it in a very personal way. "Remember your awkward cowboy? No one minded the awkwardness, because all you have to do is look at a person and it's almost as if you're commanding them to do your bidding."

Okay, this was just getting worse and worse. "I'll just be going now," she said. "I have lots to do. Research. Apartment hunting. Job-hunting."

"I'll help," he said.

"I'm capable." She stood firm.

"I know, but sometimes in a job hunt, it helps to have an objective outsider review your résumé. I'll help you with that part. And with leveraging the crew into the deal."

"The crew?"

"Nola, Lydia and John. I assume you're looking for a job managing another chapel."

She blinked. "No. I was thinking of adding more tours."

"Any luck with that?"

"No. Too many applicants, too few jobs, not enough money for us to get by."

"Exactly. Aim higher. You have skills that will be in big demand. *You'll* be in demand."

Maybe. But not with The Sutcliffe, the man who had to marry well and who turned green when babies were mentioned.

"I'll take what I can get," she said.

He frowned.

"I mean, thank you. I'd appreciate another perspective and some help with the job hunt. I'd like to do it myself, but…there's not much time. I think we both want to completely close the door when you go back to Boston."

He didn't even hesitate. "Absolutely."

She remembered the look hours later. He had looked… cold.

CHAPTER TEN

STANDING in the sparkling, glass-enclosed lobby of the Chicago Sutcliffe, Parker realized that he had never before taken a woman to one of his hotels.

He glanced down at Daisy, who was studying his creation, and realized that he was…nervous. Not a familiar feeling for him. Her pretty brown eyes looked everywhere as she craned her neck to see farther into the building. Thank goodness some of the color had returned to her face. He hadn't thought about the fact that she'd never flown before, and she had been scared. Petrified, although she hadn't uttered a peep. She'd simply hunched into herself and tried to smile.

It had been both the easiest and the most foolish thing to take her hand until they were in the air and again when they were landing. Still, despite her fake smile, the color had leached out of her cheeks. Now, she was looking alive again. Like Daisy again.

"You're very quiet."

She laughed. "I know. It's a rare occurrence."

"Want to tell me what you see?"

She looked up at him, a question in her eyes. "You want me to tell you what's right in front of your eyes?"

"No. I'm probably biased. Rose-colored glasses and all that. I want to see it through your eyes."

"All right." She turned slowly in a circle, looking up, down, left and right, her long red hair brushing against her as she tipped her head back. "It's beautiful. Aqua and white are very soothing colors, and this carpeting is so thick, it's almost like soft grass. The whole effect is of opulence, and it's also very quiet, but then it would be if we're the only ones here. Are we the only ones?"

"Other than a skeleton staff. But even once we open, the place will still be relatively quiet. Everything is built to muffle sound, to envelop visitors in a cocoon-like environment. And we've made the rooms big, so this won't be the kind of place that will ever be crowded. Space and the desire to keep the experience personal, relaxing and meditative means limiting the number of guests at any one time."

"That's interesting. You probably could have filled this place to overflowing."

He shrugged. "The idea is to make this so desirable and exclusive that people will wait to get in."

"Okay. Understood. So, big rooms, but not many people. And monastery-quiet, but without the austerity. And with lots of water."

She walked over to one of the fountains. "Oh, I like this. I love water."

He remembered her looking down on the fountain at the Bellagio and felt inordinately pleased that he had scored a point with her. "One point for me," he said.

"What?"

"I—sorry, that was dumb. I invited you here to grade the place and now I'm tallying up the things you like and don't like."

"I like it all."

"You haven't seen it all."

"So show me."

He led her down long, quiet halls, past more fountains. He showed her the rooms where visitors could be treated to mud baths, massages or the latest and greatest spa treatments available on the planet while Vivaldi, soft jazz or whatever music the visitor preferred played in the background.

Everything was ready. The low-level lighting, the spacious rooms, the plush carpeting that you sank into when you walked down the hallway, the huge fitness center. The juice bar and restaurants and shops weren't yet stocked but were otherwise completed. The whole hotel was opulent and lovely…and waiting.

For visitors. But Parker was waiting for something else.

He was waiting for Daisy to tell him what he'd missed. "I know it looks good. The design and the engineering are fine. I trust my skills enough to know that if there are mistakes in evidence, then they're minor ones. But the rest… the draw…I'm just not sure this is enough."

"Maybe that's the problem," Daisy said, after she had experienced the sights, scents and textures of the entire complex and they were seated at a nearby restaurant looking through the plans and photographs.

Parker wrapped his hands around a coffee cup and studied the concerned expression in her pretty brown eyes. "I'm not sure what you mean."

"I mean, when you were growing up and working at the company, what parts were you responsible for?"

"It varied. I started out with menial jobs, graduated to courier duties, accounting duties and, eventually, design."

"But the whole company wasn't resting on your shoulders?"

"Never before."

"Maybe you're asking too much of yourself."

"Maybe I'm just not well-rounded enough. Or maybe I'm not seeing the whole picture."

"No one can be and do everything. The Forever and a Day is a much smaller concern, but everyone has their jobs. We rely on each other."

"Sutcliffe's has a variety of employees, too, but at the helm… Sutcliffe children are raised to be self-reliant from the cradle. No tears. No whining. No excuses. No hugs. I've been told that my mother hated that at first, but she was malleable. She learned not to coddle me. When I was ten, one of the servants was teaching me a few magic tricks. Stuff like pulling a quarter from behind someone's ear. My parents said that Sutcliffe males didn't waste time on nonsense like that. The next day, the servant was gone."

"What a horrid childhood!"

He stared into her eyes. "It made me strong."

Daisy studied him. "But that's why you don't want kids, isn't it? You're not interested in treating another child that way."

He blew out a breath. "Being tough may help a business leader who has to hire and fire or deal with competition, but it's not an effective parenting strategy. My parents and I…weren't close, but I am what they wanted me to be. I have the traits they wanted me to have. And yes, I would never subject another child to that. It ends with me."

"But…" Daisy's eyes looked sad, stubborn.

He shook his head. "But we got off the subject," he said *gently*. "*I didn't come here to whine about my past or make excuses for myself*. My point was that people expect more from a hotel now than they once did, but I lack the people skills to know what they *do* want. You have those skills. Because while the Forever and a Day may be a group effort, you're the one who knows what your customers want. You're the force behind it."

She opened her mouth, then closed it again. "Tillie was up until recently."

"Exactly. You stepped in and became what she'd been."

Daisy laughed. "You wouldn't say that if you'd been here then. Tillie was wonderful, but she was more organized than I'll ever be. I could never be her, and I beat myself up about it for a while, but now...what good does beating myself up do?"

"Is that what I'm doing? Beating myself up? Pitying myself? You might be right."

Her eyes flashed fire. "I never said that. You certainly didn't seem as if you pitied *anyone*, including yourself, the first night I met you."

"Touché."

"Not complaining," she said, waving a crust of bread around. "I'm just saying that no matter how you feel, that's not the appearance you give. You always seem very much in control, a presence to be dealt with."

"Maybe I'm scaring the customers away." He was only half joking.

"Maybe you just need to lighten up and let yourself enjoy your work again."

Her voice had gotten softer as she went along. She was resting her cheek on her hand and Parker noticed that she looked very tired.

"You need rest," he noted.

"I'm just...just give me a few minutes. I'm a little tired. Probably because I was nervous and that takes it right out of me."

"Nerves because of the airplane ride?"

"A little. Mostly...I'm not used to having people solicit my opinions, especially for something this big and important. It's a bit daunting."

He shook his head. "Why wouldn't I ask for your help or care what you thought? You're a smart woman."

"Who's spent most of her life simply running or reacting. I was an unfortunate accident to my parents and an unfortunate encounter to others, including the father of my child."

"Not to Tillie."

"No. Tillie loved me. But she didn't need my help. And Nola, Lydia and John love me, too, but they know I'm just a small-time chapel operator."

"Then, they don't see what I see."

"What do you see?"

He stared at her for a moment and what he saw... He *wanted* what he saw and he couldn't have it, so he settled for the simple truth. "I see a woman who looks into the hearts and minds of people. A very wise and talented woman with the gift of being able to put herself in other people's shoes."

She raised a delicate eyebrow. "And I thought you weren't a people person."

"A man would have to be totally senseless not to see your value or to value your opinion."

Daisy shook her head, but she smiled. "That doesn't sound like the ruthless man you think you are."

He took her hand. "I'm just being truthful."

"All right. Then here's the truth as I see it regarding your spa. That's what you want from me, isn't it?"

"What I want and what I want for the company are two different things."

Her fingers shook beneath his own, and he released her. "All right. The company," she said. "Your spa is perfect. It really is. Because all those things I said? About the quiet and the fun and the visitors? The things that sounded like criticism? That's all nonsense. What I'm comfortable with...that's not what Sutcliffe's is. It's not what *you* are.

It's what *I* am, but I was right the first time. I'm not your audience. You've totally done it right. I think if you went on television and asked people to come here, they would come. Who cares if you're not your father? You're you and you designed a beautiful, beautiful building. They'll come. You'll go back to Boston, become the king of Sutcliffe's, a fantastic success, and the opening of this spa will be noted as the day you made your name as The Sutcliffe."

Her voice had dropped near the end. He noted that her eyes weren't as bright as usual. The flight and the responsibility he'd thrown on her had done her in. And her being pregnant had added a final wallop, he reminded himself. What a jerk he was. Didn't pregnant women need more sleep? And here he had dragged her across the country and all over the place.

"Time to let you sleep," he said.

"I haven't done anything major yet. Just reinforced what you already must know in your heart." Which implied that he *had* a heart. He wasn't going to argue about that anymore.

"You've done more than you know. And you're worn out. Don't feel guilty about needing to rest," he reiterated.

"I hate this part of being pregnant. Besides, I'm supposed to be paying off my debt and you paid to fly me all the way here. I darn well intended to give you your money's worth. A full Daisy Lockett consultation. Not that there really is such a thing."

"There could be."

She shook her head. "What?"

"You could hire yourself out to brides and chapels. Become a wedding planner. You already have the props. And the know-how."

"No, that's not me. I told you, I'm small-time. A tiny chapel. I'm a minor player in the field."

"You could be more. The one people come to for advice about how to run a wedding. The person who organizes events in lots of places. Weddings in hotels, anywhere, everywhere."

"That's...ambitious." She was being polite. Clearly this wasn't something she wanted to do.

"Just a thought."

"Well, thank you for the thought. So, have I convinced you that the Sutcliffe Spa Complex is golden?"

He laughed. "The Sutcliffe Spa Complex. It doesn't exactly roll off the tongue or make a person want to hop on an airplane to come here, does it? You're definitely right about it needing a better name."

"You'll think of one. Or one of your people will."

"My people? Sounds like a bad movie."

"You know what I mean. Parker?"

He looked at her.

"I'm sorry you didn't get to learn magic tricks." She sounded so sad that he couldn't help smiling.

"I learned one. Just one." And reaching out, he appeared to pull a quarter from behind her ear. Her laughter made him wish he knew more tricks.

"Do that again," she said. And he did, but this time his fingertips brushed her ear. Everything...sizzled.

Daisy gasped slightly. Parker looked deep into her eyes and remembered how exhausted she was.

He grimaced. "I can't believe I've kept you talking. I need to get you into the nearest bed."

Suddenly it seemed like one of those movies where everything in the background freezes and people start speaking in slow motion so that their voices drawl out. Parker cursed himself for phrasing it that way. Things were already dicey between him and Daisy. The air was practically electrified between them, but...they were all wrong.

She had her wedding chapel and her baby. She felt out of place in his hotels. Their Tillie quest could end badly, and no matter what she said, Daisy would be hurt if he found that what he suspected was in fact true. If Tillie really had had a shady past and he had to deny her relationship to him or bury her Sutcliffe connection even deeper, that would build the barrier between Daisy and himself even higher, especially since Daisy intended to claim Tillie as her baby's stand-in grandmother.

What kind of man placed a reputation of a company ahead of the happiness of a woman and child?

A man like me, he thought. But then he'd always known he was *that man*, one who hadn't been built for the personal relationships that Daisy coveted. He wasn't a warm man or one who could give a child what a child needed. He wasn't…a Daisy kind of man.

A businessman was all he'd ever wanted to be. And spending time with Daisy, acknowledging the chasm between them, was painful for him and possibly hurtful to her. He hated that. So, maybe he should just choose one of Jarrod's brides, send an investigator to finish up the Tillie story, hush it up and then throw himself back into repairing Sutcliffe's.

And leave Daisy alone.

Daisy had had a sleepless night, made even more restless by the knowledge that except for a tiny downstairs crew, she and Parker were the only two people in this building filled with beds and rooms with huge Jacuzzis.

Parker had been pensive when he'd insisted on walking her to her room. He'd looked around as if seeing the hotel for the first time ever.

"Lord of all you survey?" she'd asked. "How does that feel?"

He'd thought about it for a minute, then smiled. "It feels good. I'm at home with big buildings, with hotels in particular. Sutcliffe Industries made me what I am."

And she didn't think he merely meant wealthy. He was reclaiming his role, stepping back into the shoes he'd temporarily vacated when he'd come to Las Vegas as Mr. Stenson. Even reclaiming that emotionally barren life his parents had thrust on him. And she should be grateful for that. Because if he returned to his life, she could forget him, couldn't she?

Maybe. If she didn't let herself think about that silly twinge her heart seemed to have acquired somewhere in midair when Parker had taken her hand to keep her from being scared on the airplane.

Then she felt confused and angry with herself. Because she *was* attracted to this man who was so not for her.

"I'm also lost," she realized as she stared down the hallway. This was a part of the hotel she hadn't seen before.

This place was big. Seriously big. And imposing.

Daisy wandered some more. Finally, she came to a very tasteful directory tucked away in a nook by the elevators. Having been tired the day before, she hadn't noted her surroundings carefully, but she could locate the lobby. And, she thought, spying a hotel phone, use a phone. Why hadn't she just called and asked to be connected with Parker? She knew him well enough to know that he wouldn't leave her stranded in his hotel, but she'd wanted to poke around. Now she'd done that; now she just needed Parker.

A tiny ache that quickly became a bigger ache suffused her. No point in dwelling on that. She picked up the phone and asked where she could find Parker.

His room turned out to be on the floor above hers and now that she had a map, she easily made her way there.

Parker answered the door wearing his customary dark

pants and white shirt, but the shirt was unbuttoned, his sleeves were rolled up. There was a lot of Parker showing, a lot of muscle and skin.

Daisy's throat went dry.

"I—" she began, her eyes resting on his chest. What was with her? She wasn't a prude.

"I wanted to let you sleep," he said, buttoning his shirt, rolling down his cuffs. As if he needed to always be in the role of The Sutcliffe.

For some reason, that irritated her. "You don't have to do that for me. I'm not that formal."

"I know. I did it for me," he said. "Because while I *am* that formal, you also know what effect you have on me."

"Parker, who are you talking to? Are you still there?" The voice came from across the room, out of his computer speakers.

Daisy turned at the woman's voice. "I…should be going. I should have called first."

He shook his head and headed for the computer. "It's just Fran," he said. "She's heard about you."

Daisy wanted to ask what Fran had heard, but maybe that wouldn't be wise.

"Put me on video," Fran said. "I want to see this woman I've heard about."

A click of the mouse and Daisy was staring at a very fashionable middle-aged woman with beautifully high-lighted blond hair wearing a suit that had probably appeared in some designer's collection. "Hello, Fran," Daisy said, taking a deep breath, knowing she didn't look half as chic as Fran. But…that was okay. She liked her plain blue dress and flip-flops. And even fussy Parker valued her opinion.

"Daisy. I was beginning to think Parker had made you up, but you're just as vibrant as he said you were."

Hmmm, *vibrant* was one of those words that could be a

code word for *brash* or *too bold* or *cheap*. But Fran sounded sincere. And Parker liked the woman. Daisy decided to like her, too.

"Thank you," Daisy said. "Parker tells me that you're the glue that holds Sutcliffe's together."

"Parker, that's nice." Then Fran sighed. "Unfortunately, I did call for a reason." She looked suddenly hesitant, glancing at Daisy.

"I'll just wait in my room," Daisy said.

"No." Parker stopped her. "We have to catch breakfast and then a flight if I'm going to have Daisy back in time for her next wedding. Besides, she knows about what's going on at Sutcliffe's."

"All right," Fran said, but she looked a bit uncomfortable. "There's been an unfortunate situation developing here. Some of the board members aren't happy at your continued absence even though you've been in contact with me. Someone—"

She hesitated.

"Tell me," Parker said.

"Someone implied yesterday that I was being disloyal to the company by keeping your whereabouts secret and that the board might need to review my history with the company if you weren't here to vouch for me."

"What? Do they think you've kidnapped me or bumped me off?"

Fran frowned. "I suspect that they're trying to flush you out, to entrap you into revealing where you are and I said as much. Because you know that one word and there would be reporters at your doorstep. Possibly even Jarrod. And don't worry about me. I'm angry, but they can't touch me."

"You're darn right they can't."

"Oh, and Parker? The main reason I called is to let you

know that Jarrod finalized the guest list. Fifty debutantes. He released it to the press yesterday. Like it or not, he's taken it upon himself to up the ante. It's pretty much public knowledge now that the Sutcliffe ball has been turned into a marriage market. There are going to be lots of cameras."

"Thanks for telling me, Fran. I'll be back very soon. I'm not going to let them bully you."

"Don't worry about me."

"I do."

The silence in the room when he clicked off was palpable. "I'm sorry about that," he said.

Daisy lifted one shoulder in dismissal. "Hey, it's almost like reality television, isn't it? Drama? Deception? Manipulation and the battle for power?"

Parker looked frustrated. Then he shrugged. "Sins of the Sutcliffes?" he suggested.

"Parker...you made a joke."

"I know. Not my style, but the situation *is* almost laughable, isn't it?" But he didn't look all that amused.

"Will she be okay?"

"Fran? She's tough as nails. She knows her way around the Sutcliffes. Still, I don't like the fact that they're using her as a punching bag instead of me."

"You won't let them continue to do it."

"You're sure of that?"

"Absolutely."

"Why? How can you be so sure?"

Daisy looked to the side. "You held my hand on the airplane without me asking, you didn't kick us out of the apartment, and I know that was in part because you refused to throw old people on the street."

"It would have been a bad PR move."

"You've implied that before, but I don't believe it. I can't see you ordering anyone to toss Nola's things out on the sidewalk."

The man looked horrified.

"And even though you're not big on pregnant women, you worried because I was sick, and you made me rest. You're going to go back. For Fran's sake. Aren't you?"

"I'll call and give her a specific date of my return when we get back to Las Vegas. I'll email Jarrod and read him the riot act for trying to use her. I don't actually blame him for wanting more from me, you know. He was used to my father, who was Sutcliffe Industries twenty-four hours a day. My father knew how to manipulate the press and enjoyed doing it. He loved being the center of the Sutcliffe universe. Jarrod is scared. That's why he's acting like a jerk. He feels as if I've reneged on my duties and he's been forced to be Atlas, holding up Sutcliffe Industries. Only it's falling and he can't stop it. He resents that. I hate what he's doing, I don't like his methods, but I understand the whys and wherefores."

"So…are you going back to be Atlas?"

"Something like that. I'm going to try. Just as soon as we interview Liza Brett."

"What if she can't tell you anything?"

"Then—" he took her hands "—I guess there's nothing to tell."

"You don't really believe that."

"No. It's too odd that I never even saw a photo of Tillie when I was a child, not a mention of her. But if Liza isn't the connection, then Tillie's past is probably well and truly buried."

"And you won't acknowledge her?"

He frowned. "Learning of Tillie's existence was like discovering a closed door I hadn't known about. And your feelings for her make me want to keep it open, but…if I don't find the reason for her disappearance from my life, acknowledging my aunt would be like deciding to hold an unexploded grenade in my hand. Just because it seems inoperable doesn't preclude the fact that under the right circumstances, it could blow up in my face."

Daisy gave a slight nod. "I understand. So, you close the door completely. And once all of us move and I get a new job, you can quietly sell the property and also close the door on the rest of your Las Vegas connections."

And it would be as if she'd never existed in his life.

Parker gave her a tight smile. "I'd better feed you. And take you home."

She nodded. "I'm ready. I'm packed. Parker?"

He waited.

"Now that we know about Liza, can we interview her as soon as possible?" Now that she knew that Parker's departure was imminent, Daisy's entire body, her whole heart, was crying out for her to find some way to get him to stay. Which was exactly why she knew the best thing was to end things quickly.

"I've already located her," he confessed. "We'll see if we can't make an appointment within the next couple of days."

And just like that—almost as suddenly as he'd dropped into her life—Daisy found herself facing the fact that her life was going to return to normal.

Or...not normal. Just pre-Parker. Something stabbed at her heart. Hard.

She ignored it. She was used to being ill, to feeling bad and tired. Surely she could stand this, too.

"Daisy?" he said when they were on the airplane, when the fear had kicked in and he had taken her hand without even asking.

"I'm all right," she said, thinking that he was worried

about her fear of flying. It was foolish to admit it, but somehow having his big hand around hers did make the fear less stark.

"I won't push you out of the apartment or the chapel," he said. "I don't want you to have to worry about that. You and your baby and the others will have a place."

She gave a tight nod, but his words kicked at her. He was letting them stay, taking away the fear and worry. She could tell the others that they had an even longer reprieve.

But she knew she wasn't going to take it. Staying would mean maintaining the ties between herself and Parker. And she had to cut them. Break the connection. And never look back.

"I think I've found a place," she said, even though that wasn't really true. And she was pretty much planning on taking any work that she could find. Time enough later to be picky and change directions. Tillie had always told her that ripping the bandage off quickly was the best way to go.

She knew why. The theory was that the pain of removing the bandage drowned out the pain of the wound.

Please let that be true, she thought.

"It's better than your place," she said, teasingly. Because the silence had been too deep. Things were getting too serious. That couldn't happen. She needed to keep things light right up until he was gone.

It worked. He laughed. "Does that mean that it has an elevator?"

"Two," she lied.

"Good." He ran his thumb over her palm, making slick desire trickle through her. "Then I'll know that you're fine. A two-elevator building. Can't ask for more than that, can we?"

Yes. She could. She could ask for a lot more. She wanted

to ask for a lot more. But she was only allowed to think of those things—those dreams where there were no barriers between her and Parker—in her sleep.

"Everything will be perfect," she said. "You'll see."

CHAPTER ELEVEN

PARKER wasn't happy, and in some ways he should have been. Daisy's comments about the hotel had given him food for thought. Ideas were churning through his brain. It should have been a good feeling.

He knew why it wasn't. Now that he'd set a date to leave, he was having withdrawal symptoms. In a very short time he'd grown to look forward to time spent with Daisy. Leaving her would be difficult. Not that there was a choice. Lots of choices in his life had been made on the day he was born a Sutcliffe. He needed to go back to Boston. She needed to be here raising her baby with her makeshift family that would give that child all a child needed. Trying to separate Daisy from all that...well, it would be like placing an angelfish on dry land and expecting it to continue to flourish and still be a functioning angelfish. Not possible.

"So, just get it over with. Finish what you started."

Which was how he and Daisy ended up in a tiny little cottage in the next county. The woman who greeted them looked to be in her sixties. And she clearly didn't really want guests.

"I'm only letting you in because Klaus asked."

"We won't take much of your time," Parker said. "Klaus said that you were friends with Tillie Hansen."

"Once. Why do you care?" Obviously Klaus hadn't told her anything, and, of course, Klaus didn't *know* everything.

"Tillie was a good friend of mine," Daisy offered. "She more or less raised me."

The woman gave Daisy a sideways glance. "You related?"

Parker noticed how Daisy's body tightened slightly, although he doubted that anyone else would notice. He was used to noticing things about Daisy.

Belay that thought, Sutcliffe, he ordered himself. Noticing Daisy was a habit he was going to have to cut back on. Forcibly. By removing himself from her presence.

"Not by blood," Daisy admitted. They had discussed whether he should admit to the relationship but all arrows pointed to no. Throwing the Sutcliffe name into the mix could invite incorrect information if the woman turned out to be the type who would expect a reward for her efforts. Plus, not knowing anything about her, they had no clue whether Liza Brett might try to sell the story of how The Sutcliffe grilled her for family information he should already have been privy to.

"But we were close," Daisy added. "She took me in when I was sixteen."

"Yes, well, Tillie was always taking in lost animals, people in trouble, men who seemed to need saving."

"She had a kind heart," Daisy agreed.

"Sometimes. Or at least that was what I thought until I realized that she wanted the man I was in love with. When he showed an interest in her over me, then she had no problem forgetting that we were friends."

Daisy's expression turned wary, sad. "Are you saying that Tillie treated you badly?"

The woman seemed to hesitate. "I'm not saying she

sought him out, but she didn't exactly discourage him, either."

"That's why you stopped being friends?" Parker asked.

"Mostly. A man can make a woman do stupid things," she said, staring straight at Daisy and then frowning at Parker. Clearly she didn't like him. He didn't really care.

"What does 'mostly' mean?" he asked. "What else happened between you?"

"That is none of your business." Her voice was rising.

Daisy gave him a look. He had no idea exactly what that look meant, but the pleading in those caramel eyes stopped him cold. And when he stopped talking, Daisy swooped in.

"We're not interested in butting into your business, Ms. Brett," she said, soothingly. "We just want to know about Tillie. Since you were good friends, we hoped you knew something about her past. That's all we want."

Strangely enough, the woman didn't seem more relaxed. If anything, she appeared more tense. "Why would Tillie's past matter now? She's dead."

Daisy didn't even hesitate. "She still has family."

"Then why aren't they here talking to me?"

"They can't do it. They've asked us to fill in the gaps in Tillie's history. It's important. A matter of life and death."

"Hah! Now I know you're lying. Tillie's family cut her off. They sent her away because she was trouble. She was a rebel, a bit of a drinker. Finally, she robbed a store, took a whole lot of money and stuff. It was more a matter of rebellion than anything. Her sister was engaged to a rich man Tillie didn't want her to marry. She figured he'd call it off if Deanna's sister turned out to be a criminal. Only Deanna found out and followed Tillie. In trying to cover everything up and keep it quiet, Deanna ended up driving the getaway car to help Tillie escape, and Tillie let her do it. Then they both got caught and it took a ton of arm-twisting and favors called in for the police and store owner to look the other way. The deal was that they'd let Tillie go and keep Deanna's name out of things as long as Tillie agreed to leave the state and never have any contact with Deanna again.

"Deanna's fiancé was prepared to do whatever it took to keep his name clean. If Tillie hadn't agreed, he not only would have ended the engagement, but he would have drug Deanna through the dirt."

"Sounds like a man who would have simply dropped Deanna," Parker said with a scowl.

"I think she was pregnant. He wanted the baby. And if he dropped her, he would have lost his leverage at keeping his name out of it. Anyway, don't tell me that Tillie's family is interested in what happened to her. If they cared, she wouldn't have come to Vegas."

"She must have been lonely," Daisy said sadly.

"What did you mean by 'mostly' when you mentioned why your friendship with Tillie ended?" Parker asked. "You knew all this about her. That's a pretty heavy secret to carry."

The woman glared back at him. "I never told until now, and it doesn't matter, anyway. She's dead."

"But you could have held it over her head," he suggested.

Liza's eyes drifted to the side. "I loved Tillie," she said sadly. "But people make mistakes. Tillie made hers and she paid the price. So did I. Now I'm not saying anything else about her. Not even for Klaus."

"Was Klaus the man?" Daisy asked.

"Klaus was married," Liza said, but Parker noticed that she didn't deny that he was the man...which was neither here nor there. "Some men make you do crazy things.

Believe me, hon, they're not worth it." And she nodded toward the door.

Outside, Daisy and Parker got in his car and began to drive in silence. "I'm sorry," she said, her voice breaking slightly. "I—I can hardly believe it, but I guess Tillie really did do some terrible things that wouldn't look so great in the Sutcliffe history books."

Without a word, Parker pulled over to the side of the road. He took her hand and kissed her palm. "No, I'm sorry, Daisy. I shouldn't have dragged you here with me. You really didn't have to know this."

She unfastened her seat belt and turned toward him, leaning closer. "If you think I would have let you leave me at home, you're dead wrong."

"I didn't mean it that way."

"I know you didn't. You think I would have been happier not having known that Tillie once did something so bad that she nearly got her younger sister thrown in jail?"

"Yes. I do. You were happy when I met you."

"I'm still happy. I'm just...processing things."

He studied her, then reached out and slid his hand down her hair. "All right." But, of course, it wasn't all right. He'd known that while she'd thought he would find something, she'd never dreamed it would be this convoluted or ugly. Neither had he, and he wasn't sure how he felt about it. Tillie had come out of the blue, inadvertently changed his background and his whole world and now...

As if she'd read his mind, Daisy took his hand. "For you, it's not just that Tillie committed a crime. Is it?" she asked.

"No," he admitted. "And it's more than learning all these things about my aunt. My mother helped commit a crime. My father used his influence to hush things up and sentenced a woman to a lifetime of solitary confinement.

That's possibly just as bad as Tillie's crime, which was
motivated by—"

"Jealousy."

He jerked his head up. "Excuse me."

"I *think* it might have been jealousy. You know that diary
that I kept telling you was fiction?"

"Yes."

"I wanted to believe it was fiction. Maybe because Tillie
had always wanted to be a writer and inspired me to take up
writing, but mostly because…I wanted it not to be a diary,
not to be the truth. I convinced myself that it was all made
up. But now I'm not so sure. There's a story in there. It's
written like fiction, but it's about a woman named Tammy
who was jealous of another woman, Diana, who was engaged to and carrying the baby of the man Tammy loved.
Tammy tried to seduce the man into loving her instead and
when that didn't work, she did something drastic and ended
up dragging Diana into the dirt. The man ended up hating
Tammy and she ended up alone, remorseful for what she'd
done and for the fact that she could never rewrite history
or take back the hurt she'd caused. I always thought it was
a story and maybe it is, but it sounds a bit too much like
Tillie and Deanna and…your father."

Parker froze. "You think my father and mother and Tillie
were involved in a love triangle?"

"I don't know. They were sisters. I don't want to believe
it, but…"

"Then don't. I don't think it's even possible. My father—
and my mother—they were not loving people. In fact, before they were divorced, they preached about the evils of
letting one's emotions get the upper hand. Afterward, they
preached about it even more."

Daisy didn't say anything at first. Then she rose up on
her knees in the car seat and leaned over to frame Parker's

face with her hands. "Parker…maybe they were trying to protect you from what had happened to them because of an event that had been too fraught with emotions. Maybe they weren't naturally that cold and maybe they were the way they were because they did love you."

She kissed him, and her lips brought fire to his mouth, to his thoughts. For a minute he forgot everything about his parents and Tillie and only thought about Daisy. Wonderful Daisy who had just suffered a horrible blow and still was trying to comfort *him*.

With one swift move he reached down, slid the seat back and lifted her onto his lap. He plunged his hands into her glorious hair and pulled her tighter against him. He tasted her lips again and again, drowning out everything except her softness, her sweetness. He slid his hands up her body, his thumbs caressing her breasts.

She moaned into his mouth and he deepened the kiss. He wanted more of her, all of her. But when he slid his hand around and dipped lower, she suddenly bucked away. He realized that he had been touching her abdomen.

"I'm…sorry," he said. "Not for kissing you, but for—"

"I know why you're sorry, and it's not your fault. I started this. I wanted this."

"But now you don't."

"Now I've got my head back on straight. We can't do this."

He didn't answer at first. "Parker."

Parker nodded. "We can't do this."

Daisy blew out a shaky breath. "I'm sorry I didn't stop *us sooner. I didn't want to stop, and that's part of why I did* stop. The last time…when the baby was conceived, I wasn't thinking. Not that it's any excuse, but I was so miserable, I wasn't even in my right mind. I didn't think beyond that night. With you…it's different. It's…more, it's one hundred times more intense, but if anything, I'm thinking even less. And the risk is—"

Parker reached out and gently touched her lips. "Don't be sorry. I knew better than to touch you, but when you're within kissing distance I forget to be smart. I'll try not to do it again. Will that be better?"

She gave a small laugh as she moved back into her own seat and locked her seat belt again. "It won't be better—I love kissing you and having you touch me—but it will be smarter."

"I guess I'll settle for smarter."

Daisy took a deep, visible breath. "What are you going to do now?"

"Think. Work. Help you get settled, arrange for the sale of the property and—" He looked directly at her once before he moved back into traffic. "And then I'll go back to Boston and try to become what the owner of Sutcliffe Industries should be. There's nothing more to be done or said. Is there?"

"No. No," she said a bit too airily. "I think you're definitely done here. I wish I could have helped you more."

"I intend to help *you*."

"Parker, I told you that I need to find my own way."

"Daisy, you're been finding your own way for years."

"Is that a criticism?"

"That's a very major compliment. But I'm going to worry if you're not settled in your own place with a job that offers you everything you need for you and the baby. Let me pull some strings?"

She hesitated.

"Daisy, you flew all the way to Chicago to give me feedback on the hotel. You discovered the letter that led us to Liza and you provided the intro to Klaus."

"And you forgave us the rent money and let us keep running the chapel."

"I need to do this," he said. "If we're unlocking our lives, then I want to be an active participant."

She looked unhappy, but she turned to him. "All right, Parker, help me unlock our lives."

CHAPTER TWELVE

DAISY was trying to politely hustle the pregnant mother and her three children out of the chapel office. Parker was due any minute to help with her résumé, but she'd been unable to turn this anxious woman away. Now, with the interview over, the children were antsy; their departure was taking too long. She probably should have asked the woman to come back later, Daisy conceded, knowing that it was their shared state of pregnancy that had compelled her to make this bad decision.

"Come here, Bobby. Cindy, pick up your crayons. Jimmy, stop running," the woman called.

Daisy managed not to look at her watch. In the end, it didn't matter. The hallway clock chimed one. Two seconds later, as if he was there to help announce the time, Parker stepped in.

The little girl who had spilled her crayons shrieked.

Parker froze.

"Gween," the girl sobbed. "Gween." She pointed.

Parker looked down and lifted his expensive shoe. A green crayon lay smashed beneath it.

He immediately turned toward the little girl whose lip was trembling. She was staring at Parker with tear-filled eyes.

"I—" he began. The look in his eyes nearly broke Daisy's heart. He looked as if he'd killed a kitten.

"Cindy, it's just a crayon," the mother said. "It's all right," she told Parker.

That should have been the end of that. But Daisy knew that it wouldn't be. Not because of the replaceable crayon, but because Parker would remember that he hadn't known how to interact with the child. He thought he was some emotionless robot. Daisy knew different. She had to do something.

"Cindy," she suddenly said. "Did you know that Parker is a magician? If you give him a chance, he'll make you a new crayon."

Parker's head swung toward her.

"Won't you?" she asked. Then she mouthed, *Say yes.*

Immediately she wondered why he would go along with an insane statement like that. True, he had surprised and delighted her by trusting her with his hotel plans, he had made her his partner in his Tillie search, but this? This was the thing that petrified him.

But she couldn't bear for him to walk away defeated.

"Yes, I can do that," he said. His eyes looked daggers at Daisy, but his voice showed none of his concern.

"He just needs to get his magician costume, okay?" Daisy said.

Cindy nodded, all big eyes and silence as Parker followed Daisy into the costume room. She turned to him. "I'm sorry I had to do that."

He shook his head. "So am I. More than you can imagine. I assume you have a plan."

"Well...I have a green crayon. And a top hat you can use as a magician's hat."

Parker was suddenly looking amused.

"What?"

"And the reason you can't simply give the little girl your green crayon? You thought she might need a little magic?"

"Actually, I thought *you* might need some magic."

"Daisy…don't try to fix me."

He was right. She was overstepping.

"I'm sorry. You're right," she whispered. "It was probably a very bad idea. You can just give her the crayon."

"And make you look like a liar? Not a chance. Only…"

"What?"

"A crayon isn't a quarter and…I've never practiced with something longer and more difficult to palm, but mostly it's that…Daisy, she's such a little girl. What if I scare her?"

"You won't." Daisy prayed that it was true, but you could never tell with small children. She gave him the hat. Together they trooped into the other room. Parker was eyeing the child as if *she* was the broken crayon. She really *was* a little thing.

Still, Parker sat down and asked the mother to sit and hold Cindy on her lap. He managed a gentle smile.

He looked at Daisy and then away. She could see the tension in his jaw.

"Cindy," he said, his voice low and quiet. "I'm really sorry that I broke your crayon. If I could replace it with another one, I would." And he reached behind her ear and pulled out a green crayon. "Will this one do?"

Cindy's eyes opened wide. She reached behind her ear as if to see if there was a crayon vending machine there. She stared at the crayon Parker had given her. Then she smiled.

Daisy let out a breath and turned to the mother. But… too soon.

"Well, what have we here?" Parker asked. "A flower for you." He pulled out a silk rose. "And one for your mom. And two pirate patches for your brothers." One by one he pulled out the objects from the costume room as Cindy's eyes grew bigger. The little boys were whooping.

Cindy's mother turned to Daisy. "I'd heard this place was special. I see that's true."

Daisy breathed a sigh of relief...even though she saw that Parker's jaw was still tight.

"I hope you'll forgive me now," Parker said to the little girl.

"Yes," Cindy whispered, her eyes bright. Then, as Parker began to rise, she patted him on the sleeve. She wrapped her little arms around his larger arm, hugging him and resting her head on his arm for several seconds.

He went rigid. Daisy saw it. But he took his other hand and gently rested it on Cindy's hair, just for a second.

She pulled back and smiled at him. "Home?" she asked *her mother.*

Within moments they were gone.

Parker stood facing the window. Daisy couldn't see his eyes.

"I...thank you," he said.

"You were good with her."

And then he turned. "I was...a wreck."

She shrugged. "You were a wonderful wreck."

"It could have gone wrong."

"No question. Sometimes children shriek. They're small. We're big...and scary."

Then he smiled at her, and her heart flipped around. "What?"

"You are such a bold, amazing and spontaneous woman. A gambler, a woman with great ideas." The compliment made Daisy's heart sing. But they both knew that she had gambled before and lost. On her parents, on Chris, even a little bit on Tillie. Gamblers inevitably lost now and then, and Parker was a man who weighed the odds and aimed for the sure thing. And they both knew that while he had passed this test, it had been a one-time occurrence. He would never be a man who would seek out children.

Daisy walked up to him, rose on her toes and kissed him on the cheek. But even that slight touch made her tremble.

She took a step away and saw that his eyes had turned fierce. He was not unaffected, either. Passion seemed to flare between them no matter how minor the contact.

"Thank you for the compliment," she said.

"It's just…the truth." He touched her cheek, the softest of caresses, and she realized that a short time ago, she might not have believed his compliment. Being with Parker had taught her to value her quirky traits as assets. But soon he would be gone. The thought was like a fist to the heart.

"I suppose we should get down to business," she whispered. Because wasn't that what they were supposed to be about?

Parker studied her. He let his hand drop. "Yes. Your résumé."

Daisy nodded. "Let's finish it." Because she knew that finding her a job was the last thing on his Mr. Responsibility check-off list. After he was sure that she, her baby and everyone else had a place, he would go.

And she would grieve. Because despite her best efforts, she'd fallen in love with him. But she couldn't think about that now. It was time to finish up and rip the bandage off. Quickly, before she fell any further.

As if he'd read her mind, Parker opened her file on his computer. Once again, he was all business. The Sutcliffe was back.

A short time later he looked up. "This is impressive, Daisy. The basics, including your work history with the chapel and your references, look great. Now you just need to be more effusive about what you have to offer."

"You'd think that a writer would know how to do that, but that's the toughest part."

"I understand, but…you're not a shy woman. Don't go shy on me now. You have so much to offer. The way you throw yourself headfirst into everything, whoever gets you as a wedding planner will be very lucky."

She tried to smile, to forget that ending this would end her relationship with Parker. She tried to be flippant. Light. "My tendency to throw myself headfirst into things without thinking has backfired a lot. I'm not totally convinced that's a selling point."

And wasn't the proof of that right before her eyes? She'd jumped right in with Parker, and now her heart was going to break. Only this time it was going to break harder. And she couldn't even tell him how she felt, because he had so many things on his plate. Besides helping her and setting her up—again—with a real estate agent, his phone had been ringing incessantly. She realized that he must have turned it on after Cindy and her mother had gone. She also realized that these weren't normal business calls. Parker looked slightly agitated. But he said nothing and just went back to work with a fervor after each call.

The phone rang again. Parker excused himself. He took the call by the window where the reception was better. When the call ended, his eyes looked dark and stormy. And worried.

Daisy couldn't take this any longer.

"Parker, I heard her voice. That was Fran, wasn't it?"

His lips thinned. "They've accused her of theft, of falsifying records and of anything else they could think of. Jarrod has gone over the Articles of Organization and discovered that if the company president is unable to fulfill his or her duties that the next in line can, with a vote of confidence of the board, temporarily step in to fulfill those duties. It's been decided that my continued absence poses such a situation. I think he's bluffing. I don't think he'd actually try to do anything, because the public relations fallout would hurt the company, but—"

"You have to go," she said.

"Not yet."

Daisy took a deep breath. She refrained from closing her eyes even though that was what she wanted to do. "Yes. You have to go now. Today."

"There are things to do here."

"And I can do them. You've done so many good things *for us, but one of the best was showing me how I've always* been spinning my wheels, just letting life happen to me, not even trying to take control or find a direction. Now look, I'm on my way to having a winner résumé, I've taken steps to find an apartment, I've even mapped out seven new articles and sold four of them. That's more than I wrote all of last year. One of them is a fluff piece on the appeal of the flip-flop," she said, trying to draw a smile from him.

It worked. A little.

"And the one on Tillie," he pointed out.

"No. I think I'm going to shelve that one."

"You shouldn't. I saw some of what you wrote. It was moving, and it was a touching history of the good she did here. She *did* do good. Her past can't negate that, and I *think you're just the person to make that clear. You're very* talented."

"Thank you." No one had ever said that to her before. Her heart should have been singing.

"I'm not ready," he said. "This feels...unfinished."

"I know. And I know why, so...let's finish it." She walked up to him and placed her palms on his chest.

His heart was thudding. Hard.

"Daisy." He slipped one hand beneath her hair, curving

his palm around her jaw as he kissed her. "You don't want this. You just know that I want it."

A sigh slipped through her lips. "For a minute I thought you were going to tell me no."

He closed his eyes, resting his head against the top of her head. "I *am* telling you no. I just—let me do this one good thing. Let me do this right."

She pulled back. "Leaving without making love with me isn't right."

"That wasn't what you said the other day."

"I know. I was afraid. Because of what we talked about earlier. All my life I've bumped from place to place, letting things happen to me. Half the time—no, *more* than half the time—my eyes were closed and by the time I opened them, I was somewhere I didn't want to be. I didn't make choices. I just existed, like a leaf on the wind. This time, I'm opening my eyes. I'm choosing. And I know that this is just one time, so there won't be any regrets later."

"Daisy…"

But still he didn't move closer.

She stepped back. "I'm pushing you, aren't I? You don't want this, do you?"

He growled. His jaw was tense, his whole body looked tight. "I want this so much, it's all I can do to keep from acting like some caveman, throwing you over my shoulder and carrying you upstairs."

"And yet, you're not doing any of those things," she whispered. "What is it that's holding you back?"

"I was with you the other day when we learned about Tillie. You've heard from me and Liza what kind of man my father was."

"I heard. You're not him."

"He hurt people. I don't know the whole story, but my father hurt people. He punished Tillie when he wasn't without blame himself. That servant he fired unjustly wasn't the first or the last."

"You'll never be him. I'm not worried. You won't hurt me. I know that you would never intentionally hurt me."

"But unintentionally…"

"I would have to *let* you do that for it to happen. And I'm not letting anyone hurt me anymore. So just…make love with me, Parker. We promised to unlock our lives. I think that this is the key. If we don't touch, we'll always be wondering what it would have been like. There'll always be that connection, that unfinished business. Unless you don't feel the same way."

He slid his arms around her and pulled her closer. "I'll always be wondering," he agreed.

Parker lifted her into his arms and began carrying her up the stairs. "They're all gone?"

She smiled against his chest. "They said they were going to play bingo. I think they were just leaving us alone."

Parker reached the landing and made his way to her room. She leaned over and opened the door. The emerald cover on the bed called attention to their destination. "The bed's kind of small," she said apologetically.

"I don't intend to move away from you that far. We won't need a lot of space."

He lowered her to the bed and she came up on her knees, trying to unbutton his shirt and doing a poor job of it. "I don't know why my hands are shaking so."

Parker grasped both of her hands in his. "You're not just doing this for me, are you?" he asked.

She gave him a look. "If I was a slapping kind of woman, I'd slap you for that. I'm an independent woman, and you've made me realize that I need to assert myself, know my strengths, praise myself, be honest with myself. So yes, I'm a little nervous," she said, shrugging off his hands and unfastening the last few buttons, peeling off his shirt by sliding her hands down his muscular arms.

Daisy paused to swallow. "But nervous or not, I want you, and...and I deserve to have you."

His green eyes turned fierce, possessive. "Daisy, Daisy...I knew you were trouble from the moment I saw you barreling toward me in that pink dress and carrying those bubbles," he said, reaching around to unfasten the loose bow of her halter-topped sundress. The pale blue bodice of the dress dropped, and for a moment Parker just stared. "I used to hate trouble," he said, his voice hoarse. "Now I welcome trouble if its name is Daisy."

In a matter of seconds he had removed the rest of her clothes and all of his. Naked, Daisy lay in his arms, her heart pounding furiously.

Parker was nuzzling her neck, kissing her eyelids, her throat, the curve of her breast. Longing surged through her as she gasped and slid her hands up into his dark hair.

"Parker?"

"Yes?"

His lips caressed her bare shoulder and slid lower.

"I want you to know," she said breathlessly.

"Yes." He kept kissing her. She felt as if her body was going to fly apart.

"I would never sleep with you to use you like those other women did."

"I know that," he whispered.

"Okay. I just didn't want you to have morning regrets. Because your name and your money are meaningless to me."

He gazed down into her eyes. "That's the nicest thing a woman has ever said to me. Thank you."

She smiled at him. "You're welcome."

When he continued to gaze at her, Daisy squirmed in his arms. "Parker?"

"What?" He never took his eyes off of her, and his fingertips were dancing over her elbows. It was nice, but not enough.

"Are you going to make love with me?"

"Nothing is going to stop me. Unless you tell me to stop."

"I won't."

"Good. I was just waiting to see if you had more to say. You seemed to want to talk."

She laughed. "I'm done talking. Completely." With that, she looped her arms around his neck and kissed him with all the desire she was feeling. He groaned and pulled her closer.

He kissed every inch of her body. His hands were everywhere and so were hers.

"There won't be any mistakes," he whispered. "I'll make sure you're protected this time." And he was as good as his word. Tender and fierce, he encouraged her to be herself, to be as spontaneous as she wanted. He took everything that she gave him.

And he gave it back to her. He loved her for hours. Completely, holding nothing back. This was their goodbye and they made the most of every moment.

When Daisy woke afterward, she was wrapped in a sheet and Parker was beside her fully dressed.

"Go save Fran. Go save Sutcliffe's. Do what you were born to do," she whispered.

He swept her into his arms, sheet and all, for one last long kiss. "If you need me…" he began.

She shook her head. "You've given me more than I need. We'll be fine. Don't look back. Don't even think about me."

"Impossible," he said as he left her. As Daisy lay in her

empty bed, she thought that that word was one half of the two words that had categorized her relationship with Parker from the beginning.

Wonderful. And *impossible.*

And over, she thought, adding a third word. *Over.* Now came the hardest part. Trying to pretend she didn't love or miss him.

Making love with Daisy had felt absolutely right. Leaving her felt totally wrong, Parker thought. But he was going.

Because that's what Daisy wanted. Because his lifestyle would make her crazy. Because she had her own ready-made family. A whole and loving family. And because he had no question that now that she was moving farther afield, chapels all over Las Vegas were going to want to snap her up. She was finally going to have recognition and all the things she wanted and needed. Her life would be full and complete. And far away.

As for him…

He knew what he had to do. Daisy, whether she knew it or not, had, indeed, been the key, the gatekeeper. And right or wrong, smart or foolish, he knew what his place was going to be at Sutcliffe's from here on out, what he was going to try to do.

If he had Daisy at his side, it might even be an adventure. Maybe even fun…after it stopped being hair-raising.

He could already picture her jumping in with both feet. Laughing. Prodding him to do more. Be different. Be better. Let go.

Letting go. How apt. He was in love with Daisy Lockett, a crazy, silly, wonderful woman who would be punished for her best and brightest traits in his world. He couldn't let that happen.

"Let go," he told himself. He was sure he would have

to say that a hundred thousand more times before it began to have any effect.

Being with Daisy was like watching the most wonderful movie, visiting the most fantastic places, eating the best meal, experiencing bliss times one million. Everything after that just fell flat.

CHAPTER THIRTEEN

"Look, Daisy, Parker's on television again," John said.

Daisy tried very hard not to look, even though she'd watched this commercial many times since it had first come on her screen a week ago.

"He looks very handsome on television, doesn't he?" Nola noted.

"He looks handsome anywhere," Lydia said. "I have to say I like what he's saying, too. How about you, Daisy? You've been unusually quiet today."

All three of them turned to look at her. "Yes, he's very handsome, but then you already knew that. And yes, what he's saying is…"

"Refreshing," Lydia said, taking the words out of Daisy's mouth. Parker had barely left Las Vegas when everything had gone quiet on the Sutcliffe news front. Then a few days later, this commercial had appeared. Very simple. Just Parker standing in the lobby of the Sutcliffe Spa Complex, now called Silken Waters, based on an online poll Sutcliffe's had conducted. Many of the suggestions Daisy had made to Parker had been on that list. "He's telling people that Sutcliffe's will still be the first name in luxury hotels, but they have a new division, a fun division, and he's asking people to help him create hotels that meet the needs and wishes of people you meet on the street. He wants to customize each hotel from here on out and he wants the public to have a hand in things."

Daisy knew. "That's Parker. He's a man who listens and then tries to do what's right. He tries to give people what they need and want." Tears came to her heart. She missed him so much and…how had he not known that about himself? How had he ever thought he was cold and unfeeling and unable to give?

But she knew. He'd been born to the wrong people and they hadn't known what a gem they had in him. Still, they must have done some things right. A man like Parker didn't just appear out of thin air. Even if it had seemed that way when he showed up on their doorstep that day weeks ago.

Daisy was still thinking about that when she got ready for work later that day and surveyed her much larger bedroom. The rental agent had showed her this place the day after Parker had gone. There was no question that Parker had had a hand in locating it. It was in a slightly shabby but safe part of town, with a small pretty park nearby that would be perfect for a child to play in. There was a small green dog run for Romeo, and the rent was reasonable.

Her fingers had itched to call Parker and thank him. Or at least to call Fran. But she had counted to ten. To fifty. To one hundred until she had gotten past that crazy idea. And then she had gone out, handed out her résumé, interviewed at several places and found her dream job. The owner was amenable to allowing Nola and Lydia and John to help out once every week or two.

It was enough for them.

Daisy should have been happy. She'd sold more articles, the baby was healthy. Life was…easy.

And her heart was a mess. Every time that darn commercial came on, she wanted to go cry in a closet. She missed teasing Parker. Or shocking him. Or kissing him.

Seeing him all the time but never being able to talk to him or touch him was pure misery. And she felt guilty. She didn't want her friends to notice.

But she knew that they did. They watched her like three mother hawks. Even John. They didn't miss a thing. They were news watchers and they heard every story about Parker and relayed it to her. They obviously thought they were helping. How could she tell them that even hearing his name was like an arrow through the heart?

He was in his element. He was successful. She was only a memory to him. And that was as it was meant to be, as it should be. Always.

She and hers would be fine. Eventually. She hoped. Things were at least peaceful.

So when she entered the house a couple of days later to utter pandemonium and John calling her name in a panic, she was caught unawares. "What's wrong? Did someone fall? Is someone hurt? Did Romeo get out again?"

"Look! Look! I taped it. Darn machine. I couldn't remember how to do it, but I got some of it." John was pointing toward the television. He ran the player back to the beginning of where he had started taping. Parker came on the screen again. He was in Boston but he was talking about...

"Las Vegas is a wonderful, exotic and exciting place," he said. "And as I'm sure most of you know, it's known for its wedding chapels. I happen to own one of them. It belonged to my aunt Tillie, my mother's sister, and I recently inherited the property. I'd thought I was going to sell it, but it's been the site of too many happy memories for that. So I'm announcing today that I'll be reopening the chapel as the Tillie Hansen Forever and a Day Wedding Chapel." When he looked into the camera, Daisy felt as if he were looking right into her soul.

"Daisy, he's going to reopen the chapel. Isn't that wonderful?"

Daisy smiled, but inside she was scared. For Parker. Customers loved what he was doing, and even this early on, the company's outlook had started taking off. Part of it was because he looked more relaxed on camera than she had thought he would and he seemed to genuinely care about what people wanted. But he was still the president of a company that was mostly known for luxury and an exclusive clientele. When Tillie's past came out—and at least some of it was bound to come out now that the national and not just the local press knew of her existence—what would they find that she and Parker hadn't found? What if they discovered the theft and deception or even just the drinking…or the other former addictions and excesses that the diary had hinted at? They might crucify Parker. Or attempt to, anyway. All his newfound popularity with the public might be toppled.

It didn't take long for the rumors to start flying. About Tillie. About Parker's parents. About the Sutcliffes in general. Some of it was close to the truth, some a twisted version of it, some completely wrong. And a few reporters even descended on the Forever and a Day asking rude questions and demanding answers. If they were asking questions of her, what was going on with Parker?

The few newspaper articles she saw didn't seem to have many of the facts, but they did hint that the great Parker Sutcliffe might be headed for a tumble in the public eyes.

Daisy's heart hurt. She picked up the phone five times to call him. Ten times. She wanted to know how he was.

Finally, she admitted that she couldn't talk to him on the phone. But she couldn't leave this alone, either. Looking online for a Boston directory, she found what she was looking for.

If it weren't for missing Daisy and her laughter and teasing so much, Parker might have been enjoying himself. In the past, he had been so stressed about not being enough like his father to carry the company that he had missed out on a lot of opportunities just to enjoy his work. Now, keeping his dusty relatives guessing and using "the Daisy method" to open new doors for Sutcliffe's should have been special. It would have been if he could have shared it with her.

He frowned, dove into the paperwork and plans for the first ever customer-driven Sutcliffe's and tried to concentrate. It was all but impossible. Bringing Tillie back into the mix had stirred up memories of Daisy in his arms, Daisy's lips on his.

A noise outside the door broke into his thoughts, and he opened the door to find Fran standing on the other side, ready to knock. Her mouth was open. Behind her Jarrod, his other cousin, Albert, and Uncle Bill, all board members, were frowning and looking like thunderclouds in expensive suits.

"What's going on?" Parker said.

"I see what's going on now," Jarrod said. "And why you haven't shown one iota of interest in any of the beautiful and *tasteful* women we've invited to the ball. I read an article in which one Daisy Lockett was mentioned in connection with Tillie the other day. Apparently, you know her. And she's…this woman is pregnant."

Jarrod reached out and guided the woman standing slightly behind him to the forefront. He didn't appear to be hurting Daisy, but he *was* insulting her and treating her without an ounce of respect.

Parker stepped up into Jarrod's face. "Let her go. And don't touch her again, Jarrod. I mean that."

Jarrod blinked. No surprise. When they had been younger, Jarrod had been the physical one. Parker had been into math and structures.

But Daisy changed everything. Parker looked into

her warm brown eyes. He felt as if he'd been holding his breath for weeks and suddenly had been allowed to have air. "Daisy, what are you doing here?" he asked when what he really wanted to say was, "Daisy, I love you, I've missed you," and then kiss her about a million times.

She took a deep breath. "Hi, Parker. I'm probably here doing something stupid and not very well thought out. I thought I was beyond that, but…bad habits, you know?"

He couldn't help smiling then. "Maybe not such a bad habit." Because she was here. "Care to elaborate?"

Daisy looked at Fran and something passed between the two women. "If possible, I'd like to see you alone," Daisy said.

"I see," Jarrod said. "There's something between the two of you." He was still eyeing Daisy's stomach with concern.

Daisy turned around. "I am *not* carrying Parker's baby."

"You're a married woman?" Jarrod said hopefully.

"No, but Parker and I are just friends." Well, there was a total lie. Parker supposed it fell under Daisy's "greater good" philosophy. He certainly didn't like the word *friend*. But then again, maybe it wasn't a lie in Daisy's eyes. That could well be how she saw him. Maybe that one night they'd shared had been a "friends with benefits" moment for her.

He scowled, then caught himself.

"In my office," he said to Daisy. "We can talk there."

She nodded, but when he showed her inside, he was pretty sure that none of the other players were going to leave the small seating area outside his office. Fortunately, his office was secure and soundproof…almost. Because the longer he thought about Daisy being here, the more he was sure that something was dreadfully wrong. He barely got the door closed before he advanced on her. "Tell me what's happened," he said.

To her credit, she didn't back down. But then had she ever? It was one of the things he loved about her. "Why did you reopen the chapel and put Tillie's name on it?" she asked. "You had to know that when The Sutcliffe does something that public, in that unexpected a place, in a manner that is so different from anything he's ever done, the press would take notice."

He tilted his head and smiled at her. "I had to know that," he agreed.

"No one knew she was your aunt. You were going to bury her in the past...or let her stay buried."

"Did I say that?"

"Once or twice. Yes."

He blew out a breath. "What kind of a jerk does that? I can't imagine why you would ever tell anyone I was your friend. You loved Tillie. And I was going to pretend she never existed."

"I know. I know. But...you had the right. She was your relative. I wasn't even related to her."

"Yes. *You were. You were the daughter she never had.*"

"You don't know that."

"Sure I do. I read something like that in her diary. Right near the end."

"I thought you only read the beginning, because reading it made you feel like a stalker."

"That was before I decided that she was my aunt and a piece of me and I wanted to know more about her. And it was before it occurred to me that she might have written something about you."

"About me? That occurred to you when? When we first met, back when I was driving you nuts?"

"It happened last week...when thinking of you was driving me insane."

She looked up into his eyes, clearly confused. He wasn't

sure how much he should tell her of his feelings. Or if he should. "Daisy, what did you come to do?"

"I came to try to do damage control. I wrote an article about what an upstanding man you are and I wrote a story—it's fiction of a sort because I left out all the questionable parts—about what a good woman Tillie was."

"You wrote a story about me?"

"An article. Non-fiction. I have a copy here, but…"

"What?"

Her gaze slid away. "I already submitted it to a newspaper in Las Vegas. It's already run there. I was pretty sure that you'd balk at saying yes to me publishing a glowing account of all the things you've done." Still, she pulled it from her purse. "You can always ask them to print a retraction or a correction if there's something you don't like."

Parker took the paper in hands that threatened to tremble. He wasn't worried about anything Daisy had written about him. He just wanted to make sure he said the right things to her about her creation. But as he began to read the short article, he couldn't help smiling, even laughing. "Daisy, you are an amazing writer. Your personality comes through. Not that I think I'm anywhere near as nice as you've painted me. I came to Vegas, frowned at you a lot, threatened to evict you, insisted on looking for dirt on a woman you revered, and you write that I was kind?"

"You were, and not just to us. Those people at the wedding…even the children. And sweet little Cindy. I know they made you nervous, but you never let them see it. That's the mark of a kind person. I know."

"How do you know?"

"I've been lucky enough to have known some kind people."

"Nola and Lydia and John."

"Yes. By the way, they send their love. Even if you don't

want it," Lydia says. "And…Tillie loved me. She really did. No matter what she did earlier in her life. I know that. I think you know that, too, but other people won't."

"I didn't go public with the wedding chapel renovation to hurt her memory, Daisy." Despite telling himself not to touch her, he reached out and ran his hand down her cheek. "I did it because denying her was wrong. Because she *did* turn her life around and she *did* help people. Lots of people. She made others happy. That kind of thing shouldn't go unrewarded just because of something a person did when they were very young. If she did wrong—and it appears she did—then she spent the last thirty years of her life paying for it. I'm just glad that she found love. I'm glad she found you."

"If the story comes out, Tillie may fare better than your parents," she whispered. "She has people who will defend her. Who'll defend them or your family name? What if that rubs off on you?"

"I'll defend them as far as I'm able. That might be difficult to do. They did things I find difficult to forgive." He wasn't even talking about the Tillie situation, but he knew that Daisy would understand that.

"As for me, I'm not worried. A man is more than the genetic material he carries. I'm *not* him. In time I hope people will see that."

She smiled. "I see that *now*. I never thought you were like your father."

"I thought that I needed to be. But a wonderful woman showed me a better way."

Parker's heart lurched. How lucky he was to have met this woman. "Daisy…there's something I've been wondering?"

She looked up at him with those big caramel eyes, all that pretty copper hair swinging back as she waited for his question. Her eyes were glowing. She was smiling. She looked as if she'd wait forever.

But maybe that was wishful thinking.

"How did you get here? From Las Vegas?"

"I didn't have much time to lose. As soon as I saw the story, I bought a plane ticket, wrote the articles, submitted them and came here. Fran knew."

"You...flew?"

She looked up at him from under long dark eyelashes. "A train would have taken too long."

"Daisy, you're afraid of flying."

"Not when you're with me. I just...I just imagined that you were. It helped."

And then he couldn't help himself. "You flew out here to save me from myself, to save my reputation even though you don't like flying. What other woman would do something like that?"

To his surprise, she didn't smile. "I suppose in retrospect...my plan was more than a bit impetuous. And...you didn't even need my help, did you? Fran told me that even the bad publicity was bringing in customers. You're more than capable on your own. You're truly The Sutcliffe now."

She reached up to caress his cheek and then she turned to go.

Panic welled up in Parker. "You're leaving? Already?"

"I—" She closed her eyes. "I think it was a mistake to come here."

"Not for me, it wasn't."

"Parker, look at you. You're everything you ever wanted to be."

"No. I'm not. Oh, don't get me wrong. I'm happy that I was able to forge my own path at Sutcliffe's...finally, but that wouldn't have happened without you. You freed me from feeling that I had to follow a line that someone else had drawn. You made me realize that while my parents were powerful people, they were flawed just like everyone, just like me. And it's okay that I'm not perfect."

"No one's perfect."

"But you're perfect for me," he whispered. "Daisy, don't go. Don't go yet. Stay with me."

"Parker, I can't stay. I'm pregnant with a child that isn't yours. You don't want children. You especially wouldn't want another man's child, not after…"

He stopped her by taking her chin gently in his hand. He shook his head. "No. That wasn't even remotely the same as your situation. You were honest about your baby. And I know what I said about children, but…so much of that was tied up with the fear that I would repeat my parents' mistakes, make another child's life miserable. But I don't worry about that now. I've seen love, real love between you and your friends. I know how it's done."

She smiled up at him, her eyes misty. "How is it done, Parker?"

Gently he kissed her lips. "When love is between a man and a woman, sometimes it's like that. And sometimes it's like this." He kissed her more deeply. He gathered her to his heart. "I love you, Daisy. Try to love me back. Somehow we'll make this work. You and me and our baby. And…the rest of our family."

"I love you so much," she said, wrapping her arms around his neck. "I would fly across the sea and back a thousand times to get to you."

They stood there in each others' arms for a long time before Daisy raised her head. "Jarrod doesn't approve of me. What is he going to say?"

"Let's ask him," Parker whispered. Quietly he moved across the carpeting and opened the door. Jarrod and Albert nearly fell in. Fran and Uncle Bill exchanged a smile.

"Did you get all that, Jarrod?" Parker asked.

"I heard a lot. Not all. Parker, you were only in Vegas a couple of weeks. Do you even know who this woman is?"

"I do," Parker said to his cousin. "She's the woman I'm taking to the Sutcliffe ball...if she'll go. She's the woman I'm going to marry...if she'll have me. And she's the woman who's going to have my baby...if she'll let me be the one."

"*I thought you said that wasn't Parker's baby*," Jarrod said, pointing his finger at Daisy accusingly.

"I guess I was wrong," Daisy said, smiling that wonderful Daisy smile. "And the answer to everything is yes."

"Wedding at *Tillie's*?" Parker asked, raising one eyebrow and smiling at his bride-to-be.

"Please, yes."

"Bubbles? Pirates? Leprechauns? Cowboys?"

She laughed. "You said that just to upset Jarrod." And Jarrod was, indeed, looking a bit leprechaun-green. "Don't worry. I'm thinking traditional. Family and close friends only. Very tasteful. Nothing informal."

"Except for one thing," Parker said.

She looked up at him, a question in her eyes.

"Your shoes," he said. "Under a long dress, no one will even know."

Daisy laughed. "White ones? With wedding bells?"

"Perfect. Will there be children?"

"It's not necessary."

"I think it is. Maybe from a local school or church. We'll make a donation, dress them as angels. I don't want our angel to be the only child there. I don't want him or her ever to be lonely."

And in front of everyone, he dropped to one knee, leaned forward and kissed Daisy's belly. "You and I are going to love each other. I can't wait to be your dad," he said.

And then Parker picked Daisy up, tears streaming down

her face, and carried her away. "I'll expect a glowing announcement of my engagement in the paper tomorrow," he called back over his head.

"What shall I write?" Jarrod asked.

Parker paused. He gazed into Daisy's eyes. "Parker Sutcliffe, the luckiest man in the world, is marrying Daisy Lockett, the woman who holds his heart—"

"And the luckiest woman in the world," Daisy finished.

Jarrod swore. "That's not nearly formal enough. That's not how we do things around here."

"It is now," Parker said. "Thank goodness it is now." And he kissed his bride-to-be again, right in front of everyone.

EPILOGUE

DAISY paused inside the wedding chapel. She turned to look up at her husband standing by her side. "It's so hard to believe that less than four years ago this was a slightly shabby place. You did such a great job on the renovation."

"I wanted it ready for our wedding. And I wanted it to do honor to the woman who brought us together."

"Thank you. I do still miss her. I think I always will."

"I think she probably knows that. She's probably wishing us a happy third anniversary right now. Do you think I left enough of her in here?"

"I love that you hid one of her feather boas and her diary in one of the railing caps. Someday someone is going to find that and wonder about it."

"Let them. I don't think my aunt would have minded."

Daisy kissed Parker on the cheek. "We'd better get back to the guests."

"I suppose it's a bit odd that the guests of honor have disappeared." Reluctantly, they wandered out into the courtyard where a mixed group of Sutcliffes sat around the table along with Nola, Lydia and John. Jarrod was sitting with three-year-old Elise, who was smiling up at him, all golden curls and big brown eyes.

"So, what do you think, Parker? Elise as the next company president?"

Parker laughed as he took his daughter, kissed her and held her against his chest, where she lay contentedly. "Oh, I think I'll let her decide," he said, kissing her curls. "She might be a wedding planner like her mother. Or something of her own choosing."

Jarrod nodded, clearly not concerned and looking more relaxed than he had three years ago. "I know. Things change. The new hotel in town is a perfect example. Totally different from Silken Waters or any of the older more elegant hotels, but already a hit. Splash pads, playgrounds for kids and adults alike. Who would have thought that Sutcliffe's would go in that direction?"

"I think my wife might have."

Jarrod laughed. "Oh, well, Daisy. Sure, she has a lot of bright ideas, but I was a bit more...resistant."

Daisy laughed and kissed Jarrod on the cheek. "You've handled the insanity of having all of us around very well."

"I like it here. I think it was a great idea to split the offices and have half of them here."

"I wanted to be where Daisy is happiest."

"But I do like Boston, too," she reminded Parker.

"I know, but we had to make a choice. Can't go dragging our child all over the place just for the company."

Jarrod shook his head. "Daisy, I never asked... I see why Parker fell in love with you. You changed him."

"I didn't. He just found himself. The real Parker."

"Because of you," Jarrod insisted. "Don't argue. He's told me so a hundred times at least. You freed him from the stuff that was ruining his life. But...what was it about Parker that won you over? You obviously didn't care a hoot about his money or his name."

Daisy smiled up at Parker. She touched his hand, connecting herself to him and to her daughter. "He grounded me. I was always bouncing around from one thing to another, always reacting, always in motion like a tennis ball. Afraid to stop. Afraid to trust. Parker taught me to breathe. He taught me to trust. Not just him, but myself, too. He valued my ideas and taught me that I have something truly valuable to offer. Sometimes I think that when we met we just…clicked together. As if both of us had been struggling all our lives trying to reach each other."

"And now you have," Nola said.

"And it's pretty wonderful," Lydia added.

"My turn," John said, taking the child from Parker.

Parker reluctantly gave up his daughter to the man he now thought of as his second father.

Later in bed, Parker turned to Daisy and took her in his arms. "I liked what you said about the two of us trying to reach each other. Thank goodness I found you, Daisy."

"Like I said, we just clicked."

He kissed her, smiling against her lips. "Is that what they're calling it now? Clicking?"

She bopped him on the arm. "You know what I mean."

"I do know exactly what you mean."

Daisy laughed. "Good. Now that we've clarified that, love, let's click."

"You always have such good ideas, Daisy." And then he took his wife in his arms and showed her just what a good idea it was.

* * * * *

A sneaky peek at next month...

Cherish™

ROMANCE TO MELT THE HEART EVERY TIME

My wish list for next month's titles...

In stores from 18th May 2012:

❑ A Cold Creek Reunion – RaeAnne Thayne

❑ A Weaver Proposal – Allison Leigh

❑ The Nanny and the Boss's Twins & The Nanny
  Who Kissed Her Boss – Barbara McMahon

In stores from 1st June 2012:

❑ The SEAL's Promise & The Marshal's Prize
  – Rebecca Winters

❑ Mendoza's Return – Susan Crosby

❑ Fortune's Just Desserts – Marie Ferrarella

Available at WHSmith, Tesco, Asda, Eason, Amazon and Apple

Just can't wait?

Visit us Online

You can buy our books online a month before
they hit the shops! **www.millsandboon.co.uk**

0512/23

Book of the Month

MILLS & BOON

COWBOY'S
TRIPLET
TROUBLE

CARLA CASSIDY

BOOK
OF THE
MONTH

INTRIGUE...

We love this book because...

Dark, determined cowboy Jake fights against
the odds to keep his newfound family safe in this
pulse-racing romantic suspense from Intrigue star
Carla Cassidy.

On sale 18th May

Visit us Online

Find out more at
www.millsandboon.co.uk/BOTM

0512/BOTM

MILLS & BOON Book Club

2 Free Books!

Join the Mills & Boon Book Club

Want to read more **Cherish**™ stories?
We're offering you **2 more**
absolutely **FREE!**

We'll also treat you to these fabulous extras:

- 🌹 **Books up to 2 months ahead of shops**
- 🌹 **FREE home delivery**
- 🌹 **Bonus books with our special rewards scheme**
- 🌹 **Exclusive offers… and much more!**

Treat yourself now!

Visit us Online

Get your FREE books now at
www.millsandboon.co.uk/freebookoffer

0112/S2XEA/REV

MILLS & BOON Book Club — 2 Free Books!

Get your free books now at
www.millsandboon.co.uk/freebookoffer

Or fill in the form below and post it back to us

THE MILLS & BOON® BOOK CLUB™—HERE'S HOW IT WORKS: Accepting your free books places you under no obligation to buy anything. You may keep the books and return the despatch note marked 'Cancel'. If we do not hear from you, about a month later we'll send you 5 brand-new stories from the Cherish™ series, including two 2-in-1 books priced at £5.49 each, and a single book priced at £3.49*. There is no extra charge for post and packaging. You may cancel at any time, otherwise we will send you 5 stories a month which you may purchase or return to us—the choice is yours. *Terms and prices subject to change without notice. Offer valid in UK only. Applicants must be 18 or over. Offer expires 31st July 2012. **For full terms and conditions, please go to www.millsandboon.co.uk/freebookoffer**

Mrs/Miss/Ms/Mr (please circle)
_____

First Name
_____

Surname
_____

Address
_____

_____

                              Postcode
_____

E-mail
_____

Send this completed page to: Mills & Boon Book Club, Free Book Offer, FREEPOST NAT 10298, Richmond, Surrey, TW9 1BR

Find out more at
www.millsandboon.co.uk/freebookoffer

Visit us Online

0112/S2XEA/REV

Special Offers

Every month we put together collections and longer reads written by your favourite authors.

Here are some of next month's highlights— and don't miss our fabulous discount online!

On sale 18th May

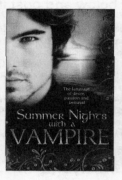

On sale 1st June

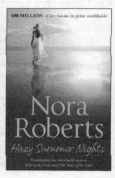

On sale 1st June

Save 20% on all Special Releases

Find out more at
www.millsandboon.co.uk/specialreleases

Visit us Online

0512/ST/MB375

Mills & Boon® Online

Discover more romance at
www.millsandboon.co.uk

- **FREE** online reads
- **Books** up to one
  month before shops
- **Browse our books**
  before you buy

...and much more!

For exclusive competitions and instant updates:

 Like us on **facebook.com/romancehq**

 Follow us on **twitter.com/millsandboonuk**

 Join us on **community.millsandboon.co.uk**

Visit us Online   Sign up for our FREE eNewsletter at
www.millsandboon.co.uk

WEB/M&B/RTL4

The World of Mills & Boon®

There's a Mills & Boon® series that's perfect for you. We publish ten series and with new titles every month, you never have to wait long for your favourite to come along.

Blaze. — Scorching hot, sexy reads

By Request — Relive the romance with the best of the best

Cherish™ — Romance to melt the *heart every time*

Desire™ — Passionate and dramatic love stories

Visit us Online — Browse our books before you buy online at **www.millsandboon.co.uk**

M&B/WORLD

What will you treat yourself to next?

Ignite your imagination, step into the past…

INTRIGUE... Breathtaking romantic suspense

Medical Romance Captivating medical drama—with heart

MODERN™ International affairs, seduction and passion

nocturne™ Deliciously wicked paranormal romance

RIVA™ Live life to the full – give in to temptation

You can also buy Mills & Boon eBooks at
www.millsandboon.co.uk

Visit us Online

M&B/WORLD